ONE SMALL STEP

Visit us at www.boldstrokesbooks.com

ONE SMALL STEP

by

MA Binfield

2019

ONE SMALL STEP

ISBN 13: 978-1-63555-596-7

This Trade Paperback Original Is Published By
Bold Strokes Books, Inc.
P.O. Box 249
Valley Falls, NY 12185

First Edition: December 2019

CREDITS
Editor: Cindy Cresap
Production Design: Susan Ramundo
Cover Design By Tammy Seidick

Acknowledgments

Huge thanks to my editor, Cindy Cresap, who improved this book immeasurably and helped this newbie author immensely. She also taught me important life lessons about Donna Noble and the importance of turning left.

Thanks to Rebecca, Debs, and Amanda for being willing and helpful beta readers before any of us even knew what that meant.

I've played for many footie teams over the years and can definitely assure everyone that Jess is a figment of my imagination—though the boozing after training definitely feels familiar!

Though Devam and his chef are not real, Dawat is an actual restaurant on Brick Lane I've stuffed myself at many times.

Finally a huge kiss and big hug for Helen, the love of my life, who fed me and did the breadwinning thing while I wrote this book.

Dedication

For Anna Chesner (who saved my life)

CHAPTER ONE

The small changing room had a smell that Iris Miller was long familiar with. Dried mud and cleaning fluids—a rich bouquet of not-very-nice aromas that Iris was happy to breathe in for once. Hazel—her teammate and oldest friend—was adding the pungent smell of muscle rub into the mix.

"You're cutting it a bit fine," Hazel said without looking up from the task of massaging the cream into the muscles in her thighs. "I thought you weren't gonna turn up."

Iris ruffled Hazel's hair affectionately. "Aren't you supposed to start by telling me how much you missed me?"

Hazel wrapped her arms around Iris in a tight hug. Hazel was a few inches shorter than Iris and stood on her tiptoes as they embraced.

"Course I missed you, stupid. It's been no fun without you, here or at work. Felt like months rather than weeks." Hazel pulled Iris down to the bench. "Now get changed quick before you get into trouble with Megan. She's got that glint in her eye that means she's gonna make training hell tonight. But I wanna hear all about your trip down the pub later."

"Yeah…if I can stay awake." Iris stripped off her jeans and started to unpack her bag. She scanned the room, checking who was there, who wasn't, feeling happy to be back amongst her teammates again. She'd only been away four weeks but didn't mind admitting that she'd missed them.

Jess reached out to put a hand awkwardly on her arm. "I missed you as well."

Iris looked back at her cautiously while subtly changing position to break the contact. "Hey, Jess. How're you doing? What've I missed?" She listened halfheartedly as Jess told her tales of office politics and new clients and, of course, of her love life. A giddying whirl of women that Iris could barely keep track of at the best of times, let alone when she felt this tired. She nodded and murmured in all the right places until Jess's phone beeped and she stopped talking to concentrate on replying to the text.

Iris felt relief at being saved by the beep. She stretched and yawned, the jet lag not yet out of her system. A good physical workout was just what she needed.

Iris noticed someone opposite her she didn't recognize. A graceful, fair-haired woman, pushing her head through the neck of a long sleeved navy sports shirt. Iris couldn't help but notice that she was in great shape, toned in all the right places, and with an athletic look that was also somehow perfectly feminine.

As the woman pulled down and straightened her top and her face came into view, Iris could see that she was also heart-stoppingly beautiful. Her pale skin was flawless, and her lips were pink and full. Iris tried not to stare, tried to move her gaze away and concentrate instead on tightening the laces on her football boots, but, involuntarily, her eyes sought out the stranger again. Iris forced herself to face up to the grim fact that, while there weren't many things that were off limits when you played team sports, staring at teammates in the changing room was definitely one of them.

Though the woman was oblivious, Iris's attentiveness hadn't gone unnoticed by Hazel. With as much subtlety as the world's most unsubtle person could muster, Hazel whispered loudly into Iris's ear. "Bloody hell, mate, I thought that you were halfway to the convent, but maybe there's life in you yet." Hazel nodded in the direction of the woman Iris had been gazing at, and Iris felt her cheeks heat.

Hazel had a loud personality—Iris loved that about her—but unfortunately it came with an even louder voice, and Iris didn't want Hazel's whispered comments to be overheard, especially not by Jess, who was sitting quietly tying her boots. "Keep your voice down, Haze. Don't embarrass me."

"Embarrass you? What with the drooling and the staring, I don't think you need any help from me."

"I was just curious that's all." Iris didn't sound at all convincing, even to herself. "I didn't know we had any new players. Is this her first time?"

Hazel seemed to relent and take pity at Iris's discomfort. "Nah. You've been away. She joined a month ago and she's played a couple of times already. Took your place in midfield while you were away. She's a pretty good player as well—nice control, a tidy finish, and definitely fitter than most of us...as you've already noticed," Hazel said with a raised eyebrow and a wink.

Iris ignored the comment, already feeling bad about her blatant checking out of the new player. "Where's she working?" She took the muscle rub from Hazel and began to massage it into her calves.

"She's in finance, works for Graham...poor sod. She was taken on to cover for Daisy's maternity leave last month. Seems nice. Came to the pub after training last week. Had a few drinks, bit quiet, but I guess she doesn't really know anyone yet."

Iris nodded and Hazel nudged her. "I tell you what though, Iris, the world ain't ready for you getting back in the game. We need notice, some time to lock up our sisters." Hazel's tone was playful.

"It'd be nice to see you interested in someone though. You know damn well that I think you insisting on staying single is ridiculous." Hazel began to stretch, first her calves and then her hamstrings.

"Don't start, Haze."

"Start what? It's true. You've become a workaholic. All work and no play. How long you gonna keep avoiding life?"

Hazel meant well, Iris knew that, but she didn't understand what it felt like to be Iris, to have to live with the mess and the pain that had happened the last time she had let herself love. She tried to keep her tone light. "C'mon, I don't want to get into this now. I've heard it all before. I just want to have a good session. Ideally, I'll score a few goals, avoid any crunching tackles from Vicki, and hope that Megan's not premenstrual enough to make us do push-ups if we miss during the penalty practice."

Iris turned her back on Hazel to signify that the topic was closed and began to stretch, pushing down on the wooden bench as she did so.

Hazel threw an arm across Iris's shoulders. "Okay, okay. I'll leave it alone, but I will say one thing, when you do decide to come back out to play, please get your gaydar fixed first. Cameron Hansen, our new temp, and the object of your attentions, is engaged, and presumably as straight as they come. Jess reckons there'll be wedding bells soon. "

Hazel raised an eyebrow. "You're a little rusty, mate." She stepped out of Iris's reach, guessing rightly that Iris would swing out with her foot and attempt to connect with Hazel's well-protected shin. Hazel's speedy reaction left Iris kicking at air. They laughed, and Jess—ever alert—demanded to know what they were talking about and whined about being left out of the fun. She scowled, looking even younger than her twenty-four years.

Iris had surprised herself by even noticing the new woman. Hazel was right. It had been a long time since she'd noticed anyone. *Cameron.* Iris tried out the name in her head. It sounded Scottish. She rarely ever crushed on straight women. It was generally a pointless endeavor, and she just wasn't one of those women who enjoyed chasing people who weren't available. Iris wondered idly if there had been something else, something other than how damn attractive she was, that had drawn her attention to Cameron. Hazel was right. Her gaydar was rusty. It shouldn't be a surprise. She hadn't used it in months.

A booming voice from across the changing room brought Iris out of her reverie.

"Iris! Where've you been? We missed you." Vicki emptied the contents of her bag onto the floor and started to get ready in a hurry.

She was loud and would be late for her own funeral, but Iris had a soft spot for Vicki a mile wide. She no longer worked at Cottoms. She left months ago to take up a more senior position at a rival solicitors', but she continued to play and train for the football team that the company supported, and Iris was glad that it gave them the opportunity to stay in touch.

Vicki was as no-nonsense as you would expect from a central defender. Tall, solidly built, with dramatic white-blond hair and pale skin. She looked Scandinavian, but when she spoke there was absolutely no doubt that she was actually Australian. Her bellowed question had caused most of her teammates to stop and listen.

"We've missed you, mate. Well, not too much actually, as she"— Vicki pointed at Cameron—"has been scoring for fun while you've been away."

Iris was aware that Cameron was watching her interaction with Vicki with an amused expression even though others had stopped paying attention and resumed getting ready.

Iris played along. "I'd heard I'd been replaced by a new improved model. To be honest, I was a bit worried I wouldn't even be allowed in tonight, but it seems that Megan still needs someone to clean the boots so you haven't seen the last of me yet."

Vicki laughed. "I missed you. I thought you must have been injured. I asked Hazel if one of those women you'd left feeling rejected had finally picked up the courage to put in a heavy tackle on you behind the ref's back, but she said you were away. Boring."

Cameron turned away and began fiddling with the bag hanging on the coat hook near where she was sitting. Iris wasn't sure, but Cameron seemed embarrassed as she was outed by Vicki so clearly. Iris was bothered for a second, but then she made herself remember that not only did she not know Cameron, and therefore shouldn't give a toss about what she thought of her, but that this was a women's football team so being freaked out by lesbians probably wouldn't get Cameron very far.

"Nothing so dramatic, sorry to disappoint. Work trip. I was in Dubai. We're setting up a new office out there. Lucky me. Four weeks away from home, working twelve-hour days and without even access to alcohol to numb the pain of being away from you lot."

"I bet British Airways had to restock that bar a couple of times on her flight home," Hazel said. "She says she's got jet lag, but I don't actually think she's been sober since she came back."

Iris was so glad to be back in London. She had missed this, missed her colleagues, her friends, her teammates—knowing that some of them fell into all three categories. And she had definitely missed the camaraderie and banter of the changing room.

Megan, the team captain, called them to order. "C'mon then, ladies. Enough chatting, it's time for training. Last one into the center circle does ten push-ups."

They clamored to leave the changing room. Those that weren't quite ready groaned and hurried themselves while those that were looked relieved to be able to head straight to the door. Iris found herself shoulder to shoulder with Cameron as they left the changing room to clatter in their boots across the pavement that led them down to the pitch.

Cameron put out her hand. "Hey, we haven't met. I'm Cameron, but my friends call me Cam."

Iris hadn't been expecting an American accent. She looked at Cam as they shook hands. She hadn't been expecting those eyes either. They were a warm and alluring sage green, and Cam was staring at Iris as if waiting for something.

Iris remembered herself. "Yeah, I'm Iris, sorry. Pleased to meet you. I've been away. Working, not on holiday." Iris was using unusually short sentences. "I missed your debut. It went well I hear."

Cam blushed slightly at the compliment. Iris thought it was cute. *Very cute.* She sucked in a breath and made herself calm down.

"It was awesome, yeah, but I feel under a bit more pressure to perform now. Megan's kind of made it clear she expects more goals." Cam shrugged.

"That's Megan for you. One of the reasons we all try so hard is that we're scared witless by her."

As if on cue, Megan strode past with a large bag of footballs slung over her shoulder and shouted at Cameron and Iris and a couple of other players who were chatting and walking too slowly to "get a bloody move on." Iris and Cam looked at each other and laughed, then quickened their pace.

Cam emerged from the steamy heat of the changing rooms and headed toward her car. It was cold outside now, colder than she had expected. London kept catching her out like that. She regretted not bothering to dry her hair properly after her shower. She pulled the hood up on her jacket in a vain attempt to keep the cold wind off her still wet head. Training had been hard tonight. Though Cam had scored again in the match last week, the team had conceded a late goal to draw the game, a game that everyone had expected them to win. Megan certainly seemed to want them to make up for it during training tonight. On top of the usual warm-up routines, and a very competitive six a side game, Megan had them running hard laps for fifteen minutes at the end of the session. She had coped with the pace better than most, though Vicki and Iris, with the unfair advantage of their long legs, had outpaced them all.

Cam was tired now. She knew it was as much to do with the sleep she'd missed last night as the intensity of the training session. Ryan had been late home from work again and they had argued—the same argument they always had—about Ryan overworking, about Cam being left alone at home, about how little point there was to being in London if they never saw any of it.

The argument hadn't lasted long and it hadn't been particularly heated, but Cam had been left chewing over things and unable to sleep. She'd been even more worked up when, after the argument, Ryan had fallen straight to sleep, seemingly untroubled by any of it. That she'd never smothered him with a pillow in those situations was a testament to her good upbringing.

Ryan was a good guy. Cam knew he was. She just wanted to see more of him, have him less stressed, and maybe have a little more fun. They would make it work; they always did.

Cam got in her car and cranked up the heater to max, willing the temperature to rise. She turned on the radio, already tuned to Heart FM, and decided to listen to some pop music and stop moping. Maybe this weekend she'd take the initiative and find somewhere in town for them to have some cocktails and a fancy dinner. She'd been wanting an excuse to wear that black dress she'd bought. The thought of it lifted her mood.

Cam noticed Iris getting into a Mini Cooper. She felt a small pang of jealousy. She'd wanted a Mini when they moved to London—the car just seemed so wonderfully British—but Ryan had insisted she get something more practical. It was hard to tell the color of the car in the dark, but she couldn't miss the Union Jack brightly painted on the roof. It was a standout feature, and a voice inside Cam's head told her that it stood out almost as much as Iris did. The thought surprised her. She had noticed Iris in the changing room straight away. It was hard not to. She was tall, athletic, and bronzed to perfection, no doubt from her recent trip. Her short black hair was wavy and unruly which, coupled with her dark brown eyes, made her look moody and handsome. Tall, dark, and handsome. Cam rolled her eyes at the cliché. But it wasn't just that she was striking to look at, the other women seemed genuinely pleased that Iris was back, and her liveliness placed her at the center of the changing room banter, her handsome features softened often by a big wide smile.

Cam had found herself watching quietly and trying to understand who Iris was most friendly with, where her alliances lay, and once Vicki had made it clear that Iris was a lesbian, if she was in a relationship with someone in the team. She didn't think so but it was hard to tell. Cam couldn't help being curious. Ryan always teased her that she was pretty nosy in that way, and she had spent the previous weeks wondering the same way about the other players, not yet discovering any pairings within the team. She didn't really care, but as much as she loved soccer, she had joined the team hoping also to make a friend or two, and she didn't want to play on a team full of established couples who had no time for new friendships.

Iris reversed the Mini out of its parking space and headed for the main road. She gave Cam a friendly wave as she passed. It was enough to make Cam want to overcome her tiredness and join everyone in the pub for the usual after training drinks. If she was going to make friends, she had to be sociable and not let her tiredness get in the way of that.

The pub was barely a five-minute walk from the sports center, but the freezing temperatures tonight made Iris thankful she had chosen to drive rather than walk.

As the players arrived in twos and threes, they settled themselves in small groups at the square tables that populated the pub's lounge area. A fire was blazing away at one end of the room and, being midweek, the lounge was empty except for a group of middle-aged men sipping pints at a corner table close to the bar. The TV near them was showing a football match, and they were watching it halfheartedly with the sound down.

The team always got a warm welcome from Jackie, the landlady of the Dog and Gun, who was glad both of the midweek business and of the company.

"Hello, darling." Jackie wrapped her arms around Iris in a hug, stopping her passage toward Hazel and the tables nearest the fire. She pulled away and looked Iris up and down, whistling softly. "Well, look at you. You look like you've been somewhere sunny."

"Dubai. For work. They worked me like a dog, but I managed a fair bit of reading by the pool on the weekends. Don't tell that lot though. I've got them all feeling sorry for me about how hard I had to work."

"Well, we missed you, and it's been freezing here so you're getting no sympathy from me."

"My hotel didn't serve any alcohol. Not even shandy." Iris pouted.

"Okay, okay, you got me. I'm finally feeling sorry for ya." Jackie pushed Iris toward the fire. "Make sure you make up for it tonight, and the first one's on me."

Iris turned back and gave Jackie a quick peck on the cheek. "Thanks." She made her way to the table.

Vicki and Hazel were sitting as close to the fire as they thought they could bear while Jess was getting the drinks. Iris had quickly pushed two of the tables together wanting to make room for Megan and Cam to join their group when they arrived. Jess's progress with the drinks was being slowed by the fact that the barmaid was showing more interest than usual in Jess's attempts to chat her up. She leaned across the bar and played with her hair flirtatiously—doing all the things she could to respond positively to Jess's presence except pour the drinks that had been ordered.

"We might have to wait a while," Vicki said. "Jess is in full seduction mode. I can't remember if she's an old flame or a new conquest. Keeping track of Jess's women is a full-time job."

Iris shook her head. "I just don't have the energy for it."

"I would have said the same, but then I met Princess Harry and I feel like a teenager again." Vicki clutched her heart playfully.

Vicki had snagged herself a posh girl called Henrietta—Harry to her friends—one of the associates at her new firm, and they were still in that madly loved up phase. Henrietta had reddish hair and a cut glass accent that made her sound like royalty so Hazel had come up with the Princess Harry nickname. Vicki had loved it so much that she now called her by it routinely and, to be fair, Harry thought it was hilarious.

"Still going well?" Iris asked, already guessing the answer.

"Yeah, totally. I've never had so much fun. And by fun, I mean sex obviously."

"As long as you're not going to go into the gory details, I'm happy to hear you say that," Iris replied.

Hazel was on the phone to Casey, her wife. She was complaining loudly about Megan, who had yet to arrive. "Honestly, babe, she was like a bad-tempered army fitness instructor tonight."

Hazel being on the phone saved Iris from being teased about the fact that she was very obviously watching for Cam through the window and had even saved Cam the seat next to her with her coat. She was just being friendly, but she knew that wouldn't matter to Hazel.

At that moment, Cam entered the pub with Megan and a couple of the other players. As she looked around to see where people were sitting, Iris smiled and waved indicating the spare chair next to her. Iris wondered where the hell all this friendliness had come from. It wasn't her normal way of behaving with strangers, but something about Cam made her feel that she was worth not being her normal self for. Cam gave a little wave back and made her way toward the table, and Iris couldn't help but smile. This time Hazel noticed.

Cam's approach was delayed by Megan inquiring what she wanted to drink, and this gave Hazel the chance to nudge Iris. "Three words, Iris—she's not interested. Don't let yourself go there."

"Thanks for the advice, Haze. Three words for you—I'm. Not. Stupid. I know she's not interested like that. I just want to get to know her a bit, that's all."

Cam reached the table and Iris took the coat off the chair beside her so that Cam could sit down. The fire in the lounge was roaring now, and it made the pub feel very warm, especially when compared to the icy temperatures outside. Cam stripped off her jacket and hung it across the back of her chair. Iris wanted to initiate conversation with her, but something about Hazel's comment had made her self-conscious. At least she assumed that was what was making her tongue-tied and it was nothing to do with how attractive Cam looked in the soft light of the room.

This is silly. I'm behaving like a schoolgirl with a new crush.

Megan joined them at the table with a drink for Cam and raised her glass to make a toast to the team.

"I'd join you in that, but I can't lift my arms off the table thanks to all those extra push-ups you made me do," Iris said.

"Is it my fault you can't put the ball in the net from twelve yards? You know the forfeit," Megan replied. "And anyway, Vicki did twice as many push-ups as you and she's still got both arms working. You're just a weakling."

Iris loved the banter of the post-training drinks—so much more relaxed than after a match when people were still worrying about chances they'd missed or how well they'd played. "But we all know that Australians have a genetic advantage with their overdeveloped biceps linked to the pints of lager they drink from childhood."

Cam offered Iris her palm for a high five. Iris obliged, pretending she had hurt her arm while doing so. Vicki joined in by flexing her muscles playfully and Cam grinned. Iris liked seeing her smile.

Megan, Hazel, and Vicki began to chat earnestly about the state of the team's finances, and whether Cottoms could be approached for more money. And this left Iris and Cam able to talk to each other properly for the first time.

"I gotta say that Megan takes the training way more seriously than any other coach I've played for."

"Have you played a lot previously then?" Iris's question was pretty stupid as Cam was obviously an experienced player. She was hopeless at small talk.

"I have. I played at school, all through college, for the varsity women's team. Soccer's much more popular with women in the US than it is here. Lots of opportunities to play." Cam sipped her wine. "I was so happy when I found out that Cottoms had a team. I missed playing so much when I moved to London that I was almost ready to just try to find a random team to join online, but I knew I'd have been a bit shy about turning up and not knowing anyone, y'know."

"When did you move to London?"

"About eight months ago now I suppose. Ryan...my boyfriend... well, I suppose I should call him my fiancé now that we're engaged... he got the chance to transfer to the London office of his company and decided he wanted to give it a go. I wasn't really doing much to keep me in Seattle, and London was a place I'd always wanted to experience, so..."

"And do you miss home?"

"I miss friends sometimes. I do the 'catching up with them on Skype' thing, but it's obviously not the same. I miss the mountains, the forests, the lakes. Washington is really beautiful. I miss my family, well, I miss my sister at least." She paused. "Mom, Dad, Alison, they're all back in Seattle. My sister and I are close. We used to cook for each other every week and make sure we were caught up on each other's news, and I really miss that." Cam looked wistful. "What about you? What do you do at Cottoms?"

Iris didn't really want to talk about herself—she never did—and she certainly didn't want to talk about work. She wanted to hear more from Cam. "I'm the operations director. As dull as dull can be. It's okay though. There are worse jobs. I like the people I work with. Most of them anyway. And I like making things work better. Plus it keeps me busy."

"And what do you do for leisure?" Cam anglicized her pronunciation of the word "leisure" a little self-consciously. Iris liked hearing it. She also liked Cam's interest and her openness. It was not natural for Iris, and she surprised herself by answering honestly.

"I do what most people do, I guess. I run, I read, I see films, I see friends, I try not to watch too much TV, and I spend too many long evenings in the pub like this. Footie takes up a lot of my time. I really miss it when the season's over." Iris felt a little nervous, worrying about how she was coming across and feeling like she sounded dull.

"And love? No time for that?"

Iris was surprised by Cam's forthrightness. She tried to determine whether the question was meant humorously or needed a proper answer, but found it hard to read Cam's expression. She decided to be herself—guarded, flippant, avoidant.

"I schedule it in every Wednesday at six just after my spin class. It's getting harder to do though—a local shortage or something. At least that's what I'm telling myself." She carried on, leaving no room for Cam to come back with a follow-up question. "And how about you? How do you spend your time?"

"Same as you really. I also like to run, I watch TV, and I read a lot. I like to cook. I try to get out to the movies, the theater, galleries. Ryan works long hours though so it's not always possible."

Cam stopped and Iris thought she looked pensive, worried even, but she still seemed very relaxed talking about herself. "I need to make some new friends. It's always difficult, but London makes it harder somehow. I hadn't expected that. Everyone's always so busy and so far away. My last place of work was a snake pit, and I didn't dare make friends there in case I ended up on the wrong side in some way. I have more hopes of this place, especially since we have a soccer team and people seem so normal and friendly."

Iris really hoped she would be one of Cam's new friends.

"Cottoms isn't all sweetness and light, but it's definitely better than most. I like the fact that we're a really diverse company. And it's not one of those macho environments where people compete to be seen working the longest hours, and it's really good that the partners support and encourage extracurricular activities like the football teams. We even have a book club, though at last count we only have four members, including me. If you like to read though, you should definitely come along."

"That sounds awesome, I will."

"We take it in turns to choose the books. I'll send you the title for next time. In fact, I can just lend you the book. I've just finished it. It's not one that I chose and, spoiler alert, I think it's absolutely terrible. Not that I'm trying to sway your opinion in advance." She leaned over to Cam and stage-whispered. "I am actually, but don't tell anyone." They both laughed.

Jess returned to their table to top up her glass from the bottle of white wine on the table. She sat down, sighed, and looked at her watch.

"What's the matter, Jess? Is she behind schedule in succumbing to your moves? Is there anything I can do to help? What I lack in charm I make up for in experience," Hazel teased her.

"Would your wife approve of you chatting up a barmaid for me? I don't think so. She'd stop baking you cakes if she found out, and you wouldn't want that would you?" Jess's response was a little snarky.

"What about telling her you've only got a week to live? Might make her hurry up a bit." Iris chanced her own joke.

Jess looked at Iris intently before responding. "I know I should take dating advice from you, Iris, considering the barmaid is probably the only woman in this pub you haven't slept with, but I'm not sure about that line, not one of your best. Of course, my favorite is 'What winks and fucks like a tiger?' It worked on me anyway, not that I like to remind myself of that very often."

Hazel put up a hand to try to stop Jess's flow, but she ignored it. "Not heard that one, Cam?" Jess winked at her.

Cam took a second to understand and then looked down at the table. Iris's own embarrassment was acute and obvious to everyone at the table.

"That's enough, Jess," Megan spoke up quietly.

"What?" Jess stood up. "Are we not allowed to remind ourselves of Iris's glory days anymore? Where's the fun in that? Surely it's important that we remember she's the only person to get awarded Player of the Year for her efforts both on and off the pitch in the same season." Jess toasted the group and returned to the bar.

An awkward silence fell upon the table. Vicki spoke first. "Hey, Iris. Sorry, mate. Don't worry. She's just having a bad night."

Iris hung her head in shame, hating being reminded of those days and dreading to imagine what Cam would think of her now. Hazel put her arm around Iris's shoulder.

"She's just used to being able to take her shit out on you because you're so tolerant of her. Don't let her get to you." Iris nodded.

"And I, for one, would like to come out and say that, to my great relief, I have never slept with Iris." Hazel nudged Iris playfully.

"Me neither." Megan lifted her own glass to join Hazel in the toast.

"So I guess we're saying it should be me that changes the subject then," Vicki said sheepishly, pulling her hood over her face.

Cam was silent and fiddling in her bag looking for something. She extracted her phone and sent someone a text message. She looked up and caught Iris watching her, then looked away quickly. Iris felt sure she was sending a message to her fiancé to say that she was coming home early. Jess's stupid comments had ruined what had been a pleasant evening up to then.

"I'm kind of tired." Cam stood as she drained her glass. "I'm gonna head off." As the group offered Cam their good-byes, Iris wondered sadly if Cam would give her a wider berth in the future.

CHAPTER TWO

Cam sat at her desk answering emails and trying to ignore the fact that Graham was sighing and tutting as he pored over the expense reports that she had just put in front of him.

After a month of working there, Cam already knew that the noises were her cue to ask him what was wrong and then receive a long lecture about the many different ways the company was "profligate" with its finances. So far this week, he had ranted about the lack of wisdom the company showed by providing free tea and coffee in the lunchroom ("encourages time-wasting") and about the needless extra cost involved in buying recycled copier paper. From her position at the desk opposite his, Cam considered the top of his bald head as he leaned over the document. It might be great for Cottoms to have such a frugal finance director, but his joyless penny-pinching made working with him less enjoyable than it should be.

Last week, Graham had asked Cam about her engagement ring and nodded thoughtfully as she awkwardly told him about Ryan, and them getting engaged before coming to London. He'd then spent twenty minutes telling her just how much money people waste on weddings and how she would do much better not bothering.

Cam had quite enjoyed that particular rant and imagined having the same conversation with her mother as a means of putting a stop to the over-the-top fairy tale wedding she'd been planning for her for years. The conversation had actually made her call her mother that night.

"Hey, Mom."

"Cameron, dear, how nice to hear from you."

They both paused. Cam wasn't really sure why she'd called. Just a feeling that it had been a while and she owed her mother some contact.

"Are you calling with news?" The way she said the last word made it clear that her mother was asking whether they had set a wedding date. She always sounded so excited at the prospect.

Face it, it's actually all she cares about. Cam couldn't stop the thought from popping into her head. She decided to deliberately misunderstand the question and started telling her mother her actual news, about her new job at Cottoms and the football team and Ryan's work. Her mother was too well mannered to interrupt, but her interest was limited. She managed some sympathy for Ryan when Cam told her how hard he had been working lately but didn't muster a single question or comment on the rest of it. It didn't matter that Cam expected it; her mother's indifference to her interests, her achievements, and her life was always hurtful. Eventually, Cam ran out of things to say and her mother pounced.

"And the wedding? Have you decided on a date? I went to the church last week and they said they need at least three months' notice. It's very popular as a venue, so close to the lake, a lovely backdrop, and the banqueting hall is divine." Her mother barely took a breath, she was so excited.

Cam sighed. She'd heard all this before. She and Ryan had been engaged for less than a year, and she was in no hurry to marry. Cam had been so surprised when Ryan had proposed the week before they left for London. It was unexpected because they had never once talked about it despite three years together.

Cam had enjoyed the deliberate cheesiness of Ryan's proposal. He'd insisted on a "farewell to Seattle" meal at the restaurant at the top of the Space Needle and ended the meal by dropping the ring into a glass of overpriced champagne, followed by a cake lit with sparklers delivered by a team of smiling waiters. She had hesitated for a second and then, swept up in the moment, said yes to cheers and applause. They had gone somewhere else for cocktails and gone home happy and wasted. Later, when reality hit, she told Ryan that the wedding would have to wait till they were back in Seattle so that family and friends could attend. She was relieved that he didn't seem to mind at all.

Cam delighted in telling her mother all about the engagement, knowing she was horrified at the tackiness of the proposal but also relieved Cam finally had a ring on her finger. Her mother adored Ryan. The fact he was an investment banker from a well off family was a big part of it, but he also had an easy charm that her mother couldn't resist. She'd never said it in quite so many words, but Cam was pretty sure that her mother thought she'd done well for herself to snag someone like Ryan. One day she would have to learn to not care what her mother thought of her quite so much. That she still did made her feel a little sad.

Cam picked up the coffee she had made ten minutes earlier and urged herself to enjoy it more knowing that it was a gift from her employers that Graham did not approve of. Her mind drifted back to the previous evening and how nice it had been to meet Iris. Cam could tell that Iris was someone who used humor to keep people at a distance, but she'd been willing to share something of herself with Cam, and it certainly seemed like they had things in common that might lead to friendship. Jess's comments about Iris's womanizing were an eye-opener though. She was obviously bitter about something in their past, but no one had really challenged what she'd said—not even Iris—so Cam figured it must have been largely true. That the drama didn't give her more pause for thought just told Cam how much she had liked Iris.

Cam put down her coffee and reverted to working through her ever-expanding inbox. The satellite office of the law firm, opened several years before to take pressure off Cottoms' main London office, was much busier than Cam had expected. The work was boring—mainly financial admin—and her boss was a total pain in the ass, but the fact that she was busy and people were generally friendly helped the days go by.

Arriving in London, Ryan had made it clear that he would support her financially and that she didn't need to work, but Cam quickly realized that being the little wife-in-waiting didn't suit her. She wanted—needed—the independence that came from having money of her own, and she wanted to meet new people. Back home, Cam had often felt bored and restless—like life was just passing her by—and she'd hoped that London would help her feel different, help her find herself somehow, but she was facing up to the fact that she had a lot of the same feelings here. She couldn't understand why it was so difficult to figure out why she was bored, and what it was that she actually wanted from her life. The role at Cottoms definitely wasn't anything she'd want forever, but for now, it was fine, and if she could make the right friends, she might even be able to start to enjoy life outside work a bit more.

Cam heard a knock on the open office door and was surprised to see first Megan, and then Iris, appear in the doorway. The office was not large—just space enough for the four desks and various filing cabinets it contained. Graham's PA, the long-suffering Sylvia, something of a Cottoms institution, usually occupied the desk nearest the door, but she was on leave.

Megan entered the room and sat in Sylvia's empty office chair while Iris remained in the doorway. "Can we have a word please, Graham? It won't take five minutes." Megan was being unusually polite.

Graham looked from Megan to Iris and back again. "That's good because I've barely got five minutes."

Like a good bean counter, Graham measured out his words carefully, speaking with a surprisingly deep voice for such a slight man.

"We've been speaking to Mr. Cottom about the football team and about the running costs going up—the pitches, the equipment, the registration and so on—and he said that he would support an increase in funding if you could identify a budget for it to come from. I wanted to ask you to see if you could."

Graham pointed at the stack of papers he had on the desk in front of him. "Times are tight, ladies. Budgets are being overspent all over the place. I'm not sure Mr. Cottom always appreciates that from his..." he searched for the right words, "rather lofty position at the top of the company."

Iris sighed loudly, and Megan shot her a look that was intended to make Iris stay quiet.

"I appreciate that, Graham, but we're only talking about a small increase. Even five hundred pounds would help us get through the season."

Cam could see that Iris was agitated. She was shifting from foot to foot.

"And what would you have me cut to find this five hundred pounds you need? Let's see..." Graham pretended to think. "I suppose I could have the sanitary bin contract in the women's lavatories canceled. An eye for an eye—that sort of thing."

It was, Cam supposed, a joke, but it was hard to tell with Graham and it certainly wasn't funny.

Before Megan could respond, Iris stepped into the room. She addressed her comment to Megan, but her eyes were focused on Graham. "I knew this was a waste of time and that he'd use us asking as some sort of power trip. Let's leave it and find the money some other way. I don't think we should have to beg." Megan held up a hand as if to say "Let me deal with it" and spoke again to Graham.

"We've heard that the men's team has a lot more funding than we do, and we thought maybe one option might be to equalize the spending a bit between the teams—only seems fair."

Graham regarded Megan coldly. "Not sure where you heard that, Megan, but let me assure you that we're cutting back in all corners of the business. Times are tight, as I've already said. I can only promise that I'll do my best to identify something that will help. Is that all?"

Megan was showing what Cam felt was masterful composure in the face of Graham's dismissive behavior.

"That's all. Thank you, Graham." Megan moved toward the door.

Iris stood back from the entrance to allow Megan to pass her into the corridor, but before moving off after her, she popped her head back into the office.

"I really hope it isn't the case that the men's team gets more funding, Graham, because that sort of blatant gender discrimination would not reflect very well on the company, especially given that it's a company full to the brim of female lawyers who enjoy nothing more than litigating that kind of injustice."

Iris left before Graham could respond. Cam couldn't help but think they'd tag-teamed Graham pretty well, leaving him with little room to maneuver around the funding. He stood up, causing Cam to start slightly.

"The cheek of it. Who the hell does she think she is? They think that I don't know that they use that team as a women's social group. Half the players don't even work for Cottoms. They don't take it as seriously as the men's team do. I don't see the comparison as a helpful one. Not at all." He jabbed his fingers at his desk to emphasize the words. "I know you're engaged to be married, Cameron, but I would think very carefully about continuing your membership on the team under the circumstances."

"What's that supposed to mean?"

"I'm just saying that I have my sources of information too, and I know that Iris—and certainly one or two of the other players—use that team as a way of meeting like-minded women, and I'm sure your fiancé wouldn't want you exposed to that."

"I don't know anything about that except to say that people meet people in all areas of life—work, sport, the supermarket, pottery classes—so I don't see why it's so wrong that women would connect through the team. And as for taking it seriously, we've won three of the last four matches we've played, are third in the league, and my legs feel like they won't get me up the stairs given how hard the training was last night. Before you judge, I suggest you come along and watch one week. We totally take that team seriously."

Cam had kept her composure, but the effort meant that her hands were shaking when she picked up her cup. "I'm going to get a coffee." She had to get out of there before saying something more that she might regret.

On her way out of the door, a little voice in her head reminded Cam that Graham was the second person in as many days to suggest that Iris was a real player. She had been very friendly, but Cam hadn't got any kind of vibe that made her worry about Iris's intentions. Maybe it'd be better if Iris was with someone, but as soon as the thought landed, another collided with it. *That might mean she doesn't have time to become my friend.* And Cam really wanted Iris to be her friend. As she reached the kitchen, Cam decided to swap her coffee for a chamomile tea and the hope of a peaceful afternoon.

CHAPTER THREE

Iris leafed through the pamphlet she'd been given with her ticket on the way in. This bookstore was one of her favorite places to waste time in Hampstead. She loved the atmosphere. It was one of those bookstores that made clear that browsing and sitting were still approved of, and she'd spent many happy hours occupying one or other of the comfy armchairs that were dotted around the store. It had an impressive selection of books spread over three floors and a poetry section that occupied half of one whole wall of the store rather than a few volumes tacked on to the end of the fiction section like you might get elsewhere. She'd discovered so many new writers there, and that just made her love it more.

As usual, she had snagged a seat on the back row, her back to a wall of large bookcases containing travel books of all shapes, sizes, countries, and continents. She picked up a book at random to browse while the room filled up and put it straight back when she saw it was the *Eyewitness Guide to New York*. Typical. Another unhelpful reminder of the past.

She looked around the room and saw that the chairs crammed in rows in this half of the second floor were nearly all taken. It was close to seven thirty, and there were just a few empty seats at the front. Iris tried, as she often did, to imagine herself standing in front of this audience, reading one of her own poems. She would be terrified of course, but also, she liked to hope, exhilarated at giving life to something she had created, to bring the words off the page and plant them in people's hearts and minds where they might germinate and grow. It saddened Iris that she wasn't writing as much as she used to. It had just gotten too hard after Amanda. Iris sometimes blamed Amanda for not encouraging her to perform when they were together and Iris was at her most prolific, but she usually pushed the thought away, reminding herself that Amanda had done nothing to stop her from performing either. She needed to have her own courage.

When Iris and Amanda had separated, after the initial period of losing herself in drinking and sleeping around had passed, Iris found herself writing to give an outlet to the pain she felt, but the poems were so personal, so raw, that she knew she could never perform them. Now she just found it hard to write at all, and coming to events like this was as much an attempt to find inspiration as a way of spending an enjoyable evening.

Iris tried to find a comfortable position in the fold-up chair and sipped the tea she had bought from the café on her way upstairs. She could tell from the way that the middle-aged woman next to her kept glancing at her that she wanted to start up a conversation, but Iris avoided her gaze. She felt a little mean, but she wasn't in the mood to chat. Being on her own meant that she often attracted conversation from other solo attendees who wanted to discuss the poems. Iris hardly ever agreed with them but was always too polite to say so. To her, poetry was an emotional experience, as personal to each person as the kind of sex they liked to have, but in this bookstore in genteel, well-heeled Hampstead, she doubted that pointing out that comparison would go down well.

On the small makeshift stage at one end of the bookstore floor, the evening's emcee was waiting for the room to come to order. She was looking at a sheaf of notes attached to a clipboard as if to remind herself of what should happen and what she should say. As Iris felt the room settle down around her, she saw the woman impatiently wave at a couple who had just entered the room and urge them to sit in the seats immediately in front of her. The man and the woman began to pick their way across the front row, muttering apologies as they tried to creep as unobtrusively as possible past those already seated, obviously flustered to be arriving so late.

Iris sat up in her chair at the realization that the woman, now seated and trying to take off her coat without attracting even more attention, was Cam. The dark haired man she had arrived with said something in her ear. You didn't need to be an expert in body language to see from Cam's response that she was annoyed. She shook her head, refusing to look at him and stared fixedly ahead at the low stage, just a couple of feet away from them. Iris was so surprised to find Cam here, so taken with watching the interaction between Cam and, she presumed, her fiancé that she missed the introduction of the first performer. Cam clapped enthusiastically, and Ryan—Iris finally remembered his name—did not. *So Cam likes poetry. What a lovely surprise.*

Throughout the first half of the evening, Iris caught herself looking across at Cam more than once. Cam seemed rapt, sitting upright in her seat, quite still and only seeming to relax when each performer left the stage. Her fiancé looked bored. He was slouched in his seat, still wearing his jacket as if he didn't really mean to stay very long and constantly checking his phone.

The emcee announced a fifteen-minute break, and Iris stood up for a stretch. The rickety wooden chairs, packed closely together, were never especially comfortable. She nodded in recognition at an old couple she had chatted with at length last time she was here. She knew they were both heading down to the café for tea and a slice of cake. A tempting idea if only she wasn't trying to stay in shape for the rest of the season. By the time Iris had thought to check whether Cam was going or staying, she noticed that the seats they had been occupying were empty. Iris hadn't been sure if she should make the effort to go over and say hello, and Cam's departure had spared her the need to decide. Iris wasn't sorry not to have to make small talk—it really wasn't her strong suit—but she was sorry not to have the chance to at least say hello and find out whether Cam came to these kind of events regularly. As she completed the thought, Iris became aware of a presence next to her.

"Hey, fancy meeting you here." Iris turned to see Cam smiling sweetly at her. "It's great isn't it? I really enjoyed that last poem. So moving. I could see that she was really nervous, but she had no reason to be, as she was so good. I loved the way she described her feelings about her son's illness. So dark, but so poignant."

Cam took a breath and leaned against the back of the chair in the row in front of Iris, her feet crossed at the ankles. She looked relaxed. Her fair hair was worn loose, and she was wearing a brightly colored knee length open knit jumper over faded jeans. Iris couldn't help but approve. She also appreciated Cam's enthusiasm for the poetry and the refreshing lack of small talk.

"I know. I guessed it was her first time performing, but the poem was so good, I figured she must be quite an experienced writer. I know it was long, but I just didn't want it to end." Iris paused. "Do you come here…I mean…have you been here before?" Iris stopped herself from asking the obvious question.

"No, not here. I used to go a lot back home—my sister writes and performs—so, well, I used to go and see her. I love these kinds of things, but Ryan"—she turned to indicate the chairs where they had been sitting—"well, he doesn't. He hates it actually so we don't come very often." She frowned. "He owes me tonight though because I did some awful dinner party with him at his boss's house last week."

"That's a real shame…I mean if it's something you enjoy you shouldn't have to not do it."

Cam nodded but looked uncomfortable. "Who are you here with?"

"No one," Iris replied softly. "I usually come on my own. I try not to miss one unless there's a really good reason, but I wouldn't let not having anyone to go with keep me away."

Iris sounded more pointed than she had meant to be. "I'm sorry. I didn't mean to suggest…it's just that I don't know anyone else who likes it, and I don't seem to mind doing things on my own is all. Though I know plenty of people who would though."

Cam made no effort to hide her surprise. "I'm sorry too. I assumed, I mean, I just expected you to be here with a date for some reason."

Iris could have taken Cam's words the wrong way and gotten offended and defensive. She decided not to.

"I've never been lucky enough to date a woman interested in poetry. Not sure why. My last girlfriend was worse than Ryan. I couldn't even get her to come and sit and fidget. She hated it so much. So I just started to come on my own. No one really cares. Look around you. There are so many people here on their own. Sometimes I'm glad of it as I don't have to try to externalize my feelings about what I've heard, but sometimes I really want to talk about how the poems have made me feel. It depends on my mood, you know?"

"Yeah, I get that. Do you write?" Cam asked.

"I do. I mean, I try to. I like to. I don't always have the time or the inspiration, to be honest."

Cam nodded. "Do you perform?"

"I don't." Iris wondered if she looked as uncomfortable as she felt. It was partly the questions and partly the way Cam's earnest attention made her feel.

"I want to but don't think I have the nerve. It feels so...exposing, and I guess I'm not the kind of person who likes to expose their feelings. Kudos to your sister for doing it. She's braver than me." Iris tried to sound less bothered than she felt at having to acknowledge her lack of confidence to Cam before they really knew each other.

Ryan waved a coffee cup in Iris's direction and pointed at Cam.

"Your fiancé is waving at you."

Cam turned to look in Ryan's direction and gave him the universal sign that meant "I'm coming."

"I'd better go. I'm sorry."

"Don't be. I don't want your half-time cuppa to get cold." Iris felt regret at not being able to chat to Cam for a little longer.

"Well, it was nice to see you again, anyway." Cam sounded oddly formal, almost British.

Iris nodded and Cam headed back to her seat. As she got to the end of the row, several seats away, Iris called out.

"Really nice to see you again too. See you at training or work or somewhere soon." Iris mentally face-palmed, wondering where all that friendliness had come from. It wasn't like her at all.

Cam turned back and smiled. Iris caught it before looking away feeling a little embarrassed.

"Iris?"

Iris turned back toward Cam's voice, and their eyes met across the chairs.

"Next time, we could save Ryan the trauma and come to one of these things together."

Iris took a beat before replying. "That sounds like a really cool plan."

Cam picked her way through the rows of chairs back to her seat. And Iris watched her go, happy that Cam had been so friendly.

"Who was that you were talking to?" Ryan asked.

"Just someone from work. Iris. Plays on the soccer team."

Ryan made a listening noise and Cam continued.

"Surprised she's here really. Didn't seem the poetry evening type, but it might let you off the hook if we can come to these things together in the future."

Ryan looked in Iris's direction. He raised an eyebrow as he looked at Iris properly.

"She's cute. And I'll gladly buy her a beer if she gets me out of poetry duty. My ears are already complaining and it's only halfway."

Cam could have gotten annoyed with him, but her mood had improved since arriving, and she chose to punch him playfully on the arm instead. He grabbed her and pretended to bite her neck in retaliation. Cam drank her coffee, looking forward to the second half and feeling more at peace than when she'd arrived.

As Ryan was parking the car in front of their rented semidetached house, a delivery driver on a moped pulled up next to them, dismounted at speed, and knocked on their door. Ryan jumped out of the car and intercepted the man, taking possession of a brown paper bag full of Chinese food. He waggled his phone at Cam.

"Ordered during the break. Got your favorite stir-fry with king prawns and a side of spring rolls." He looked pleased with himself.

"I have prawns in the fridge. I could've made us a stir-fry if you'd gotten home on time," Cam replied coolly.

She walked past Ryan and slipped her key in the front door, realizing she sounded churlish but not really caring. She hung up her coat and kicked off her shoes into the storage space under the stairs without waiting for Ryan and made her way along the long hallway into their kitchen. Her earlier annoyance with him had returned, and she felt tension in her body as she reached up to pull plates from the cabinet above the sink.

Ryan put the bag of food on the counter and then snaked his arms around Cam's waist, nuzzling the back of her neck.

"I thought you'd forgiven me?"

So did I, thought Cam.

"I'm sorry about making us late, honey. It's hard. It's not like Seattle here. They're real hard-asses. It's just not the kind of place that's gonna let me go in the middle of some important call just because

I have plans. I told you that already. I got home as fast as I could." He sounded genuinely sorry.

Ryan turned Cam around, making her face him. "We didn't miss anything, huh? Not a single word. No harm done." He brushed the hair from her forehead tenderly.

"We missed our dinner. That's why we're eating takeaway at nine o'clock." Cam didn't want to argue again, but she also wasn't going to let him brush away her annoyance so easily.

She slipped out of his arms and busied herself spooning food out of the containers. It smelled heavenly and her stomach rumbled.

"Let's just eat."

Cam carried the plates across to the dining table.

Just every now and then, putting me before work would be great. She really didn't want them to have another argument so, this time, Cam didn't speak the complaint out loud.

CHAPTER FOUR

I'm sorry. Will it disturb you if I join you?" Iris looked up from her iPad, and Cam looked for signs of annoyance. She was relieved to see none.

Iris moved her things to make room. The colorful tables in the small lunchroom at Cottoms each had four chairs arranged around them, but they were tiny and would only really ever seat four if two of them happened to be toddlers.

"Of course not, please take a seat." Iris pulled out the chair next to her.

Cam knew that things were still pretty formal between them. But it was something she hoped would change as they got to know each other better.

Cam sat and began the process of unpacking her lunch. Iris's gaze made her feel a little self-conscious. Ryan had put the lunch together—as he often did—but he was up and out to work so early that she rarely saw him prepare it and never knew what to expect. Inside a large sandwich box, Cam found a couple of chunks of focaccia bread wrapped in foil, a generous portion of pâté in a smaller lidded container, and lots of crudités scattered across the bottom of the box, looking colorful and very healthy. Set to one side, Ryan had tucked in a small Kit Kat—her favorite chocolate bar. The thoughtfulness of the lunch made Cam feel fondly toward him.

"Yours kind of puts my shop bought tuna sandwich to shame." Iris indicated the empty triangular cardboard box next to her.

Cam liked how Iris's face softened when she smiled.

"I'm spoiled. Ryan always makes me a lunch when he's home. He's on a health kick, and I get the benefits."

"Lucky you." Iris sipped her coffee. "He sounds like a keeper."

Cam nodded. She was feeling oddly lost for words.

"Hey, I really enjoyed the book club yesterday. Thanks for inviting me." Cam blurted it out as Iris focused her attention on her.

"No problem. It was actually really good having someone there who agreed with me for once. I'm usually the odd one out." Iris chewed her lip. "It was a pretty awful book, let's be honest."

"It was god-awful. Sometimes I think people pretend to like books because they know they've sold well and been hyped so much that they don't want to be the person to say they're actually not any good."

Iris stole a piece of pepper from Cam's lunchbox. Cam raised an eyebrow and got a wink in return. Not so formal now. She liked it.

"I know I'm not exactly the demographic for those *Fifty Shades of Grey*-type books, but you are and you hated it even more than me. That's got to tell you something about how bad it is."

Cam spread a too thick coating of pâté onto her bread, wondering how she was going to get it into her mouth without dropping half of it onto the table.

"Jeez, I hate to think I'm the demographic. Surely it's just bored housewives who want to spice up their love lives." A thought crossed her mind that Cam pushed away. "Not that there was much that was sexy in there. It mainly made me cringe." Cam knew she sounded more bothered than she felt about the book, but she was just happy to prolong the conversation, to keep Iris talking.

At the book club, Cam enjoyed hearing Iris explain her views, picking out passages to illustrate her points, listening respectfully to the others even when, Cam could tell, she vehemently disagreed with them. "Jess isn't exactly the intended readership either, but she seemed to like it, until…well, until you said you didn't and then she decided she hated it. I'm sure you noticed."

Iris looked uncomfortable but said nothing. Cam wasn't sure if she'd said too much or struck a nerve. The thought was interrupted by a lump of pâté falling as predicted from the overloaded bread and landing on the foil in front of her. Before Cam could react, Iris moved to scoop it up and pop it into her own mouth. She raised her eyebrows at Cam playfully.

"What? I'm still hungry. I had a long run this morning and it always leaves me ravenous, and all I had…" She pointed ruefully at the sandwich wrapper next to her. Cam passed her a cherry tomato.

"I'll tell Ryan to pack me extra tomorrow. He obviously didn't know that I was eating for two."

"You've got him that well trained?"

"It's about the only thing I can get him to do. He's pretty strong minded. You're right though, I'll have to add 'and forever make me a healthy lunch' into his wedding vows to make sure he doesn't slack off after the wedding."

"Is it soon?"

Cam passed Iris another piece of pepper and watched as Iris finished it off in one bite.

"Not really. We don't have a date. We're going to wait till we get back to the States so our families can attend. It'd be silly to have it here when we don't really know anyone and they'd all have to travel. My mom is super anxious that it's soon though. She's been planning it for years. I'm the elder of two daughters and she can't wait. She keeps telling me I shouldn't wait too long as my biological clock is ticking."

"She's worried about that at your age? What are you, twenty-five, twenty-six?" Iris shook her head.

"I'm twenty-eight in March."

"You look younger than that. But twenty-eight's not exactly ancient."

"It's desperately old according to my mom—especially since she had me at twenty-one."

"Rubbish. You're in the prime of life. Don't let anyone tell you different."

"Are those kind of flattering comments how you get all those women to fall for your charms?" Cam chanced a joke, but regretted it when Iris's jaw tightened.

For a moment, neither of them spoke.

"I don't have women falling for my charms. Probably best not to listen to Jess on the subject of me. She tends to exaggerate." Iris sounded weary and let out a breath.

Cam wanted to get Iris talking again…about safer things.

"Where do you run? And more to the point, how the hell do you get yourself out of bed to run on winter mornings like this one? I find it impossible and I love running."

Iris ticked off her responses on her fingers. "One, I love my food—other people's food too as you might have noticed." She stole another piece of pepper. "I eat so much that if I don't run, I'll get out of shape. Two, I'm scared to get out of shape because Megan will notice and she will punish me with extra training and push-ups. Fear is a very powerful motivator. And three, I live close to Hampstead Heath, which is one of the most amazing places in London to run. Sometimes when I don't want to get up, I think about the views and being out there as the Heath wakes up and it gets me out of bed."

"Oh," Cam exclaimed. "No way. I live near there too. We must be neighbors. That's amazing. I've walked over the Heath so many times but just never thought to run there. It's so dark in the mornings, I'd be a bit nervous of getting lost."

"It's dark all right, but it's got a good network of paths and, anyway, the light from all the luminous running jerseys of the other early runners out at that time of day means you never really have to worry about the dark."

Cam looked pensive.

"Ryan and I used to run together before work. Not on the Heath, but there's this park closer to the house. We'd run laps together. He stopped a while back, too busy to fit in the early runs and preferring to play squash on the weekends. I guess running is something else I don't much like doing on my own so I kind of stopped too. I miss early morning runs actually. They used to set me up for the day." Cam blew out a breath, feeling frustrated that she had let herself go without something else that she really liked doing.

"That's funny, I sort of prefer—" Iris stopped halfway through the sentence.

"What?"

"I was going to say that I prefer running alone. That I love to put on a playlist and lose myself for an hour but, actually, I'm not even sure that's really true. I guess it's just what I've got used to." Iris shrugged.

"Considering we live close by, and considering we're both too scared of Megan not to maintain peak fitness, don't you think it'd be neighborly of us to run together sometime? I have plenty of luminous stuff in my closet. I would love to run on the Heath with you. Or I could show you the little park where Ryan and I used to run." Cam waited, worried she had been too forward, too quick to ask.

"That sounds cool."

Cam sat back, satisfied that her boldness had paid off. She had a good feeling about Iris. She unwrapped the Kit Kat and offered half to Iris.

Iris raised an eyebrow. "You sure you're not just being polite?" Cam shook her head and Iris took the offering happily.

Cam pointed at Iris's iPad. "Working during your lunch hour? Not good."

Iris sat back in her chair. Her expression was thoughtful, like she was deciding about something. Finally, Iris sat forward.

"I was working on a poem, been working on it for weeks actually. I just can't seem to get it right. I thought I'd got hold of what the problem was an hour ago and snuck off for an early lunch to see if I could make it work. Turns out to have been a false dawn." She pushed the iPad farther away from her.

Cam leaned forward conspiratorially. "I totally approve of you thinking about poetry during the team meeting. You looked like you were paying attention, but you were actually being all creative and not listening at all. Graham would be very offended."

"Graham is a Grade A pillock."

"A what?" Cam frowned.

"Pillock is British for jerk. Or asshat. It's politer than wanker but stronger than moron," Iris clarified. "I'm enlarging your British cursing vocabulary. You can thank me later."

"Pillock." Cam tried out the word, it sounded strange in her mouth. "I'll give it a try and let you know how it goes."

"Extra points if you try it out on Graham," Iris said. She put her sandwich wrapper in the trash can to the left of their table.

Cam didn't want her to leave so soon. She sat forward in her chair. "Do you...I mean, can I..." She pointed at the iPad. "Can I help? Can I look at it?"

The look of horror that passed across Iris's face was all the answer Cam needed.

"Of course not. Sorry. You barely know me. Put it down to me being a socially forward American or something. My sister used to let me help by reading hers...never mind, sorry, Iris." Cam focused on putting away her lunch and trying to hide her embarrassment.

"It's not that, it's not that it's you I mean. It's just…I'm sorry, but I don't show them to anyone. They're just for me really. I write about personal things."

"It's okay, don't worry. Sorry for intruding. I'm kind of jealous actually. I used to write…not poetry…I always considered poems too hard, maybe a little too creative for me. But I wrote nonfiction. A lot of articles, reviews, that sort of thing. I was a journalism major in college, and I wrote for the college newspaper." Cam hesitated.

"But I kinda lost my way with it all. I sometimes think that it's a shame because I think that…" Cam stopped again, not sure she knew what she thought, knowing that she tried not to think about it at all. "I think being a journalist would have suited me. I'm very curious about things, and I really like words, reading them, writing them."

"How'd you lose your way?" Iris asked quietly.

They were interrupted by the sound of the door swinging open and Hazel stepped in.

"James decided he wants you in this meeting after all." Hazel spoke from the doorway. "Sorry."

Cam looked on forlornly as Iris stood up—wishing she'd had the chance to apologize again for her tactlessness in asking to see the poem. Iris picked up her iPad.

"Got to get back to work I suppose."

"See you at training later?"

Iris nodded. "Yeah, definitely."

Cam smiled hesitantly, really hoping she hadn't made a mess of things by trying too hard to be friendly. She really liked Iris and knew they had lots in common, and as Iris turned toward the door, Cam realized that she hadn't wanted someone to be her friend this much in a really long time.

Chapter Five

Cam looked across the table at Ryan. It was barely eight, but he was already showered and dressed. His dark hair was still a little damp, and she couldn't help but notice how pale he looked, the dark rings around his eyes giving away that he wasn't sleeping enough. He had his head buried in the *Financial Times* like most weekend mornings. When they first got together, Cam would challenge him to put the paper aside and be more sociable over breakfast, but these days she didn't bother.

Cam knew she should be more worried about the change than she was, but like everything these days, even the worrying had become routine and she didn't have enough energy for it. When she'd confided to her sister a few months ago that she was concerned at how little she and Ryan did together, how disconnected they sometimes felt, Alison told her it was natural for a couple with four years on the clock to not be sparking off each other all the time. Alison wasn't exactly an expert though. Her longest relationship had been nine months, and she'd always told Cam that she was too easily bored to manage anything longer. Despite that, Alison seemed to think it was absolutely the right thing for Cam to stick it out and make her long-term relationship work. Like always, they reverted to their childhood roles. Cam was the sensible one and Alison was younger and wilder.

As close as Cam was with her sister, and despite the many tawdry tales Alison had shared about her own love life, Cam had never had the nerve to confess that her sex life with Ryan had also stopped sparking. She felt it was something shameful and not something to admit, even to Alison. Weekends were when she felt the loss of the intimacy most. Earlier in the relationship, they'd make a point of staying in bed to have breakfast and then "fooling around." Cam used the euphemism her mother used, the words sounding prissy even to herself. Cam missed those times even though she didn't always think of herself as a very sexual person.

Cam shook the thought away and concentrated on the task of introducing a thin coating of Marmite to her bagel. The brown goo had become her breakfast topping of choice since coming to London and discovering it all those months ago. She'd tried to describe the unusual taste to Alison, found it impossible, given up, and mailed her a jar. She got a text message two weeks later that simply said: *Hate it. The devil's invention.* Cam missed her sister; she missed their chats. She should call her soon.

Cam crossed the kitchen to top up her coffee, automatically doing the same for Ryan and receiving a similarly automatic "Thanks, babe" by way of acknowledgement. Too much in her life was automatic these days. Roles, tasks, even meals like this. She hadn't ever questioned it, but lately she had begun to wonder when it had all started, when she had started to feel like everything was so routine and her life was emptier than she'd like. Would she be happier back in the States, with friends and family closer? Or would the dull routine and respectability of all that feel stifling? Cam always tried to be honest with herself so she didn't want to deny that she had felt some of that boredom and absence of purpose before they left for London, and in agreeing to come with Ryan, had hoped that the change of scene might be good for them. The first few months did feel different, more exciting, but then the same feelings had reemerged. Maybe her sister was right and things feeling a little routine was a natural part of any long-term relationship, regardless of the partner or the setting. Cam tried to imagine herself five years from now or even ten years from now, having the same breakfast with Ryan for all that time. Maybe at some point there'd be kids she'd need to feed a breakfast to as well. It should have been a good feeling, something she looked forward to. It wasn't, and the thought made her feel gloomy.

Cam wondered what Iris was doing and whether she would ever choose to read the paper rather than talk to her girlfriend over a meal. *Where had that thought come from?* Cam chided herself for being ridiculous. Especially given that everything she'd heard about Iris said she was the kind of person who conquered women for fun and probably wouldn't even stick around for breakfast, let alone sit and offer sparkling conversation over a Marmite bagel.

Cam did know that Iris had had at least one relationship—the woman who hated poetry—but she didn't know if it had been anything serious. The idea that Iris might have been referring to Jess jarred for some reason. Jess would definitely hate poetry, and Jess had already suggested that she and Iris had had something. Try as she might though, Cam just couldn't see Iris and Jess together. Iris was funny and creative and...she searched for the right word...careful. And Cam already knew that Jess was the opposite—unkind, impulsive, and indiscreet.

Cam sipped her coffee, not really understanding why she was thinking about Iris, why Iris was the person she was comparing Ryan to. *But she was.* She was a new friend and there was lots about her still to know. It was understandable that Iris was on Cam's mind. *Wasn't it?* Cam chewed the last of her bagel. She had only known Iris for a matter of weeks, whereas she and Ryan had four years under their belts. Surely she'd be in this position with anyone she had spent that length of time with.

"Can we do something later?" Cam broke the silence of the breakfast table, wanting to banish the thoughts that were roaming unhelpfully around her mind. "Maybe a museum or a gallery. Or a movie."

To her own ears, she sounded a little whiny as if she were already expecting Ryan to find an excuse to say no. He put down the paper.

"I'd love to, honey, but I'm going to Frankfurt later, remember? We have that big presentation first thing tomorrow." He shrugged as if sorry about it.

Cam hadn't remembered. She felt a wave of annoyance.

"The car's coming for me at three thirty. Sorry, babe. Next week, definitely. We can go and see that new Bond movie if you like. It's supposed to be good." Ryan took his plate and mug to the sink and started rinsing them.

Cam was not willing to be dismissed so easily.

"What about lunch before you go? We'll have time for that after your squash game. There's a new veggie café up in the village. We could try that out. Iris said it's great."

Ryan turned from the sink. "I said I'd have lunch with Rory after we played squash. He needs a bit of a pep talk. It's not going well for him at work and he's having a few problems at home. If he doesn't up his game, he's going to cost the whole team our bonus this month." Ryan looked a little shamefaced that he had made plans.

Cam couldn't believe that, knowing he was going away again, he would not have arranged things so as to spend some of the day with her. She could easily say as much, make him feel bad, and he would tell her wearily that she didn't understand the pressure he was under. She just couldn't see the point.

"Aren't you going running with Iris this morning?" Ryan didn't wait for an answer. "Ask her to try out that café with you. She might not have plans."

"Good idea," Cam said flatly. She crossed to the stairs, leaving her breakfast things on the table. "I'd better go and get ready actually." As she left the room, Cam offered up a halfhearted, "Enjoy your game." Ryan sighed as she left the room. She was determined not to care.

Though it was December and still only a quarter past nine, the day was a clear one, and the sun had managed to get itself up and was sitting low in the sky. Iris closed her eyes and enjoyed the feel of it on her face. It was about the only part of her that wasn't covered. She was dressed for the cold weather in leggings and a long-sleeved top over a short-sleeved base layer. Iris had arrived at the allotted bench at the bottom of Preacher's Hill fifteen minutes early, which, given that she lived ten minutes away, was no mean feat. It also meant she was already starting to feel the cold.

Iris didn't want to use the word excited to describe how she felt when she woke up and remembered she was meeting Cam for a run, but she had to admit that she'd looked forward to it all week. She had something close to butterflies over breakfast, and they hadn't vanished until she got here and sat on the bench. Iris had chosen a northeasterly route that took them away from the road that crossed the Heath, up past Hampstead ponds, across Parliament Hill, and then farther up to Highgate.

The sun was soothing Iris's nerves in a way that no amount of telling herself that them running together wasn't a big deal hadn't. The truth was that it wasn't a big deal. Cam had said Ryan never had the time to go running with her and wanted the company. Iris made herself imagine that she'd have said the same to Hazel or Vicki or whoever she happened to be talking to when the subject came up. It helped.

She was delighted when Cam stopped by her desk on Friday saying that, as they didn't have a match this week and Ryan was playing squash, she'd love to go for a run on Sunday morning if Iris was free. Iris had agreed happily. Very happily.

"Hey, shouldn't you be stretching or doing push-ups or something." Cam's voice startled her.

"Hey, Grandma, you look like you're having a little snooze there. Do you want me to come back later?" Cam teased her.

"Well, it is pretty early for a Sunday and I did have a very late night." Cam frowned slightly and, for some reason, Iris felt a need to clarify she wasn't out with a woman. "I mean I was writing until about one—got in the groove somehow—and then of course I couldn't sleep afterward."

"I'm glad you're writing. Anything unbelievably personal that you want me to read?" It had become a joke between them that Cam would offer to read the poems and Iris would refuse. "Maybe it's a love poem about someone you like?" She faltered. "Ignore me, sorry. Just needlessly fishing for information I don't have a right to have. That American thing. I'm gonna keep blaming that until someone stops me."

"It's funny you should ask." Iris paused for effect. "The poem was all about my unrequited love for Graham actually. Far too personal to share of course. Though if you can help me find a rhyme for pillock I'll forever be in your debt."

Iris started to stretch her calves, leaning on the side of the bench for balance. Cam took up a similar position opposite her and began to do likewise.

Iris was mid-stretch, her head pointing down to her knees, her leg up on the bench.

"You sound like Hazel actually. She's always asking me about my love life and I always say the same thing back—nothing to report I'm afraid. Sorry to disappoint everyone who wants to see me happily paired off."

"I'm not sure that's what I want." Cam paused. "You'll have someone else to run with and talk to about poetry...where would that leave me?" Cam's matter-of-fact possessiveness surprised Iris.

"Funnily enough, I was chatting with Diane in the pub after training last week and she was paying me a lot of attention, and I thought I'd have to have one of those conversations about liking her as a friend, etc., but then I realized that she was actually just talking to me so she could pump me for info about Jess, who she seems to have the total hots for." Iris lifted her eyebrows. "She's far too young and far too sweet for me. I'd worry that my cynical self would simply crush her under foot, but the old ego still took a bruising when I finally figured out I was just her way to get to Jess."

Iris looked at Cam, who was observing her closely, biting her lip and looking as if she wanted to say something and then thinking better of it. Iris wasn't sure whether to be relieved or disappointed. Cam's openness was refreshing but still a little disconcerting sometimes.

Despite the coldness of the morning, Cam had opted for running shorts, and Iris couldn't help but admire her legs. It wasn't the first time she had acknowledged just how damned good Cam looked in shorts. Her running top was a bright fluorescent yellow color, long-sleeved, and fit Cam perfectly, accentuating the shapeliness of her body. Cam had her hair tied up, as she did for football, but some strands had broken free, and Iris had to fight an urge to reach out and tuck them back into place. She sought to pull herself together and concentrate on the tightness of her own hamstrings rather than the tightness of Cam's top. Cam had this power to occasionally reduce her to thoughts best suited to a teenage boy. Happily, the last year had meant that Iris had gotten pretty good at closing down feelings like that. She wanted to build a grown-up friendship with Cam without anything getting in the way.

"I've planned a circular route that's about five miles if that's okay? Takes us past the ponds. There'll be naked bathers so try not to look."

"Of course I'm going to find it impossible not to be staring now." Cam rewarded Iris with a wink.

"Well, the men and women have separate ponds, so we'll have to diverge paths at that point to get the view we want."

Iris raised both eyebrows to signify she was joking. Cam reacted, looking like she was going to say something but presumably thinking better of it.

"Then we'll take the path up Parliament Hill toward Highgate. It's a clear day so we should get great views."

"Sounds perfect. I'm completely in your hands." Cam nodded.

Iris wasn't sure whether she imagined the faint blush that colored Cam's cheeks as the double meaning of the comment landed. If Hazel or Vicki had said it, Iris would have answered back with a smutty remark, but she didn't know Cam well enough to take the chance and let the comment go.

"Okay, I'll hum the theme from *Rocky* and you set the pace." Iris pointed in the direction they needed to go. They set off along the narrow path, a low railing on one side and a line of tall oak trees on the other.

❖

Iris and Cam had passed the ponds and were striking out now on the steady climb that would get them to the top of Parliament Hill. They were almost there, and the sky was still completely cloudless

"This view is incredible. Ryan and I walked up here a couple of times, but both times it was cloudy and we couldn't see much of the view."

"Have you and Ryan always lived around here?" Iris tried to sound like she had more breath than she did.

"It's the only place we've stayed. His company found the place when he agreed to relocate to London. The house is one of those things that's making Ryan think about leaving. We have to decide in the next couple of months whether to renew the rental or pack up and go home."

Iris felt a pang of disappointment stronger than she had expected at the news that Cam might be leaving.

"Do you think you will? Leave, I mean."

Cam waited a long time before replying. "I don't know. I think Ryan is of two minds. He's hating his job but also hates the idea of admitting defeat and going back home. Talking about it doesn't seem to get us anywhere. I suggested renewing for six months rather than a year, give ourselves more time to see how things go, but Ryan hates compromises. He's a bit do-or-die, you know?" She looked across at Iris as they ran.

Iris didn't know Ryan, but she was starting to really dislike him for threatening to take Cam away before they'd had a chance to really form their friendship.

"The worst of it is that I don't really feel ready to leave London. You know what it's like. Working takes up all your time and you realize there's so much you haven't seen, so many places you haven't visited." Cam slowed her pace. A woman with a stroller was ahead of them on the path, and they had to pass her in single file.

"When we first came we did a fair bit of sightseeing—the obvious places like Madame Tussauds, Buckingham Palace, the big museums—and then Ryan's work got busy and he seemed to find it impossible to find time. I...well...you'll say it's lame I'm sure, but I don't really know anyone here, so I stopped exploring too."

Iris could feel Cam's sadness. It made her wonder about Cam's relationship with Ryan. They'd obviously been together a long time, and Cam had followed him here and now seemed prepared to follow him home again to get married, but where was she in all this? Ryan didn't have time to run with Cam and he didn't have time to take her out to see London. Cam deserved better than that.

"Well, I hope you'll stay. I'd love to show you London." Iris said the words without thinking. "Not all of it. I mean that would take ages... obviously. But some bits of it are really worth seeing. The East End has some really quirky old houses and museums that are a bit off the beaten track. I used to live there and always want an excuse to go back. Oh, my God." Iris was animated. "There's this amazing curry house that I loved when I lived there. The food is to die for. If you like curry."

"I love curry."

"Well, I'll take you there if you promise not to complain about the service and the slightly strange decor." Iris was stupidly nervous for someone who was just offering to show a friend around town.

Cam slowed down, leaned across, and touched Iris's arm. "You know, I'd really like that. I really would."

Iris smiled, her self-consciousness gone. She was rewarded with a nudge from Cam.

"I'll race you to that bench." Cam pointed at a bench on the crest of the hill about a hundred yards away and set off sprinting along the path. Iris followed, sure that she wouldn't be able to catch Cam, but surer still that she wanted very much to do this again. Instead of the warning bells that should have been sounding, Iris heard only her own breath in her ears as she quickened her pace to catch up.

As Cam reached the bench a few yards ahead of Iris, she lifted her arms in mock celebration. She laughed as Iris flopped down onto the bench breathing heavily. Her black hair was damp, and her face, flushed red with the effort of the run, was…radiant. Cam couldn't think of a more perfect word. Her phone beeped with a text alert, and she could feel Iris watching her as she fished around in her pocket for it. She wondered if she looked anywhere near as appealing as Iris did or was simply just pink and sweaty.

Cam opened the text. *Got time to talk to your little sister?* It was Alison. Cam typed out a short reply feeling regretful. The time difference often thwarted their attempts to stay in touch. She put her phone away.

"My sister. Wanting to chat. But it'll be far too late by the time we get home so we've missed our chance now." Cam shrugged.

"That's tough. Do you find it hard to stay in touch?"

"We're close, we make it work. You can…I mean, if you want to. Though the time difference is a good excuse to never speak to my mother…we're not nearly as close."

Iris was watching her silently. Her gaze had an intensity that Cam imagined would have drawn in plenty of women over the years. The thought almost made her lose the thread of what she'd been saying.

"We're very different I think. It's hard for us to be close. My mom's a snob, so concerned about what things look like, about what people will think of her, think of us, that it affects everything she does, and I hate it." Cam knew she sounded bitter. "It's all about being seen to do the right thing."

"That's also tough."

"Yeah, tougher for my sister than me. I'm semi-respectable these days. Fiancé, office job, even living in London gives her something to boast about. My sister, on the other hand, won't knuckle down. She works on and off at shitty jobs while she prioritizes her writing, she has casual relationships with no one my mother has ever approved of, and she lives close enough to feel the pressure of putting herself through regular visits where my mom can make it clear just how disappointed she is with her choices." Again, Cam found herself able to easily talk about personal things to Iris. It felt good.

"Do you have a good relationship with your mom?" Cam asked.

Iris tensed slightly. A tiny muscle in her jaw twitched.

"Not really. I haven't seen her since I was five. She walked out."

"Jeez, sorry, Iris. What an idiot. Sorry."

"Don't be. It was a long time ago. And how could you have known? I have a great relationship with my dad. He brought me up on his own. It was just the two of us, and I had a great time having all of his attention for myself. I never felt like I missed out on much. I guess I must have, but it never felt that way. And he was way more relaxed than your mom sounds. He encouraged me—encourages me—to do what I enjoy regardless of what others might think. He taught me how to play football as a kid. He loves that I write poetry; he thinks it's soulful. He even taught me the best way to cope with menstrual cramps." Iris raised an eyebrow.

"And he didn't bat an eyelid when I came out as gay at seventeen."

"At seventeen? That's amazing. I don't think I knew anything about anything at seventeen."

Iris ran her hands through her hair. The dampness had made it even more unruly than normal. It looked cute.

"Oh, I knew about that, but probably not much else. At seventeen, I'd already had my heart broken." Iris placed a hand over her heart and pouted comically.

"Spill the heartbreaking details," Cam said.

"Her name was Rachel. We met working in a youth club. She was eighteen and taking a year out before uni. I was seventeen and still at school. She was so cool, a hundred times cooler than me, and I fell for her hard. We were inseparable for two months, and then, as I always knew would happen, she went away to study in Edinburgh, while I stayed at school in London. She was my first, but I couldn't believe we weren't going to be forever and I cried for about a week after she left, played nothing but sad songs. My dad…he knew I think. He helped me to tell him what had happened. How I felt. He was so great, didn't once try to tell me it was a phase. Even took me to the gay pride parade in London the next summer. A top bloke."

"He sounds wonderful."

"He is. Dad of the Year every year in my book. He even took me camping in the middle of nowhere when I was suffering after I split from my last long-term girlfriend. He took my phone away so I wasn't tempted to make contact with her. He knew the break was just what I needed, even when I didn't."

"Sounds like she really broke your heart."

Iris nodded. "Not that I didn't play my own part in it." Iris spoke so quietly that Cam could barely hear her.

Iris sat up in her seat, sweeping her arm out in front of her. "So, what do you think of the view of my city? Not a cloud in the sky. Almost like I planned it that way."

The modern shiny office towers that made up the Canary Wharf complex were clearly visible on the left of the vista.

"Ryan works somewhere close to that building," Cam pointed to a torpedo-shaped building in the middle distance, "I know they call it the gherkin, but it looks nothing like a sandwich pickle to me."

"If you look really closely, behind that fairly hideous tower block, you can just about make out the London Eye." Iris pointed at something dead center in the view.

"I don't think any of it's hideous. It all looks beautiful to me." She pushed her toe against Iris's foot. "Hey, thanks for bringing me up here."

"My pleasure."

Cam felt more disappointment than she had a right to when Iris stood up.

"Not sure if you've clocked it yet, but we still have to run home. You can't get an Uber from up here, not yet anyway." She bent down and touched her toes.

Cam wanted to stay sitting, wanted a few more minutes of the view and the companionship.

"Do you have plans after this? Ryan has to have lunch with some guy from work and then he's going to Frankfurt. Maybe we could do something?" Cam's plan had been to ask Iris to meet her for lunch at the new café as Ryan had suggested when he was trying to palm her off on someone for the day. But now she felt silly, like she was being too eager, too needy.

"I have plans for lunch myself. Sorry. I thought we were just running or I'd have kept the time free. I'm seeing my dad. We try to have a Sunday roast together as often as we can."

Cam was stupidly relieved that Iris wasn't meeting a woman, not really understanding why.

"We could stop for a coffee on the way back though. I'll even get you a muffin if you promise not to tell Megan I'm feeding you carbs."

"Sounds great. Blueberry. Or pecan pie. Or maybe both. I'll need them after this." Cam patted her stomach happily.

"And if we've got time, we can talk about the book you chose for next week's book club so I can get my observations in early. Five hundred pages and translated from French. I'm no psychic, Cam, but I'm guessing you're not going to be popular with the other girls with that choice."

Cam couldn't think of a better way to spend an hour on a Sunday. Her mood lifted, and she and Iris set off down the opposite side of the hill and onto the circular path that would wind them back toward their starting point.

CHAPTER SIX

Megan stood with the team sheet in her hand in the center of the changing room. The players sitting on the benches running around the edge of the room had stopped chatting as she ran through the team for the match they were about to play.

"Iris. You're staying in the center of midfield. Diane, you're on the bench this week. I'm giving Priti a run out. Sorry, but you know how it goes. Cam, you play on the left wing again. Watch their right back. You don't know her, but she'll try to intimidate you early on with a few strong tackles. Don't let her get close to you. Everyone else, same positions as last time, but a better result would be nice." Megan looked around the group with a determined look on her face.

"C'mon, Cottoms, let's get out there and win this one," Vicki's voice boomed out across the room.

Iris ran up and down on the spot, willing her muscles to stay loose, her boots clattering noisily on the tiled floor. She was relieved that Megan had switched things up so she and Cam could play together. Though fairly confident in her own ability, she'd been a little worried that Cam's obvious good form during her absence would see her lose her place.

As Iris got ready to follow her teammates out onto the pitch, Megan took her to one side, her expression even more serious than usual.

"I've got the team sheet for the other side." Megan rubbed her forehead. "Amanda's playing for them."

Iris shook her head slightly, unsure she had heard properly.

"I asked the manager, and Amanda joined them last month apparently. Are you going to be okay? I mean, I really want to you to play, but if you feel you can't, I can switch you out for Diane." The question sat between them. Iris realized how stupid this was.

"No way. Thanks though, but I'm fine. I was bound to run into her like this sooner or later. It's okay. Water under the bridge and all that." Iris headed toward the door, then turned back to Megan.

"Gina?" Iris held her breath and felt a wave of relief in her body as Megan shook her head.

"Not even on the bench."

Iris nodded and held the door open for Megan, and they walked to the pitch. It was freezing today. She could already see her breath, feeling the cold air hit her lungs. They jogged slightly to catch up with the others and Megan leaned in slightly.

"You never know, you might even enjoy putting a couple past her." She raised her eyebrows at Iris, a challenge in her eyes. Ever the motivator, Iris thought wryly.

Iris's legs felt steady. She was going to be fine. It was all water under the bridge. A lot of water, a rickety bridge, but it would be fine. Ahead of her, she could see Jess walking with Diane, who was dressed as if for an Arctic expedition in what looked like layers of polar survival gear. She didn't blame her. The life of a substitute was a tough one in this weather. Jess had an arm slung around Diane's shoulders, and Iris hoped she was giving her some encouraging words about being dropped to the bench rather than bitching about Megan's team selection. You never knew with Jess.

The atmosphere was always more subdued on a match day, the pre-match nerves meaning that there was none of the banter present during training sessions. The walk from the changing rooms to the pitch they had been allocated took them past four other pitches.

They passed goalkeepers saving practice shots from teammates and dodged the occasional wayward ball fired in their direction. All the other pitches contained men's teams, as was usually the case. As they neared their allocated pitch, Iris was close enough to recognize Maxine, Cottoms' goalkeeper, warming up with Hazel in the goal closest to her. Hazel was taking practice shots, forcing Maxine to dive first to her left and then to her right. She scrambled back to her feet after each dive, her tracksuit bottoms already covered in mud. Iris was glad Amanda and her team were warming up at the far end of the pitch. If she had been closer, Iris would have felt obliged to say hello. It would probably have been awkward, and she really didn't want her mind distracted ahead of the game.

Reaching the pitch, Iris was happy to see Cam waiting for her a few yards away, looking cute in the royal blue of the team's colors. Megan gathered the players together. The team they were due to play was likewise huddled in their own half, and Iris could make out Amanda in the middle of the group in a bright orange goalkeeping jersey. She had her back to Iris. It was hard not to seek her out. They hadn't seen each other in months. The last time being an awkward, and very brief, bumping into each other at that summer's Pride march. Iris had been with Hazel—Casey hated to march—and Amanda had been with a group of friends. They had simply exchanged a few awkward words of greeting and moved on, but the memory was not a good one.

The ref and linesmen were already in position, and Iris felt the tension in her belly that she always felt just before a game. It was usually a welcome feeling, but she knew that this time Amanda's presence on the opposing team was adding to it.

"Let's see if we can get a round of drinks out of Megan by winning this one." Cam nudged Iris.

"Yeah. My ex is in goal for the other side so if you could put a couple of goals past her, that would also be kind of satisfying." Iris wasn't sure what had made her tell Cam that. Cam scanned their opponents looking for the goalkeeper, and her brow furrowed slightly. Iris had the feeling it had been the wrong thing to say, but Cam just bumped her shoulder.

"I'll definitely try, but there's absolutely nothing stopping you from doing the same." Cam headed off to take her position ready for kickoff.

They were almost thirty minutes into the game and up 1-0. Cam ran up the left hand side of the pitch with the ball at her feet. She had good speed, but more than that, she seemed in complete control of the ball, never letting it get too far away from her feet as she dribbled. Cam's head was slightly bowed as she concentrated on keeping possession, but she lifted it occasionally, looking for a teammate to make a run into space that she could pass the ball into. Iris was hanging back slightly, ready for the give-and-go from Cam. Iris could see that Cam was now level with the penalty area and closing on the right back who had come across to cover Cam's run. The right back, a fearsome woman oddly named Mabel, covered the distance between the edge of the penalty area and Cam with surprising speed. Iris could see the defender wasn't going to stop, and her shout to Cam to release the ball or get out of the way was truncated as the crunch of Mabel's tackle and Cam's cry of pain rendered the warning shout pointless.

Iris and Jess were the first to her side. Jess pushed Mabel in the chest.

"You didn't even try to play the ball. What the fuck is wrong with you, you fucking psycho." Jess was shouting as players from both sides tried to pull them apart.

Iris's priority wasn't Mabel but Cam, who was rolling around on the ground, hands covering her face and making all sorts of noises that illustrated just how much pain she was in. Iris gently pulled Cam's hands away from her face. She was a not-very-reassuring shade of gray.

"Show me where it hurts," Iris said gently. "Is it bad?"

Cam nodded and reached down to her right ankle. Iris could already see that it was swollen—badly swollen. She said a silent prayer for nothing to be broken and gingerly prodded the anklebone. Cam yelped at Iris's touch.

"I'm sorry, but I'm going to try to move it. It'll hurt, but we need to see if you need an ambulance." Cam looked at Iris. The intensity of the stare made Iris feel a little disconcerted. Cam nodded.

"My left leg's fine though, so hurt me too much and I'll kick you with it." Cam grimaced but still managed a joke.

Iris grinned back at her, relieved and impressed at the same time. She took the ankle's weight with one hand and carefully and gently rotated Cam's foot with the other, moving it slowly in wide circles. Cam winced, the pain seemingly linked to every rotation, though Cam was nodding at the same time. A good sign. Iris caught a flash of orange. It was the orange of Amanda's shirt. Iris hadn't been aware of her leaning over the two of them. Iris glanced up at her, and their eyes locked for a moment before Amanda touched Cam on the knee.

"I hope you're okay. I'm really sorry about that."

Iris watched her trudge back toward the goal at the other end of the pitch and brought her attention back to Cam who was studying her curiously. Iris jumped slightly as a red bucket dropped to the ground next to them. Megan had set it down and was now crouched next to Cam.

"I'm going to report that tackle to the football association." She fished a sponge out of the bucket and wrung it out so that icy cold water poured onto Cam's ankle. Having passed a first aid course some years before, Megan was the closest thing they had to a team physio. She took over examining Cam's foot.

"That's not the first time she's tried to hurt another player. The ref sent her off, and I suspect Jess will slash her car tires later if she doesn't have the good sense to leave before the end of the match."

Iris shook her head. "She'd better be out of here before we get finished."

Megan gave her an arched eyebrow of disapproval. Iris felt silly. Megan was right; this was a time for cool heads not retaliation. Megan liberally sprayed Cam's ankle with a can of Deep Freeze.

"Can you get up if we help you?" Megan asked. Cam nodded unconvincingly, still looking as gray as the winter sky.

"It's badly swollen and the bruises will be impressive but probably nothing more serious than that." Megan sounded reassuring, to Iris at least.

Megan grabbed the red bucket with one hand and took one of Cam's arms with the other. Iris took the other arm and encouraged Cam to lean on her as she very gingerly got to her feet. She tried to walk but clearly couldn't put any real weight on her right foot.

"I guess I'll just sit out the rest of the game. Give someone else a chance to shine." Cam winced again as she tried to put her foot down. "But at least the bruises will give me something to show Graham the next time he says that women don't take the game as seriously as the men."

Iris's regard for Cam continued to climb. Leaning on Iris and Megan, Cam slowly hopped to the touchline. Diane had been hoping for the chance to play but obviously hadn't expected it to come so soon. She peeled off her layers of clothes and quickly began to warm up. Iris grabbed one of Diane's coats for Cam to sit on and covered her with the rest of the clothing.

"Try not to get hit with the ball while you're sitting there and we'll try not to throw away this lead without you." Iris placed a hand on Cam's shoulder.

"Thanks." Cam gazed back at her.

Iris jogged back to her position on the field, trying to concentrate on the remainder of the game and to stop worrying about Cam. Jess passed by on her way to take the free kick that the referee had awarded for Mabel's foul.

"I'm not sure we'd all have gotten that much sympathy from you, Iris. Still trying to impress the new girl I guess."

There was definitely something edgy underneath Jess's comment, and Iris was already annoyed enough by the tackle to react. She wheeled around ready to tell Jess to screw herself, but Jess had moved quickly out of range and Megan was close enough to hiss a quick "Ignore her and get in the box" at Iris. Iris did as she was told, determined not to get involved in any more drama and even more determined to make the other team pay for hurting Cam by winning this match.

At the touchline, three of the spectators gathered around Cam and helped her awkwardly get up off the ground, supporting her to hop off in the direction of the changing rooms. Iris was happy to see Cam get out of the cold but inexplicably jealous that they were the ones caring for her while she had to play the remainder of the game.

Before she could ponder it further, the ref blew her whistle, and Jess floated a lovely ball into the box. Iris used her height to climb above the defender at the far post and head the ball in the direction of the goal. She had just enough pace on the header to force the ball past Amanda's outstretched hands and into the far corner of the net. The whooping that greeted the goal came not just from her own teammates but from the little band of spectators that were carrying Cam. They were still close enough to have seen the goal go in, and Iris led her teammates to the side of the pitch to celebrate with Cam. The broad smile and high five Iris received from Cam when they got there was all the reward she needed for the goal, and she skipped back to the center circle for the restart feeling pleased with herself.

❖

There was excitement amongst the chatter on the way to the pub. They enjoyed the 2-0 win as much as any of their recent victories, and the extra drama caused by the vicious tackle that Iris thought had badly damaged Cam's ankle added to the feverish atmosphere.

As everyone got changed after the match, Iris had stepped in and insisted that she would take Cam straight home so that she could rest, ice her ankle, and let the painkillers do their work, but once they were in the car, Cam begged Iris to take her to the pub.

"Please," Cam said, her voice imploring Iris to do what she wanted. "I don't want to miss the celebrations."

Iris was at the junction leading onto the main road. Left would take her toward Hampstead and Cam's house, and right would take her toward the pub. Cam leaned across Iris's body and flicked the lever to indicate a right turn.

"I bet Jackie can find some ice for my foot."

"Painkillers make you bossy, you know," Iris said, turning her steering wheel clockwise.

Despite the cold December temperatures, colder still now that the sun was down, a few of them braved the cold and sat outside the pub trying to stay warm under the feeble patio heaters. The beer garden was not large, housing six rectangular picnic tables, and at one end, a large built-in brick barbecue—an extravagance of Jackie's that got used for barely three weeks every summer when the sun poked through the clouds and everyone got their shorts on and starting grilling sausages like mad.

The outside space sat behind the pub and was surrounded by a low wall. Regents Canal ran along the longest side. The towpath was popular with cyclists and dog walkers, and a gap in the wall halfway along made it possible to stop in for an impromptu drink on their way along the canal.

Cam had refused to sit inside, convinced that the smell of the Deep Freeze that Megan had insisted on re-spraying all over her ankle would be off-putting to the other drinkers. Iris was unwilling to leave Cam and go inside. This was partly out of concern for Cam's well-being, partly because she was starting to love Cam's company, and partly a consequence of the fact that Jess and Vicki had sat outside with them and were offering up anecdotes that again made Iris sound like some kind of sex addict. Iris winced as the discussion had turned to the time that a couple of defenders on a team they were playing against got sent off after they came to blows with each other in a jealous fight over Iris who had, so the story went, bedded them both in the same week. The fight between them was actually nothing to do with Iris, but Jess and Vicki weren't about to let the facts get in the way of a good story.

Cam had looked as uncomfortable as Iris felt at hearing the story, and Iris badly wanted the chance to redeem herself with Cam in some way. Iris had slept with both the women—she couldn't deny that—but it was important to her that Cam understood that she was no longer the Iris who did that kind of thing. She didn't want old Iris, as she thought of her, to put Cam off being friends with the person she was now. Iris changed the subject, but she felt that Cam was still looking at her a little oddly.

Waiting at the bar to get some drinks, Iris felt Hazel sidle up to her and put an arm around her shoulders.

"Amanda's not coming, in case you were wondering. She texted me half an hour ago and said she had plans. I don't think she did. I think she just didn't want it to be awkward." Iris felt her blood pressure drop a few points.

"I wasn't sure. She'd have been within her rights to come."

It was often the case that the two teams drank together after a match, and some of their opponents today—with the obvious exception of Mabel, now cemented as Public Enemy Number One with the Cottoms women—were sitting with the players enjoying a drink.

"I don't know why I was worrying about her coming. It's not like we haven't spoken since the split. We spent hours, days even, going over everything at the time, and we left things in an okay place. I think." Iris ran her hands through her hair. "It'll be fine. I just wasn't expecting it. It's been ages since I've seen her and I hadn't prepared myself for it." Iris blew out a breath. Hazel gave her a squeeze.

"I know, babe, it's okay. I'm just sorry I didn't get the chance to warn you. She didn't say she was playing this week."

Hazel turned back toward the lounge with her drinks in hand and Iris called after her.

"Next time, tell her she should come. I'm sure we can be civilized around each other after all this time."

Hazel nodded, and Iris paid the barmaid and picked up her own drinks. What she hadn't said was that while she was prepared to see Amanda, Iris wasn't at all ready to see Amanda out with Gina, the woman Amanda had replaced her with. She wasn't sure when she'd be ready for that, but definitely not while she was single and still feeling so bruised by it all.

The number of players sitting at the outside tables had reduced. The falling temperatures meant that the inside of the pub was proving too much of a draw.

"Where is everyone? I was only gone five minutes. What ridiculously forward American questions did you ask them to make them all leave?" Iris smiled as she sat and waited for Cam to suggest they follow the rest of the team indoors for the warmth, and when she didn't, she felt relief.

They were now the only occupants of a table sitting at the edge of the pub's garden. Beside the low wall next to them was the narrow canal path. It was dark already and the canal surface looked murky and still.

"Vicki's gone home to get ready for a night out with the Princess. Apparently, Harry's taking her somewhere very fancy for dinner. She sounded excited but seemed worried about eating with the wrong fork." Cam took the drink that Iris pushed in her direction. "She said she was pretty surprised they were getting on so well what with Harry being so posh and Vicki being so common." Cam paused to sip her drink. "I'm paraphrasing obviously. She also said she's been Instagram stalking Harry and found out that she's still friends with her most recent ex and said she's gonna put a stop to that. She told me that staying friends with the ex is an 'awful lesbian tradition' that she's always resisted." Cam looked at Iris with a guilty expression before looking down at the table briefly.

"Tell me you didn't?"

"I just said she'd obviously made an exception by staying friends with you, and she just looked a bit sheepish. What's wrong with that?" Cam put her hands out trying to look innocent.

"You are the worst." Iris shook her head, pretending to be cross.

"You never tell me anything. That's why I have to do my own investigating."

"There's nothing to tell. Especially about Vicki. Though obviously I wouldn't tell you if there was." Iris tipped her glass in Cam's direction and popped out her tongue.

"True. I've learned more from Jess than I have from you."

"And most of that is fake news." Iris sighed. "Where is the little troublemaker anyway?"

"She's gone inside with Diane. They looked pretty darn cozy I have to say. Jess looked about ready to make a move."

"Yeah, I bet. She's pretty damn relentless. I keep thinking she'll get bored of it, but she never does." Iris shrugged.

"I suppose it's one way of keeping fit. It's got to be easier than running up Parliament Hill."

"You enjoyed it. I know you did. And I'm taking you up there again after we've tried out your park. I'm actually looking forward to going running with you now that your ankle's bruised. It's got to slow you down. We both know I couldn't keep up with you last time."

They sat quietly for a few moments, both watching the ducks on the canal's surface, barely visible in the murk.

"When did you get bored of it all?" Cam's question confused Iris. She assumed Cam was still talking about running. But something in her expression helped Iris to understand she was talking about something else.

"I mean the relentless womanizing that Jess won't shut up about. When did you tire of it? And why don't you date anymore? I can't believe you don't get offers." Cam sipped her drink and regarded Iris closely.

Cam had a knack for asking the most disconcerting questions. Iris hesitated before responding. She knew that Cam's question was the chance she wanted to state clearly that chasing women she didn't really want was a soulless activity and one she was glad was definitely in her past, but she also knew that making clear she'd put it behind her meant owning up to the truth of it all, and she still felt pretty shameful about the whole thing.

"I got bored of it almost instantly. I realized that sex without a connection is, well, just sex. Empty and oddly unenjoyable, and sex with a connection, well, that's a relationship, and I feel like I've proved

I'm not very good at those. I figure that staying single means I don't have to expose myself to either, and that seems like a good thing. For me and the women involved, less damaging all round." Iris wanted to say more, but she felt a hand on her shoulder and stopped. It was Hazel.

"We're going home now." Hazel was hand in hand with Casey. "We've got an early start tomorrow. Casey's making me go on a stupid o'clock flight to Dublin to visit her family." She paused. "Save me, Iris, there's hundreds of them." She spoke in a mock whisper and was rewarded with a playful nudge from Casey.

"I already promised her unlimited Guinness, and she knows that my family always treat her like visiting royalty. My ma will have been baking for days, but no, she still wants to moan about it."

"I do. I like milking the sympathy." Hazel pulled Casey into a kiss.

Iris hugged them both good-bye.

"So cute. Like teenagers in love even though they've been together for ages. It's pretty inspiring actually." Iris remembered the way that Cam and Ryan had been play fighting at the poetry evening. "I guess you and Ryan are the same though, and you guys have a few years under your belts, don't you?"

Cam looked really uncomfortable at the question and Iris wished she had kept her comment to herself. It was a joke among her friends that she had an uncanny ability to divine what would be the worst thing to say in any given situation and then to say it. It was one of the reasons she generally tried to say as little as possible. Iris waited for Cam to find a way to avoid answering the question. They were now the only two people left outside. The cold had finally driven everyone else inside or home.

"I'm sorry. I didn't mean to be intrusive."

"It's not that. I don't mind the question. I'm just not sure I want to give a truthful answer."

For a second, Iris didn't understand. Then she did. Or at least thought that maybe she did.

"It's freezing out here." Cam pulled the zip on her training top as high as it would go. Cam was only wearing a windbreaker, and the jersey she was wearing underneath didn't look very thick. Iris had seen the projected temperatures and chosen a warm coat over a thick fleece-lined hoodie. She knew she should suggest that they go inside, but she didn't want to. A small voice in her head told her that Cam was using the weather to get away from her inappropriate questions anyway. She felt deflated. She was enjoying the evening, enjoying getting to know Cam, and she didn't want tonight's chat to come to such a quick end.

Iris gestured with her head toward the pub. "Do you want to try to get a table inside?"

"No, thanks, I'll tough it out. I'm quite enjoying it out here." Cam shook her head as she spoke and gave Iris a sweet smile. Iris felt the warmth of it register in every corner of her body.

"Can I at least offer you my gloves? I'm wearing a lot more than you so your need is definitely greater than mine." Iris handed over her gloves and Cam took them happily.

"That's very gallant of you. They told me before I came here that the British were very well mannered, but you're the only person that's come close to proving it." Cam wiggled her fingers at Iris in the gloves, which looked far too big for her.

"You have very big hands though compared to mine." Cam paused. "Actually, that's not very complimentary is it? Sorry." Cam's eyes sparkled, and Iris found it hard not to stare.

Get a grip, Iris warned herself, willing the coldness of the air to counter the heat she felt when Cam looked at her like that. Cam looked down at her drink—a soft drink she had complained about, but which Iris had forced on her given the painkillers she had taken. Cam took a small sip and rolled her eyes at Iris as if to signify how unsatisfactory the drink was. She leaned forward and adjusted the bag of ice Jackie had propped on top of her ankle.

"Ryan is lovely and I really do love him a lot, but sometimes I think we have so little in common that I don't know how we've built a life together. Or even if we have built a life together. He works, I work. He sees people from his work, I see people from work. He wants to stay home, I want to go out. He wants a big wedding, kids, a dog, and a big yard, and I can't quite believe that that's going to be my future. Forget the rest of it; I'm not even sure I'm ready to get married yet if I'm honest." Cam seemed to have found her voice, and Iris stayed silent, letting her talk.

"I don't know why I'm talking to you like this. I have a lot on my mind, and maybe because you don't know him, I can say it to you. If I say it to my sister, she just tells me he's lovely and I'll never find a sweeter man. My mother adores him and always takes his side. She thinks I've done well to snag an investment banker and should just be grateful." Cam toyed with her watch, and then her engagement ring.

"Don't get me wrong, he is sweet and I've spent four years loving him, it's just that sometimes we seem like such different people and I don't feel like he gets me at all. I don't get myself sometimes so I can hardly blame him, but still…" Cam looked down at the table, seeming self-conscious. When Cam looked up, Iris could see sadness. Iris had the impulse to make her feel better.

"Trust me, Cam. I know all about loving someone despite what you don't have in common, not because of what you do. Love works funny like that. You just have to focus on the things that you do really like about him, the things that you do have in common. And keep talking about the difficult stuff. Never stop talking. When you stop talking is when you're in trouble." Iris had realized this far too late to save her own relationship but always gave the advice to others, believing that maybe she and Amanda would have found a way through had they only talked to each other.

"I tell you what, tell me three things you really love about him. It can't hurt to remind yourself." Iris leaned forward, wanting to show Cam that she was ready to listen.

"It wasn't this cold last winter. What happened to that global warming we were promised?" Cam shivered and rubbed her hands together.

Iris wouldn't blame Cam if she was trying to change the subject; they'd managed to get onto very personal ground somehow.

"I love lots of things about him. He's driven and he's decisive, and I think that's good for me because I'm a bit of a drifter. He loves to eat and I love to cook. I like the way he looks when he sleeps, like a little boy version of his adult self, so sweet and vulnerable and with all the stress he usually carries in his face completely gone." Cam picked up her drink and took a swallow. "But I don't want to talk about Ryan. I feel like you're trying to distract me. Let's talk about you. Tell me why grown women fight over you, why you don't date anymore, and tell me about your—very attractive by the way—goalkeeping ex-girlfriend who I assume is the one you stopped talking to." Cam leaned forward to mirror Iris's posture, holding her gaze.

Iris spluttered her beer with surprise, almost spitting a mouthful onto the table in front of them.

"Wow, that's very direct, even for you."

"Oh, I know. I'm generally not as bad as this, and I can't even blame the drink tonight. You can either take the blame for being so easy to talk to or I can try to claim concussion from the knock to my ankle. What do you think?"

"Might work except I'm sober too and definitely not concussed so have no real reason to lay out in front of you the sorry story of my prolonged singlehood. The sad bleakness of that emotional landscape will make you shiver even more than you are already." Iris paused, not sure whether to continue. "But I will take the chance to say that my love life is nowhere near as exciting or terrifying as Jess likes to make out."

"You definitely sounded like a poet then." Cam studied Iris closely, her gaze making Iris nervous. She hated talking about herself at the best of times, and this was not a subject she expected to get out in the open so soon.

"But your love life was exciting and terrifying at one point?"

"It was out of control…I mean, I was out of control, and that is pretty terrifying. I'm not sure it ever felt very exciting. There was far too much self-loathing for that." She took a breath. "What's to say? I had a bad breakup. With Amanda, the attractive goalkeeping ex. It was a long-term relationship that ended before I expected it to, and I went off the rails in the weeks afterward. I'm not proud of it. I really was an idiot. I was thrashing around and I did as much harm to myself as I did to the women I got involved with. And then I stopped. It wasn't fun, it wasn't fair, and I figured out I didn't want to do it anymore." Iris had been speaking to her beer bottle. She dared now to look at Cam who was nodding and chewing her bottom lip in thought.

"And now I'm a model citizen. More sober, more boring, no girlfriend, and absolutely no women fighting over me." Cam nodded. Iris wanted to know Cam heard her, that Cam knew that was the old Iris, but she didn't know how to make sure.

"When did it stop?"

"Amanda and I broke up about nine months ago. I lost the plot for a couple of months after that maybe, drinking to numb the pain, and sleeping with women I wasn't really interested in to avoid being alone. While actually feeling as alone as it's possible to feel."

"Why'd you break up?"

"If I sound like a poet, you sound like a journalist. So many questions."

Cam started to apologize, looking a little guilty. Iris held up a hand. "It's okay." She took a breath.

"What can I say? We grew apart, didn't talk about what was wrong. She…there was someone else. Mutually assured destruction. It was hard."

"And now?" Cam looked at Iris kindly.

"I've been focusing on work mostly." She indicated the phrase ironically with speech marks in the air. "And avoiding the efforts of well-meaning friends to set me up with someone." Iris managed a smile. "I trust myself with myself, that's probably just about it."

"And Jess?"

"Someone I hurt at that time. I think…" Iris tried to find words that didn't sound arrogant. "She had feelings for me. But I was never interested. After Amanda, all I was capable of was hooking up and never staying around afterward. We had a very brief thing. A couple of nights really. I ended it, as gently, as soon, as I could. She took it badly." Iris put her palms up as if to apologize.

"She still has feelings for you. It's obvious really. It's partly why she's so hostile all the time. It can't be easy for her working and socializing with you. I think if I had someone I was in love with who I couldn't have, I'd need to take myself far away from them, you know?"

Iris nodded. She was surprised both by how much Cam had noticed and her willingness to be so up-front about it.

As if reading Iris's thoughts, Cam spoke up. "I like talking to you. It's been a while since I felt this comfortable with anyone, even Ryan."

The mention of Ryan's name had a sobering effect on Iris. He was, she reminded herself, Cam's fiancé, the one Cam would go back to tonight and maybe even relay parts of this conversation to. He was the one she was really intimate with despite their growing friendship.

"Can I ask you something?" Iris asked. "If you love reading and writing and you were a journalism major, how come you're working in finance now? How come you've stopped with the words and chosen the numbers?"

It was a harmless question, an obvious one maybe, but this was the question Cam always dreaded. The one she got at job interviews as people looked through her résumé, the one that friends she hadn't seen in a while asked her innocently. She left journalism behind when she left college, because it reminded her of her cowardice, because she didn't know how to get back to the person she was. But how do you explain that to people you barely know?

Cam concentrated on steadying her breathing, on figuring out a neutral way to explain.

"I just lost my way with it. Lost my writing mojo or whatever you call it. You know what that's like I guess. I left Chicago after college." The lie slipped out easily. "I went back home to Seattle and got sucked into other stuff, then I met Ryan. My mom said…" Cam didn't want to finish the sentence. "I just figured that finance is a better, more solid career choice." She knew how lame it sounded. Especially to Iris, someone who loved words, books, poems just as much as Cam. She tried another angle.

"Making a career out of writing is hard. My sister is trying…and struggling. I guess I agree with Mom that we don't need two failing writers in the family."

Iris nodded. "It is hard to make a career of. I guess that's why we all have boring day jobs. I mean look at mine, as boring as they come. Maybe you could do it as a hobby though?"

"I could, if I had the energy and some encouragement." Cam sighed, knowing she sounded as frustrated as she felt. "I miss it sometimes, but mostly I don't even think about it."

"A bit like me and relationships." Iris lifted her beer as she spoke. Cam thought she looked a little sad. She hadn't meant for things to get so serious, but something about Iris made her want to reveal herself.

Cam reached across the table and stole a swig of beer from Iris's bottle.

"Maybe we can go to the next poetry night like we said we would and I'll nag you about performing, and in return you can nag me about not writing. Sound fair?"

"That's a deal. I tell you what though, if I lose any fingers to frostbite out here then writing poetry is going to get very difficult. Maybe we should go inside now that you've stolen my gloves. We can eat packets of pork scratchings in front of the fire to warm up before I drive you home and you show your impressive bruises to that man of yours."

"Pork scratchings? I don't even wanna ask. Is that another British culinary triumph I'm gonna regret ever allowing past my lips?"

"Too bloody right."

Iris supported Cam as she walked, still hobbling, toward the pub door.

"I'm keeping the gloves on for now though," Cam said as she leaned on Iris. "So you'll have to open the bag for me."

CHAPTER SEVEN

Iris knocked on Hazel and Casey's front door, pausing to admire the winter plants that were thriving in a row of colorful pots dotted along the space under the wide bay window. Casey swung the door wide open and pulled Iris into a big warm hug.

"I'm in the middle of cooking. Go and help Hazel decide if she wants a party for her thirtieth or if she's just gonna hide." Casey pushed Iris in the direction of the living room.

"Hey." Iris dropped onto the couch next to Hazel. "Casey said you're having trauma about entering your fourth decade. Sorry but… well…I'm just too damn young to understand, y'know?"

"You're not that far behind me, babe." Hazel stuck her two fingers up at Iris. "Though your enforced celibacy makes you seem like an even older old maid than that."

Iris tapped her watch, her wry expression letting Hazel know that she had beaten her own record for the shortest time taken to bring up Iris's lack of a love life.

"Actually, seeing Amanda the other day was a pretty good reminder of why I'm still single. Wasn't really expecting it." Iris paused. "Did you know she was playing again?"

They never really talked about Amanda and the friendship that Hazel and Casey had maintained with her.

"She said she was thinking about it. She…well…she said she was a bit in need of stuff to do now that she's single again." Hazel spoke uncertainly. "Though I feel bad chatting her business with you."

"She broke up with Gina?" Iris couldn't keep the surprise out of her voice.

Hazel shook her head. "Gina? No, not Gina. This was someone else, the one after Gina. Happened last month. We saw her last week. She wasn't the one who ended it so she's pretty cut up about it all obviously."

Iris didn't know what to say. She had deliberately never asked Hazel about Amanda, but she'd just assumed that she and Gina were still together. In the weeks after she and Amanda broke up, it was Gina that she blamed, Gina that she hated. It was ridiculous given that it was Amanda's choice to cheat on her with Gina, but she wasn't exactly feeling rational at the time. The idea that Amanda and Gina hadn't made it was a real surprise.

"When?" It was all Iris could manage.

"What?"

"Amanda and Gina. When did they break up?"

"I don't remember exactly. They barely lasted a month or so after you guys split. I was surprised. They seemed well suited." Hazel quickly added a sheepish, "Sorry, mate. Bit tactless."

"Do you know what happened?"

"She told us some of it at the time...but...y'know...it's kind of private stuff really." Hazel looked a bit uncomfortable.

Iris felt stupid. Of course it was. She had no right to ask and not really any right to know. "Yeah 'course. Sorry. Just reacting, not thinking. I always thought they were pretty right for each other too if I'm honest. I think it made Amanda choosing her easier to take somehow. They seemed like they had so much more in common. I'm glad you're being discreet anyway. Surprised but glad. I wouldn't want you gossiping about me over dinner with Amanda either."

"Mate, me and Casey would have to make up stuff about you, your love life is so boring. If only there was something there to gossip about. ..."

"Not that again." Iris playfully threw a cushion at Hazel, who caught it adeptly without spilling a drop of her drink.

"You forget I used to play in goal myself." Hazel threw it back at Iris.

"I hadn't forgotten. I think that was the season we nearly got relegated."

"We nearly got relegated because you were too busy writing love poems for that center forward you had a crush on to concentrate on playing properly."

"God, that was so long ago. Maybe we are old." Iris shook her head. "And those poems were awful as well."

Casey joined them in the living room. "Half an hour and we can eat. What did I miss?"

"Poetry," Iris answered first. "Hazel was saying how much she'd love to come with me to a reading one time."

"Yeah right." Hazel stuck her tongue out. "Maybe when hell freezes over...twice."

"Actually, I've found someone to go to poetry readings with." She said it very matter-of-factly.

"You're dating?" Hazel sat forward. "More than that, you're dating a woman who actually loves poetry? Well, you kept that quiet."

Iris felt stupid. She hadn't meant it to sound like that.

"No, I mean, not like that anyway. It's just Cam. She really likes poetry. When I went to that reading in Hampstead a few weeks ago, she was there and we got talking. Her sister's a poet, and turns out she's really into it as well. I didn't know."

Hazel and Casey exchanged glances.

"Told you," Hazel said to Casey.

"What? What are you on about?" Iris asked. Casey looked at Hazel and shook her head.

"Hazel thinks you have a little crush on Cameron. But I defended you and told her that, at twenty-nine, you're far too old and experienced to crush on a soon-to-be-married woman," Casey said.

"And I told her that Cam is very attractive and very friendly, and you've had your libido on ice for so long that anything's possible...and that was before I knew the two of you had been doing poems together." Hazel waggled her eyebrows, aiming for a tone that was teasing, but Iris was already annoyed that they had been talking about her and Cam in that way. Joking or not.

"C'mon, Hazel, I'm single but not desperate enough to go after women that aren't even available. Cam was there with Ryan—her fiancé—and we just agreed that it'd be nice to go again together. In a friendly way. You know, in that way that women who get on well can be friends?"

"Okay, okay, sorry, mate. Just teasing."

"Yeah, and gossiping about how pathetic I am."

"No, no, not at all." Hazel held her hands up in an apologetic gesture. "I am sorry. Honestly, it was just that you guys looked a bit cozy down the pub, and, well, Jess was saying that she'd seen you having lunch together a couple of times at the office. Shouldn't jump to conclusions I know, but I just don't want you making a fool of yourself."

Iris scowled. "Well, you definitely shouldn't be listening to Jess. You know what she's like, always making things seem more dramatic than they are." She sighed. "And I'm only going to make a fool of myself if Cam decides that I'm just too boring to make a friend of."

Casey put her hand on Iris's arm. "It was worse for me, Iris. I had to hear my own beloved tell me just how damn irresistible Cam was and how she didn't blame you at all for being interested in her." There was a glint in her eye. "I even had to come down to the pub to see for myself."

"And?"

"Well, I definitely have a crush on her now even if you don't. She's gorgeous, her eyes are irresistible, and her accent is so sexy."

They all laughed, the tension gone. Iris couldn't deny that Cam was beautiful, but much more importantly, she was smart and open and interesting, and Iris wasn't going to allow Hazel's suspicions about her feelings make her feel bad about trying to make a new friend. Maybe she hadn't felt this interested in spending time with someone in a while, but so what? Fate brought Cam to Cottoms, and Iris wasn't going to pass up the opportunity to hang out with someone who loved poetry as much as she did.

CHAPTER EIGHT

Jess had announced Amanda's return to the Cottoms team over lunch on Friday, and Cam still couldn't quite believe it. She spent all of Friday afternoon and evening worrying about it and the concern was still there when she woke on Saturday morning. Iris hadn't been in to work on Friday so Cam hadn't had a chance to talk to her about it, even assuming she'd have felt comfortable doing so, and she couldn't stop wondering how Iris was coping with the news.

According to Jess, Maxine had decided to stop playing, and Megan, knowing good keepers were hard to find, had asked Amanda to come back and play for Cottoms. Amanda had agreed, and her first match was going to be tomorrow—no training, no easing in, just straight into the team. It was pragmatic and sensible of Megan in the circumstances but really tough on Iris. Cam assumed that since Amanda had readily agreed to switch teams, she didn't think seeing Iris regularly would be difficult. Amanda's obliviousness to Iris's feelings made Cam not like her at all.

Cam wondered if it had been Jess or Megan who had told Iris about Amanda coming back. She hoped it had been Megan. She didn't trust Jess to have been sensitive about it.

Cam worried it would be too difficult for Iris to play with Amanda given their history and she'd decide to change teams. It would be a real blow for Iris, but all Cam could think of was how it would also mean she'd see much less of her. The strength of her worry surprised her. The time they were spending together was cementing a growing feeling that Iris could become—was becoming—someone special to her. Someone she really liked. But she just didn't have the confidence in their friendship yet to reach out and see how Iris was doing with the news without it seeming intrusive. Cam didn't really know if Iris would even welcome her making contact without having arranged to. She sighed and made herself forget about contacting Iris and think about how she was going to spend her Saturday.

"What about the South Bank?" Cam was sitting on the edge of the bed, leafing through her guidebook. "There's a riverside walk with lots of stopping points." She raised her voice so Ryan could hear her from the bathroom.

Cam circled the mention of secondhand book stalls on the Embankment near Waterloo Bridge and Shakespeare's Globe Theatre museum, which sounded fascinating. She also circled the recommendation of a pub near the Globe that she thought Ryan might need after the museum.

"There's a fifteenth century pub halfway along the walk that the book says used to have bear baiting in the beer garden. How crazy is that?" The idea of it made her smile. London was so damn old.

Ryan appeared in the doorway. "I'm playing squash. I told you last night."

"I know. I was thinking of after."

"I dunno, babe. How about we stay home and chill? Watch a movie or something. I've had a big week and I'm really tired, and I won't feel any less tired after my games." Ryan was looking in the dresser for something to wear.

"Are you kidding? Stay home all weekend? The weather's good. It's a great day for a walk. Come on, Ryan, we haven't been into town for weeks." Cam couldn't keep the complaining tone out of her voice.

"Yeah, and there's a reason for that. I'm crazy busy at work. It's not a nine to five job like yours. And anyway, London is so crowded on the weekend. I hate the crowds, and the traffic, and the tourists are so fucking rude." He sat next to her on the bed as he pulled on a pair of socks. "It would be nice just to hang out here and spend the rest of the day with you and a huge pizza." He leaned across and kissed Cam's cheek.

"I don't wanna do that." Cam kept her tone even. She didn't want them to argue again. "I want to see the city that we've chosen to live in. And I don't want to spend the weekend hanging out in this house." She swallowed her frustration. "I'm going to go by myself if you don't feel up to coming out."

"Don't do the emotional blackmail thing, Cam." Ryan sounded annoyed. "I can't help it if I don't like London as much as you."

"I'm not. I just think the South Bank sounds cool, and I'm going to do that walk whether or not you come. I don't need an escort. Go play squash and I'll see you later. Maybe we can have that pizza." She stood and kissed the top of his head before moving toward the door. She was upset with him but determined not to let it show.

The saddest thing wasn't her Saturday plans being ruined, but that Cam felt them drifting apart with every passing month and she just didn't know what to do about it. She had no idea how she was going to spend the day, not sure she'd feel like going to the South Bank on her own, but sure as hell, she wasn't going to waste it by sitting at home waiting for Ryan to decide how they spent the day.

Cam decided to walk down into the village and treat herself to cake and browse around the bookstore while she figured out what to do with the rest of the day. She knew Iris would tell her to not be silly and to go on her own to the South Bank, and she might, she was a grown ass woman after all, but she wanted some time to think about it first. And the bookstore had cake. Cake always helped her think.

The overcast morning had given way to a bright and sunny day, and it was just about warm enough for her to leave her jacket unbuttoned on the walk down the hill. A small miracle that improved her mood. Seattle was a rainy city and everyone had said the same was true of London, but her experience already told her that it rained less but was much, much colder. She wrapped the bright scarf she was wearing a little tighter around her neck and enjoyed the feel of the sun on her skin.

The bookstore was not too busy, and she browsed the biography section for half an hour, treating herself to a book about Barbara Ehrenreich, before decamping to the café to browse through it. She was halfway through her latte and had demolished most of a huge slice of walnut cake when a wave of decisiveness overcame her. She pulled out her phone. What harm would a text do? She typed out a quick message. *Hey, I'm in your/our favorite bookstore. If you're free this morning, come join me for a bit of cake. Or actually a lot of cake. The portions are deadly here, as I'm sure you know! Cam x*

Cam put her phone facedown on the table. She tried to calm herself. No one in their right mind would think a casual offer of coffee was coming on too strong. *Friends texted each other all the time, right?* She and Iris might not be at the texting each other to hang out at the weekend stage yet, but Cam was determined to be there for Iris if she was suffering. She remembered the pained look on Iris's face as she spoke about Amanda when they'd sat outside the pub and could already tell that Iris was not the kind of person who found it easy to reach out when she needed to talk.

Cam's phone buzzed and she picked it up seeing the message from Iris. *The portions are indeed huge. I was going to suggest splitting a cake with you, but I can see I'm too late ;)*

Cam frowned at the text. Why was Iris too late? A cough and then a chuckle made Cam look up. Next to the table, books under her arm and a phone in her hand, stood Iris.

Tall, dark, and handsome. They were the first words that came to Cam's mind, and they were spot-on, if more than a little surprising.

"Hey." Cam felt strangely nervous.

"Hey back," Iris said, smiling at her. "Are you following me? I mean, I know I'm adorable and all, but this is the second time you've followed me to this bookstore, and stalking is actually a crime here in the UK." Iris flopped into the chair next to Cam, piling the books she'd been carrying onto the small table.

Cam couldn't take her eyes off Iris. Seeing her so unexpectedly made her feel a little giddy.

"Actually, it's good you're here." Iris pointed at the books. "You can save me from myself by helping me whittle down this pile of books into ones I should buy and ones I should regretfully put back. I'm completely unable to resist splurging here. Too much good stuff." Iris picked up some crumbs of cake from Cam's plate and licked them from her fingers, smiling at Cam, seeming to dare her to object.

Iris seemed to be full of energy, happy, playful even. Cam was a little surprised in the circumstances but also relieved. Iris at work was thoughtful and generally serious, Iris in the pub was witty and guarded, but this Iris—weekend Iris—was even better. She was wearing a thick burgundy hoodie with the words *The Dogs Trust* emblazoned across the front above a logo of a cute spaniel. It was worn over tight but faded black jeans and black Converse sneakers. She looked kind of...Cam knew the right word was "hot" but she made herself replace it with "cute" which seemed like a much better word to use about a friend.

"Let's see." Cam pulled the pile of books toward her and began studying them one by one. She was happy for something to do that wasn't simply staring at Iris. Iris pointed at her coffee.

"Do you want a top up? I'm gonna get myself a tea."

Cam shook her head, watching as Iris chatted and laughed with the server, then making herself look away as Iris turned to come back to the table. She returned her attention to the books. A couple of poetry anthologies, a couple of novels, a biography about a war poet Cam had heard of but never read, and a big colorful Sicilian recipe book. The last one surprised her and she held it up with a quizzical look as Iris slid back into the chair next to her.

"I didn't have you down as a cook."

"No, I'm not. I can barely manage cheese on toast. Though I probably should be offended you wrote me off on that so quickly." Cam enjoyed the teasing tone in Iris's voice.

"It's for Casey actually. A little gift to thank her for always cooking for me. They went to Sicily in the summer and loved it." Iris ran her fingers across the cover.

"I can't help you then. That was the only one I was going to tell you to put back." Cam sat back in her chair, waving her hand across the pile of books. "I think you'll have to spring for all six." Iris groaned playfully.

"Do you think Graham will spot it if I put them on my expenses?" Iris was clearly joking. Cam frowned.

"I'm pretty sure he would. He seems to pay attention to anything that relates to you. If I didn't know you better, I'd suggest he's one of those vengeful brokenhearted paramours you've left in your wake."

Iris shuddered. "God help me. I'm not even sure I know what a paramour is, but I do know that I don't ever want the words Graham, me, and 'amour' in the same sentence. Ugh."

She pointed at the bag next to Cam changing the subject. "What did you get?"

"A biography. She's a journalist, very political, an activist really. Bit of a heroine of mine." Cam fished out the book and passed it across so Iris could read the cover. She passed it back to Cam after a few moments, nodding as she did so.

"And books involve words not numbers, so I approve." She smiled shyly at Cam. They were both silent for a moment.

"How do you know Hazel and Casey?"

"Met them both at university. Casey first and Hazel a little later. I like to say that I brought them together. Sort of. Though Hazel always refuses to give me credit for it."

"So you're a secret matchmaker?"

Iris laughed and threw her head back. Cam noticed, as if for the first time, her perfect white teeth and wide smile.

"I wouldn't go that far. They'd probably have got together sooner if it wasn't for me." She lifted a shoulder in a shrug. "And anyway, Hazel reckons that anything I had to do with bringing her and Casey together is more than made up for by her introducing me to Amanda years later…though of course she keeps a little quieter about that one since we did the whole crash and burn thing." A slight furrow appeared on Iris's brow.

Cam wondered whether a bad memory was passing through.

"You actually seem in a much better mood about the whole Amanda thing than I expected." Cam had been waiting for an opportunity to ask Iris about it. "Half my reason for texting was to see if you wanted some company and the chance to talk about it."

"That's nice of you, but I only have to see her twice a season, once now that the home game's already been played. It's not like we have to hang out all that much. How bad can it be?"

Damn, is it possible she doesn't even know? Cam really didn't want to be the one to tell her, as cowardly as that felt.

"Did you…I mean, I know you weren't in work yesterday, but did you get to speak to Megan? Or Jess?" Cam tried to keep her voice level.

Iris sat up a little straighter in her chair. "About what? What do you mean? Has something happened at work?"

Cam had no way out. "Oh, Iris, I'm sorry. Jess told me. She told everyone actually. Maxine doesn't want to keep playing. She can't fit it in with her studies and everything so…" Cam knew she was making no sense. Iris was looking at her in confusion.

"Megan told Jess that Amanda is taking over in goal for Cottoms. To replace Maxine for the rest of the season. She's playing tomorrow. She'll be playing every week. I can't believe no one told you. I thought

Megan would call you at least." Cam waited for Iris to react. She didn't. Her face was closed, a complete blank. They sat in silence for a few moments.

Cam had no idea what to do or say. Iris stood up, and Cam felt a little panic settle on her chest, assuming Iris was heading home. She really didn't want her to.

"Iris, don't go. Stay and talk to me about it."

"There's really nothing to talk about, Cam." Iris sounded calm enough, but there was something uncertain underlying her words. "We were together and then we weren't. She chose to be with someone else, and now she's not. She stopped playing football, and now she's back. It's really got nothing to do with me."

Iris sat back down. She was silent for a beat or two, tracing the outline of her teacup. "If anything I'm just embarrassed. It's a little harder to put a breakup like that behind you when the person who knows better than anyone what an idiot you are is back in your friendship group. Not that Jess ever lets me forget my part in it."

Cam wanted to ask Iris about being an idiot, needing to know what had happened between them, but this wasn't the right time. Cam felt a little spellbound sometimes when she was with Iris. It was a strange feeling, one that she hadn't felt for a very long time.

"Amanda's single again?" Cam asked.

"She is. According to Hazel anyway. I don't know the details. I guess it's why she's playing again. At a loose end or something."

"I don't want her to hurt you again." Cam placed her hand over Iris's.

"She won't, she can't. She doesn't mean anything to me now. Whatever hold we had over each other was broken a long time ago." Iris blew out a breath. "It's just going to be weird, that's all. We spent a lot of time playing together. It's going to be hard sitting across from her in the changing room or in the pub and not think back to those days. They were—mostly—happy ones until…" Iris hesitated. "For a long time we were good together. But now it'll be awkward, a little, I think. Maybe not for her but for me."

"Isn't that just because she hurt you when she went off with what's-her-name?"

"Gina."

"I think she should feel more awkward than you about coming back."

"It's not like that. It's never that simple when two people break up. There's usually blame on both sides. She hurt me, but I sometimes think that maybe I deserved it somehow. And I didn't exactly behave well." Iris pulled her hand away. "And I don't want to be judged for my part in it. I want to forget all about it. I've spent the last nine months trying to do just that to be honest. Actually, can we talk about something else? Split another piece of cake and maybe talk about the weather." There was a sadness in Iris's eyes, and Cam felt bad for making her recall painful memories when all she'd wanted to do was let Iris know she was there for her.

"Hey, I can do better than that." Cam said. "Pork scratchings. In a riverside pub. Hopefully with a roaring fire. I...well...I don't have anything to do today, so I was going to go to the South Bank, go to the Globe, and go to a pub that used to bait bears. Though if I'm honest I don't really understand what that is." Cam smiled at Iris, trying to lighten the mood. "Come with me if you're free. I mean, I'm sure you have plans so don't worry if you can't. Bit last minute on my part obviously."

Iris leaned forward. "My plans involved cleaning the rug in my lounge and then trying, and probably failing, to finish one of the poems I'm struggling with so I'm definitely up for not doing either of those things. I tell you what though, the South Bank will be mad busy on a Saturday, so how about I show you some of the East End like I said I would? It'll be quieter and just as interesting. I'm sure we can find pork scratchings somewhere, but if you want, we could try that curry place I was raving about."

"Sounds fantastic," Cam replied. And it did. Cam felt happy— happy that she'd chanced the invitation, happy that Iris had said yes, and happy that Iris seemed able to manage the news about Amanda.

"Oh, I forgot." Cam pulled a flyer out of her bag and handed it to Iris. "I picked this up for you downstairs. End of next month, they're doing a 'first-timers' poetry event for those new to performing." She paused. "I'll come with you if you want to give it a try. Get one of those poems finished and I'll sit on the front row and clap proudly."

Iris looked at Cam, holding her gaze for a beat.

"I know you're nervous about it, but it would be so cool and I figured that if I encouraged you to perform, I'd finally get to hear one of your poems."

Iris carefully folded the flyer and tucked it into her back pocket. "I'll try, but I can't promise. It's such a terrifying thought."

She hadn't said no and Cam nodded as if satisfied with that.

CHAPTER NINE

"When you said you'd show me East London, I was imagining museums and historic houses, not the back alleys of Whitechapel in the twilight," Cam mock chided Iris. "Are we going to get killed here? Because I've got a really good book in my bag that I was hoping to finish."

"Two more victims and I promise we're done."

They rounded a corner and walked along a narrow passageway to the back of a tall office block that sat on a square courtyard. The courtyard backed on to a small park—no more than an enclosed patch of grass really. The courtyard housed half a dozen large trash cans, one of which had been pushed over and spilled its contents onto the gravel. The smell was not appealing, and the overall air was one of squalor, though it was still just about light enough not to feel afraid. Iris beckoned Cam across the courtyard and they skirted around the side of a small park. Give it an hour and the place would be dark enough to lure out the local drug dealers and their customers.

Iris and Cam had taken their time getting here, chatting in the bookshop café while splitting a cake, dropping the books off at Iris's flat, and giving her the chance to pick up the guidebook she wanted.

Iris had made them get the bus rather than the Tube from Hampstead, and they had sat happily on the top deck, crawling along in the traffic, with Iris pointing out random landmarks along the route, including Cam's favorite, a pub called the Blind Beggar where someone called Jack "The Hat" McVitie was shot by one of the infamous Kray twins, apparently for calling him a homosexual. It wasn't at all funny yet it somehow made them both giggle like children.

Now they were in Whitechapel, in what even Iris described as a bit of a rough neighborhood, wandering around alleys behind office buildings and between shops, overlooked by endless low-rise apartment blocks. Iris stopped and pointed at a bollard—a stout iron bollard about eighteen inches high, quite ornate and old-fashioned looking. It was painted black with gold lettering etched around the top.

"And this," Iris pointed at the bollard, searching for the right paragraph in her guidebook, "was where Elizabeth Stride's body was found. She was also a local prostitute, originally from Sweden—which is kind of random—and understood to be Jack's third victim in London. Historians think that Jack was interrupted while murdering Elizabeth because, while he killed her with a scalpel, he—" Iris stopped and looked at Cam. "Maybe I'll skip the description of how she was killed. You went a bit green the last time and I'm still hoping for that curry."

"Thanks. It's all a bit gruesome."

"You did say you liked scary movies. I figured you'd be able to handle it."

"Yeah, I do, but scary movies are on a TV screen in the safety of your own house, and there's popcorn and cushions to hide behind and you can scream without worrying you're going to scare up the ghost of Jack the Ripper." She took Iris by the arm. "I don't care if you mock me all week for being too scared to carry on. I'd rather suffer that and get out of here alive."

Cam pulled on Iris's arm, leading them back toward the lights of the high street, wanting to leave the alleys behind.

"Don't know why you're worrying. He mainly only severed the arteries of prostitutes y'know, so you're safe unless there's something you need to tell me?"

"You're funny, Iris. Very funny. And now you're definitely making it up to me by buying dinner. I'm going to recover my appetite just as soon as we get somewhere where there's streetlights and actual living people and I stop thinking about Jack and his scalpel."

"No problem. The curry place is only a fifteen-minute walk from here, so start recovering quickly."

They fell into stride next to each other, Iris leading the way up Brick Lane and steering them through the crowds with the movement of her body. The street was thronged with people moving in both directions. Many, like them, looking for somewhere to eat. Groups of tourists, blocking the street with their matching backpacks, were joined by couples out for the night. Both sides of the street were populated with Indian restaurants, their lights and colorful frontages jostling for attention. Most had young men standing outside, dressed as waiters, holding menus and promising discounts or free drinks. Shouting over each other to compete for the attention of passersby. Would-be diners occasionally stopped in front of them to consider the menus offered.

Cam loved the bustling atmosphere of the place. Iris had not paused once, had met all the entreaties they had received to try out individual restaurants with a polite, "No, thank you." And then, a few minutes later, at the door of a restaurant with a huge vertical neon sign spelling the word Dawat in purple lights, Iris stopped. A middle-aged man stood outside the front door. He was holding menus but not offering them to passersby with quite the same enthusiasm as the others they had passed. He smiled when he saw Iris.

"Iris. Goodness me, it's been ages." His voice was deep and sonorous. He stepped forward and pulled Iris into a hug.

"I know. I'm sorry. I moved away, the most northern bit of north London. It's too far and I'm too busy. Rubbish excuses I know. Sorry." Iris was smiling just as broadly.

The man released Iris and turned his gaze toward her.

"And this is not your Amanda." It was a statement, not a question though he looked with a raised eyebrow in Iris's direction as he spoke. The man was still looking at Cam, and she felt a little uncomfortable under his gaze. Iris spoke up.

"No, of course not. This is Cameron. She's a..." Iris looked at Cam, biting her lip. "She's a friend. We work together. She plays on the team too." He said nothing but simply nodded in Cam's direction.

"Cam?" Iris touched her on the arm. "This is Devam. Dev to his friends. He manages this wonderful place." She waved her arm in the direction of the restaurant.

Dev shook his head, his eyes crinkling. "I wish that were true. That crazy chef of mine is unmanageable. And, yes, he is still here. No one else will put up with him." He moved aside and opened the door. "Come, ladies. I have a nice table for you in the window. Your beauty will attract the customers."

Dev held Iris in front of him, his hands on her shoulders. "You look good, my dear." He whistled softly. Iris actually blushed, and Cam saw her properly for the first time since they'd left Hampstead. She did look good. She had changed out of her hoodie when they'd stopped at her flat and was now wearing a dark gray sweater over a black shirt with a very fine silver gray check. A fitted leather jacket hugged her figure. She looked handsome, very handsome. Cam refused to acknowledge the slight pulsing that this realization caused in her body.

Iris refused to be steered by Dev to cross the threshold into the restaurant. She leaned across and whispered in his ear, pointing to the restaurant opposite with a grin on her face. Cam saw the affection in his eyes as he patted Iris's cheeks.

"If they offered you ten percent off, my dearest, I will give you the same. And free papadams, as many free papadams as you can both eat." Dev pulled Iris into the restaurant and waited for Cam to follow, bowing gallantly as she entered.

The inside of the restaurant was not large. There were probably only twelve tables in total, with a scattering of diners occupying around half of them. The lighting was low, and soft music played. Cam loved that Iris loved this place and was happy that she thought enough of their friendship to bring Cam here. Cam followed her to the vacant table in the window and they sat.

Iris had a slightly faraway look in her eyes, and Cam wondered if being here was bringing back memories of being with Amanda. Every time they talked about her relationship with Ryan, every time someone commented on Iris's concerted singledom, every time Jess made yet another snide remark about what an emotional car crash Iris was, Cam wanted to ask Iris what on earth had happened with Amanda, but so far she just hadn't felt able to. Trouble was, the desire to know was getting greater in proportion to how much Cam found herself liking Iris. She knew that the comments and stories got under her skin, making Iris sound reckless and destructive, and while Cam couldn't quite see Iris that way, she couldn't help but notice all the times Iris herself had talked of being an idiot, of blame on both sides without really saying what had happened. As Iris's friend, she had a right to ask but no real need to know. Trouble was Cam really needed to know. She didn't know what that meant, but she did know that her feelings were confusing her mightily.

Dev interrupted Cam's thoughts by handing them both a large menu and disappearing behind a curtain at the back of the room.

"The chef might well be crazy—I only met him once—but he's also a genius because the food here is incredible. There's nothing on the menu I wouldn't recommend, and I feel like I've tried most of it."

"Did you and Amanda...I mean, you must have come here often to have worked your way through the menu...though Dev didn't know about the two of you breaking up so I guess you haven't been back here since?" She couldn't help herself asking but wished that she hadn't. She started to apologize, but Iris surprised her by replying before she had time.

"Yeah, it was a favorite place of ours. We lived ten minutes away, over in Stepney Green, a little bit to the east of here." Iris pointed out the direction through the window. "Dev always had a bit of a crush on Amanda I think. The welcome she always got from him..." Iris hesitated and seemed to blink away a memory. "And, no, I haven't been back here since. She stayed in the area, stayed in the flat. I didn't know if she still came here to eat after we...y'know...if she ever brought Gina here...but I guess not given Dev's reaction."

Cam wasn't sure if Iris had anything more to say, but the moment was gone anyway as Dev approached the table with two beers, a basket of papadams, and a carousel containing four little jars of chutneys and sauces. He placed them on the table, arranged them carefully, and walked away whistling softly to himself. Cam was hungry. She brought her side plate onto the tablemat in front of her, spooned some mango chutney onto it, and broke off a large piece of papadam, all thoughts of murdered prostitutes a million miles away.

Iris looked across the table at Cam. Her eyes, had Cam looked up at her at that point, would have given her away. Iris was unsure exactly when the fondness she had started to feel for Cam had given way to these feelings of attraction, but she couldn't deny, sitting here admiring the soft skin on Cam's shapely arms and shoulders, that attraction was what she was feeling. She hated herself for it almost as much as she hated the idea that Hazel was right about her developing crush.

The restaurant was warm, and Cam had cast off not just her coat but the wraparound cardigan that she had been wearing, leaving her arms exposed in a green sleeveless top that brought out the color of her eyes beautifully. Iris couldn't help appreciating the bitter irony of the situation. Old Iris, the one who went off the rails after her split from Amanda, would have loved the challenge of Cam. Not caring who she hurt, she'd had some success seducing seemingly unavailable women. It had become almost a sport to her in the weeks after Amanda, but she had quickly come to hate the person she had turned into, and almost overnight, closed down whatever receiver it was that she had been relying on to identify women she knew were bored and interested in trying something a little new.

What remained of those instincts told her that Cam had been nothing but friendly toward her, and Iris needed to manage her feelings away as quickly as possible. She knew she could do that, she'd had crushes before. She watched with a slight flutter in her belly as Cam broke her papadam into small pieces, spooned chutney onto a sliver, and brought it to her mouth. Iris was captivated by the sight of Cam's mouth when she was eating, and that was definitely not a good thing. Iris wondered if maybe this crush would be a little more difficult to manage away. She groaned inwardly; having Amanda around would certainly help, just the sight of her reminding Iris why getting stuck on Cam would be so wrong and just why she had chosen to stay single for so long.

Iris tried to concentrate on the menu, but her thoughts kept drifting. She wanted to tell Cam about Amanda. Jess and the others had talked of the old days so many times, and Cam had asked around the topic several times, but Iris couldn't decide if it was a good idea or not. She hated the version that she assumed Cam had pieced together from Jess's comments over the previous weeks, but telling her the truth would probably be worse.

She made herself study the menu. A voice inside her head telling her to face up to the fact that they were building a friendship, not a relationship, and it shouldn't matter to either of them what had happened in the past. The trouble was that Iris still felt so ashamed of it, that she felt sure that Cam—even sweet Cam—would judge her harshly, and it made her feel sad to think it might affect what Cam thought about her.

"I'll have the chicken achari I think. I've never tried it, but it sounds wonderful. I love ginger and I love pickle." Cam's words cut through Iris's drifting thoughts. "What do you think? Is there anything else you'd recommend?" She looked at Iris, her eyes open and inviting, and Iris felt a flush rise from her neck to her face.

Willing herself to get a grip, Iris composed herself. "I always want the same thing when I come here, the lamb pasanda. It's wonderful, probably about nine thousand calories, but definitely worth it."

Cam laughed, delighting Iris as she did so. "You don't exactly need to worry about your weight. You're in great shape."

The compliment pleased Iris, but the matter-of-fact tone made it clear that Cam wasn't flirting. As ridiculous as it was, she couldn't help but be disappointed. Iris needed to get her mind off Cam's bare arms, her lips, her eyes, and start acting more like a friend.

"Whenever I've visited the States, I've found good Indian restaurants really hard to come by." Iris tried small talk, feeling like it was safer.

"Yeah," Cam said. "One more thing in favor of staying in London. Though Ryan needs some convincing that London has anything that puts it ahead of Seattle. I sometimes think he's done his list of pros and cons without me and already made his mind up that we're going back."

Iris felt a tightness in her chest at the idea of Cam following her fiancé back to the States, and she was pleased when Dev came over to take their order, breaking the tension she was feeling at the idea of losing her before they'd really gotten started.

CHAPTER TEN

As they sat back and waited for their coffee, Iris continued the conversation they'd been having about performing.

"I just don't think I'm bold enough to do it, to stand up there and believe that people would want to listen to something I'd written. The only person I've ever shown a poem to was my dad when I was a teenager and a lot braver than I am today. It's okay for you. You're just much bolder than me."

"I might seem bold, but I'm not. Not when it matters. I mean, I haven't been in my life up to now. I accept less for myself than I should."

"Like what?"

"If I'm being honest, all of it. I've always done what's expected of me, done what people like my mom approve of. Not done things they disapproved of. It's meant I don't have things, things I want. I let journalism go when I shouldn't have. I...I let somebody go that meant a lot to me, before Ryan I mean. I wouldn't stand up for them, for us, when it got tough." She let out a sigh. "And I let Ryan decide how we live our life, where we live our life even. I'm not bold at all. Not really. I mean, I won't even go to a poetry evening on my own for fuck's sake. And I've started to realize that the reason I accept second best for myself far too much is because I often don't know what it is that I actually want." She ran a hand through her hair. "I'm sorry. I didn't mean to get so personal. You...you kind of have that effect on me. You make me want to face up to things." Cam spoke softly.

Iris hated hearing Cam sounding so sad. She leaned forward. "It's definitely not too late to be bolder, to have more of what you want." Iris wanted to help Cam be happier. Cam nodded.

"And it's not too late for you to stop hiding from whatever it was that happened with Amanda. Don't you think it's time you let yourself move on?

"I…I guess so." Iris was surprised by Cam's question. She seemed so serious.

"I know you mean well when you say things like that, Cam. And trust me, I've heard it enough times from Hazel, Casey, my dad, but you don't know what happened. If you did, you'd maybe see things a little differently, be glad I'm hiding and not out there having my heart broken and hurting people for the hell of it."

"I just don't believe you would do that. I know we haven't known each other for long, but I know you, Iris. You're kind and careful and sweet. And I've hated sitting by while you let Jess say the things she says about you." She paused. "And you're far too much of a catch to stay single."

Hearing Cam's words, Iris felt a shiver run down her spine. She had let Cam in, let Cam get under her defenses, gone out of her way to get close to her when she should have known better. Cam thought Iris was "careful and sweet," but Iris had been anything but and, even now, she was finding it hard to be friends with Cam and not feel attracted to her. She had kept herself single for a very good reason.

"Relationships go wrong all the time, Iris. There's no reason why you should still be the one suffering while Amanda moves on. It's too much."

There wasn't really a question there for Iris to answer, and she could have avoided responding, changed the subject, told a lie even. But she knew, sitting there with Cam, in the soft light of the restaurant and after a lovely evening together, that she should tell Cam what happened. Cam would either understand and it would be a relief, or she would figure out what an emotional fuck up she was and give her a wide berth in the future and, as much as that would hurt, maybe it would be for the best. Iris believed she could fight her attraction to Cam, but if Cam walked away it might be safer for both of them.

Iris had hold of the almost empty beer glass in front of her. They had football tomorrow, so she'd only had a small beer. She couldn't even rely on alcohol to give her the courage to get through this.

"I was very much in love with Amanda. At the time of our relationship and for a long time afterward. I don't know why I need you to know that, but I do. In some respects it makes it worse, but maybe it also partly explains things."

Iris picked up her beer and drained what was left in the glass. Rather than put it down, she cradled it in her hands and tried to find a way to tell this story truthfully—Cam deserved that—but also in a way that wouldn't actually make her run a mile in the opposite direction. Despite everything, she really didn't want that.

"We'd been together nearly two years, and Amanda had her thirtieth birthday coming up. As a present, because I knew she'd always wanted to do it, I booked places for us to run the New York marathon. We'd never visited and Amanda had *running a marathon* on her bucket list. It seemed like a good idea, and she was so happy when she opened the gift. It felt good to be the cause of that happiness. It wasn't that we weren't getting on—we were—but I had this feeling that we weren't having as much fun, that we were drifting…though sometimes I think I only see that with hindsight." Iris sighed deeply.

"Within days, she'd developed this training routine to make sure we were in marathon running shape in time for the race. Some friends of ours—Gina and her girlfriend, Anna—were also racing so we were all in it together. Trying to eat well, cutting down on our drinking, lots and lots of running. Too much actually. It seemed to completely take over everything, but, well, Amanda was excited and happy and that was enough for me." Iris flinched slightly at the words she had unconsciously chosen. "Well, I thought it was enough for me. Guess I was kind of wrong about that."

"You don't have to do this, not if it's going to upset you. I don't want that," Cam said.

"No, I want to. It's okay and you should know this about me… from me." Iris took in a breath. She really didn't want to cry. This story made her seem pathetic enough already.

"We were still playing football alongside all the marathon training. It was pretty hard going. If we had a game that coincided with one of our heavy training weeks, I found it hard to keep up. Often Megan would take me off at half time. Amanda struggled too, but it was easier for her, playing in goal." Iris paused. "I resented it getting in the way of football and I should have said something. I didn't. I let the resentment eat at me."

Cam nodded.

"Gina was really into it. She and Amanda were the ones who put the training routines together, researched the route, and planned the things we'd all do in New York after the race. I was busy at work and, honestly, just not as enthusiastic about it. I always felt like I was a bit of a passenger actually." Iris stopped, losing her train of thought slightly.

"Anyway, to cut a long story short, a couple of months before the race Amanda asked me to stop playing football for a while, worrying it was interfering with the marathon training and even more worried that I might get injured. She was just being sensible, but I wouldn't accept that. I felt the race was taking over our lives. I was fed up we'd stopped doing other things and annoyed that I had to share Amanda with Gina, who was a third wheel at home. I refused to stop playing. I loved it of course, but it was also stubbornness on my part—wanting to retain something for me. Drinks after footie became the high point of an otherwise barren social calendar, and I took a perverse delight in watching Amanda watch me drink more wine than was allowed in our 'dietary schedule.'" Iris emphasized the words.

"I was behaving just like a rebellious teenager. To this day I don't understand why I didn't just talk to Amanda about how I was feeling about it all. We'd never really had any problems up to then, but I figured we were grownups, that we'd handle things like grownups. I know I should have said something but, afterward, when I was hating myself for not saying something, I realized that she didn't try to talk to me about any of it either. This gap had opened up between us and neither of us tried to bridge it." Iris looked at Cam. She was finding the words from somewhere and Cam was listening to them.

"About this time, Gina split up with her girlfriend. It was one more pressure, one more problem. Gina was ever-present. If I was too busy at work to go and run, Gina wasn't. If I was bad at sticking to the diet, Gina wasn't. I'm sorry if I sound self-pitying, but I was struggling. I felt this race had exposed some failing in my relationship with Amanda, some failing in me. Gina had had to give up her place in the race as her girlfriend was taking someone else, and this created extra pressure thanks to Gina's constant comments. 'If I was running, I wouldn't eat that' or 'If I was running, I'd be worried about playing football.' The two of them were beating a drum, and try as I might, I couldn't find their rhythm."

Iris stopped as Dev placed their coffees on the table. She picked up the cup, put it to her lips, and put it down again without taking a sip.

"I thought we had this perfect relationship so when all this was happening I didn't know where to go, what to do. It didn't have to become a problem, but in not acting, in not telling Amanda how resentful I was, how left out I felt, I made sure it became one." Iris spoke softly. "And please know that there's no part of this story that reflects well on me."

"I don't believe that." Cam leaned across the table and took hold of her hand. Iris withdrew it, surprised at her own reaction. Cam looked hurt, but Iris couldn't afford to care if she was going to get the rest of the story told.

"So, what happened next—you can probably guess—is I got injured. A bad tackle that, at first, didn't seem too bad, but then turned out to have damaged my Achilles. It was one of those moments that happen in football all too often. I should have been upset that it meant I couldn't run the race, but I wasn't, not at first. I was more bothered that it might mean the end of my season. Amanda took me to hospital, and she acted all concerned, but underneath all the caring words, I could feel how disappointed she was in me, how much she wanted to scream at me that she'd told me this might happen. It was horrible." Iris was twisting the napkin in her lap, her heart beating loudly in her chest.

"My injury wasn't as serious as it might have been so I guess, on one level, I was lucky. It meant being off my feet for a few weeks—no football and, obviously, no running. The race was four weeks away, and it was clear I wouldn't be fit enough to run. For a while, I felt relief, but I didn't dare tell Amanda that. Just something else I didn't talk to her about. She and Gina carried on regardless. Running together, obsessing about nutrition, aches and pains. And I closed down and isolated myself. I didn't see the point of post-match drinks if I wasn't playing. Friends came to see me, but I wasn't much fun to be honest. And I was drinking a bit more when we did go out. It wasn't good for us. We argued more. Amanda didn't like to see me drinking and self-pitying—who would? I wasn't very nice and I wasn't doing a thing to try and sort things out between us.

"But I thought about New York a lot, about how nice it would be to at least have the holiday. That maybe me and Amanda would start to get on like we used to after the race was out of the way, enjoy the trip, reconnect…" Iris was aware she was on the point of tears.

"Amanda had other ideas. One night, she said we needed to talk. I should have known something was up because Gina had disappeared so quickly after their run. Anyway, we sat down. I didn't know what to expect. I knew Amanda was struggling to find the words she needed. She was fidgeting. I remember it really clearly. Turning this bottle of mayonnaise she had picked up over and over in her hands. We both got quite fixed on staring at it and then she spoke up and asked me to give my place in the race to Gina. I was so relieved. I mean I was hardly going to limp around the course in my state. I said as much." Iris paused for a second before continuing. "You know the dread you feel when someone says 'we need to talk'? Well, to be honest, I'd expected worse. Amanda got up from the table and started to fix herself a sandwich. She was saying stuff like, 'I know it's a disappointment not to be able to go, but we can go together next year,' and 'Gina says you'll just get annoyed with all the hanging around if you're not running,' and then finally, she just said, 'Apparently, it doesn't even cost that much to change the name on the tickets.' I just sat there as the meaning sank in. Amanda had meant that I should give up my place on the trip to Gina, give up the hotel, the flight…the whole holiday, not just my place in the race. And I'd agreed, without really meaning to. And the most awful part was that she was so relieved I'd agreed. I could hear it in her voice."

Iris was crying now. Cam took Iris's hand. This time Iris did not pull it away. Iris shook her head sadly.

"I should have said something, told her it was our trip and that we should see New York for the first time together, but I didn't. I stopped listening and just sat there as she put mayonnaise on her sandwich, feeling sick and confused about what was happening and where we had gone so wrong."

"Why didn't you tell her you wanted to go with her?" Cam spoke softly. For the first time in a while, she focused on Cam, seeing concern and curiosity on her face. And, not for the first time, Iris thought how lovely she looked, how open she was.

Iris shrugged. "I don't know. I've thought about it often. Spent nights wondering why I gave up so easily. Sometimes I think it was pride. I didn't want to be the one who needed things, who couldn't cope with everything. Sometimes I wonder if I knew me and Amanda together were wrong. I had no idea of that at the time and, afterward, well...I thought I couldn't live without her...but now I do kind of wonder. If it was as right as I thought it was I'd have fought for it surely? I didn't. I was a passenger who sat and watched the train crash. I could have pulled the emergency cord, stopped the train, but I didn't."

"So they went to New York and you didn't?"

"Yeah. The conversation in the kitchen didn't really change anything. I suspect Amanda called Gina that evening. They would have been happy that I'd agreed to the plan of course. I had no idea right then just how happy it would have made them. " Iris swallowed a small sob.

"A couple of weeks later, I'd been out and got home a bit earlier than I'd said. I'd been drinking and I got a taxi to drop me at the end of the street. As I walked toward the flat, I could see Amanda saying good-bye to Gina on the doorstep. The light from the hall making them both easy to see. I wasn't surprised Gina was there; she was always there." Iris was rambling a little, trying not to get to the point. This wasn't something she'd ever told anyone. "And then I saw them. Amanda reached out and brushed some hair from Gina's cheek, and Gina just leaned in to her hand. It wasn't anything much really but, at the same time, it was everything and I knew then. It was all so fucking clear to me.

"I was ten yards away, Cam. I could have called out, I could have let them see me, let them know they'd been seen. But I froze. I watched Gina get in her car. I watched the front door close and the hall light go off. And I just carried on standing there."

Iris felt Cam wipe the tears from her cheeks with soft fingers, but she didn't move. She was somewhere else.

"The thing that bothered me was my reaction. I was devastated obviously. Realizing that Amanda was sleeping with Gina was a punch to the gut just like they say, and I had never felt pain like it. But those feelings lasted minutes, and then I completely shut off. And I mean completely. I went home. We watched TV. I feigned tiredness and went to bed and then we carried on as normal. I sat next to Amanda at breakfast and at dinner for two days after seeing them that night, and made myself think about all the ways in which Gina was better for her than I was, all the ways in which I had driven her to cheat by being so miserable and difficult. I wanted to tell her I knew about them, that I loved her, that what we had was worth fighting for, but I didn't. I let her go to New York without saying a thing."

Iris looked up at Cam. Her wide eyes showed surprise but also concern. "Would you have helped me not to be such an idiot if you'd known me then?" Iris asked.

"I...I don't know. I hope so, but I don't know Amanda. I didn't know the two of you. Maybe...Maybe I would have felt like it was worth you fighting for it, but maybe I wouldn't. I don't know." Cam sounded almost as upset as Iris.

Iris sat here with Cam—the woman she was worried she was falling for—talking about the woman she had loved more than anything else in the world. She felt sick, scared, and shameful. She gulped the coffee, knowing there was more she needed to say. "They went to New York. The night before they left, I didn't go home. I couldn't watch her pack, not knowing what it meant, what they were going to be doing without me on that trip. I stayed out, ignoring all of Amanda's worried messages. Instead of being a grown up, I sent a text message from some bar. One line that just said, *I hope New York is everything you both hoped for*. It was the final act of destruction. In not going home, in not talking about any of it, I had made sure that Amanda would choose the safety of a relationship with Gina. A relationship where it was possible to talk about stuff, where they could want the same things." Iris let the tears fall.

"What happened next?" Cam's voice sounded strange, and Iris imagined disapproval written into the three words of her question.

"What you'd expect really. Amanda came home from New York. I wasn't there when she came back. I couldn't bear the idea of her continuing to lie to me about Gina, telling me about the trip. I went to my dad's. I didn't know what else to do. Then we met and got everything out in the open, hours and hours of recriminations, tears, anger. I told her what I'd seen. She didn't deny any of it. She said she hadn't meant it to happen of course, but that we were different people, and basically implying that it was my fault for being impossible. We went our separate ways. She left the team—it was a decent thing for her to do actually—she knew I'd need it more than her, need our friends. And she got on with building a new life with Gina. Or so I thought." Iris hesitated, taking a moment to dry her eyes.

"And I…well…after we broke up, I became the person that Jess loves to talk about. I was destructive. I went back to the team when I was fit, played and trained with an absolute fury, and I numbed the pain I felt at losing Amanda by chasing women I didn't want and having lots of meaningless sex, not caring who I hurt, who I used, and hating myself more than ever. When Jess talks about the things I did, the person I was, I feel nothing but shame and a sense that all I can do to make amends is to make sure I'm not in a position to be that damaging to anyone ever again." Iris had her arms crossed. She was feeling tired now, the effort of retelling the story taking its toll.

Dev's shadow darkened the table as he placed a round silver platter containing the bill onto the table.

"Here you go, ladies. Ten percent off as promised." He touched Iris on the shoulder, the gesture was kind, gentle. He couldn't have heard what they had been talking about, but somehow it seemed he knew she needed it.

Iris looked at Cam, waiting for her to say something. She had badly wanted to explain to Cam what had happened with Amanda, had wanted her to understand why she had behaved so badly afterward, to not want the story to reflect badly on her but of course it did.

"I've got so many questions I want to ask you." Cam leaned back in her chair. "I don't dare to though. I'm worried I'll upset you or that I'll sound judgmental."

"You couldn't judge me any more harshly than I've judged myself. I know there's no point saying it, but I want you to know that I'm not that person any more. I haven't been for a while. It matters to me that you know that though I won't blame you if it changes things. I wouldn't really want to be close to someone like me either."

Iris fished out her wallet and left enough cash to cover the bill and a generous tip for Dev.

"Shall we go? I'll get us a taxi." Iris stood, wanting to be anywhere but sitting there facing Cam. She could see concern on Cam's face mixed with something else; she imagined it was disappointment, disappointment in her.

"I guess we should," Cam replied quietly but didn't move.

Iris put on her jacket, tugging at the sleeves, unable to meet Cam's eyes, wanting and not wanting her to ask whatever was on her mind.

Outside the restaurant, after they had said their good-byes to Dev, they waited at the curb for their taxi. The street was as busy as it had been when they arrived. They were standing side by side, but Iris felt like she was miles away, hunched in her jacket, her face turned away from Cam's. She felt arms wrap around her body as Cam pulled her into a tight hug.

"Thanks for dinner, Iris. It was lovely, just like you said it would be." Cam pulled away. "And I don't know what to say about the rest of it, but it's not your fault that you were cheated on, whatever you think you did to deserve it. And it's not fair that Amanda let you take the blame for it." Cam paused. "And I know you probably did some things you're not proud of when you were hurting, but…"

Iris pulled away from the hug.

"Iris?" Iris didn't react. She couldn't look at Cam. She didn't want to see pity reflected back at her. Cam said her name again, a little more emphatically, and Iris lifted her head slowly, seeing Cam's earnest gaze. "We've all done things we're not proud of, Iris. Don't let yours define you…please."

Cam put a hand on her arm and squeezed gently.

"Amanda coming back doesn't mean that old Iris is any more relevant than she was a week ago. I don't care about her. I'm here for new Iris. I like her and I trust her, and I'm going to be her friend whatever."

Iris pulled Cam into a hug, both arms wrapped around her, letting herself dare to believe that their friendship could survive Cam knowing the worst about her. The beep of the taxi horn at the curb gave them both a reason to retreat. Cam opened the door and ushered Iris inside.

They had been largely silent on the way home. Iris looking out the window, and Cam watching Iris, trying to find something to say that matched her desire to offer Iris reassurance. Everything she tried out in her head seemed lame. She wanted to tell Iris that Amanda cheating and then blaming her was a shitty thing to do. She wanted to say that she didn't care how many women Iris had fucked around with afterward, friends didn't turn their back on friends and she would never turn her back on Iris. And, above everything else, she wanted to tell Iris to start trusting herself and other people again. Starting with her.

Despite the thoughts and questions buzzing round her brain, Cam eventually decided that talking didn't feel right and settled for taking Iris's hand. She found herself stroking it soothingly, trying to use the contact to let Iris know she was there for her, despite it being clear that Iris had now retreated behind a defensive wall.

At one point, when they were close to home, heading up through the village, Iris looked across at her and, even in the dark of the car, Cam could see from her eyes that Iris had something she wanted to say.

"I don't know how I'm going to feel being around her every week." Iris said the words quietly. "It doesn't hurt anymore, and I don't even feel angry with her, but she reminds me of who I was then...of how stupid I was for not realizing how broken we were, and how much I hurt people after, people that didn't deserve me treating them like that. I was no better than her in the end." Iris took in a breath, her voice trailing off before completing the sentence.

"It was a long time ago, Iris. If you've forgiven her, you can forgive yourself."

"Would you?" Iris held Cam's gaze.

"Forgive her or forgive myself?"

"Both. Either. I dunno really." The car was slowing to a stop; they had reached Cam's house.

Iris was finally letting her in, and Cam knew she had to be honest but that she also had to be careful. Iris was hurting and Cam didn't want to add to it.

"I think all of what you did was human. Maybe it wasn't great, but it seems to me like you've made yourself suffer far too much for it ever since. So, yes, I think it's time you forgave yourself." She poked Iris on the leg for emphasis. "And I'd definitely expect you to forgive me if the shoe was on the other foot."

Iris nodded and they sat silently for a beat until Cam realized that the taxi driver was speaking to them, telling them they had arrived at their first stop. Cam gathered up her bag and pulled away from Iris to exit the cab. She felt a tug on her arm and turned back.

"Thanks, Cam." Iris let go of Cam's arm, looking slightly embarrassed. "I mean it."

"No problem." Cam nodded back at her. She had the door slightly ajar and the back seat was now illuminated by the overhead light. Cam could see Iris's dark eyes staring back at her and she was frowning. Cam felt a strong urge to lean across and drag her thumb across the frown, smoothing the skin. Instead, she stepped out of the cab onto the pavement in front of her house and waved a good-bye at Iris as the cab headed off down the street. The renewed darkness in the back of the car not allowing her to see if Iris had waved back.

Cam looked at her watch as she put her key in the door and saw that it was past ten. She blinked as she realized the time. She left her bag, shoes, and coat in the cabinet under the stairs and moved along the hallway to the living room. The landing light was on, but the downstairs of the house was dark. Ryan had already gone to bed. She headed to the sink and poured herself a glass of water before treading softly up the stairs, not sure if Ryan was awake or asleep but feeling a little guilty that she hadn't texted before heading home to let him know that they had stayed a little later than intended at the restaurant.

Cam gently pushed open the door to their bedroom and was greeted by the sight of Ryan sitting up in bed, his bedside lamp shining softly and the small TV on top of the chest of drawers giving off a flickering light. There was no sound, but Ryan had the remote control in his hand, and Cam glanced across to see football on the TV.

"Match of the day...just started if you're interested." He pointed at the TV with the remote, sounding a little weary.

Cam nodded, peeling off her clothes and placing them on the chair in the corner of their room before crossing to the dressing table to put down her watch and necklace.

"You're a lot later than I thought you'd be." Ryan's tone was pretty even. Cam had expected him to be more annoyed than this.

"Yeah, we went to the East End and ended up having a curry. Lovely place actually. We..." she hesitated. "We got to talking, lost track of time a bit...and the cab home took longer than I expected. Sorry." Cam felt a slight resentment at having to explain herself to him, when he spent so much time away or out with other people, leaving her home alone far too many times. She honestly couldn't remember the last time he'd stayed in waiting for her, but there was no point in saying that now.

"I should meet her. She must be really good company. I mean, what was that, twelve hours together? That's some serious hanging out. And, hey, only twelve hours till you get to see her again for tomorrow's match." Ryan's tone had hardened, the sarcasm hard to miss.

"Of course, you'd rather I'd stayed in and waited for you I suppose, and spent another Saturday doing nothing." Cam dressed for bed, hating this, hating the way he was looking at her, but determined not to feel guilty.

"Not at all, I'm just surprised you could find so much to talk about. Or maybe there were long periods of just gazing at each other to pass the time." Ryan didn't wait for her to respond. "I mean everyone's bisexual these days, maybe you've got a woman-crush. She's hot. It's not like I wouldn't understand. I just didn't know you had it in you." He was trying to provoke her and they both knew it.

"And I'm kind of surprised that you can't just be happy that I've found a new friend to do stuff with without being such a fucking ass about it." Cam left the room without looking back. As she stalked back down the stairs, Cam could feel her insides churning with anger and upset. It was bad enough that he was sulking and selfish, but to accuse her of having a crush on Iris was pathetic and unfair. She liked Iris, and that was not something she should have to justify to him.

Cam sat in darkness on the couch, a blanket across her legs and her phone in her hand, checking emails, checking Twitter, looking for something to do that would distract her and calm her down. She just didn't understand what was happening with her and Ryan these days, and if she was honest, she couldn't stop thinking about Iris and how upset she'd been. Midway through an article about Donald Trump's latest outburst, Cam was surprised to see the door to the living room open and light spill in from the hallway. Ryan appeared in the doorway in his boxers. They looked at each other for a while.

"I'm sorry, Cam." He ran a hand through his hair.

She sat, looking at him silently, needing more from him than that.

"I am sorry. I know I was a jerk, I was just feeling a bit resentful. Stupid I know." He paused. "Please come to bed." He sounded like he meant it, but Cam couldn't be sure. She shook her head in reply.

"Not yet." Cam was still wide-awake.

"Okay then." Ryan crossed the room to where she was sitting and planted a soft kiss on her forehead. "G'night, babe. Sorry for being such a grouch."

"Good night." Cam gave him a weary smile and watched as he disappeared back out of the room, the hallway light briefly shining into the room before the darkness settled in again.

❖

It was just after midnight before Cam finally readied herself for bed, the argument with Ryan finally out of her system. She'd spent an hour of thinking about Iris and was pretty clear in her own mind that Amanda had a lot to answer for. She had broken Iris's heart, while leaving her feeling responsible for the relationship ending. That, and Iris going off the rails afterward, had left Iris unwilling to trust herself to love again. Cam just couldn't imagine how hard it was going to be for Iris to be around Amanda again.

Cam chanced a text to Iris. *Amanda was a fool and you didn't deserve what happened. You deserve to be happy.* She didn't know exactly why she needed to say it, why she wanted to reach out to Iris, but she did.

The reply came almost immediately, letting Cam know that Iris was also still awake. *Thank you. I think I like your version of my life better than mine.*

A minute or two later, Cam received another text from Iris that simply said, *In case you were wondering.* The short message was accompanied by a URL. Cam clicked on it and was taken to a Buzzfeed list: *50 Reasons Why Britain is Better than America.* She read through the list—better at queuing, the National Health Service, better at understatement and irony, better at making tea, invented the Spice Girls. The list was perfect and Cam knew it was Iris's way of telling her not to leave London, and thinking that she cared enough to find and send it made Cam feel stupidly happy, happier than she had a right to be lying in bed next to her fiancé. She didn't want to face the fact that the happiness Iris made her feel was something she wasn't sure she could be without anymore.

CHAPTER ELEVEN

Cam was one of the first to arrive at the changing rooms. She shook out her umbrella and hung it on the hook above her usual spot on the bench, trying to make sure it didn't drip all over her. In the opposite corner, a red bucket was catching the drip drip drip of rainwater coming through the roof. The changing room was in a terrible state—the word primitive was what came to Cam's mind—and it was nowhere near as well maintained as the one they used for training. According to Hazel and Jess, who had been on several spying missions, it was also nowhere near as well maintained as the quartet of men's changing rooms sitting alongside it.

It was a tiny space, but still no one could be bothered to paint it or keep it clean. The main window was cracked, allowing in a cold breeze, and unless a plumbing miracle had occurred in the last week, Cam knew the water in the showers would alternate erratically between scalding hot and heart-stoppingly cold.

Megan was trying to sweep the worst of the dried mud into a corner. The Cottoms team had this changing room to themselves, but the showers were shared with the other women's changing room next door, and Cam could hear the noises on the other side of the showers that signaled that their opponents were starting to arrive. She began to change, willing herself to move slowly so she wasn't ready too soon, not wanting to sit and shiver in her shorts if she got the timing wrong.

Megan had stopped sweeping and was now fiddling with the medical supplies, emptying out the huge first aid box and counting the items back in. Cam cleared her throat and spoke across the short distance between them.

"Jess told me…about Amanda coming back I mean. I know we need a goalkeeper, but I don't think it's fair to Iris. Is there really no one else who can play in goal?" Cam wasn't sure Megan would welcome the challenge, but Iris was her friend and someone had to be willing to stick up for her.

Megan sat next to Cam on the bench.

"Being captain means making decisions for the good of the team, not for the good of individuals. It sounds naff, but it's true. It's the same when you have to leave out someone who really wants to play for someone else who plays better. It's not easy, but someone's got to do it, and unfortunately, that person is me. We need a keeper. Someone solid. We have a real chance of winning this league this season, and a good goalkeeper will make all the difference. I can't afford to worry about past relationship dramas. Iris knows that."

Megan sighed. "Look, Iris is a big girl. She'll be fine. They don't have to be the best of friends, just play on the same team."

"You should have told her though. She should have heard it from you, since you're the captain and all. It wasn't fair she heard it from me."

"You're right, I should have. It was all a bit sudden and I was scrambling to get things sorted for today. I didn't manage to get hold of her till really late on Saturday, and she already knew about it by then. I'm sorry for that."

Megan looked at Cam as if assessing something, as if assessing her. "It's good that you have her back though. She needs that. She needs people. On her side I mean. She doesn't ever admit to it, but she does."

Cam nodded, realizing that she did really want to be on Iris's side, wanted to be someone that Iris could lean on. She hadn't understood, until Megan said it, just how damn much she wanted it.

As if on cue, Iris walked in the door. A few steps behind her came Vicki and Priti, and then, moments later, Jess, Diane, and three of the other players. The noise level in the room went up by what seemed like a few hundred decibels. Iris smiled at her, dropping her bag on the ground. The smile was hesitant but seemed genuine, and Cam couldn't help but return it.

"Here we are then," Iris said as she sat down, pulling a towel out of her bag to dry off her hair. She had gotten wet even in the short walk from the parking lot to the changing room. "A chance to beat the league leaders. I bet Megan hasn't slept all night with the excitement of it all."

"For sure. Check that out, she's even bought oranges for halftime, it must be serious." Cam pointed at the table.

Iris looked tired, slight shadows under her eyes. Cam imagined it was because of her, because she had all but forced Iris to recount what had happened with Amanda, and probably because Iris knew she'd be playing with Amanda today.

"You okay?" Cam leaned in and touched Iris's arm gently.

"I think I am actually." Iris returned the touch, squeezing Cam's arm. "But thanks for asking. And thanks for yesterday, by the way. Not just for listening but for all of it. I know it probably didn't seem like it with the way it ended, but I had a good time, a really good time. And obviously the best bit was watching you squealing with fear about Jack the Ripper." She gave Cam a wink.

Cam let Iris lighten the mood, feeling ridiculously pleased that Iris had had as good a time as she had. And that she'd been willing to admit to it.

"Reminding me of my Whitechapel trauma makes you a very mean girl." Cam punched Iris playfully on the leg.

"Ow." Iris acted like it really hurt and made Cam rub her leg better. They both laughed, and Cam couldn't measure the relief she felt that Iris seemed okay.

The changing room door opened, and Hazel came in with Amanda close behind her. Amanda looked uncomfortable for a long moment until Vicki crossed the room to give her a bear hug and a warm welcome. Jess waved Amanda over, making space for her on the bench to her left. It was a friendly gesture but probably calculated to allow Jess to get as much information as possible out of Amanda in the process.

As Amanda sat down, Cam saw her look across toward where Iris was sitting, before quickly looking away again and getting on with the business of getting ready. Cam could feel Iris's tension beside her, the lightheartedness of a few moments ago gone. She nudged Iris with her leg and reached down to squeeze her hand gently, getting a small nod in return.

Hazel headed to her usual position on Iris's right hand side. She snaked an arm across Iris's shoulders and gave her a squeeze.

"Cheers, mate." Iris spoke quietly.

"All good?"

"Yeah, completely."

Iris finished tying her boots and walked slowly over to where Amanda was sitting. The room seemed to grow quieter.

"Hey." Iris stuck out a hand in Amanda's direction. "Good to have you back."

Amanda blinked up at Iris slightly before taking the hand she had offered. "Yeah, Megan's pretty hard to say no to, you know what she's like."

"I definitely do. You joined at the right time. We might just be about to win the league," Iris said.

"Yeah, I figured, thought I'd join now and see if I could grab a bit of glory right at the end of the season."

"Anyway, good to see you."

"You too."

Iris sat back down next to Cam and blew out a breath of relief.

"Well done, that can't have been easy." Cam was impressed by how Iris had handled Amanda's arrival, and she was rewarded for her comment with a shy smile from Iris and a slight shrug as if to say, what else was I supposed to do?

Cam found it impossible not to pay attention to Amanda, knowing more than she had a right to about the new player and her breakup with Iris. It was easy for Cam to imagine just what an attractive couple they'd have made. Amanda was not as tall as Iris, but she had the same dark good looks and she carried herself gracefully. Her lighter hazel eyes made her seem less brooding, less intense than Iris, and she had certainly been very friendly toward Cam and the others in the team she didn't know as Megan had made introductions before they headed out. Cam wanted to dislike her, she'd broken Iris's heart for fuck's sake, but that was silly. If Iris could rise above it, then so could she.

Cam stood with the other players as Megan brought them together in a huddle for their pre-match pep talk. She and Iris had their arms linked as part of the circle, and Amanda was directly opposite them. *Hurt her again, though, and you'll have me to deal with.* Cam wondered where the tribal feelings had sprung from. She shook her head, shaking away the ridiculous protectiveness.

❖

Ryan had arrived pitch-side a couple of minutes before the start of the second half and far too late for him to do anything other than wave at Cam across the pitch. Cam should have been pleased he'd come at all, but instead she couldn't help being annoyed he'd come so late. He was standing and chatting with Diane and Priti. It was still raining steadily, and though Ryan had an umbrella, Cam could see he wasn't at all dressed for the terrible weather. She guessed that coming to watch had been a real last-minute decision for him.

Ryan had watched her from the sidelines many times when they'd first got together. Cam liked having him there, enjoying his compliments about how she'd played, and laughing as he made silly jokes about their opponents. Over time, he found better things to do with his time. Cam frowned as she tried to remember, but it must have been a couple of years since he'd last watched her play.

And since he'd shown no interest at all in her excited tales of how well her new team here in London was doing, Cam couldn't help but wonder if Ryan turning up today was related to the argument they'd had on Saturday.

"C'mon, Cottoms. Let's do this." Hearing the shout from across the pitch brought Cam out of her reverie. It was Vicki of course, her loud voice carrying to all corners of the pitch. Cam turned and clapped in Vicki's direction, hearing Jess and Hazel return the shout. She made herself stop thinking about Iris and Amanda, stop wondering why Ryan had turned up, and simply concentrate on the game they really wanted to win.

Iris was standing with Jess at the center spot, waiting to kick off, a picture of stillness and concentration, as she waited for the ref to get them underway again. The team was winning 2-1, but the first half had been tight. Megan had scored Cottoms' first goal—a confidently taken penalty—awarded after a heavy kick to the back of Iris's legs from the center half—who had received a yellow card for the foul and an earful from Hazel for good measure. The second goal had been Cam's. She had run on to a pass that Iris had threaded through the two central defenders, controlled it with one touch, and then deftly lofted it over the advancing goalkeeper and into the back of the net. Even Amanda had sprinted half the length of the pitch to join in celebrating that goal, seeming genuinely delighted.

In the ten minutes before half time, the other team got a goal back and could have scored more, but Cottoms had defended tenaciously, and Amanda had made a couple of really good saves, surprising Cam with how well she had played and by how easily she had slotted back into the team.

Their opponents were tough, top of the league and unbeaten in six matches, and Cam knew that this made the halftime lead even more impressive. It was also one of the reasons—along with the steady rain—why Cam felt like the second half was going to feel like a very long forty-five minutes. She jumped up and down on the spot, willing her muscles to warm up and her mind to clear, determined to take any chances that came her way in the second half.

With only a few minutes to go, and with the score still at 2-1, the opposing team's right back was caught in possession by Jess and had no option but to kick the ball into touch for a throw-in.

The other team's goalkeeper was tall and clad in a lime green shirt that made her look even more imposing. She was waving her arms in the air, trying to attract the ref's attention to complain about how close Hazel was standing to her. It was something Megan had made them practice often, and it was perfectly within the rules of the game. Hazel would stand in front of the goalie, hoping to impede her ability to come and claim the ball, and Iris and Vicki would stand on the penalty spot and run toward the goal as Megan launched her throw hoping to connect with a header while the goalkeeper was stranded. Cam could see them both in front of her now, being closely marked. Their height always made Vicki and Iris a threat in the penalty area, and she knew that the defenders had no choice but to focus on them.

Cam ghosted toward the back post, hoping her movement wouldn't be noticed with all the attention on the taller players. Megan looped the ball into the box, and Cam watched, almost in slow motion, as Iris jumped, rising above the defenders to get her head to the ball and glance it behind her. As the ball came in Cam's direction and landed at her feet, Cam nipped in to turn it into the net with a simple tap-in to take the score to 3-1.

Her teammates crowded around Cam happily, hugging each other, slapping her on the back and high fiving jubilantly. She could see Iris being congratulated by Hazel and Vicki and ran the few yards toward them, jumping onto Iris's back in celebration. Iris waited for her to jump down and enveloped her in a big hug, ruffling her hair affectionately and then holding her head with both hands on the side of Cam's face and placing their foreheads together.

"Nice movement, nice goal," Iris said with a big grin.

"You put it on a plate for me," Cam responded happily.

They fist-bumped and trotted back to take their places for the kickoff. The team was pumped, knowing the third goal would be decisive given how little time was left and pretty certain that they were about to register their most important win of the season.

The full time whistle blew moments after they had kicked off after the goal, and the two teams began mingling on the pitch, shaking hands and offering congratulations and condolences where they were needed. It was obvious from the dropped heads and gloomy faces of their opponents that this was a loss they hadn't expected. Cottoms had spent last season puttering along without much attention, finally ending up in sixth place. This season something was different, and they were playing some impressive football as well as picking up some good wins, and they had moved stealthily up the table without anyone really expecting it.

Across the pitch, Amanda patted Iris on the back in celebration. To Cam, they seemed friendly enough, if a little awkward, but Iris looked tense as she turned away to shake hands with the opposing team's goalkeeper. Just ahead of Iris, trudging off the pitch toward the changing rooms, Jess was in earnest conversation with the other team's striker—a tall, graceful player with a mop of peroxide blond hair. Cam had already made the assumption that Jess was in the early stages of making a move, but maybe she really was just being friendly. For all Cam knew, they might already be friends. Surely even Jess had to have female friends, women she'd never slept with, women she didn't want to sleep with.

Of course she did. Cam shook her head at her own stupidity, feeling embarrassed that maybe she was guilty of a little homophobia for assuming that a gay woman couldn't be capable of a close friendship with another woman without it meaning something else. Cam's mind drifted to her own experience with Iris—they were becoming close, and Iris was gay, yet her feelings for Cam seemed completely platonic. Cam cut herself some slack as far as Jess was concerned. After all, given her track record, it was much more like wisdom than homophobia to assume she was looking for a new conquest.

She looked for Ryan where he'd been standing. In all the excitement of the late goal, and the end of the game, she had forgotten he was there. He was no longer in the same spot, and Cam cast her eyes around the pitch, wondering if he'd moved position, but there was no sign of him. She felt a bubbling of annoyance that he'd left before the end of the match and missed her late goal. *And he missed the one I scored in the first half too.* She let out a deep sigh of frustration.

On the side of the pitch where Ryan had been standing, Iris was helping Megan gather up the various bits of surplus equipment, medical supplies, and so on. Cam had had a good game and was psyched that she'd scored another two goals, but she knew that it was the understanding she was developing with Iris, who always seemed to know where she was on the pitch that was making her play so well and, more importantly, helping the team win more games this season. At the final whistle, Megan had hugged both Iris and Cam in a very un-Megan like display of affection. "You two carry on like that and we might even win the bloody league." Her enthusiasm explained by the fact that they were now just two points behind the league leaders.

Cam jogged across the pitch toward Megan and Iris. "Can I carry something?"

"No way. We need you lying on a bed of feathers and wrapped in cotton wool till the end of the season. I'm not allowing our star player to pull a muscle." Iris's eyes danced as she spoke, the tension of earlier completely gone.

Cam felt herself blush at the silly compliment, liking the fact that Iris did not seem at all jealous of the praise that came Cam's way and liking more the fact that this praise came from Iris.

"I'm only as good as the service I'm getting from you, so give me one of those buckets before you pull a muscle and everyone figures out you're the one making me look so good." Cam took one of the buckets and mimed it hitting the floor due to its heaviness.

"What's Megan got in here? Bricks?"

"Close. She always brings ankle weights. Makes the subs warm up while wearing them. You'd know that if you'd ever sat on the subs bench." Cam looked across and saw that Iris was smiling, teasing her.

"I've been substitute plenty of times, thank you. I wasn't always this appreciated in teams I've played in."

"And do you feel 'appreciated' by us, Cam?" Iris raised her eyebrows flirtatiously. "Because, speaking for myself, I certainly do appreciate you." She looked Cam up and down appraisingly before she let out a chuckle.

Cam felt a rush of blood to her cheeks. Iris was just teasing, of course she was. She pushed Iris ahead of her, toward the changing rooms, so she couldn't see that Cam was blushing furiously and working hard not to worry about just how much the idea of Iris appreciating her was suddenly so appealing.

CHAPTER TWELVE

Cam sat quietly as the players headed out of the changing room in twos and threes looking all showered and pink and thirsty for a celebratory pint. For a bunch of athletes, they sure liked a drink. It was a British thing, Alison had explained to her once. Her sister considered herself an expert on all things British having spent a summer here once touring music festivals with a Brit she'd met back in Seattle. Her not-very-scientific theory was that British people were naturally so reserved that only the consumption of a certain amount of alcohol enabled them to function socially. There was some truth in it, but Cam had always suspected this was wisdom born only of Alison's experience of having her heart broken by the same heavy drinking emotionally stunted British boyfriend at the end of that summer.

Before showering, Cam had checked for a text from Ryan explaining his sudden disappearance. There was nothing. She felt annoyed, hoping he had a good excuse. If she was being honest though, she was happy to escape having to go home with him and miss the post-match celebrations. Maybe she was going native, but a pint of warm ale in a cozy pub sounded like heaven right now.

"Ready?" Iris zipped up her bag and stood, slinging it over one shoulder.

Cam nodded in response and looked up at her. She was completely surprised by the jolt of arousal she felt at the sight of Iris, her cheeks flushed from the shower, her dark hair still damp, the very shape of her, framed against the light, seeming to be something Cam couldn't help but notice as attractive. *Very attractive actually.* She willed herself to stop staring, willed herself to stop thinking what she was thinking, and then watched as Iris frowned. Cam worried that Iris somehow understood what she had been thinking, and she felt a stab of panic.

Iris reached behind her, prodding at the back of her right calf and wincing. "It's bloody sore and a nice shade of purple already." She grinned. "Totally worth it for that penalty though."

Cam exhaled. She made herself smile back, trying to ignore the tight feeling in her belly.

"I know, I got whacked too. I think that's how they've won so many games, intimidating their opponents with a few kicks when the ref's not looking." Cam rolled up her tracksuit and turned her leg to show Iris, insanely relieved that they were talking about bruises.

Iris dropped her bag onto the bench and knelt in front of Cam. She turned her leg slightly with one hand and gently probed Cam's calf with the other. Cam felt every touch of Iris's fingers. Her skin was alive, sparkling under the soft pressure. She felt a little too warm and understood that it wasn't the temperature in the changing room.

"There's some faint bruising and it feels a little swollen, but nothing too bad. Is it sore?" Iris looked up at Cam as she spoke. Her eyes were hard to read in the dim light, but Cam couldn't see past them. She nodded, words beyond her, and Iris nodded in response, holding Cam's gaze before returning her foot to the floor slowly, then gently rolling the tracksuit back into position. Cam stared at her fingers as they moved.

"Well, at least you can walk this time," Iris said, not moving. The air seemed heavy between them, but Cam wasn't sure if that was her imagination. Last night they had shared something, something much more important than a curry. It had made them closer, and Cam could feel it. She swallowed, her throat seeming full, her eyes unable to look away from Iris's. The two of them just looking at each other.

"Ryan came to see us play today." Something made Cam say the words; they were unexpected, even to her.

"Oh," Iris responded neutrally. "I didn't know, I mean, I didn't see him. I should have said hello." Iris stood up slowly and Cam did likewise. They were the last players to leave the changing room, and Cam badly needed to get out into the air. She picked up her bag.

"He arrived at the end of halftime, but left before the end. Missed both my goals." She tried to sound breezy, like she didn't really care.

"Probably got pneumonia out there in the rain and had to go to the hospital." Cam was trying to be humorous, but none of it was funny. Iris being so close had made her feel something she didn't want to feel, and it had made her want to remind herself of Ryan, to remind Iris of Ryan, and all she'd done was make herself feel short-changed by him again.

Iris and Cam left the changing room side by side.

"Muscle rub," Iris murmured.

Cam looked at her, not sure she'd heard correctly.

"Hazel always has some muscle rub. Ask her for some for your leg. And then you can buy me a pint of shandy for setting up both your goals." Cam was relieved that Iris seemed completely unaware of whatever it was she had imagined had just passed between them.

❖

"Cam," Ryan yelled from the parking lot. "I'm over here. I've got the heat on."

Cam and Iris exchanged a glance. "I guess he did stick around after all," Iris said quietly.

They both changed direction and headed toward Ryan and his car.

"Hey, Ryan." Iris spoke first, putting out a hand which Ryan shook firmly. "We've not met. I'm Iris. How did you enjoy the game? Pretty wet and cold day for spectating. Hope Cam's performance made up for the weather."

"Hey, Iris, I've heard a lot about you." Ryan regarded Iris closely. Cam wasn't sure, but she thought she detected a little edge to the statement. Whatever it was, it passed quickly. "Yeah, I'm soaked through but happy I came."

Ryan looked very wet. Jeans and shoes sodden, neither given any protection by the umbrella he had been holding. Cam felt affection for him, happy he had come. Her annoyance now only an itch.

"You missed my goal right at the end." Cam scratched the itch.

"I didn't. I saw it from a distance. I thought the game was about to finish so I went to find a bathroom. Sorry, babe." Cam let Ryan pull her into a hug.

"I played well didn't I?" She looked up at him.

"You certainly did, my sweet. You all did actually. I was quite proud. That last goal was a peach, even from a distance," Ryan said. "But now I need to get out of these wet clothes." He waved his hands down his body, drawing attention to the state of his clothes, and Cam felt him turn her in the direction of his parked car.

"I don't wanna go home." Cam felt a slight rush of panic. "I want to go for a drink."

"Babe, I'm soaked through." Ryan patted his jeans.

Cam held her ground but sounded uncertain. "They'll probably have the fire going in the pub. You can dry off there. I think we've all earned a pint." Cam looked pleadingly at him, and then sideways at Iris. Cam was waiting for him to decide what they were going to do, and they all knew that she'd acquiesce if he said they had to go home. Ryan looked from Cam to Iris and back again.

"Okay, okay, a quick pint sounds good. And it's about time I met all those people you talk about, except maybe that Graham guy." He lifted his eyebrows, and Cam felt relief as Ryan kissed her on the top of the head and remotely unlocked his car. "Need a lift, Iris?" He didn't look at Iris as he spoke.

"No, thanks." Iris shook her head.

Cam threw her bag onto the back seat and turned back to Iris before getting in. "See you there?" Iris nodded and walked slowly away.

Moments later, Iris was sitting in her car, not yet having pulled away, feeling the loss of Cam by her side, and missing her usual excited chatter about all the key moments of the match as Iris drove them to the pub. They had fallen into an enjoyable routine over the past few weeks. Cam would leave her car at home, and Iris would pick her up and then drop her off after they'd finished. They lived so close, it made sense to share cars, and Cam loved the Mini, saying that it made her feel like she was in an Austin Powers movie. Iris tried not to be too alarmed by the fact that she minded very much that Ryan had swept in tonight and ushered Cam into his car, ruining their routine and her post match good mood at the same time. The small stab of jealousy that she felt as Cam allowed herself to be pulled into Ryan's arms, as Ryan kissed the top of Cam's head, was something else she didn't want to face up to.

Last night, Iris had worried that things wouldn't be the same between them once Cam knew what had happened with Amanda and how she had behaved after their split, but Cam had surprised her by being so damn solid about it all—she'd been amazing actually—and today Iris was the one in danger of ruining things by not controlling her feelings. The irony being that, before Cam, she'd had them under supreme control for months. Iris sighed. She shouldn't have let Cam get so close, should have realized the attraction from the start. The tense, sparking feeling in her body as she had knelt in front of Cam in the changing room just now was the clearest proof yet that she was in over her head. She might be telling herself that she and Cam were just becoming good friends, but her body clearly hadn't gotten the message.

She thumped her steering wheel in frustration and turned on her engine, watching as Ryan pulled out ahead of her, waving as he passed. Iris returned the wave halfheartedly and seriously contemplated driving home rather than to the pub. She'd started the day wondering how she'd feel being around Amanda again, and she was ending it by worrying more about how she'd handle seeing Cam with Ryan, her actual fucking fiancé. And that wasn't a good thing at all.

Damn, damn, damn. Iris put the car into first gear. *Am I really dumb enough to be developing feelings for my soon to be married friend?* She took in a breath. *A sweet, smart, sexy friend...with eyes you could swim in.* Iris slowed the car at the junction, chiding herself for her own ridiculousness. She flicked the indicator for a left turn, intending to go home. As she waited for a gap in the traffic so she could pull out, she found herself pushing down on the indicator lever to signal right, deciding at the last minute that seeing Cam canoodling with Ryan would be good for her stupid crush. It'd be like aversion therapy, helping her to face reality and get back to being the friend to Cam that she really wanted to be. As Iris got closer to the pub, she rolled her shoulders against the tension she felt knowing that, if it got a bit too much with Cam and Ryan, for a bit of light relief, she could make awkward conversation with the woman who broke her heart by cheating on her. It was gonna be a great night.

When Iris entered the lounge, Ryan and Cam were already seated, and Ryan was shaking hands across the table introducing himself to the other players. Someone had moved a few of the small tables together so that everyone was sitting in a big group.

Cam waved at Iris and pointed at the seat next to her. It was a sweet gesture and she could hardly refuse, even if it would mean a close-up view of the future newlyweds all night. Inside, Iris groaned and then reminded herself that was the point. She was here to be cured. She approached the table, her hand on her wallet.

"Anyone missing a drink?"

"Hazel's already had a whip round and is getting a round in. Go and chip in, mate." Vicki's voice carried above the din.

Vicki was with Harry, the two of them sitting close, fingers entwined and obviously finding it hard not to keep touching each other. It made Iris remember how crazy the first few weeks of any relationship were. Unsure, intense, and passionate. She made her way to the bar, wondering if something of that was going on with her and Cam. Not a relationship, she wasn't that dumb, but new friendships could also be intense, could involve wanting to spend a lot of time together, even involve being jealous. Maybe that was what was going on. Iris liked the explanation and tried to convince herself it was plausible, but then she remembered the wave of arousal that had coursed through her body when Cam had looked at her as she'd knelt before her in the changing room, and had to face up to the fact that even intense friendships didn't usually involve those kinds of feelings. It was a nice try though.

"Hey, bud, add a pint of shandy to that order will you?" Iris threw an arm around Hazel's shoulders.

"Sure thing." Hazel passed on the request to the barmaid.

"Great game today, eh? Really enjoyable to beat that lot." Iris didn't sound all that convincing, even to herself.

"Yeah, really enjoyable. They're an arrogant bunch, nice to put one over on them. So why does your face look like we lost?" Hazel nudged her affectionately.

Iris shrugged.

"Seriously, mate, what's up?"

The barmaid was lining up the drinks on two round trays in front of Hazel.

"Dunno, really. Probably nothing."

"Uh-oh, not premenstrual are we? You know how evil you get." Hazel made devil horn signs in Iris's direction.

Despite herself, Iris laughed. "Nah, that was last week. Thanks for asking though."

Iris decided to tell a half truth to Hazel knowing she'd get a proper telling off if she confessed even the smallest smidgeon of jealousy about Cam and Ryan.

"I guess it's just weird having Amanda here. Weirder than I thought it would be. Seeing her play, her being here in the pub, it kind of makes me think of the old days, and I've spent a lot of time trying not to remember the old days." Iris shrugged again.

"Oh, mate, you should have said. I'm sure she would have stayed away from the pub. The first thing she said when she told me she was coming back to play was that she didn't want it to be awkward for you." Hazel paused. "I honestly thought you guys were past it all."

"I am, I guess. I just hate everything about the person I was then, but since I haven't allowed myself to prove that I'm not that person any more, I can't even trust that I'm any better now." Iris took a gulp of the shandy, wondering where that tortuous clarity had come from.

It was true. Iris hadn't shown that she'd learned any lessons from it; she had just shut herself away. It sometimes felt as if she didn't trust herself to have changed. The realization landed heavily and deepened her dark mood. And now she was moping because Cam—the sweetest woman she'd met in a very long time, someone who'd been nothing but kind and supportive—had a fiancé she loved in a way she would never love Iris, and it made her jealous as hell.

Iris made herself think straight. So what if it had felt special when she and Cam had shared that cab home after the curry. So what if she had knelt in front of Cam in the changing room and dared to imagine that Cam's gaze contained something of what Iris was feeling. She had to get over it. She and Cam could be great friends whether or not she had a fiancé, a husband or even six kids.

Hazel touched Iris's arm. "I'd trust you with my life, Iris. Shit, maybe even with my wife. You're a good sort. Get back out there and prove to yourself that you're a catch and far too tame and sweet to be a danger to anyone. Please."

Iris nodded, unable to respond with words, wanting Hazel to be right. Hazel pushed one of the trays in her direction.

"Now, let's deliver our precious cargo before we get shouted at. A thirsty Vicki is not a pretty sight." Iris picked up one of the trays, now full of various shaped drinks, and carefully maneuvered her way back to the group.

She sat next to Cam, with only the window on her right hand side. It meant she was slightly on the edge of the group, but it suited her odd mood. She chatted happily with Cam for a while about the game and answered Ryan's questions about Cottoms, about her role, about whether she hated traveling for work. She didn't, but he clearly did. He made that crystal clear, and Iris couldn't help but feel a little sorry for him.

"And do you have a girlfriend?" Ryan's question came out of left field. "I'm amazed I don't know actually. I feel like Cam talks about you a lot, but she's never mentioned that." Cam looked at him with a warning in her eyes before switching her gaze to Iris.

"Not at the moment, no," Iris replied.

"I'm surprised, a good-looking woman like you." Ryan raised an eyebrow. "Cam tells me I'm not supposed to make comments like that, but I hope you'll take it as the compliment it's meant to be." Iris forced herself to play along for Cam's sake, but she resented him asking, and resented him passing comment, however complimentary he thought he was being.

"Well, you know what they say. Lucky at cards, unlucky in love." She paused for effect. "Just don't ever get into a poker game with me, I'll clean you out." She wanted Ryan to let her joke the subject away.

"Understood." He held a hand up as if in surrender.

Ryan was handsome. The kind of handsome you don't see straight away but that comes into view slowly. He had dark hair and pale blue eyes, perfect teeth and a nice smile. He was tall and obviously in good shape. Iris could see why Cam would like him.

"Is Graham really as bad as Cam makes out, or is she complaining for the sake of it?" Ryan asked Iris.

"I guarantee that he's at least twice as bad as anything she's told you." She didn't like Ryan dismissing Cam's feelings.

"Hmm. And how do you work that out?"

"In my limited experience of Cam, she always tends to see the best in people, to try to understand them, and she's probably found all sorts of empathetic excuses for why he's the complete arsehole that he is, when actually he's just a horrible person."

"You think she's tolerant of bad behavior? That's interesting." Ryan tilted his head, suggesting he didn't agree.

Cam put up a hand. "I'm sitting here you know, right here." Ryan looked like he hadn't heard her; he was focused on Iris.

"Like you say, Iris, your experience of Cam is pretty limited, despite you guys doing your best to play catch up. I'll just say that I could do with a bit of that empathy you think she's famous for every now and then." Ryan delivered the comment lightly, with an attempt at passing it off as a joke, but Iris saw Cam react, a hurt look in her eyes, and she withdrew the hand she had been resting on Ryan's leg.

"I just meant that Graham is genuinely horrible, and if I had to work for him, I'd either have quit by now or be in prison. Cam does well to put up with him." Iris looked at Cam, who was now gazing out across the pub, seeming like she was ignoring them both.

Ryan simply nodded, looked at Iris for a second, and then turned the other way in his seat, returning his attention to Megan, who sat on the other side of him.

Iris nudged Cam's leg under the table. "Are you okay?" She spoke quietly not wanting to make things worse. Cam nodded but didn't look convincing.

"I'm sorry if I said the wrong thing."

Cam looked at her. "You didn't, you were sweet. Ryan's just being a pain. He didn't really want to come, and he's paying me back for getting my own way by being an ass." She shrugged.

"And you think that's okay? 'Cos I don't."

Cam's body visibly tensed. "I think it's what people in long-term relationships sometimes do to each other, get annoyed, be annoying. You can't make every little thing a big deal or you'd be arguing constantly. Don't pass judgment on my relationship, Iris. Not when you can't even be bothered to try for one of your own." Cam ran a hand through her hair, then put it on Iris's knee. "I'm sorry—"

Iris held up a hand, cutting her off. "It's okay. I'm the one that should be sorry." She deserved the jab from Cam. It absolutely wasn't Iris's business how Cam and Ryan navigated their relationship. Cam was right. Iris was so bad at relationships, so unable to cope with the difficulties and the compromises that she had given up. She was in no position to judge Cam for not doing the same.

They sat there in silence for a minute. She tried to find a way back into conversation with Cam, but she was looking like she wanted to be anywhere but where she was.

"Hey, the pool table's free, fancy a game?" Iris looked up to see Priti in front of their table, pool cues in hand. She didn't really want to leave Cam's side, feeling like she owed Cam another apology and that they had more they needed to say, but she also felt that giving Cam some space might help rather than hinder. She nodded, took one of the cues from Priti with one hand, and fished in her pocket for a pound coin with the other.

They played two games and Iris was well on her way to losing them both. Truth be told, Iris was a terrible lesbian. She couldn't play pool, was unimpressed by cats, and couldn't stand Ellen. Priti wasn't a bad player, but Iris was definitely making her look good. Priti pocketed another ball, giving Iris a slightly sheepish look as if to say sorry. Iris just shrugged.

Priti was new to the team, and Iris hadn't made much effort to talk to her before tonight. She said she'd been working at Cottoms for a few months as a paralegal but didn't know about the team until Jess had invited her to come along a few weeks ago. Iris didn't feel too bad about not having noticed her. Cottoms had so many paralegals working in the offices on the floor above hers that she could never keep track of them all. Priti was petite, shapely, and had a sweet face framed by luscious dark brown hair. She was also really easy to talk to, surprising Iris more than once with her astute observations about the people they had in common.

And, unfortunately, Iris didn't feel attracted to her at all. Though she was probably not that much younger than Cam, there was something about Priti that seemed a little too young, a little too sweet. Iris made herself agree to the second game, telling herself that spending time with a single woman who was showing her some attention had to be better than being all angsty with Cam and her fiancé, but the attempt at positivity was punctured by annoyance when Hazel gave her a cheeky thumbs-up as if approving of Iris being with Priti.

Iris let out a breath. Hazel could be really annoying sometimes. Iris was being friendly to Priti but that was all. When Priti asked hesitantly whether Iris was single, she had said yes but quickly made it clear she liked it that way. After the end of the second game, Priti politely thanked Iris for playing, and they went to their seats at opposite ends of the table. No harm done and hopefully not too devastating an outcome for Hazel. And playing pool had at least gotten Iris away from Cam and Ryan for half an hour.

She crossed to the bar, intending to get a couple of packets of pork scratchings in the hope of making Cam smile, and found herself standing shoulder to shoulder with Amanda. Iris had expected Amanda to come for drinks—it was part of the ritual of playing, and she had no right to object—but knowing that Amanda was in the pub, knowing they would have to interact had definitely added to her strange mood. Iris nudged Amanda with her arm, knowing they had to do this at some point. Amanda turned toward Iris.

"Has the place changed?"

"Not really, I was just saying that to Jess actually. The decor's the same and Jackie's still as crazy as ever." Amanda spoke lightly.

"The pool table's new though." Iris nodded toward the corner. "Though the chance to practice hasn't improved my game any."

"Yeah, you always were pretty bad." Amanda paused. "That's where the stage used to be, no? I'd almost forgotten about that."

"You forgot Jackie's attempts to bring music to the masses? I fear my eardrums never will."

"Wasn't she also keen on putting on poetry evenings? Did that ever happen? Did you do any of your poems?"

"I think she did it once or twice, but I wasn't involved." Having to admit she still hadn't overcome her fear of performing made Iris feel silly, made her feel she hadn't made any forward progress in her life since their breakup, and of course Amanda was the last person she wanted to admit that to. Amanda had always had an easy confidence that made Iris feel inadequate by comparison. Even as they chatted briefly about how good it was for Amanda to be playing again, about her feeling in a rut and wanting to be a bit more sociable, Iris felt out of her depth, while Amanda seemed open and unafraid. They hadn't mentioned Gina, or Amanda's recent breakup, and Amanda hadn't asked Iris if she was seeing anyone. It was all very civilized, if a little tense, and Iris was sure that they both felt relief when the barmaid put Amanda's drinks in front of her and they murmured a polite good-bye.

Returning to the other end of table with the snacks and taking her seat next to Cam, Iris could hear Ryan telling Megan about his job—something about investing in start-ups and then selling them when they became more profitable. He said something Iris couldn't hear and Megan laughed. His mood seemed to have improved while she'd been away.

Iris slipped the pork scratchings into Cam's lap and was rewarded with a squeal of delight that caused the conversation to stop and everyone to turn and look at them.

"Sorry." Cam waved the packet in front of her goofily. "Just overreacting to pork scratchings."

Ryan looked at her. "So this is what you've been raving about. Let me try one." Cam opened the packet and offered it to him. He took one into his mouth and grimaced.

"They're a bit of an acquired taste maybe," Iris said.

"A heart attack in a packet maybe." He clutched his chest.

"Good, I'm glad you hate them. I don't want to share." Cam poked his arm playfully and he leaned over and kissed her on the head before turning back to Megan to carry on the conversation they'd been having.

Iris couldn't help but wonder about the two of them. Cam had not exactly been negative about Ryan, but Iris had filled in the gaps when Cam had said she wasn't entirely happy and assumed Ryan was a big part of the problem. Ryan reached down for Cam's hand as he talked and stroked it softly. Cam leaned into him slightly. Iris made herself face the fact that, while they sometimes bickered, Cam and Ryan actually seemed pretty solid. If the goal of the evening was to kill off her burgeoning Cam crush, reminding herself that Cam had a fiancé she seemed pretty fond of was helpful. Iris nodded to herself, knowing that having more going on in her life would help. And that maybe—just maybe—it was time to stop being so concertedly single. She felt a panic wash over her at the very thought of it, and then felt Cam nudge her leg. Iris brought her focus back to the table as Ryan spoke to her.

"Cam's got a lot of good things to say about you." Ryan's tone was neutral, and this time, Iris couldn't detect any edge to the statement. "She says that not only do you form a pretty unbeatable midfield partnership but that you guys are going to do poetry stuff together." He smiled at her.

"Yeah. We…it's been good." Iris felt inarticulate. She was half paying attention and half wondering what else Cam had said to him about her, not liking the idea of them talking about her at all.

"I promised her I'd buy you a beer for saving me having to go listen to poetry in the future. I'm sure she's moaned to you about how uncultured I am. I can't even pretend to like it. Nor those awful movies with subtitles that she used to try to make me watch when we first got together." He smiled at Cam as he spoke, and Cam tugged at his arm, seeming embarrassed. "Actually, you saving me from poetry is worth much more than a pint. Come to dinner. It'd be nice to get to know you better, and Cam's always telling me we should be more sociable and I should get to know her friends. I promise not to ask you to recite any poetry, and I'll even promise not to cook."

"That's a blessing. He's a terrible cook," Cam said. The invitation was unexpected. Cam had made Ryan sound so busy, so anti-social. Iris looked at Cam, trying to read if she wanted this, if she wanted an evening with Iris and Ryan. She couldn't think of anything worse, but she guessed that, for Cam, having her fiancé and her new friend get along would be something she'd want. For Cam's sake, she made herself accept.

"That's sweet of you, and of course I'd love to. Though maybe we could go out to avoid Cam having to cook. There's a new Italian place that opened up a few streets away from you guys if you'd rather do that."

"Nonsense. Cam will cook. She enjoys it. Don't you?" Ryan spoke for Cam, but she simply nodded, smiling at him. But it was a smile that didn't reach her eyes.

"I do like to cook. Though not as much as you like to eat." She patted his stomach teasingly.

"Nonsense, woman. I'm a fine figure of a man." He flexed his muscles playfully.

Iris didn't want to banter with Ryan and Cam tonight. Her mood was strange, had been strange since Ryan had arrived after the match. She had an impulse to get away. Her eyes darted toward the door and Ryan caught the movement.

"Don't tell me you're craving one too. I thought all you soccer players would be health fanatics. I gave up smoking years ago, but sometimes, when we're out drinking, I still get the craving and have to have one. I usually have to beg one from complete strangers. Cam hates it, says it's embarrassing." He shrugged.

"That's because it is embarrassing," Cam said.

Iris was resentful that Cam and Ryan had these anecdotes, that they had years of shared stories, shared experiences, and she had nothing. It wasn't just that she was single—she'd had relationships, she had stories she could tell—it was something about Cam and Ryan, something about never being able to compete with him where Cam was concerned. And she hated herself for even wanting to.

"No, not a smoker. Never have been. Actually, I was just worrying that I'd left my car lights on." Iris stood. "I think I'll check. Excuse me." She headed for the door. So much for not moping.

Outside, Iris looked up at the moon. It was full tonight. It made the car park at the front of the pub seem lighter than usual. She could make out the top of the hedges that surrounded it on two sides. It was cold but not unbearably so, and she leaned on her car trying to find the will to go back inside. This evening had been an eye-opener. She wasn't stupid, she knew she found Cam attractive, but she had honestly believed that her feelings were platonic and friendly and that any desire she felt to hang out with Cam related simply to how nice it was to spend time with her as a friend.

Despite being single for several months now, Iris didn't ever think of herself as lonely, but she wondered if Cam had ignited something inside her, some desire she had buried that wanted to be close to someone, to be special to someone.

Someone would come along when she was ready—the platitude was one she had told herself many times—she just wasn't sure she knew what ready would feel like.

As she pushed herself away from the car, ready to go back inside and leave her stupid jealousy in the car park, the side door to the pub opened and, in the light spilling out, she saw Amanda come outside and walk toward her.

"Oh, hey, I thought you'd left, but Cam said you'd come out to check on your car. Everything okay?"

"Yeah, just thought I'd left my lights on. Didn't. Old age beckons."

She wasn't a great liar, and Amanda considered Iris with a curious expression.

"I wanted to see if you were okay actually. You seem a bit quiet tonight. I wondered…" Amanda faltered slightly. "I wondered if it was because I'm here. I don't have to be. I mean, I wasn't going to come, but Hazel said you were completely cool with it, but maybe it's not a good idea."

"It's not you. Don't think that. I'm probably just a bit tired I think." She pushed her toe at a loose stone. "There's just a few too many people in there is all. Bit overwhelming having to do the talking thing with people I don't know very well. You know what I'm like with small talk." Iris was trying to be truthful, without being completely honest.

"Tell me about it. I apologized for you leaving social events early more times than I can remember. I think we used to pretend you had sudden migraines."

"Yeah, we did, sorry about that."

"Hey, it was a long time ago and, if I'm honest, I sometimes wished I'd had the nerve to join you. Too polite I think."

"You're calling me impolite?" Iris smiled.

"I guess I am." Amanda chuckled.

They stood silently for a while.

"I broke up with my girlfriend. I'm sure Hazel told you." Iris didn't respond, guessing that Amanda wasn't expecting her to.

"She…I mean, there was someone else…it's been awful and a bit…" Amanda searched for the word, "unpleasant. Makes me realize how badly I behaved myself. I'm not sure I ever said sorry to you properly at the time. I was so lucky with the way you handled our thing. You weren't ever nasty."

Iris didn't know what to say. She'd been so hurt by Amanda. Being cheated on had made her lose herself. She didn't want that for Amanda, despite everything.

"I'm sorry too. You don't deserve that." She paused. "And I wouldn't say I handled 'our thing' all that well, but I know what you mean. I did go quietly. I think I saved my unpleasantness for all the women I fucked over afterward." Iris let out a small bitter laugh.

"Don't." Amanda put her hand on Iris's arm. "We've all done things we regret, and treating you like I did is definitely one of mine. And after what happened between us…I mean, a lot of people would have reacted like you did. I just haven't got your energy obviously." The joke fell flat between them.

"Jess been keeping you in the picture has she?" Iris ran her hands through her hair. Amanda looked a little sheepish.

"Yeah, sorry, I wasn't asking, she just had plenty to say about you. Couldn't wait to tell me that the two of you, you know, after we broke up."

"Great."

"It's nothing to do with me obviously. She also told me you'd been single for months. But she basically warned me off trying anything now that 'I'm back.' Tried to make it sound like you two still had some kind of connection that I'd be foolish to get in the way of. She's a very strange girl."

"I know. Just try to ignore her, that's what I do. I didn't…I mean…I didn't tell them all what happened between us. I didn't want them feeling sorry for me."

Amanda nodded. They stood silently for a while.

"We played well today, eh? I've never seen Megan so happy." Iris changed the subject.

"I know. She's already focused on next week though. Says that we can go top if we win and the other results go our way. She's so focused. And we have a great chance. Cam's a very good player. You guys have a good understanding."

It was a casual comment, but Iris felt herself tense, even though she knew Amanda couldn't know Cam was anything but a teammate to her.

"She seems sweet as well. Though she seems a bit awkward around me for some reason."

Iris felt weird. She didn't want to talk to Amanda about Cam, and she felt guilty that if there was any awkwardness, it was because she had told Cam more than she should have about her breakup with Amanda.

"She's just a little shy, that's all." Iris changed the subject again, moving off toward the pub door. "Anyway, never mind all that, let's get to the important stuff. Are you still happy to be beaten by me at pool?"

"You know you never won a single game we played when we were together don't you?"

"I think I've blocked out those painful memories. But, for all you know, I might well have improved my game since we last played."

"Have you?"

"Not at all. I'm still awful." Iris opened the door for Amanda to enter ahead of her.

This felt okay. The idea of being this friendly with Amanda seemed a little less crazy than it had done twelve hours ago and maybe even something positive. They had been good friends before they got together and been good together for a long time before it went so wrong.

They crossed to the pool table. Iris was happy to try and get onto an even keel with Amanda and, if she was being honest with herself, just happy to have something to do that wasn't sitting with Cam and Ryan.

❖

As Iris took her seat next to Cam, having lost the pool game as expected, Cam put a hand on her leg and squeezed, asking a question with her eyes. She had obviously seen Amanda and Iris together. Ryan was mid-anecdote, and Iris knew Cam didn't want to talk across him so she just nodded, a gesture that said "everything's fine." Cam held her gaze for a beat and then lowered her eyes.

"I swear it was a complete accident." Ryan was telling Jess a story about the last time he'd been to see Cam play football and he scraped his car door against the car of the player who had feigned a dive in the penalty area to get Cam sent off. "I honestly didn't even know what car she was driving, but Cam was convinced it was vengeful." Everyone laughed.

Jess told Ryan about the tackle that had hurt Cam a few weeks before and how she had squared up to Mabel afterward and would definitely have scratched her car if she'd stayed around afterward. They were both being a little too macho for Iris's liking. She was pretty sure Cam could look after herself and didn't need either of them fighting her battles.

"Actually, it was Iris who was the real hero of that story." Cam interrupted them. "Checked out my ankle, got me safely off the pitch, and made sure I was warm enough. Even introduced me to the medicinal power of pork scratchings afterward. More useful than fighting anyway." She looked at Iris intently, offering her a fist to bump. Ryan looked at Cam with a questioning look on his face, while Jess scowled furiously, not even trying to hide how annoyed she was to hear Cam praising Iris. Jess was so transparent with her emotions and had so little impulse control. Not counting those few weeks after Amanda, Iris had spent a lifetime being the opposite, trusting no one but her father with her emotions. Sometimes it left her unable to understand what it was she wanted, what it was she was actually feeling. Of course, it also meant she felt safe, but maybe she'd started to want something more than safety.

A thought popped into Iris's head. Could it be that seeing Amanda again after so long had thrown her off balance and made her question whether she was happy being single, made her long for some form of meaningful connection with someone and that was why Cam had come to mean so much in such a short time? If it was that, then it would settle and she and Cam would be okay. She drained her glass and decided to go home, satisfied that she had come up with a reason that was as plausible as anything else she cared to contemplate for why seeing Cam and Ryan together was so difficult for her.

CHAPTER THIRTEEN

Iris was making tea for them both at the counter that ran along one side of the kitchen at Cottoms. Cam could hear Iris humming a song gently to herself as she stirred the drinks. It was cute. Iris was fairly dressed down by her normal standards—in a patterned purple shirt worn loosely over black chinos. Even dressed casually, she looked good. Cam wondered briefly when she'd started to pay such attention to what Iris was wearing. She dispelled the thought, not really wanting to examine what it meant.

Cam had a container full of food in her bag, and she'd already seen Iris put a huge baguette on the table next to her, but she still had the urge to go out somewhere for lunch. With Iris. Just the two of them. Graham had been a real grouch all morning and she wanted to treat herself. And if she was honest, she just wanted to spend some time with Iris.

Iris turned and set the drinks on the table. Before she could sit, Cam spoke in a rush.

"Let's go out somewhere for lunch, ditch this place for an hour, get some hot food."

Iris sat down with a sigh. "That sounds so tempting, but I can't, sorry. It's the last day of the month and that usually means a twelve-hour day for me making sure all the offices have filed what they need to with head office. I was just gonna speed eat that baguette and get back to my desk. I'll be here till late as it is." She ran her hand through her hair, a gesture Cam now recognized as a sign of tiredness. She started to unwrap her baguette. "You definitely should go out though if you feel like a break. It's healthy." She tapped the baguette in front of her with a finger. "Unlike this baguette."

"No, it's okay. I'll eat here with you. I kind of wanted the company more than the change of air."

Cam took her food out of her bag and busied herself with unwrapping it. Ryan had surpassed himself today with a giant chicken and avocado sandwich on ciabatta layered with crispy strips of bacon. Iris bit into her baguette. Cam could see thick slices of brie sticking out and red smears of what looked like cranberry sauce. Iris had a streak of it on the corner of her mouth. Without thinking, Cam reached across to wipe it away with her thumb. Iris's eyes darkened with surprise, and Cam was left feeling that the touch hadn't been appreciated. They were quiet together, their usual chatter missing. Iris seemed a little preoccupied and Cam wanted to ask her if she was okay.

And she really wanted to talk about the other night, about Amanda, and if she was really honest, about Priti. Cam had watched Iris with Priti, seen them laughing and talking, looking like they were getting on well. She had assumed that Iris wouldn't be interested, was just being friendly, but the thumbs-up she caught Hazel giving Iris across the pub had made her think again. Maybe Iris was getting back in the dating game. The thought of Iris and Priti getting together made Cam feel unsettled, anxious even. She started in on the sandwich in front of her as Iris scrolled through emails on her phone. Iris had put down her baguette and was concentrating on drinking the tea she had made.

The door banged open and a group of staff including Jess and Hazel came rushing in bringing noise and movement. A long meeting had just ended and the shouts of "Get me coffee" were interlaced with moans about needing the loo. Jess sat next to Iris, pulling a fifth chair over from the adjacent table.

"Don't bother with milk for my coffee," Jess shouted across to Oliver as she fished a sandwich out of her bag. Oliver was an intern but Jess seemed to think this meant he was her personal slave.

Hazel crossed to the fridge to retrieve a Tupperware container, grabbed a fork from the drawer, and plopped herself down next to Cam, forking pasta salad greedily into her mouth.

"I'm starving. That was two and a half hours of account reviews and not even a comfort break. I think Mr. Cottom has had his bladder surgically sealed. In the end I had to put my hand up and ask if I could go. Felt like a school kid. I swear he looked at me like he disapproved of the weakness of my bladder."

"He did," Jess said. "That's why I told Oliver to pee in his Coke bottle under the table if he wanted to make a good impression."

"He didn't?" Cam said.

"Of course not, it was obviously a joke." Jess glared at her like she was an idiot, her hostility was so open that Cam blanched.

Oliver came back to the table with the drinks. "You should have seen me sprint to the toilets as soon as the meeting was over though. Broke the one-hundred-meter record." They all laughed, except Cam who resented them interrupting her lunch with Iris. She picked up her sandwich. Next to her, Iris licked away a smear of cranberry sauce on her fingers. The sight caused an unexpected jolt deep down in Cam's insides.

"You're joking, right?" Hazel's raised voice brought Cam's attention back to the group. She'd missed something.

Hazel leaned toward Oliver. "Just to be clear, he's paying for your team to have a physio attend every single match and he's agreed to buy you a new kit?"

"I'm sorry, it's not…I mean, I'm not sure, just something Liam said at training, I don't know all the details."

Hazel leaned back in her chair. "Not your fault, mate, don't worry." She paused. "That sexist little prick. Wait till Megan finds out about this. She'll go ballistic."

"Graham will just deny it's outside of the budget that's already been agreed or he'll get Liam to lie about it. I don't see how we can get the fucker on it." Iris sounded as angry as Hazel.

Liam was the captain of the men's soccer team, and he and Graham were on very friendly terms. Cam had plenty of experience of what a dick Liam was, hanging around her desk, telling her how pretty she looked in whatever she was wearing like he was God's gift to women, like he had a right to comment on a coworker's appearance and, of course, Graham had not once stood up for her.

"Liam and Graham are thick as thieves," Cam said. "I could ask Liam, see if he admits to it without realizing. He kind of, well, he's always flirting with me. Obviously I hate it but, well, it might be useful for once." She looked across the table toward Hazel.

"That's a great idea." Hazel nodded.

"He's too smart for that," Iris said. "If he already knows that we're agitating Graham about the unequal funding given to the teams, he'll see you coming. And anyway I don't see why you should have to do that." Iris held her gaze for a beat.

"Couldn't you do some spying for us? You could find out from Liam just how much funding the men's team gets." Jess nudged Oliver.

Oliver looked terrified. "No way. It's bad enough that I blabbed about this to you. If Liam finds out he'll make my life a misery. Sorry."

"We'll think of something," Hazel said. "He's not going to get away with treating us like second class citizens."

Iris picked up the remains of her lunch and stuffed it into her bag. "Got to get on. End of the month today and I'm off tomorrow. Catch you guys soon."

"I'll come with you." Hazel picked up her tea and the remains of her lunch. "I'll find Megan and give her the latest on Graham. If you hear any breaking furniture, you'll know I've told her."

Cam stood awkwardly, not sure she would see Iris again today.

"Iris?"

Iris turned back to face her.

"Are we still doing that dinner thing tomorrow?"

"Yes, we are." Iris said the words quietly. "I mean, if it's still okay with you." She left the question in the air.

"Yeah, totally. Okay, so, see you then," Cam replied, her relief competing with a bit of anxiety. Iris left the room, and Cam sat back at the table, aware of Jess gazing at her with even more hostility than normal.

"Well, well, well, so you have a dinner date with Iris tomorrow? I guess you two have been getting a bit friendly. You're taking a chance with that though."

Cam said nothing, biting into her sandwich and hoping Jess would let it go.

"I mean, you know what she's like. It's not as if we haven't warned you, but seducing women is something she's very good at so don't let your guard down and," a malicious look passed across Jess's face, "don't feel at all special. She won't return any of your calls afterward." Jess leaned back looking pleased with herself.

Cam felt her face burn. In her reaction, she recognized the part that was anger, but there was something else too. She didn't think Iris was interested in her that way, but the idea of Iris hurting her just didn't compute. She was sweeter than Jess would ever know.

"I'm sure she'd love to hear you talking about her like this, Jess. Is that what friends do, do you think? You say you're her friend, but every chance you get you make all these nasty bitter comments about her, making her sound like a monster and trying to sabotage her friendships. I can't believe you haven't moved on after all this time."

Jess's eyes narrowed.

"She's a friend, Jess. We're having dinner because we like spending time together, because we have things in common. I know it's hard for you to believe, but it is possible for that to be the case with no one getting laid." Cam could have told Jess that it was Ryan who had made the invitation to Iris, and that he would be present throughout the evening, but she didn't want to explain herself to Jess.

"But I tell you what, the Iris I know, today's Iris—not the one you want to keep talking about from months ago—is sweet and kind and not the slightest bit interested in seducing me, so stop with the stupid comments please." Cam took in a breath. "We've all done things we regret, but usually our friends let us forget them and help us move on. Iris deserves your support for what she went through with Amanda, not your constant snide comments."

Cam wrapped the remains of her sandwich into the foil and shoved it back into the container.

Jess was silent and she looked at Cam coldly. She leaned forward. "So Iris told you a sob story did she? I bet she made you feel sorry for her, and I bet you feel all protective toward her now. Don't you know that means she's halfway there already? Trust me, I should know. It's a good job I let your fiancé know that you hanging out with Iris was something he needed to keep an eye on. Seems like you're not capable of protecting yourself."

Jess summoned Oliver to follow her and strolled nonchalantly out of the kitchen.

What the hell am I supposed to make of all that? Cam rubbed her forehead, a headache developing. She wasn't good with conflict but was happy to have at least tried to stand up to Jess...to stand up for Iris.

A niggling voice told her that maybe, just maybe, Jess knew Iris better than she did. Cam shook the thought away. She might not have known Iris for long, but she knew her well enough to know that Iris hadn't told her about Amanda to gain her sympathy. She had owned her part in what went wrong and been clear that she'd behaved badly afterward. If anything, the way she told the story would have made most people run in the opposite direction. Cam sighed and wondered what it said about her that it had pulled her closer.

But why the hell didn't Ryan tell me that Jess had warned him about Iris?

Cam thought about the evening they had spent in the pub and tried to remember a time when he and Jess had spoken privately. She wasn't sure they'd even had the chance and wondered if Jess was making it up, simply saying it to hurt her. Knowing Jess, the lie was perfectly possible.

Cam stood and pushed her chair under the table, ready to go back to work. On her way back into the annex, she stopped, remembering just how unlike Ryan it had been to invite Iris to dinner. It had surprised her at the time, and now she was convinced Jess had said something and that Ryan intended to use the dinner to scrutinize her relationship with Iris. Her annoyance with him grew. Not only had he not told her what Jess had said but he was clearly pretending to have a nicer motive in arranging the dinner.

CHAPTER FOURTEEN

Iris stopped for a minute to catch her breath, leaning on her shovel. This was bloody hard work. Her dad plowed on ahead of her, turning over the soil in his corner of the allotment, occasionally bending down to pick out a large stone and flinging it onto the pile they had accumulated between them close to the fence. It was cold and damp. Though it had stopped raining hours before, the soil was still wet, and Iris's boots were covered in mud and her jeans were streaked with it up to her knees.

God, she loved this. Being outside, being with her dad, getting ready to plant things. She even loved the effort of it, enjoying the feel of her muscles straining. Her own flat didn't even have a balcony, so the closest she came to growing things were the herbs she had in little pots set out across her kitchen window ledge. Nowhere near as satisfying as this. Being with her dad out on his allotment, getting the soil ready so he could grow real stuff like rhubarb and cabbage and squash.

"Hey, Dad," she called across to him. "When do we stop for that tea break you promised me an hour ago?"

"Struggling, sweet pea?" He swiped his gloved hand across his brow, leaving behind a smear of mud.

John Miller was nearly sixty, but he looked closer to fifty. He had aged well and kept himself in good shape. Despite the cold, he was stripped down to a T-shirt, now soaked in sweat, the hard work keeping him warmer than the jumper and rain jacket he had discarded. He put down his shovel and picked his way across the allotment toward the shed at the far end of the plot, its double doors wide open. He rummaged in a rucksack hanging on the back of one of two camping chairs, and fished out a flask and a large square Tupperware container.

"I might even have something for us to eat." He waved the container at Iris.

Iris dropped her own shovel and came quickly to his side. She dropped into one of the chairs, glad to give her aching back a rest and more than happy to help eat whatever was in the container.

"I reckon we're about halfway." He was an optimistic soul.

"If you mean halfway to death, then yeah. When you asked me to help with planting, I was imagining scattering a few seeds, maybe plugging in some plants. I didn't realize we'd have to dig the whole thing over first. And if I'd known your new allotment was this big, I'd have insisted we rent a couple of diggers." Iris pulled a face at him.

Her dad leaned over and ruffled Iris's hair in that way that only he was allowed to do. She pretended to object, knowing his hands were covered in mud, but not really minding at all. He poured tea into two tin cups he had fetched from inside the shed.

"It's good for you. Better than a gym trip. Fresh air, exercise, time spent with your old dad."

"Your energy levels make me feel old," Iris said.

"But you are old, sweet pea. The big 3-0 isn't too far away."

"Great, thanks for the reminder, Dad." She grinned.

He grinned back at her. The two of them were unmistakably related. Her dad had the same black hair, no sign of it thinning even at sixty, and the same brooding demeanor. But when he smiled, his open wide smile made him seem less surly, less intimidating.

He passed Iris a thick slice of banana loaf. Homemade, of course. Iris's dad was a carpenter by trade, but he was also a man who could cook, clean, and cry at soppy films.

"I'm just glad you came. I wasn't expecting the help on a weekday, and I knew turning it over the first time would be hard."

"Day off, I'm owed loads of flexitime, and I'm trying to take some of it back. I worked till eleven last night. I could probably take a month off and Cottoms would still owe me time."

He frowned. "Still working too hard?"

"Maybe. I don't know anymore. The long hours have just become so normal." Iris paused. "Though I have been doing a bit more social stuff lately. It feels good."

"Oh yeah, like what?" He said it through a mouthful of cake.

Iris put on the sweater she had tied around her waist; sitting down had let the cold back in.

"Oh, this and that. Remember I said someone new joined the team? Cam. I mentioned her I think?"

"The American?"

"Yeah, we've been getting on well, hanging out a bit, y'know?" He nodded.

"We have stuff in common. She likes poetry, she reads a lot, and she wants to find out stuff about London. She's invited me to dinner later actually. That's assuming my arms recover to the point that I can actually pick up a knife and fork. I'm looking forward to it." She picked a corner off the cake and popped it into her mouth.

"Though I'm also kind of worried about it." Iris looked at her dad. "She's so cool. I mean, she's funny, she's smart, she's curious. She's everything you'd want in a new friend." Iris stopped.

"Is there a 'but'?"

"Not a 'but,' no. Maybe an 'and' though."

"And?"

"And if I keep eating this I won't want the dinner she's cooking for us." Iris wasn't sure now that she wanted to talk about it.

"Nice try, sweet pea. What's making you anxious about making a friend who sounds as cool as you are?"

"She's also beautiful. Really beautiful. Like your heart kind of skips when you catch her in a certain light kind of beautiful. And…I'm attracted to her. I know I shouldn't be and I know it's not fair to her because she's engaged and been nothing but friendly, but I can't help it." Iris exhaled. "I hate that I'm attracted to her. It's so unexpected and I really wish I wasn't."

"You can't help who you find attractive, Iris. It's not something to be ashamed of. People always find people attractive, even people they shouldn't. I know I do. I always had the hots for your geography teacher. Remember her? Married, about ten years younger than me, but I couldn't help myself. Used to spend ages choosing a shirt whenever it was time to attend parents' evening." He leaned across to put a hand on Iris's shoulder.

"The important thing isn't what you feel when you catch sight of her looking beautiful, it's what you do, what kind of friend you are. Are you treating her well, with respect, and acting like a friend, or are you trying to act on your attraction?"

"God, no, Dad, I mean, of course I wouldn't try. She's got a fiancé. I've met him. He's the one that invited me to dinner. I just…well, it makes me anxious. I think that I'll give it away by saying or doing the wrong thing, and she'll be appalled and it'll stop us being friends. I really don't want that to happen. I don't wanna be that person, the one who can't control her feelings and I don't want to lose her friendship." She didn't want to be having this conversation but knew it was exactly what she needed, why she had come.

"Iris, love, cut yourself some slack. I know what this is about and I think you do too." He looked into her eyes and Iris looked down at her feet.

"Amanda."

"Exactly. This is about Amanda being back, reminding you about the breakup. I know you did things you weren't proud of, but that doesn't mean you should stop trusting yourself. Honestly, sweet pea, it was a long time ago and it's time to forgive yourself. I trust in who you are, and I bet Cam trusts you too." He squeezed her shoulder as he spoke.

Iris let his words sink in, willing herself to believe them. "I told Cam about Amanda cheating on me, how awful I'd been to live with, how I didn't even try and work things out, all the stuff I did afterward. Stuff I've never even told you. I think I told her because on some level I wanted to push her away, wanted her to reject me so I didn't have to face up to the fact that I'm attracted to her and it's likely to fuck up our friendship." Iris shook her head slightly. "But she didn't hate me for it. She was so supportive, so solid about it, and it just made me want her friendship even more than I did already." Iris bit her lip. "I think she's gotten under my defenses and I've freaked out a bit because I haven't let anyone get this close to me in so long."

He put his hand on Iris's arm. "There you go then. There's your answer. She sounds great. You showed her you at your worst and she still likes you enough to be cooking you dinner. Sounds to me like you don't have to worry too much about her."

Iris nodded, believing him, believing it could be okay. And then she leaned over and kissed her dad on the cheek. He was the best. The absolute best.

"How's it been seeing Amanda again after all this time?" He sipped his tea.

"Okay actually, better than I expected. Of course it reminded me that I wasn't good enough for her back then. It made me doubt myself—is making me doubt myself—but she was nice to me, and we both acted like it was all forgotten and over with. We were fine around each other. Cam helped I think. She's been completely on my side and made me hate myself less."

"I'm glad you have someone who you can talk to, who sounds like they understand you." He picked at his fingers, at the blisters that were developing.

"Yeah, maybe she does."

They sat in silence for a few minutes drinking their tea and watching the birds swooping down into the overturned mud hoping for worms.

"And she really likes poetry." Iris smiled at her dad. "She's been encouraging me to perform. I've been complaining about it to her, but actually it feels great. It feels like she sees that part of me and thinks I'm worth paying attention to."

"Even if you don't?" He said the words gently.

"Even if I don't."

He topped up both their teas, then put the empty flask back in his bag.

"Is Cam the one that's also joined the footie team?"

Iris nodded. "She's also brilliant at football. Actually, if I could find one damn thing about her that wasn't perfect, it'd be a bit helpful right now."

"Maybe she's a terrible cook. And keeps a slovenly house. And farts after dinner." He chuckled.

"Yeah, let's hope so."

Iris clinked her metal cup to her dad's. "To my wise old dad."

"To my worrisome sweet pea." He drained his tea. "Now, get yourself over there and start digging over the rhubarb patch before the rain comes back. You'll need to work up an appetite if she's as bad a cook as we're hoping."

CHAPTER FIFTEEN

Cam stopped chopping the vegetables on the wooden board in front of her, her mind drifting back to Iris, to what Jess had said in the lunchroom. Jess was jealous and clearly trying to sabotage things, but that didn't mean she hadn't thought a lot about what she had said. Cam didn't think Iris would make a move on her, not for a second. It wasn't just that Iris had been clear that she'd sworn off women, it was that she hadn't given any indication that she was attracted to Cam.

Cam's mind drifted back to the moment when Iris had knelt before her in the changing room, examining her sore leg. Was there something in her eyes then? Cam had felt something intimate between them, but had Iris? Cam had no idea. All she knew for sure was that Iris had been nothing but sweet, sincere, and completely appropriate, and that Jess was a troublemaker who still had designs on Iris.

Cam sighed and switched on the radio hoping for a distraction from her thoughts. Cam had bought juicy steaks for the three of them to eat but yet another last-minute work trip meant Ryan couldn't join them for dinner so she'd changed her mind and decided to cook swordfish with ratatouille. Ryan hated fish, and Cam was going to take advantage of his absence to eat what she wanted for a change. And happily, that was also what Iris wanted. Cam had given Iris the choice for dinner and she'd texted back. *Swordfish sounds great to me* adding a cute fish emoji.

Cam scraped the vegetables into the pan and added some stock. Her phone beeped and she reached into her pocket. *White wine or red?*

Cam typed a quick message back. *Red.* She was looking forward to seeing Iris and felt slightly disloyal that she was happy for once that Ryan had been called away.

Of course his absence meant she didn't have to worry about whether he and Iris would get on over the course of an evening—especially given the added tension of whatever baloney Jess had told Ryan about Iris in the pub—but her real happiness was about getting Iris all to herself for an evening. They had so much to catch up on, and the time they'd had together last week—in the bookshop, in the East End, even in the curry house, despite the way the evening ended—was some of the best she'd had since coming to London. Or for a long time before that if she was being really honest. Cam wanted more of that, perhaps wanted it a little more than she was prepared to admit. And her past experience meant she couldn't exactly deny what those wanting feelings really meant.

She looked at her watch. She was just about on schedule. She had twenty minutes for a quick shower and to change. She went up the stairs telling herself it was a blessing she'd have no time to obsess over what to wear.

Iris pushed the doorbell. She had a wine bottle under her arm and a gigantic bag of caramel popcorn in her hand. She'd managed to find a nice bottle of Côtes du Rhône in the supermarket after a stupid amount of time choosing. The nervousness she felt on the walk over evaporated when the door opened and a smiling Cam stood in front of her. It was replaced by a pang of attraction as she looked into Cam's eyes, but Iris had promised herself—and her dad—that she wasn't going to worry about it tonight. Yes, she found Cam extremely attractive, so what? It would eventually fade and maybe they'd even laugh about it one day.

Cam ushered Iris into a small hallway that faced onto a long, straight corridor.

"You can leave your coat under there." Cam nodded at a cupboard under the stairs, the door slightly ajar. "And follow me into the kitchen. I'm just about to burn the ratatouille."

Cam hurried along the corridor and disappeared into a door at the far end. Iris watched her go. She looked slightly flushed, no doubt from the cooking. She was also very casually dressed—barefoot, in worn jeans and a checked flannel shirt, worn loosely and rolled up at the sleeves. Iris looked down at her own outfit. She had spent ages deciding what to wear and then opted for something casual and comfy—dressing for a girls' night in rather than a dinner party—and she was glad she'd abandoned the smart clothes for her favorite hoodie and jeans.

At the door to the kitchen, Iris heard the faint sound of music. She pushed it open. Cam had her back to her, stirring a pan and moving in time to the song. It was nice to see her so relaxed.

She moved into the room determined to ignore the fluttering low down in her belly that she knew was caused by the sight of Cam's swaying figure. "Shall I open the wine?" Iris wanted something to do.

Cam nodded and leaned across to point at a drawer to her left. "In there." She was concentrating on seasoning their swordfish steaks.

Iris pulled out the corkscrew and set to work on the wine. The end of the room where Cam was attending to the fish was taken up with a modern, U-shaped kitchen. She let her gaze roam across the living area at the other end of the room. She couldn't see any photos or other knickknacks and the only books visible were a handful of paperbacks sitting on a small bookcase under the window. It had the feel of a rental property, a very temporary rental at that, and it reminded Iris that Cam might not be in London for too much longer. It was a horrible thought, and as Iris carried the open wine bottle to the dining table and placed it next to the salad, she felt a little less happy than when she'd arrived.

Iris moved to a stool next to the breakfast bar. On the bar was a small plate of bread rolls of various colors and shapes. Iris picked one up, tore off a piece, and popped it in her mouth. Cam turned at that moment, catching her with her mouth full. She gave Iris a look that told her she'd been caught.

"I'm starving, sorry. Spent most of the day working on the allotment with my dad. He worked me pretty hard. It's given me an appetite." She shrugged, hoping Cam would take pity.

"You always have an appetite. Don't try and blame the gardening." Cam studied her with a raised eyebrow, her eyes teasing.

"True. You got me there." Iris grinned.

"I've gotten a bit of a head start on you with the drinking though." Cam waved a tall glass in Iris's direction. "Gin and tonic. You've probably got time to catch up if you're quick. Want one?"

Iris nodded. "Please." She needed something to take the edge off her insane nervousness.

"Watch the fish." Cam handed her the spatula and Iris did as she was told, crossing to the cooker and half watching the pan and half watching Cam as she fixed the drink. She seemed at home here, capable and comfortable in her kitchen, and Iris remembered her saying how much she loved to cook. She took the glass Cam offered and sipped it, moving back from the cooker to her stool.

"Do you do this often? Have people over for dinner I mean. You look like you know what you're doing in that kitchen."

Cam turned and faced her, leaning against the sink and cradling her G&T. "Not so much, sadly. My sister came to stay in the summer. My mom came at Christmas, and Ryan made me host a dinner party for a few of his work buddies a while back. Mostly, I just cook for me and Ryan, when he's home on time." She paused. "If he's not, I rustle up some pasta or a salad and eat with a book in my lap. What about you?"

"Dinner parties are not really my thing. Not only am I a terrible cook but I'm a lousy conversationalist."

"You are not difficult to talk to."

"I'm fine one-on-one or even with a small group of people I know if it's casual, but dinner parties are different. They require you to have opinions on everything, and everyone gets all intense and competitive for attention. I'm wrong for that. Here with you I'm fine, but introduce people I don't know or, worse, people I don't like and it goes wrong for me. I either get too involved or go silent. I don't really have an in between." She was being honest. Honesty was something Cam brought out in her.

"And if Ryan had been here? Would we have gotten silent Iris or too involved Iris?"

"Well, I don't really know him so that is a little off-putting, but I think I'd have managed to be chatty and polite for your sake." She chewed her lip.

"For my sake?"

Iris felt like she'd said the wrong thing. She waited for Cam to pull her up on it. She didn't, seeming to let it go.

"Didn't you ever cook for Amanda?"

"Not really. She was the cook in our relationship. She'd have gotten tired of me a lot sooner if she'd had to eat my cooking. I do a really good fried breakfast though. Perfect hangover food. Next time you have a hangover, give me a call and I'll cure it with my special fry-up. It's almost worth getting drunk for."

"Now there's an offer that's hard to refuse."

Cam turned back to the fish and pronounced it ready. She turned the swordfish steaks onto large dinner plates, spooning a generous helping of baby potatoes and ratatouille alongside each before artfully arranging some fresh parsley on top. It looked and smelled heavenly.

Cam carried the plates to the table and placed them carefully down. Iris followed her and, without thinking, pulled out Cam's chair for her to sit down. She hadn't meant the gesture to be anything but polite, but Cam reacted, looking slightly flustered and gazing at Iris with an odd expression. Iris felt silly, wondering where the hell that gallantry had come from. She tried to remember the last time she had pulled out a chair for Hazel or Casey and, of course, the answer was never. The gesture was much more than polite. She knew that; she had to hope Cam didn't.

Iris sat in her own chair, self-conscious now, and poured them both some wine. Cam tasted it and darted her eyebrows upward. "Nice wine."

"That was lovely, Cam...cooked to perfection." Iris sat back in her chair.

Cam blushed at the compliment. "I love fish, but Ryan totally hates it, even the smell drives him crazy, so I don't really eat it much at home. It was a real treat for me too." She sipped her wine.

"I know what you mean. I had a girlfriend who hated eggs. I used to wait till she was out for the day and make myself egg on toast. It became this really guilty pleasure. I had to open the windows afterward and hope the smell didn't linger. It was like trying to hide the fact I smoked dope from my dad."

"And what happened with you and your egg-hater?"

"We wanted different things and not just menu-wise. It didn't last very long."

"Yet you lived together so it can't have been that casual."

"We did. Something you might not know about lesbians is that we tend to become very quickly committed in relationships. Take a removal van along on the second date is the standard joke, get a rescue cat on the third." Iris raised her eyebrows playfully.

"So does that mean that you and Priti are moving in together soon? Two games of pool and a ton of flirting has to count as a first date." Iris had expected all of Cam's questions about Amanda, about how they'd managed to get along on Sunday night, about how Iris had felt seeing her again, but she'd forgotten all about Priti, hadn't expected it to have registered with Cam.

"Priti is a very sweet girl, but I don't know what to say other than anytime anyone starts off by describing anyone as 'a very sweet girl,' it's not a good start. Plus, she beat me, twice. I swore that my next relationship would be with someone I could beat at pool. It's not good for my self-esteem otherwise." She held Cam's gaze, wondering why she looked so unsure of herself.

"You always do that."

"What?"

"Make jokes to avoid answering questions seriously."

"I do. I know. It must be frustrating." Iris held up her hands as if in apology.

"Not frustrating. It's more that I feel that it puts up a barrier between us." Cam hesitated. "A barrier I don't want, that I think we should be well past by now."

Iris felt the challenge was a fair one, but something about the way Cam said it, the way she was gazing at Iris, made her heart beat a little faster. She liked that Cam wanted them to be honest with each other. She had the same feeling.

Iris took a breath. "Okay, being serious, I'm not at all interested in Priti, and that's not just because she's a teammate and I don't want to cause any drama, it's because I'm not interested in Priti that way. I don't find her attractive."

Cam nodded and did the lip biting thing again. Iris had come to understand it meant she wanted to say something but felt she shouldn't.

"And what do you find attractive?"

Iris blinked. Cam's curiosity shouldn't surprise her anymore but somehow it did. "I don't know. I don't really have a type. It's a cliché, but it used to be the connection that I was looking for. Not so much the physical attributes, though I can obviously appreciate an attractive woman." She smiled but Cam did not. She was looking serious.

"And you've really not met anyone you felt that way about since you and Amanda split up?"

Iris badly wanted to make a joke, push Cam and her questions away, but Cam had a way of making her want to be known.

"I dunno. Maybe I got choosy along the way or maybe I'm still a little scared, but there's been no one. I want someone who challenges me, someone smart and interesting, and funny. Someone who gets me, even when I'm being weird and inconsistent and proud." *Someone like you*. She pushed the thought away. "But maybe that's too much to hope for and I should compromise somehow."

"Maybe. But maybe…well, maybe it's worth waiting for the right person rather than just settling because you feel you should." Cam hesitated before leaning forward and pouring them some more wine. Iris saw a shadow of what looked like sadness pass across Cam's face.

"Anyway, what about you?"

Cam looked surprised at her question and Iris cocked an eyebrow at her. "What? You think you're the only one who can ask questions? Just because you're soon to be an old married lady doesn't mean you don't get to fess up." She pointed her glass at Cam. "If you weren't with Ryan, what would your type be? And don't describe Ryan, that's too obvious."

"Do you want the glib answer or the honest one?"

"Either…both. I don't mind."

"Okay, the honest answer is that I'd want someone who would really see me, support me in my choices, and make me alternate between shivering with lust and sighing with happiness when I catch sight of them across a room."

Iris felt the impact of Cam's words in the tightness of her chest and the slight pulse between her legs.

"And the glib answer?"

"They'd have to be tall, dark, and impossibly handsome." Cam's expression was hard to read. It was wistful but also maybe a little angry. "Though I guess in reality I'd settle for half of that."

"Didn't you just tell me that settling was a bad idea, and that it was worth waiting for something better? You can't give me advice and not follow it yourself."

"That's exactly what I do, haven't you realized that yet?" Cam put down her glass, picking at the edge of the tablecloth. "I'm all about talking the talk, rather than walking the walk." She seemed lost in thought for a moment, before lifting her head.

"Anyway, changing the subject for my own sake, I might have created a bit of drama at work with Jess yesterday without meaning to."

Iris sat up straighter. "What happened?"

"Well, you know how she's still so in love with you?"

"I am irresistible." Iris waggled her eyebrows.

"I'm serious, Iris. Sometimes the way she looks at you, the way she talks about you…it's not right. At lunch, when she heard we were having dinner, she said all this stuff about you, about me, about us hanging out all the time. She said I should 'watch myself' around you and you'd probably make a move on me tonight." Iris felt herself grow warm with embarrassment. She had done nothing to feel bad about, yet Cam's words made her feel ashamed.

"I didn't stand for it of course. I told her not to be so nasty and not to make assumptions about people who just want to be friends. But you could tell she was so jealous. She looked at me like she really hated me."

"What? No way. I'm sorry you had to be on the receiving end of that. But she's just being Jess. She loves to create a bit of drama."

"Tell me about it. She also said she took Ryan to one side in the pub and told him he should watch me around you, or you around me, or some such BS, basically that you shouldn't be trusted."

"What the hell." Iris felt shame and rage mingling in her veins.

"I don't know exactly what she said. I asked him about it last night, but he brushed it off though I could tell he was annoyed."

"Oh, Cam, I'm sorry. I'm sure Ryan will know it's rubbish. I mean, he knows we…that you're not…like that. First chance I get I'll speak to Jess, tell her to lay off." Iris wanted to strangle her.

"I don't need you to speak to Jess on my behalf. I can handle her. But you should talk to her for your own sake. She trashes your reputation constantly because you won't give her what she wants. You shouldn't put up with her. You deserve better than that."

Iris couldn't argue. Cam was right. More than right, she was inspiring. She inspired Iris to believe that maybe she did deserve better.

"It's just that she's between girlfriends right now. Normally, when she's in love, I don't get a look in."

"I don't think it's that, Iris. It's me, it's us. She hates that we've gotten so close. She's trying to sabotage it."

Iris liked hearing Cam say that they'd gotten close. Iris had felt it, but she hadn't assumed Cam felt the same way. "You might be right. She's a pain in the arse and I let her get away with far too much because I feel bad about how I treated her."

"That was so long ago, Iris. You need to start living in the present." Cam sounded so serious, looked so beautiful, that Iris felt things tilt a little.

"I know, I know. As long as living in the present doesn't mean moving in with Priti and getting a cat." She fell back on humor to move them onto safer ground, happy to be there with Cam and not wanting to sour what had started off as a lovely evening together.

❖

Iris watched from the couch as Cam made them coffee. She was moving slowly, as if a little distracted, leaving pauses between the various stages in the process. Her mind not seeming to be completely on the job.

For a moment, a long, pleasant moment, Iris felt at home. Here, in this place that wasn't her home, she felt the pull, the desire, to sit across from Cam every night and watch her make coffee. So mundane a wish but so appealing. A voice inside Iris's head reminded her that she didn't belong here with Cam, Ryan did. She was just visiting the possibility of this life and the visit would end soon. Iris welcomed the cruel reminder, knowing she needed to stop herself from feeling this way.

Cam turned back to her, coffee cups in hand, moving across the room. Iris had the remote control and was cueing the DVD.

"This movie had better not be too scary." Cam's eyes widened.

"It's supposed to be creepy rather than scary. I read all the reviews, tried to make sure there was no slashing. And it's Spanish so if we close our eyes when it gets scary, we won't even be able to understand them screaming."

"Very funny. If I can't sleep after this and my game is off on Sunday, I'm going to tell Megan it's your fault."

Cam went back to the kitchen to get a large bowl down from a shelf. Iris took the bowl as Cam grabbed a large purple blanket from the back of the adjacent armchair. Iris poured the popcorn into the bowl while Cam draped the blanket over their laps.

Iris felt the room warm up several degrees, and she knew it wasn't just the blanket. *How was sitting this close to Cam for two hours going to help her manage her attraction?* Cam leaned across and tucked the blanket in on Iris's side and she felt an involuntary flutter in her stomach.

Iris tried to talk, to take her mind off the physical effects caused by being this close to Cam. "How come you're scared of scary films when you're so gutsy otherwise?" Iris had been thinking about it, about how Cam was often right, handled difficult things well, how she encouraged Iris to be better. "Sorry, I don't mean that in a challenging way. I mean…I was just wondering. You give good advice, you challenge me. It seems kind of brave, at least compared to me anyway." Iris willed herself to stop talking.

"You think that's what I'm like, but maybe that's because you don't know me very well."

Iris hated hearing Cam say that. She wanted to know Cam well, was trying to know Cam. "What don't I know about you?"

Cam seemed surprised by the question but she held Iris's gaze, her eyes seemed sad, her expression cautious. She sighed and sipped her coffee.

"I don't know. I sometimes think I'm an observer, a drifter poking about in other people's lives rather than living the life I might want to. I tried to live that life once. It didn't go well." Cam swallowed. "You said you felt like a passenger when it was all going wrong with Amanda. I feel like a passenger as well. Watching life go by, the people, the places, the years—not feeling that any of it is something I really chose."

Iris didn't know what to say. She wanted to offer comfort, show Cam she cared, but she doubted herself, doubted that getting physically closer to Cam was a good idea.

She reached across and took Cam's hand anyway. "Want to tell me about it?"

"I don't know how it would help to tell you about it. It's done. It's the here and now I need to be thinking about. Making sure I have things for me, that I stop living some life Ryan wants for us, a life my mom wants for me."

Iris felt Cam entwine their fingers. "But thanks for asking." Iris knew she should move but she couldn't, she didn't want to. She wondered if the life Cam wanted for herself would include more nights like this, whether it would have room for her.

"Oh shit, I forgot." Iris jumped up, breaking the contact, breaking the spell. "I got something for you."

Iris got her bag and fished out a folded magazine. She opened it out and held it up for Cam to see. "I remembered it finally."

"What the hell is it?"

Iris sat and pulled the blanket back over their legs, her hand grazing Cam's thigh as she did so. Cam couldn't tell if it was an innocent gesture or if this was Iris making a move. They were alone, under a blanket, they'd had wine, and Iris had taken hold of her hand just moments ago. The thought made her scared, but also, she couldn't deny, impossibly aroused. Iris spread out the magazine on their laps. Her face was open and excited, not showing an ounce of desire.

"Cottoms has an in-house magazine. They produce a thousand copies a month, send it out to clients, and it goes out to the various offices to sit in reception, that sort of thing. Like an airline magazine." She sounded animated, and Cam couldn't help but smile.

"I was chatting to Janie—she's the head of Comms, works in the Bloomsbury office. She's in charge of it." She looked Cam in the eye. "They want contributors. She said they're always struggling for good content."

Cam finally understood.

"You could…I mean, it might be a good way to get started again. I know it's not very glamorous, but it might get you back in the groove and it's…" Iris hesitated. "Well, it's words, not numbers." Her eyes were shining. "Go on, Cam, you'd be great. I'd love to read something in there that you'd written."

"I don't know. Maybe. What the hell would I write about?"

"Write about what you know, do book reviews, an advice column, an interview with Sylvia. I don't know, Cam, but I believe in you. Do words. Make that curiosity of yours count for something."

"Is that your way of calling me nosy?"

"This could be something you do for you, only for you, not your mom, not Ryan, not even me really."

"This is the sweetest thing, the nicest thing." Cam could feel tears welling.

"Hey, I'm sorry. I didn't mean to…"

"No, it's okay, I'm okay. It's just so nice of you. And you know what, it's an awesome idea. I don't know where to start, but I'll try." Cam felt a light bulb switch on. "Maybe I'll write about the football teams. We're so close to winning the league, and I heard Liam complaining to Graham about the men's team being close to relegation. It'll make quite a story. Women's team succeeds against the odds sort of thing. One condition though." Cam looked at Iris.

"Anything."

"Anything? Are you sure about that?"

"Er, maybe?" Iris sounded nervous and Cam laughed.

"The poetry event at the end of the month. You have to perform. If I'm gonna do this," she pointed at the magazine, "then you have to do that. You'll be wonderful. I know you will. And deep down I think you know it's time."

"I think I've just been played." Iris said.

Cam waited.

"You'll come with me?" Iris sounded adorably shy.

"Of course I will. I'll even help you choose something, if you like." Cam smiled as she said it, knowing Iris usually pushed her away whenever she took too much of an interest in her poetry.

"I kind of have something actually. It's about my mom and dad. About growing up with him, without her. I...I mean I've been working on it for months, and I've lost sight of whether it's any good, but it's finally finished—I think. If I send it to you, will you tell me if it's good enough?" Iris spoke uncertainly.

"It'd be a privilege." Cam paused, not wanting to push but knowing Iris needed it. "And you'll perform it?" She looked at Iris expectantly.

Iris blew out a breath. "Okay, I'll do it, but only if you absolutely, definitely promise to come."

Cam squealed and hugged Iris before pulling away self-consciously. "I will, I absolutely will, I promise." She offered Iris her pinkie finger and they shook on it.

"Shall I start the movie?" Cam had her hand on the remote control. Iris reached across to the coffee table where Cam had left the big bowl of popcorn and placed it on the blanket in between their knees.

"Yep, let's do this. And no digging your nails into my arms during the scary bits."

"You said there weren't any scary bits."

"Oh yeah, so I did." She winked at Cam.

Cam reached down for a handful of popcorn, feeling like this night had turned out even better than she had hoped.

Cam opened her eyes, expecting the movie to still be playing but found that the TV screen was dark. Next to her, she could hear Iris breathing, the breaths deep and even. And then she felt the weight of Iris's head against her shoulder. She was fast asleep. Cam looked down at her, trying not to move, not wanting to wake her. She looked so peaceful, her eyelashes long and dark against her pink cheeks. She was so damn stunning. Cam's heart skipped and she wasn't sure if it was desire or panic. Iris's hand was resting on her arm, the long fingers curled around Cam's wrist possessively. Cam enjoyed the feel of it more than she had any right to.

The room was warm and the blanket covering them made it even more so, but some of the heat was coming from inside Cam. She allowed herself to sweep a few strands of dark hair from Iris's forehead with her fingers. Her touch was light and Iris didn't move. Iris at least had the excuse of hours of heavy gardening whereas Cam had spent the day at her desk. She wondered if her excuse for falling asleep was simply feeling so at home with Iris on the couch.

Cam moved slightly, the arm that Iris was leaning against was tingling with pins and needles. The movement caused Iris to stir. Her eyelids fluttered and then her eyes opened.

"Hey, sleepyhead." Cam smiled at her and watched as a look of confusion was followed by a jolt of comprehension as Iris moved quickly into a more upright position, breaking the contact between them.

"God, sorry, Cam, I didn't mean..." Iris's words were swallowed in a yawn. She stood, and the tangled blanket fell to the floor.

"Sorry, I didn't mean to fall asleep on you." Iris had a worried frown on her face that Cam couldn't understand.

"You mean literally or figuratively?" She aimed for a light tone, wanting to reassure Iris that it was okay.

"Both I guess. I think maybe the gardening took more of a toll than I expected. Sorry."

"Don't worry, I was asleep too. I woke up barely a minute before you. Guess the movie wasn't scary enough to keep either of us awake."

Iris shuffled from one foot to the other. "I should probably go. It must be late." They both checked their watches. It was well past midnight.

Iris fished under the couch for her shoes, and tied them hurriedly. She picked up her bag, and headed for the door to the hallway. "I'll pick you up Sunday for the match, normal time."

Cam had never seen Iris move so fast. She had no idea what had just happened, but Iris was acting like there was something she was running away from. "Erm, sure, yeah. Big game for us." She followed Iris into the hallway.

"Hey, Iris." Iris turned to her, her eyes wide-awake now, but cautious and guarded for the first time all evening. "Don't worry about falling asleep, please. I really didn't mind. And I had the best time tonight." She didn't know what else to say.

Iris waited a beat before moving along the hallway toward the front door. Cam wasn't sure she'd heard her, wasn't sure she'd respond, until she turned to her.

"Me too." Iris's eyes held Cam's for an instant and then she opened the door and left.

Confused about what had happened to cause Iris's sudden departure, Cam moved back into the living room and picked up her phone. She yawned and stretched. The memory of her fingers brushing Iris's hair from her forehead causing her to flush slightly. Iris's skin had felt so soft, her face in sleep so peaceful. When Iris stood up and broke the contact, Cam felt the loss of it too much.

She really needed to face up to the fact that her feelings for Iris had crept well past platonic. She'd never really thought of herself as bisexual and she rarely found women attractive but she'd been with a woman before and she understood what feeling like this about Iris meant. She shook her head at her own stupidity in thinking she could sit under a blanket with Iris and watch a DVD like friends do without it meaning more than that to her.

Knowing what was happening didn't help her figure out what to do about it. Having the feelings wasn't fair to Ryan or Iris and, if she wasn't careful, they would ruin everything. Ryan was her fiancé but she just couldn't imagine making herself see less of Iris. The idea of that seemed unbearable.

Cam looked at her phone screen. It showed several text messages from Ryan. The person she was supposed to have these kinds of feelings for. She sighed. She'd slept through the beeps. She scrolled through them. The last one simply said, *Okay I'm going to bed now.* She knew Ryan would be pissed at her for not responding, but it was much too late to call him now.

On her way up the stairs to bed, Cam typed out a quick reply. *Sorry. We fell asleep watching the DVD and I didn't hear you text. Speak tomorrow xx.*

Almost immediately, she received a text back. It was a shrugging emoji. No other comment and definitely no kisses. *Yep, he's definitely pissed at me.* She frowned, pushing open the bedroom door and throwing the phone onto the bed as she headed into the en suite. Her mind was racing and her body was tense. She wasn't a fool. It was the kind of tension she hadn't felt in a really long time and she decided on a shower to wash it away before trying to sleep.

CHAPTER SIXTEEN

Cam poured herself a glass of prosecco. The team was sitting together in the pub, and everyone was in a buoyant mood. Cottoms had enjoyed an easy 3-0 victory, and their main rivals had only drawn their match today, meaning that Cottoms was now top of the league on goal difference. Two games left in the season and a real chance of winning the title.

Iris knew her mood was off. She had felt agitated all weekend, and while the exertions of the match had taken the edge off, she still felt weird. She'd gone home on Friday feeling embarrassed and couldn't quite shake the feeling that she shouldn't have allowed things to go so far. It was one thing to have a crush on a friend and quite another to allow yourself to sit next to them under a blanket in the dark and fall asleep in their arms with them having no idea just how good it felt.

She wasn't being fair to Cam by having the feelings and not keeping more of a distance until they dissipated, and hell, she wasn't even being fair to herself. It didn't matter how many times she told herself that she hadn't been the one to suggest sitting under the blanket, she still felt like a creep. Dreaming of Cam kissing her and then waking up to see Cam's face leaning toward her was confusing and affecting in equal measure. The fact that Cam had seemed oblivious to it all was the only silver lining to the cloud.

By Sunday morning, Iris had narrowed her options down to two— say nothing and hope the crush burned itself out before Cam noticed, or say something and hope for Cam's understanding while waiting for it to wear off. Neither option seemed great. She knew there was a third option that she was refusing to consider. It involved putting some real distance between her and Cam so that she could be sure to completely get the feelings out of her system, but to Iris, that felt like a doomsday option and she didn't want to push that button. She just didn't want to lose her connection with Cam, to sacrifice the friendship because of her stupid feelings. Not yet anyway. Probably not ever.

Cam leaned across to Iris. "It's not fair that you can't have a proper drink because you're driving. Let's leave the car here and get a cab home. I want you to be able to celebrate as well." Cam's face was a little flushed, her eyes were sparkling.

"I dunno. I'm not even sure we should be celebrating so soon. We're not champions yet."

"Are you trying to poop our party, party pooper?" She poked Iris as she said it, and pouted, and despite herself, Iris laughed. "Seriously, Iris, cut loose a little. C'mon, please."

Cam poured some of the prosecco into a glass and pushed it across the table toward Iris. Her eyes contained what looked like a challenge, and Iris already knew that she would give in. Maybe a little alcohol would make her feel more relaxed.

She picked up the glass, raised it in Cam's direction, and took a sip. "To premature celebrations."

Cam raised her glass in return, seeming satisfied, before excusing herself to go to the bathroom. As soon as she departed, Hazel slid into Cam's seat. "How goes it, bud? Not drinking and driving I hope."

Iris looked at the glass. "Drinking but not driving. Cam persuaded me to go home by cab so I can join in the fun, though I think we might jinx things celebrating this early."

"That's just what Megan was saying. She'd have refused to accept Jackie's free prosecco if she didn't think it would have caused a riot."

"She knows Vicki well," Iris said.

Hazel looked at her with a hesitant expression. She obviously had something on her mind.

"Mate, don't take this the wrong way, but is everything okay with you? Even Megan noticed your mood was off today. Jess was saying—"

"I'm really not interested in anything Jess has to say."

Hazel held up her hands. "This is me, Iris, your best mate. I'm not Jess. I'm not here to gossip, I'm here to ask if everything's okay. You know I love you, right?"

"Yes, I know you love me." Iris sighed.

"Good. Then just know that you can talk to me, about anything. About anyone, y'know." She nodded in the direction of the bathroom.

"Jeez, Hazel, were you at the back of the queue when they handed out subtlety?"

"What?" Hazel feigned ignorance but had the good grace to look a little guilty.

"If you're talking about me and Cam, and I guess you are, because I know Jess is and probably everyone else for that matter, then don't worry. She's straight, she has a fiancé, and she's perfectly safe around me. And it feels kind of shitty that everyone thinks she's not." Iris was trying not to lose her temper with Hazel, but she did want to make a few things clear to her.

"Even if I did have feelings for her—" Hazel started to speak, but Iris didn't let her. "Even if I did have feelings for her, I can control myself. I'm not gonna jump on her you know. You can all chill the fuck out."

"I know you, Iris. I know you won't do anything. Trouble is, I don't know Cam, and I can't say the same for her. How's that self-control of yours going to hold up when she comes to you one day, tells you she's unhappy and bored, tells you she has feelings for you?"

"That's ridiculous. I'm not gonna get involved with someone who's in a relationship. You should know me better than that, Haze. I've been cheated on, remember. I know how shitty that is. And, anyway, she's not interested in me that way."

"You don't know that. You guys have got really close really quick, and I've heard the way she talks about you. She's like a one-woman fan club. Maybe it's not all that ridiculous. Don't tell me you haven't noticed."

"Are you talking about earlier?"

Iris was being teased by Vicki and Hazel for missing an open goal, and Cam had jumped to Iris's defense, sweetly pointing out that Iris had created all three of the goals they had scored and the team would be lost without her.

Hazel nodded but shook her head. "Yeah, but not just that, other stuff. She was telling Jess earlier what a capital G great time you guys had the other night at dinner. Made it really clear that Ryan had gone away for the night."

Iris let out a laugh, feeling relieved but also, crazily, a little disappointed. "She's joking, Haze. She's just messing with Jess. Jess said all this crap to her about being careful around me, and I wasn't to be trusted to have over for dinner because I'm so dangerous. Cam's just paying her back, knowing how jealous Jess gets." Iris approved of Cam tormenting Jess like that.

Cam was walking toward the table carrying two pool cues.

"And did you?" Hazel asked.

"Did I what?"

"Have a great time at dinner without Ryan?"

"We did. We get on well. I don't think I should have to apologize for that."

Iris waved at Cam over Hazel's shoulder, using the gesture to let Hazel know that Cam was heading back.

"Just be careful, Iris. I don't want you to get hurt." Hazel stood and nodded at Cam before heading back to her seat at the other table, leaving Iris in a state of confusion.

"Look what I've got." Cam waved the cues. She seemed so happy, so relaxed. "You said you wanted a woman you could beat at pool. I am that woman." She bowed with a flourish.

Was she flirting? Was Cam looking at her right now in a way that would make Hazel worry? In a way that should make her worry? Iris honestly couldn't tell. She thought she was just being Cam. Sweet, open, friendly.

"Believe it or not, I've never actually played before so if you can't beat me there really is no hope for you." Cam chuckled as she handed a cue to Iris.

"You're on. But be prepared for this to be a very long game." Iris followed Cam to the pool table. Hazel was watching them. Iris waved in her direction a little pointedly. She decided she would play pool with Cam, would enjoy Cam's good mood tonight, and tomorrow she would worry about things. It didn't matter whether Hazel was right or wrong about the way Cam might be feeling, Iris knew her own feelings and she wasn't always on an even keel around Cam. It wouldn't hurt either of them if she slowed things down a little.

❖

Cam stood next to Iris, leaning against the table, watching Iris rack up the balls for another game. She was standing quite close, but when Cam spoke, she spoke so softly that Iris still couldn't hear her above the noise of the pub. Iris leaned in and asked Cam to repeat it.

"I said, I'm very disappointed in you. I thought you were someone I could rely on." Cam spoke more loudly.

Iris heard the words but didn't understand the meaning. She gave Cam a puzzled look.

"I mean that I've already started sketching out the magazine article, but you haven't sent me the poem and you said you would. You even pinkie swore." Cam's tone said she was teasing, but her eyes took Iris's breath away. They were darker than usual in the low light of the pub, the gaze so open, so intense, that it reached right to Iris's center, pulling her muscles tight.

Iris had never been more relieved to talk about a poem. "Oh right, sorry, yeah. I hadn't forgotten. I've been tweaking it again, trying to perfect it. It's an endless task." She put her hands on the cue and leaned her head down, willing her lustful thoughts about Cam to clear.

"Are you okay?"

Iris willed herself to say something that wasn't, *I'm falling for you and I hate myself for it and I fear you'll hate me for it too.* She blinked herself back into the moment. "Sorry. Yes, I am. Just a bit tired. I'll send it soon I promise."

Cam put a finger under Iris's chin, using it to lift Iris's head and turn it slightly so that they were face to face. "I promise to be careful with it." Cam's eyes showed such kindness that Iris wanted to run away. She just couldn't wreck this friendship with her stupid feelings. She needed to be careful too.

"Okay." She swallowed the feelings. "Okay. I trust you."

The fact was that she did. She just needed to believe that she could trust herself with Cam.

Cam picked up her phone from the bedside table and groaned. It was nearly two a.m. *This is ridiculous.* She was tired enough to sleep, but the wine, the headache, and her whirling thoughts were conspiring to keep her awake. She eased herself out of bed, being careful not to wake Ryan slumbering soundly beside her, and crept downstairs, her phone still in hand. The house was cool, and she picked up a jersey of Ryan's from the back of the couch and slipped it on over her nightshirt. She had a lot on her mind. She'd argued with Ryan again tonight. He still refused to tell her exactly what Jess had said about Iris, and when she didn't let it go, he accused her of being a "bit too bothered" about it all with a slight sneer.

He'd been in a spiteful mood since coming back from Frankfurt and seemed determined to keep punishing her for neglecting his texts and calls on Friday night. The trigger for tonight's argument had been his matter-of-fact admission that he had met up with his old boss from Seattle in Frankfurt and that he'd practically begged Ryan to go back, promising a pay rise and a promotion.

"I'm seriously considering it," was Ryan's final comment, paying Cam back for her indifference with indifference of his own. She felt a surge of panic at the idea of them leaving London, but she hadn't been able to articulate it in the moment, worried that her reasons wouldn't stand up to his scrutiny. On top of all that, she was finding it hard to be around Iris and harder still not to be around Iris. Right now, she felt like the world's worst friend and the world's worst fiancé at the same time.

Cam picked up the kettle she had set to boil and poured hot water over the chamomile tea bag she had placed in her mug. On impulse, Cam unlocked her phone and called her sister. Her brain did a quick calculation—two a.m. in London meant six p.m. in Seattle—a good time to call. She waited, hoping she'd get Alison and not her voice mail.

"Hey, big sis. How you doing?" Alison's voice rang out clearly.

"Are you on your way out or do you have time for a chat?" Cam sat on the couch with her tea, pulling her feet up under her legs to keep them warm.

"I do. I'm going out later, but I've come home to eat first. Greg and I are going to some experimental theater thing that his friends are involved in. He said it's going to be a bit weird. I figure I'll need a full stomach."

The phone went quiet. Cam could almost hear her sister doing the math.

"Hey, isn't it the middle of the night there?"

"It is. I can't sleep though. Thought I'd take advantage to make the time difference work for us for once."

"Well, amen to that, I've missed you calling. How's things in dear old London town?"

Cam told Alison about the team, about their chance of winning the league. She talked about Graham, and Vicki and Harry, about the book club and the poetry readings, about Jack the Ripper and East End curries, and it sounded even to her own ears as if she was having a great time, but there was a reason she was awake at two a.m., and she needed to talk to her sister about it.

"Wow, seems like you've been plenty busy. Last time you were moaning about not having enough going on, now you're the opposite. It's good, yes?"

"Uh-huh." Cam was unsure of what to say. It was good but it was also bad.

"Uh-huh, yes or uh-huh, no?"

Her sister was a wise ass sometimes.

"Both I guess. I'm doing okay. I'm probably just a little frustrated with Ryan. He's working constantly and away a lot. He's—" Cam was going to say, "he's away more than I'd like," but then realized with a wave of sadness that that wasn't even true anymore.

"I feel like he's away—mentally I mean. We're just not very connected. I do my stuff and he does his. We can't seem to get into any sort of groove."

"Hey, sis, you've been saying this for a while now—"

"Don't tell me it's normal and just a symptom of being in a long-term relationship. I don't need to hear that tonight."

"I wasn't going to. Actually, I was gonna say that maybe you should be worried that you've been feeling like this for so long. Have you guys tried talking about it?"

"We've talked around it. He says it's just his work being busy and he hates London and we'd be okay otherwise." Cam sighed.

"You don't agree?"

"I don't know. Alongside everything else, we've stopped having sex." She made herself say it. "And I don't even know if I care, not really. I feel like I've wasted so much energy trying to fix things, find things for us to do together, to try to get us back to a good place, and now I've stopped trying." Cam took in a breath. "And I've met someone who makes me feel really good so I'm prioritizing that. It doesn't really help and yet it does, y'know."

"You've met someone? Hot damn. I never thought you had that in you sis. You're the monogamous, marrying her first serious boyfriend type. I thought I was the little hussy."

"I haven't met someone like that, dummy." *It wasn't like that was it?* She wasn't sure, she just wanted to be able to talk to someone about Iris, about how great she was and what fun times they were having. That was all. Right?

"I mean I've made a friend—at work—someone I've been doing all that cool stuff with. We have so much in common." Cam felt herself smiling. "She's so cool and…well, I've been spending time with her and she's made me realize that I am a decent human who has something to offer and who doesn't deserve to sit around and beg her fiancé to show her some attention."

"Cam?"

"What?"

"Are you really okay?"

"What do you mean?"

"I mean it's the middle of the night and you're calling me to tell me that you've given up trying to make things work with Ryan in favor of hanging out with a woman named…what's her name?"

"Iris." Cam felt butterflies as she said the name out loud, feeling faintly ridiculous, not wanting to imagine how Iris would react if she knew Cam was talking about her in this way to her sister.

"Yeah, Iris." Alison repeated. "Iris, your new friend, who you have so much in common with and who's so damn cool. Is there some shocking revelation coming next, sis, because you know how much mom hates the gays and I definitely want to be the one who tells her that you're coming out. It'll take the heat off me for decades."

Cam felt the sharp and painful memory of a conversation with her mother many years ago. She pushed it away.

"Don't be silly. It's not like that. I'm just saying that when you spend time with someone new and they like getting to know you and you have a good time together, it makes you question why you accept so little from the person who's supposed to love you the most."

Alison waited.

"But it's not just that. She's kind of amazing as well, she's funny and creative and strong, and she's got these dark, surly looks that draw you in, that seem a little dangerous, but when you get to know her, she's sweet, and soft, and just adorable really."

Alison was quiet. Cam waited.

"Well, I think you and Ryan should go and see a counselor, try and figure out what's going wrong. Four years together must mean something works, and you agreed to marry him less than a year ago. It can't be something you can't fix."

Cam wasn't very experienced in relationships. She didn't know what falling out of love felt like. Right now, she didn't even trust herself to know what falling in love felt like. She wanted to ask Alison, but it seemed silly.

"You're really not having sex?" Alison asked gently.

"Nope, it's been weeks. Neither of us is looking for it, and neither of us is talking about it."

"That sucks."

"Maybe. Or maybe it's a sign. Maybe it says something about where we are, something important." Cam hadn't thought of it like that until she said the words. She didn't care they weren't having sex and she should, surely?

"And, Iris? I mean, are you sure you two aren't gonna…y'know? Is she married, engaged?"

"No, it's not like that. We're just friends, we just 'get' each other. It's…nice." Cam felt tired, and a little embarrassed, wanting to go back to bed, not sure the chat was entirely helping. She wasn't ready to tell Alison about her feelings for Iris. She had no right to have them. She should focus on making things work with Ryan. Doing anything else would make her as bad as Amanda. Suddenly understanding things that way shocked her, but it wasn't unhelpful.

"Cam?"

"Yeah."

"If you did find you liked this Iris in that way, it'd be cool by me. I mean, I'm a millennial, we're all for that kind of thing. I'd only be upset if she was a Republican." Alison chuckled softly.

Cam knew that she meant it, that she meant well. Her sister was all about following her heart whatever the consequences. She imagined introducing Iris to her. The two of them bonding over poetry.

"I think you'd think she was amazing actually. And she's so damn attractive, she'd probably have even you in love with her." Cam was aiming for a teasing humor, but saying the words out loud made her feel strange.

"Is she gay?" Alison waited a beat before asking.

"Yeah."

"Is she seeing anyone?"

Cam hesitated. "No. She's kinda sworn off women for a while, bad breakup."

"Then be careful, eh? I mean, if you're getting close and spending all this time together and she's gay, how do you know she won't end up liking you as more than a friend?"

Cam felt the hammer drop. She hadn't really thought of that, had been so wrapped up in her own feelings about the friendship. "I think I'd know if that was the case." Cam thought that was probably true, but then she remembered Iris leaving her house in a hurry, acting all scared and embarrassed. *Was that a sign of something?* Cam shook her head. No, Iris wasn't interested in her that way. She'd be able to tell.

"Just be careful, sis. You might think being with her is something that picks you up when you're bored with Ryan, but she might not see things the same way."

Alison was wise beyond her years, and Cam could do with a bit of her savvy sometimes. She wished her luck with the experimental theater—pretty sure that she'd need it—and drained her cup, knowing she should get back to bed.

Cam had denied her feelings about Iris were feelings "like that," but sitting here on the couch, with the purple blanket draped over the arm next to her, it was hard to keep away the image of Iris waking in her arms, and gazing up at Cam sleepily. The wanting to pull Iris back to her when Iris had pulled away had only lasted seconds, but it had been there.

Even if she was falling for Iris in some way—and she wasn't sure that she really was—Iris had made it clear she was someone who didn't do drama, and her friendship with Iris was the most important thing in her life right now. Cam took in a deep breath. The simplest thing to do was to make herself stop having the feelings, to remember that she was engaged to be married, and that she had a lot to lose. She let out the breath and headed up the stairs to bed.

CHAPTER SEVENTEEN

C am sat at her desk rubbing her temples knowing she should try to do some actual work but finding it near impossible to concentrate given the headache that the lack of sleep and the prosecco had left her with. All of it was compounded by the email that Iris had sent her late last night.

In Cam's mind a whirlwind of thoughts were jostling for space. The email had a time stamp of one thirty-four a.m. Iris must have agonized for a long time after getting home on Sunday before finally sending it to her.

They hadn't exchanged personal email addresses so Iris had sent it to Cam's Cottoms account, and it had sat waiting for her until she'd arrived at eight thirty that morning and it was the main reason why she hadn't done a stroke of work since she'd opened it almost two hours ago. It said:

Hello you

I know I owe you a poem. I've attached the one about my dad that I told you about and also another that is a bit older. Maybe you can help me choose which one is best if you're really going to make me perform #panicattack

Oh, and thanks, Cam. You're a good friend for making me do this x

PS: If they are bad, you need to please tell me. I hate the idea of performing, but performing bad poems is even worse. I'm relying on your American bluntness ;)

Cam loved the poems, and she hadn't been able to stop reading them. One was simply called "John" and was a moving account of Iris's relationship with her dad and the things her mother had missed out on by leaving them, and the other she had to admit that she was kind of obsessed by. It was called "Bridge to Nowhere" and talked of a relationship breaking apart that she could only assume had been inspired by what happened with Amanda. The imagery was so bleak, so dark but somehow still beautiful, and completely and utterly relatable. And of course it made her think of her relationship with Mia. And if she was being honest, it made her think even more often of Iris, which wasn't entirely helpful. The poems showed a sensitive and creative side to her that Cam had often imagined but never seen. And Iris sharing them with her made her feel special.

More than once that morning, Cam had drifted into imagining Iris standing on the bookstore stage reading the poems to the audience and Cam sitting alone in that audience hearing them for the first time, not knowing who Iris was. She would think them amazing and she would probably think the handsome poet reading them was awesome and fall for her straightaway. Cam should have felt bad about the daydream, but she didn't. She'd denied herself so much over the years, and lived in the shadows with Ryan for months, so if spending time thinking that way about Iris was what got her through a bad morning, she wasn't going to feel bad about that. There were worse things than a crush on a friend that she had no intention of doing anything about.

Cam read the email again. Iris had said that Cam was a good friend, and above all else, she really wanted to be. She shook the lustful feelings away and went to her Sent folder to open the email she had sent Iris in reply a few minutes ago.

Re: Hello you

Wow. What can I say about the poems? Wonderful, poignant, and a privilege to read. I'm not just saying it. I mean it. I've read them over and over. You have a way of describing feelings so authentically, so imaginatively that it's impossible not to understand, not to identify with them and that's a real gift. Literally awesome.

And I can't actually choose between them. They are so different. I looked on the website and it says that performers are restricted to ten minutes each max (not one poem each) so you could actually do both. So I guess if you still want me to help you choose, I choose both.

Thanks so much for sharing them with me. How about lunch today so we can have a proper chat about them? (And also because I like watching you eat!)

C x

She was happy with the email overall. She worried she'd been a bit over-the-top but couldn't help herself. And the comment about watching Iris eat was a joke. Sort of. *Iris would know that, right?* The computer in front of her beeped to signal the arrival of a new message. It was from Iris.

Re: Re: Hello you

Thanks, Cam, for the encouraging words. I'm sure you know it's hard for me to believe them, but I'm trying really hard to let them land. And don't think I haven't spotted that you're trying to make me perform two poems now rather than one. Very crafty, very crafty indeed. I'd love to have lunch with you, but I've just been told I'm needed in Bristol this afternoon. I'm going to be there all week. I'm even gonna miss training, which is crappy. Hopefully, back in time for the dinner dance thing on Friday though. The food is usually pretty good. Can't always say the same for the dancing!

Cam felt annoyed that work was taking Iris away. She sighed at just the moment that Graham dumped a pile of invoices on her desk on his way out the door, asking her to scan them. She didn't particularly care if he thought the sigh was directed at him. His processes were so old-fashioned, and she knew that the task would take hours.

Cam looked across the room at Sylvia typing into her computer. Graham's departure had provided an opportunity for Cam, the would-be journalist, and she took it.

"Hey, Sylvia, do you happen to know what funding the men's soccer team receives from the company?" She tried to sound casual.

Sylvia looked up from her screen and fixed Cam with a questioning look. "Who wants to know?"

Sylvia had a scary demeanor, but she'd always been friendly to Cam and they'd shared many an eye roll in Graham's direction over the weeks so Cam felt okay about asking.

"We're just curious. Oliver said that the men get a lot of extras that the women's team doesn't, and it doesn't seem fair. I tried asking Liam, but he just said I shouldn't worry my pretty little head about it."

"Ew." Sylvia had made it very clear how much she disliked Liam, and he tended to avoid the office when she was around. She peered at Cam. "That kind of information wouldn't be in the shared files. I imagine Graham would hide it away somewhere. I mean, I'd probably have to look in Graham's inbox to find out, and while I do have access for when he's absent, I'm sure a fishing expedition like that would get me into trouble."

Sylvia sounded like she was serious, but then she smirked at Cam and gave out a little chuckle. "And I wouldn't want to blot my copybook so close to my retirement date."

"No worries, I understand." Cam worried she shouldn't have asked. She picked up her cup. "Coffee?" Sylvia nodded and looked back at her screen.

Cam headed to the kitchen still wondering about the article and feeling a little stuck. Iris's poems were so good that she felt they had raised the ante and now she wanted to write something that would make Iris proud. All she had so far were the stats on how the teams had performed in each of the last six seasons, since both teams had been formed. The women's team had improved their position year by year and were now top of the league and the men's team had an opposite trajectory and were second from bottom with two games to go. There was a real chance that the women would win their league, and maybe the story should simply be about that—a celebration of something positive, of victory against the odds. She felt sure it was the kind of story that Cottoms would like their clients to read. She could even imagine a picture of the team looking victorious on the front cover. The idea of it made her smile.

Cam headed back to her desk with the coffees. Graham was sitting back at his desk. He lifted his eyes toward her and semi-scowled. The drinking coffee thing really did make him mad. Cam sat at her desk and noticed a folded piece of A4 paper on top of her keyboard. She was sure it wasn't there before and wondered if Graham had tired of verbally giving out orders and resorted to paper notes. It wouldn't surprise her. She unfolded the sheet of paper. It was a printout of an email, an email from Graham to Liam.

Liam,

I've managed to increase the funds for next season by a further £300. You know I'm supportive, but that's probably about the limit. It just needs Iris or one of her man-hating friends in the women's team to find out that you're now getting three times the funds they do and we'll have them being all hormonal and #metoo about it. If you could try to win a few more games that'd help. It's embarrassing that you're getting all the money and they are winning all the games.

Regards, Graham

Cam was holding her breath. *Damn, this was dynamite.* Not only was Graham admitting that the men's team had way more funding, but he was being offensive about Iris and the women in a way that she knew no one in the senior team at Cottoms would tolerate.

And she had a copy of the email.

Cam coughed and Sylvia looked up at her, giving her a small nod and an imperceptible wink.

Cam tucked the piece of paper into the inside of her bag, wondering what on earth she should do with it. She couldn't use it for her article. Janie would never let her use the in-house magazine for a whistle blowing story, and giving it to Megan or Hazel would mean they'd raise hell and Sylvia might get into trouble. She needed time to think. She picked up the pile of invoices that needed scanning and headed out of the office. Having Graham's unfairness and misogyny confirmed chafed at her, and getting out of his presence was as important as scanning his stupid invoices.

On the way along the corridor to the main office, Cam told herself that her elevated heart rate was simply the bombshell of an email she had in her bag and had nothing to do with the chance of bumping into Iris before she left for Bristol. She couldn't believe they wouldn't see each other all week. The feeling of loss was strong, stronger than she was entitled to feel, and it made her feel uneasy. By the time she'd reached the copy room and scanned the first few invoices, Cam had made herself believe that a few days away from Iris was exactly what she needed. She'd cook a nice meal for Ryan and try to talk properly to him about their plans.

CHAPTER EIGHTEEN

Iris stood at the threshold of the upmarket country club where the league was holding its annual dinner dance. She was facing out into the grounds. It was dark, but the gardens were tastefully lit with soft golden lights allowing her to see the wide, manicured lawns, the sculpted bushes dotting the paths that crisscrossed the lawns and the sweep of the long driveway that led from the edge of the grounds to the bottom of the main stone staircase she was standing on. Iris breathed in deeply, inhaling the fresh, cold air and not wanting to make her way back into the banquet hall.

People were still arriving. Most of them were dressed up for the fancy dinner. The tickets were expensive and the place was kind of high end, and for most of the players, it was the highlight of the season, a chance to get dressed up and cut loose. The season wasn't quite over, but it wouldn't stop the teams from playing hard this evening.

The year before, Iris had attended with Amanda of course, feeling proud of having her on her arm. It was before they'd started having problems, and they'd danced until their feet hurt, drank until they couldn't stop giggling, and gone home happy. Iris remembered it fondly, and not even seeing Amanda arrive with someone else half an hour before made her feel any sadness about it. Amanda deserved happiness, and Iris knew that out there was someone better for her than Iris ever could have been. The thought wasn't as self-pitying as it might have been a few months ago. There was someone out there for everyone, even her. Trouble was, right now, Iris couldn't see past Cam. Her very unavailable and uninterested friend.

She sighed for the thirtieth time that day. Not seeing Cam all week had not had the cooling effect Iris had hoped for and she knew that, despite telling herself that she needed to cool things down with Cam, it was the prospect of seeing her tonight that had made her make the effort to come.

The fact that she was standing out in the cold regretting it wasn't because she was alone, wasn't even the fact that she hated formal dinners, it was that her own stupidity had stopped her from realizing that Cam would turn up with Ryan. Of course she would. Most of the players brought their partners. And Ryan was Cam's partner. Iris made herself say it out loud. "Cam is Ryan's fiancée." The words were important even if they made Iris feel things she didn't really want to face.

Iris had already been seated at one of the Cottoms tables when Cam and Ryan arrived hand in hand. Cam turning heads in a fitted navy blue dress that showed off her figure, and Ryan looking handsome in a lounge suit. He looked pretty pleased with himself to be arriving with Cam. As they approached, Iris wondered if it was too late to change tables. The team had three that had been reserved for them, and if she hadn't gotten there so ridiculously early—and hadn't badly needed that aperitif—she could have joined one of the other tables at a much later point. Now she'd made it possible for Cam and Ryan to choose to join her table, which they did, and that meant she'd get to spend the entire evening watching them, trying not be jealous.

Cam greeted Iris with a sweet wave that made Iris's heart skip, and Ryan did the handshake thing as they said hello. Iris looked for some sign he was going to be hostile, but his face was open and unconcerned. Iris beckoned the waiter for another gin and tonic.

"I'm trying to make up for my lack of social skills with G&Ts." She was self-conscious about drinking so much so early

"How was the journey back from Bristol?" Cam looked pensive, slightly awkward even.

"Fine," Iris replied flatly.

Ryan looked at Iris curiously. "Oh, that's right, Cam said you'd been out of town for work, had to drive herself to training and complained like a teenager about it."

Cam shot him a look. Ryan ignored her.

"She doesn't seem to like her routine disrupted by little things like work." Cam darted an even darker look in Ryan's direction.

Iris stood up. "Sorry I need to go outside for something." She hurried toward the main doors.

After several minutes, Iris knew she should rejoin her table, but she really, really didn't want to. Cam's look of hurt as Ryan sniped at her was nothing Iris could do anything about, but Ryan making comments like that made her feel protective of Cam and, worse, it made her feel stupidly hopeful that Cam would tire of him. And Iris knew that was not a helpful way to be thinking at all.

At the top of the stone steps, lost in her thoughts, lost in the view of the grounds, Iris felt someone slide their hands around her waist and turn her around.

"Gemma." Iris hugged her friend. "I wasn't expecting to see you here."

"I'm here with Erica, the hot new captain of the Hackney Lions. She isn't the brightest but she's very good company if you know what I mean." She smirked, before putting her arm through Iris's and steering them into the doorway. Most of the diners had arrived now, just the odd stragglers dribbling in.

"I'd better get to my table, but find me later and we can catch up and have a dance."

"Okay, assuming I'm still capable of coherent thought and coordinated movement." Iris pointed at her glass and Gemma laughed, leaning in to kiss Iris's cheek.

"And come and say a quick hello to Erica. She has the cutest German accent. You're going to love it." Gemma put her arm around Iris's waist and steered her toward their table.

❖

Cam watched Iris in the doorway, aware of only that spot in the entire room. A woman of similar build to Iris, but with a fairer complexion and blond hair, had her arm around Iris's waist. Iris said something into the woman's ear, and the woman threw her head back and laughed. Cam felt a knot tighten in her stomach, and the feeling was accompanied by a rising sense of panic that told her, without words, that she shouldn't be feeling like this.

Ryan had stood up and was leaning over her. Cam tried to focus on what he was saying, tearing her eyes away from Iris and her "friend," the word heavy with speech marks even in her own mind.

"What do you want to drink? I can't seem to get the waiter's attention and I want to get started." Cam could tell Ryan was in the mood to drink, ready to party amongst all these people.

"Dry white wine." Cam managed to say the words. Ryan set off for the bar alongside the west wall of the massive dining room. Her gaze returned to the doorway, but she could no longer see Iris and her companion. She scanned the room. Iris was walking with the woman toward a table near the edge of the roped off dance floor. For a horrible moment, Cam thought she was going to sit with her date at that table, that Cam wouldn't be able to talk to her all night. She couldn't decide if that was worse than sharing the evening with Iris and whoever the hell that woman was, especially if they were going to be as loved up as their display in the doorway had suggested.

Cam chided herself. She had no right to feel resentful, no right at all, but she just couldn't believe that Iris would bring a date—someone she already seemed close to—without first mentioning it to her. They were friends, weren't they? They talked about stuff. Why wouldn't Iris mention that she was dating? She wasn't being honest with herself. Cam wasn't just upset that Iris hadn't mentioned it, she was upset about the fact that Iris had a date at all. She shook her head to shake some sense into herself and stopped as she felt Ryan's presence next to her.

"It's as expensive as it looks. We should have smuggled in a hip flask." Cam smiled at him. His meanness was a topic of fun between them.

"I'll drink slowly," she promised before taking a large swig of wine.

Ryan playfully snatched the glass away, and Cam pouted at him until he gave it back to her. When Cam returned her attention to the table, Iris was standing with her hands on the back of the chair she had earlier been sitting in. She was alone and had a look on her face that made Cam want to ask her if she was okay.

"Hey again." Iris sat down a little self-consciously and sipped at the tall drink that the waiter had left for her.

"You two have scrubbed up well." Iris looked across at Casey and Hazel and waved her fingers in greeting. Cam felt a small pinprick of jealousy that Iris hadn't offered her a similar compliment.

Cam wanted to ask Iris who the woman was, and why they weren't sitting together, but Jess arrived with Diane and quickly claimed the vacant seat next to Iris.

"You look gorgeous." Jess spoke to Iris as if the others were not even there, as if she had the right to pay Iris such lavish compliments. Iris did look good, but Cam hated the fact that Jess felt able to say it when she didn't dare. Iris said nothing, simply shaking her head at Jess and turning away.

Iris was wearing a fitted black shirt; the material was sheer in places, and Cam knew that she had noticed as much as Jess probably had, how it clung to Iris's abdomen and arms, showing off her toned physique. Despite the formality of the evening, Iris was wearing a pair of low-slung red jeans. Her hair was tousled and her makeup was understated. Cam wasn't sure how she managed it, but despite being one of the least dressed up women in the room, Iris was by far the most captivating.

Iris lifted her arm to signal to the hovering waiter that she wanted to order some wine, revealing to Cam a strip of torso, taut and tanned, in the gap between Iris's jeans and her shirt. Cam had seen Iris's body—they changed together every week before and after football—but this unintended glimpse of skin made her feel hot to her core. A feeling she needed to tamp down. Once again, she shook her head, physically hoping to shake some sense into herself. Ryan leaned over and put his hand on Cam's neck.

"Are you okay, babe?"

"I'm fine. Bit of neck ache from being hunched over the computer all day. Don't worry."

The lie came out easily and Cam hated herself for it. She made herself stop staring at Iris, trying to regain a sense of control and grasp the fact that she was here having dinner with her fiancé and some friends, one of whom just happened to be Iris.

Cam tuned back in to what Jess was saying to Iris. "Was that Gemma you were chatting to? Who is she here with? I had the biggest crush on her for months. You never went there did you? I don't know why. She obviously wanted you to."

Cam spoke to Iris, into the space she had left by not responding to Jess's questions. She couldn't help it.

"I thought she was your date for some reason…Gemma, is that her name? I saw the two of you at the door and you looked, well, like you were together. You looked pretty good together actually."

Ryan, oblivious to any undercurrents, spoke up. "Iris and the blond woman? For sure. Go for it, Iris. She's hot."

Cam gave Ryan a look of disapproval that would have knocked him off his feet had he been standing.

Iris's cheeks flamed. Cam hadn't meant to embarrass her. She just had been so affected by the idea that Iris might be dating. The table was now focused on Iris. Only Diane—staring off into the middle distance while playing with her hair absent-mindedly—was not looking at her expectantly.

"Sorry I'm such a disappointment, guys, but I came alone. The hot blonde…Gemma, as she probably prefers to be known, and I are old friends, and no, Jess, not 'old friends' like that." Iris punctuated the air with her fingers to make clear the speech marks. "And she's here with her girlfriend."

"Like that ever stopped you." Jess made the remark under her breath.

Iris flashed a look in Jess's direction but didn't say a word to stick up for herself. Cam wanted her to. She actually wanted to do it for her, but of course she had no right to.

"You never know though, a few more of these," Iris picked up her glass, "and I might find the courage to ask Ryan for a dance. It's been quite a while since I've danced with someone taller than me." She drained her glass. "In fact the last time was probably when I danced with my dad when I was fifteen and he embarrassed me by agreeing to be a parent chaperone at the school disco."

"Oh God, I remember that story," Hazel said. "Didn't he find you in the closet with some boy and pour a lemonade over you both?"

"He did. Last time I was in any kind of closet."

The others laughed; the tension was broken.

Ryan picked up the ball and ran with it. "Okay I'm in, but only if it's a slow one so we can snuggle up real close." There was more laughter, but Cam saw his eyes dart in her direction, wanting to see her reaction.

She ignored him and returned her attention to Iris. Her eyes were fixed on Cam but clouded with something that she couldn't read. She really was inscrutable. Cam wanted so badly to lean across the table, take Iris's hand, and ask her to please tell her, in words as simple and straightforward as she could manage, what she was thinking when she looked at Cam that way. Instead, she gratefully sat back as the waiter poured some more white wine into the glass bowl in front of her that passed for a wine glass.

❖

Ryan put down his knife and fork and leaned across to Cam, whispering something in her ear. Iris watched as she mouthed the word "Don't" in his direction and then felt embarrassed as Cam looked up and caught her watching them both. The wine Iris had drunk, on top of the G&Ts she had started with, was making her feel looser and less guarded, and she knew herself well enough to know that wasn't always a good thing.

"I hope the dessert is as good as the dinner." Priti pushed her plate away. "And I'm glad the food is living up to the ticket price."

Iris topped up her glass. Across the table, Hazel widened her eyes at the amount of wine she was drinking, and Iris shrugged, happy Hazel hadn't arrived early enough to see her drink the three G&Ts.

Casey sat back in her chair as the waiters arrived to begin to clear the plates of those diners that had finished eating. "I'm going to have to dance all night to work off those potatoes." Casey stroked an imaginary paunch.

"Good luck with finding a dance partner. I'm too full to move." Hazel leaned her head on Casey's shoulder.

"You know the rule my sweet—one dance for each potato. I counted six." Casey patted Hazel's arm playfully.

"No way." Hazel shook her head, her eyes wide and disbelieving.

Iris couldn't help but be charmed by their obvious affection for each other, but felt bitter about being in the presence of such loved up couples, especially when she was feeling so miserably single and halfway to being miserably drunk.

"Ryan's not full," Cam said. "I had to stop him from asking if he could finish Jess's dinner. He's such an embarrassment when it comes to food."

"The portions were too small for a growing boy like me. If I'm going to have to dance, I'll need three desserts." Ryan looked a little sheepish.

Iris blanched at the easy banter between Ryan and Cam. She hadn't expected it to hurt quite so much. She willed herself to be happy for Cam that Ryan was in a better mood and they seemed content together for once. But it was hard, harder than it should be.

"I think Iris had four potatoes so she owes the table four dances. Ryan and I will take one each, any other volunteers?" Her eyes met Iris's.

The look Iris received from Cam was mystifying, lingering but with a meaning she couldn't quite read. It was like trying to communicate with someone who didn't speak the same language. If Cam wasn't so happily engaged, Iris might have read the looks Cam was giving her very differently, but as things stood, she was simply confused. Confused, tipsy, and impossibly aroused every time Cam looked at her that way.

"I'm always happy to dance with Iris." It was Jess, of course, throwing her hat into the ring. Though Iris wasn't yet drunk enough to let that happen. And she was still mad as hell at her.

"Sorry, Jess, but if I've got to dance with Mr. and Mrs. White Picket Fence over there, my card is full. I've already promised Gemma and Priti a dance, and I'm certainly not dancing any more than the potatoes I've eaten." She knew the sarcastic comment about Cam and Ryan was needless, but she was feeling the effects of the drink and finding it harder to stay away from her feelings. Jess muttered something inaudible but clearly grouchy in Iris's direction and yanked Diane to her feet, pulling her toward the large dance floor at the far end of the room.

Iris let Ryan see her to her seat. His gentlemanly behavior made her want to tease him, but she thought better of it, unsure whether he would take the joke or get defensive. He was actually a pretty good dancer, and it had felt strangely comfortable to allow him to twist and turn her as they performed what might have passed for disco dancing to a song by Madonna.

"You and Ryan have inspired us." Iris looked up to see Casey and Hazel get up from their seats. "We're going to throw some shapes as I believe the kids probably never say." Casey nudged Hazel in the back in the direction of the dance floor as she spoke, and they departed to the sound of Hazel muttering about never eating potatoes again.

"So, when was the last time you had a man in your arms?" Ryan's tone was light and obviously playful, and Iris was surprised to see Cam nudge him and give him a dirty look.

"I'm sorry, Iris. He has no social skills at the best of times and especially not when he's drinking. Ignore him."

"I'm the same, don't worry. Actually, I was trying to remember. I gave first aid to big Tony when he slipped on a teabag and fell down at work last month. Does that count?"

Cam and Ryan both laughed, but the mood soured again when Ryan made a comment about resuscitation being a form of foreplay in his book. Cam didn't look amused, and even Iris thought the comment a little crass. Ryan appeared to be quite drunk, more than he had seemed when they were dancing.

"Maybe we should give it a whirl?" Priti leaned over and spoke to Iris quietly. "I'm a little anxious Jess will stab me if I dance with you, but I'm willing to take the risk if you are."

Iris stood, holding up her hands as if apologizing.

"I mean, it doesn't exactly take Hercule Poirot to see she has the serious feels for you. I don't know how Diane puts up with it." Priti shook her head.

Iris walked with Priti to the dance floor. "The irony is that I actually think Jess is quite keen on her."

"But she can't get you out of her system, eh? You must be quite the lady-killer." She raised an eyebrow as they approached the edge of dance floor.

"Mind control. Got it from a library book. Makes me irresistible." Iris stood to one side so that Priti could pass in front of her.

"So that's why you're here tonight on your own."

"The library made me take the book back." Iris shrugged, enjoying the aimless banter, and Priti nudged her as they found a place for themselves amongst the other dancers, moving happily together as a Beyoncé track was replaced by Taylor Swift.

❖

Cam joined Iris at the bar, standing alongside her, their shoulders touching. Iris and Priti had just finished dancing, and Cam had taken the opportunity to finally get some time alone with Iris.

"Can I have a pint of water please?" Iris asked politely.

The young woman serving her smiled as she turned away. She looked handsome in her waitress tuxedo, short blond hair, and piercing blue eyes. Cam wondered if she was more Iris's type than Priti and a hot flash of what felt a lot like jealousy passed through her body.

"I didn't have you down as a dancer."

"Why not? I could get insulted by a comment like that." Iris's tone was playful, and her eyes gleamed. Cam felt pulled in, speaking suddenly getting more difficult.

"I don't know. At work…I mean…well, you just seem so serious sometimes." Cam's heart was beating in her ears and she felt slightly tongue-tied.

Iris tilted her head, her eyes not leaving Cam's face. "Are you complaining that I don't dance enough at work?" Cam wondered if Iris was flirting. She felt heat rise from her feet and settle somewhere unexpected.

"Next time I come to see Graham, I'll try and throw in a little rumba for you." Iris moved her hips from side to side.

Cam could only stare, enjoying the movement of Iris's mouth, her white teeth, her full lips. Her eyes impossible to look away from. Cam hoped she was a little drunk because feeling this way sober would not be good at all.

"Come with me a minute. I want to gossip and I need some air." Cam took Iris's arm and pulled her across to the fire exit a few yards away.

They stood outside against the wall, enjoying the cool air of the evening. Cam wanted to talk, that much was true, but she also wanted Iris to herself, even if only for a few minutes. She told Iris that Amanda's date wasn't a date but a friend. She passed on the news of Vicki and Harry's breakup. She tried to say the words "irreconcilable differences" but stumbled every time, until she gave up and they dissolved into laughter. And now Cam had stopped talking and they were just looking out across the grounds.

"England is so old. This house, these gardens, they're older than Seattle. That tree." She pointed and Iris looked in the direction of her pointing finger. "Not that one, that one." She grabbed Iris's finger and aimed it at a large fir tree. "It's probably older than my mom's house." She paused. "I'm a little drunk I think."

"I think you're probably right."

"And I'm not thinking straight." The choice of words registered somewhere in Cam's brain and she frowned. "In fact, I'm sure I'm not." She looked up at Iris with a shrug, wanting her to understand, wanting them to talk about just how not-straight Cam was, but knowing that it was all forbidden, and that none of it mattered a damn.

Iris smiled at her.

"What are you smiling at?" Cam loved the way Iris looked when she smiled. Her features softened and she looked even more beautiful.

"You. You're a very cute drunk."

Cam groaned.

"Are you okay? You're not going to be sick are you?"

Cam shook her head. "A cute drunk? That's really what you're thinking? Well, that's no use, that's no use at all."

"Well, what kind of drunk were you aiming to be?"

Cam paused, daring herself to answer, and then shrugged, offering no response. She wanted Iris to find her attractive, she wanted to be an irresistible drunk, but how could she say that? She shivered.

"I'm cold, but I don't want to go back inside." Cam knew she sounded truculent. She wanted something but couldn't admit to wanting it. Iris didn't respond, but their closeness made Cam's nerve endings vibrate.

"You're nowhere near as bad as they all make out, you know? Jess said you were dangerous and you'd make a move on me, and all you did was fall asleep. And that's no good for my self-esteem."

"Cam?" Iris's voice sounded like a warning.

Cam wanted to talk about that evening, about what Jess had said, about the two of them falling asleep nestled on her couch.

"And then you just ran away." Cam was tipsy enough to chance saying things she would probably regret.

"Come on, Cam. Let's go back inside. Let's get your cute drunk self some coffee to warm up." Iris's voice was calm and even. Cam hated how unreadable she was. She pushed herself off the wall and followed Iris toward the fire door that led back into the hall.

Cam headed back to the table and Iris went to the bar to get coffees. They both needed one. As she waited to be served, Iris felt a presence at her elbow, and she turned. Jess was staring at her, pulling at her lip with her fingers nervously, looking like she had something on her mind.

"You're going to make a fool of yourself." Jess spoke as if they'd been in the middle of a conversation.

"Sorry?" Iris didn't understand.

"She's just bored and enjoying the attention. Even you must know that." Jess nodded toward their table. "I still care for you. And I don't want to see her make a fool of you."

Iris suddenly understood. She felt the anger and the embarrassment clash. "And that 'care' you have for me, is that why you've gone out of your way to mess in my life. Chatting shit to Amanda about me, trying to sabotage my friendship with Cam by telling her fiancé a load of bullshit about how I can't be trusted to be around her?" Iris didn't care how bitter she sounded. "I mean, I'm just trying to figure out what you caring for me looks like and how I'm supposed to recognize it. Because it looks to me that you're just being spiteful and jealous."

Jess stepped back as if Iris had slapped her. Iris felt a second's regret and then remembered that Jess had had it coming. There was no part of her warning about Cam that was meant kindly. She just wanted to cause trouble.

The coffees were ready, and Iris turned to pick up the tray and stalked off, dismayed that Jess had somehow picked up on something. She headed back to the table, wishing desperately that people would just leave her alone. The table was empty except for Hazel. She put the coffee down with a sigh.

"Hey, what's up?" Hazel looked concerned.

"Nothing. I'm fine." She rubbed her forehead. "Just Jess being Jess." Iris gestured across the table. "Where is everyone?"

"Dancing, toilet, bar. Who knows? I'm just glad of the rest." Hazel peered at Iris. "Sure you're okay, mate?"

Iris wanted to talk to her, to tell her about her feelings for Cam and the confusion she felt. Even about what Jess had said. But she didn't dare.

"Is there someone for me do you think?" Iris took a long drink of her wine.

"Of course there is. You, mate, are an absolute catch. But to make an omelet you have to crack an egg. An available egg. Or several available eggs probably." She shrugged. "I don't know. I can't cook, and I'm rubbish with metaphors. I just mean that you need to get out there, meet some new people, y'know." She leaned across and squeezed Iris's arm.

The music in the room seemed to be getting louder, and the dance was getting fuller as the tables were emptying after the meal. Iris remembered how much she'd been dreading and looking forward to the evening in equal measure. The truth was that she loved to dance, loved to lose herself in the music with others who felt the same way. She didn't do it very often now that she was single, but that didn't mean she didn't miss it.

Jess headed back to the table, Diane at her side. "Diane says she can't keep up with me so she's come back for a drink and a rest." Jess looked at Iris. "Iris, you're not dancing. Could we?" Jess pouted slightly, and Iris couldn't tell if this was an attempt to appear seductive or a form of petulance that would mean she would throw a tantrum if refused. After what had just happened, she couldn't believe Jess would still have the nerve to ask. Before Iris could react, Cam stood up at the other side of the table.

"I think you'll find it's my turn actually, Jess. I was promised a dance, and I've been waiting patiently for my chance." Iris looked from Jess to Cam, unsure of how to respond. The look on Cam's face confused Iris. She was biting her lip looking unsure, but her eyes were more certain and they held Iris's gaze. She stood and nodded in Cam's direction.

"You're on, but remember we've got a big match on Sunday so no treading on my toes." Iris moved around to Cam's side of the table, hearing Jess grumble and not caring. Cam took her by the arm and steered her across the room, and she was aware of nothing but the feel of Cam at her side and the blood pulsing through her body.

Cam leaned in to Iris. "You owe me big for saving you from Jess." Her voice was teasing, flirtatious, but the words made Iris stop still yards away from the dance floor. She wondered if Cam had actually wanted to dance with her or just done the right thing for a friend in need. Cam held her gaze and gave her a shy smile. It was all the answer she was going to get.

They maneuvered their way into the heart of the dance floor, surrounding themselves with people. Everyone seemed lost in the music and occupying their own world. An up-tempo song—something by Rihanna—came to an end as they arrived and was replaced by a slower, more rhythmic track that Iris didn't recognize. Around them, people began to move as the song started in earnest.

Cam started to sway. Iris let the music wash over her. She began to move, but she couldn't take her eyes off Cam who was turning slowly from one side to the other, moving her hips in time to the beat. Cam closed her eyes, and Iris began to doubt that Cam was as aware of her presence as she was of Cam's, but almost before the thought could complete itself, Cam put her hands on Iris's hips. The movement seemed so natural, and Iris felt the tender pressure of her hands as they sought to pull her closer and to help them sway in time with each other. Iris had her hands at her sides and felt self-conscious, not sure what to do.

Cam opened her eyes and looked at Iris searchingly. Cam's eyes showed a need that Iris saw clearly for the first time, a need that was very similar to her own. The realization shocked her, and her face must have betrayed her surprise, because she felt Cam stiffen in front of her. Iris moved closer then, wanting to reassure. She rested her arms on Cam's shoulders so that they were now dancing together half an arm's length apart. Iris was oblivious to everything and everyone around them. The music had the effect of loosening her muscles. The alcohol had already washed away her good sense. Iris couldn't help but stare at Cam's mouth. Cam bit her lip—an unconscious gesture—but one that made Iris want to cross the small distance between them and crush her lips with a kiss.

Cam's hands moved from Iris's hips to the small of her back, drawing them even closer together. Cam's eyes were open now, shining and clear. She held Iris's gaze, the two of them locked in their embrace, moving slowly, barely. Iris was aware of nothing but the two of them. She was dangerously close to losing control, to leaning the few inches she would need to in order to touch her lips to Cam's, not knowing whether Cam would push her away or respond by returning the kiss.

The feel of Cam's hands on Iris's back created spots of tingling warmth, and Iris felt the awareness of their touch drown out all her other senses. Cam reached beneath her shirt and stroked the bare skin of her back. Cam's touch was electrifying, shooting lightning bolts through Iris's body that grounded between her legs. Iris groaned. It must have been obvious to Cam that this signified arousal. Her reaction to it was not to pull away but to pull Iris tighter to her, to lean her head on Iris's shoulder. Her mouth was next to Iris's ear, and Iris could hear Cam breathing raggedly in a way that suggested she was just as turned on by their closeness, by the touching.

Iris couldn't fight off her need to respond. Her arms were around Cam's neck, her hands loosely clasped. She moved so that her hands were touching Cam's neck. She used her thumbs to gently massage the top of Cam's spine, to stroke her soft skin. She let her fingers explore Cam's hair at the neckline, running them through it, lacing them in Cam's hair. She felt Cam arch at her touch and moan in Iris's ear. There were words, as well as soft moans, as they enjoyed the feeling of each other's skin, the touch of each other's fingers. Iris was lost. She'd wanted this but had no idea that Cam felt the same.

Cam lifted her head from Iris's shoulder and faced Iris. She was so very clearly as aroused as Iris was. Her hand moved to touch Iris's mouth. Her thumb stroking Iris's bottom lip, her own lips parting, their heads moving closer together.

All at once, the music changed. The new song was an old Abba classic, and some of the dancers around them cheered as they recognized the beginning. It was enough to break the spell. Cam stepped back, dropping her arms to her side. The reality of where they were and what they had been doing seemed to land with Cam. Iris tried to put a reassuring hand on her arm, but Cam looked at her with such confusion that she felt the need to withdraw it.

"Cam, it's okay. It's…" What could Iris say? They had both been aroused, dangerously close to doing something that would have had terrible consequences. They had crossed a line.

"It's not okay. I shouldn't…I'm sorry. I…need to go. I need to go."

Iris stepped back slightly as Cam turned away, hurrying back toward their table.

Iris's heart was pounding and her skin was alive. She was happy to escape to the bar. She needed to clear her head and process what had just happened. Cam had touched her, touched her in a way that you don't touch a friend you're dancing with. Iris had responded and…she shivered as she remembered the look in Cam's eyes. The desire was unmistakable. She could only imagine that her own eyes would have betrayed the same thing to Cam.

Fuck. That wasn't supposed to happen. Cam wasn't single and neither of them were the kind of people who wanted to do what they'd come so close to doing. She needed to sober up, needed to get back in control. Cam had been drinking too, but what the hell just happened? Iris had spent the early part of the evening feeling like a fool, seeing Cam with Ryan, the two of them looking happier together, feeling like she was reading too much into every gaze in her direction, but now this. She drained the glass of water that the bartender had placed in front of her and asked for another, wanting to wash away the alcohol as fast as possible.

She saw Ryan approaching. Her body tensed. He stood next to her, his back to the bar, mirroring her posture.

"Hey." She willed herself to behave normally.

He nodded back at her. "How you doing?" Ryan's tone was neutral, but his body language suggested he was as tense as she was. Iris swallowed down the panic that told her he must have seen her with Cam, seen them dancing, or worse, that Cam had told him what happened and he was here to confront her.

"I was feeling a bit squiffy. Just taking on some water so I can last the night." She pointed at the glass.

"Yeah, good idea, not really sure that drunken pining is a good look on a woman, even one as good-looking as you."

He held her gaze. She couldn't look away, knowing it would give her away.

Iris pretended to misunderstand. "Priti? No, you've got that wrong. That's just Jess mischief-making. We're friends. Not even that really."

"Is Jess making mischief when she tells me I need to watch you around Cam? I thought she was, assumed she was exaggerating, but then tonight I saw you." Iris's heart beat loudly in her head. She waited for it all to come crashing down.

"You were looking at her and I thought about how gorgeous she is and how it'd be perfectly natural if you'd noticed that." He spoke softly. It sounded more menacing somehow. "She's a little sweetheart, maybe a bit too naive sometimes, always sees the best in people, y'know. She likes you, Iris. She's always telling me how cool you are and how much she's enjoying getting to know you."

It was a warning. But even in warning Iris off Cam, Ryan was patronizing, not taking Cam seriously. She felt her hackles rise.

"She wants to be your friend, Iris, that's all. Don't imagine it's anything more than that." He pushed himself off the bar and stood in front of her. "And I hope you won't be the kind of person who tries to exploit how much she likes you. I know you can be, have been."

"That's not fair. I'm not like that anymore." The memory of them holding each other, touching each other on the dance floor made her stop. "I would never do that. Cam is my friend." The words sounded hollow. She couldn't deny she wanted Cam, but she also knew now that some part of Cam wanted her back. This was a fucking mess. But it was not all her mess and she was going to do everything she could to sort it out.

"For Cam's sake, I'm going to walk back to our table now and pretend we haven't had this conversation, but maybe, just maybe, you should concentrate on making her happier, happy enough that you don't have to worry about people like me." She downed the second glass of water and slammed it down on the bar, before striding back to the table. Her legs felt unsteady and her heart was hammering in her chest, but she felt more sober than she had all night. She was ashamed of her part in what had just happened but hated Ryan warning her off like it was all on her. Did he really think Cam wasn't capable of making her own choices in life? Cam was the one who sat them under a blanket and let Iris sleep in her arms. And Cam had touched her on the dance floor like she wanted more. Iris wasn't really the one he needed to worry about.

CHAPTER NINETEEN

Cam?" Ryan's voice brought her back. For a second, she had been somewhere else, in Iris's arms, on the dance floor, feeling the touch of Iris's hands on the back of her neck. "Can I have decaf? I don't wanna be up all night with the caffeine." Ryan was on the couch, talking to her over his shoulder, flicking through channels with the remote.

Cam had reached for Iris and Iris had responded, her eyes full of desire. She hadn't dared to think Iris felt that way about her, but her actions said she wanted Cam, and Cam had wanted…what? Her hands had wanted to touch Iris, her mouth had wanted to taste her, her body making it clear, even now, hours later, that it would have betrayed her, betrayed Ryan, given the chance. They were both drunk. Cam was still feeling the effects of the alcohol even now. Was it really as simple as that? Alcohol, dancing, their close friendship, conspiring to trick them both into doing something stupid they both knew was wrong.

She put on the coffee and crossed the room to stand behind the couch. Ryan had found a real life cops documentary to watch. She tried not to be annoyed by it, reaching down and running her fingers through his hair, scratching his neck softly. He reached a hand back and stroked her fingers and, without thinking, she crouched down to scatter kisses across the back of his neck, in the hollow behind his ear lobe, remembering what a sensitive spot it was for him. He turned and gave her a quizzical look. She knew why. She never initiated sex, was never usually this bold. She leaned in to kiss him properly, her mouth hungry for contact. He kissed her back, his hand in her hair, pulling her into the kiss. She could taste the wine he had drunk, feel the slight stubble on his cheeks. He pulled her over the side of the couch and into his lap. They kept kissing. His tongue was in her mouth, he grazed his hands across her breasts as he reached behind her for the zip on her dress. She could feel him growing hard underneath her. She willed herself to want this, to give herself up to it. It was something they both needed.

Cam closed her eyes as they kissed, but it was the wrong thing to do. When she opened them again moments later, the eyes looking back at her were a pale blue, not dark, not dark as she had expected, as she had wanted. She felt the shock like a physical jolt in her body. She put her hands on his chest, no longer wanting to do this, knowing she was doing it for all the wrong reasons.

"I'm sorry, Ryan," she stammered, tears in her eyes. "I don't feel well. I need to—" He let his arms drop, and she moved quickly, climbing out of his lap and heading quickly for the stairs, hearing his curse of frustration as she left the room. She locked the bathroom door behind her, sat on the toilet in the house she shared with her fiancé, and she sobbed.

She had lost herself. She knew Iris was cool, funny, sweet. She had become a really good friend, and Cam had to face up to the fact that she also wanted her more than she had ever wanted anyone.

She leaned back, stiffening as her bare back touched the cold porcelain of the toilet tank. Her mind played her a movie—Iris waking up next to her, blinking her way out of sleep, Iris across the table as she suffered telling her the story of what happened with Amanda, Iris doubled over with laughter at how bad Cam was at pool, and finally, Iris's mouth. Cam tracing her lips with her thumb, her only thought being how damn much she wanted to kiss them. She had a fiancé who wanted to take her home to get married, but she had fallen for Iris, and the whole thing made her feel completely dismantled. She closed her eyes and cried more quiet tears.

Iris woke to find the light in her bedroom still on, and looking down, found that she had slept in her clothes. Her alarm clock told her it was only four a.m., but her mind felt wide-awake as soon as she opened her eyes. Thoughts and memories associated with the previous evening collided with each other as they darted around her mind. Dancing with Priti, seeing Gemma, arguing with Ryan, until her brain finally settled on remembering her dance with Cam. A feeling similar to butterflies accompanied the recollection, except these butterflies didn't stay in her stomach; they fluttered uninvited between her legs, the arousal unwelcome.

She went to the kitchen, knowing that if she didn't eat something, and drink some more water, she'd feel dreadful, and she wanted, needed, to be clearheaded about the evening, about the dance, to be sure she'd remembered it properly. Iris drank a pint of water without pausing, filled her glass, and crossed to the dining room table. She picked up her phone. She had both a missed call and a text message from Cam sent at one thirty a.m. Iris opened the text.

Tried calling. Wanted to talk. Probably best that you're not answering. Of course it is. And my voice mail should be deleted without being listened to. Please do that. Really, Iris, please do that for me. Thanks.

Iris read and reread the text. It contained none of the answers she was looking for about what happened tonight. She guessed that Cam would simply apologize, blame the drink, tell Iris she got carried away, and say she didn't mean anything by it. Maybe with the added hope that they could forget all about it and still be friends.

It was the right thing to say and the right thing to do. Trouble was, Iris couldn't just forget about it. She was deluding herself to think her feelings for Cam were manageable. And she had fallen asleep feeling even more shame than she had expected thanks to Ryan's humiliating comments at the end of the evening.

She'd made herself go back to the dinner table and pretended to be okay for what seemed like the longest thirty minutes of her life before feigning tiredness and leaving. A thirty minutes in which she sat and suffered as Ryan claimed Cam, putting his arms around her, touching her needlessly, showing Cam more affection in that short time slot than he had done all evening.

And Cam let him. She drank coffee and looked blankly across the table, avoiding Iris's eyes and avoiding all conversation. Her only reaction came as Iris stood and put on her coat, announcing her departure. Cam looked at her then, her gaze impossible to read.

Hazel wrapped Iris in a hug and Casey followed suit, and then Iris nodded to the rest of the table and slipped away without saying any kind of good-bye to Cam. And it didn't seem as if Cam even noticed.

Iris put the kettle on to make some tea and popped some bread into the toaster. Sleep wouldn't come now, she was sure of that. She decided to try to embrace the early hour and do some writing.

As the kettle began to boil and Iris fished in a drawer for some painkillers, she thought about the voice mail. If Cam had called intending to explain away what had happened when they danced, to blame it on the drink somehow, why had she asked Iris to delete the voice mail without listening to it? It made no sense. She would surely want Iris to hear it, to hear the excuses.

She felt the increased pulsing of her heart in her chest. Perhaps Cam had been drunk enough to say something else, something that Iris did need to hear. She wanted to do the right thing, to delete the voice mail as Cam had asked her to, but she also wanted to know what it was that Cam had said that she didn't want her to hear.

The toaster popped and Iris added a thick layer of peanut butter to the dry toast. Her own hangover cure, tried and tested too many times. Iris sat at the table to eat it, absentmindedly turning her phone over and over. Iris read the text again. Cam definitely did not want her to listen to the voice mail and Iris knew she should respect that. Maybe there would be a chance for them to talk about what happened on the dance floor, openly and soberly, so the message would become irrelevant. And if there wasn't, would she regret not knowing? Iris couldn't answer her own question.

She dialed the mailbox and, when prompted, selected the Delete all Messages option. She might never know what was on Cam's mind that night. It didn't really matter. If her heart was going to survive how she was feeling about Cam, she needed to never let it happen again. Cam was engaged and had a fiancé who'd reminded Iris of the fact, and, right now, Iris felt like a hurt fool. Someone Cam had picked up to play with in the dark and put down as soon as the lights came on.

And unless she could stop wanting Cam, she couldn't even see a way for them to be friends. That was the thing that made Iris's breath snag in her chest, bringing tears to her eyes.

She logged on to her laptop, deciding to try to write the pain away. She had several unfinished poems sitting on the desktop. She scanned the document names quickly recognizing with a sharp stab that most of them were about Cam in one way or another. She clicked on one called "Green" and started to read back what she had already written. It made her think of Cam's eyes; it was supposed to. She had written of the green of the trees, the leaves and the grass and how falling in love would mean reminders of her everywhere. Iris closed the document, wanting to delete it. Wanting to delete them all, knowing that writing about Cam wouldn't help at all.

She had ignored every one of her instincts and brushed Hazel's warnings aside, but had to accept that if the song had been thirty seconds longer, they would have kissed. The kiss wasn't the problem; they could have explained that away with the drink and been sheepish for a few days. The problem was how much Iris wanted it. She knew they couldn't come back from that. She could only think of a future where they kept their distance. She held her arms across her body tightly, physically holding herself together. It didn't matter whether they had kissed. She had fallen for Cam, and she couldn't just dismiss the dance by pretending she'd been too drunk to know what she was doing. Iris wasn't the kind of person to lie to herself. They could try to talk about it, but Iris had to accept that staying away from Cam was the only way to save herself—and to save Cam—from further hurt.

CHAPTER TWENTY

Oliver fiddled with his camera and adjusted and readjusted his tripod. Cam had been stupidly nervous about asking everyone to pose for the photos, playing down the importance of the article and minimizing her role in pulling it together, but of course, her teammates had loved the idea of a starring role in the Cottoms magazine.

When Cam had finally plucked up the courage to pitch the idea of an article about the football team to Janie in Communications, she'd loved the idea and Cam had been excited to hear her say, in her thick Scottish accent, that she'd even put them on the cover if the team actually won the league.

"We'll need photos to go with the article of course. Color and professionally done. It'd be up to you, but I think it'd be great to have one of you girls in your footie kit." Cam loved the way she rolled her r's. "And one of you looking all smart in your office finery next to it. Och, I love the idea of this." She had given Cam a deadline and a word limit and rung off wishing her luck.

For a few days, Cam had fretted about how to get the photos taken and what it might cost, but Oliver was her savior. He'd overheard her talking to Megan and offered to step in, explaining that his dad ran a photography studio that he'd worked in every summer.

Cam had persuaded him to bring his gear to the match to capture the team in their kit. It was a picture that Janie would love, the professional women of Cottoms muddied and sweating after the exertions of a game. Their easy victory meant no one minded the delay in getting to the pub afterward.

They were top of the table with a game to go and needed only to avoid a heavy defeat in the last game to seal the championship. The atmosphere in the changing room had been boisterous to say the least, and Oliver had looked ready to bolt for the door on several occasions, especially when Hazel had suggested he get a shot of everyone in the shower, teasingly heading over in that direction with Vicki. Eventually, though, they behaved themselves long enough for him to get some great photos.

Everyone had agreed to reassemble for more photos this morning. Cam had asked them to come in their smartest office wear so the contrast with their sweaty sporting selves was more noticeable, and Megan, unable not to assume the role of team captain even when they weren't anywhere near a soccer pitch, was helping Oliver arrange the women, using a copy of one of the photos from the changing room to replicate the arrangement of the group.

It was a great idea, and Cam felt sure Janie would love it. They'd moved the kitchen tables to one side of the room and Oliver had them either sitting on chairs, standing, or leaning on the wall of the dining area looking serious and professional, just like the kind of lawyers you'd trust with your life.

"I don't want to sit down. I'll look better standing," Jess whined.

"You can't, you sat down yesterday and we need the photos to match," Megan said.

Cam looked at her watch. There was still no sign of Iris. She felt a bite of anxiety, the memories of Friday evening pushing through constantly. She had remembered the dance more times than she cared to admit, but now her memory was full of Iris, sitting at the table afterward, looking lost and embarrassed. Cam had been unable to look at her, unable to handle the fact that she had almost kissed her, had very badly wanted to kiss her, while her fiancé was in the same fucking room. And then Iris had rushed off home without Cam managing to say anything, without any kind of good-bye.

The fact that the only contact they'd had since was an awkward hello as Iris arrived late for the match on Sunday made her worry that Iris had listened to her voice mail message and was running a mile in the opposite direction. Cam didn't blame her. After everything Iris had been through with Amanda, she was hardly likely to be anything but pissed that Cam had told her she was developing feelings for her.

She could blame the drink, but that wouldn't be the truth. She'd called because it was something she had wanted to acknowledge, wanted Iris to know, before she'd got sober enough to be scared about saying it.

Iris had texted her Sunday morning to say she couldn't pick Cam up for the match as she had "things to do" and she had avoided the pub afterward, going home immediately after the photos had been taken.

It was obvious Iris was avoiding her, but they needed to talk. She needed to apologize, to try to explain how she was feeling and convince Iris that she could manage her feelings and still be her friend.

"I think we're ready, Cam." Oliver was speaking to her.

"Sure, yeah, okay. I guess so. I mean we're missing someone, but I guess we should carry on." As Cam spoke, the door opened and Iris stepped in. She was greeted with a chorus of comments and catcalls from everyone.

"Late I know, sorry, guys."

Cam felt time slow down. Iris had clearly taken Cam's request seriously when she had asked them all to dress as smartly as possible for the shoot. She was wearing an expensive-looking, fitted suit in bottle green and a geometrically patterned shirt that added an edge to her outfit. Her hair, so often beautifully unruly, looked as if it had been styled, and in the hollow of her neck, she wore a silver moon-shaped pendant on a fine chain. Cam felt her breath catch in her throat. Iris moved into the group. Hazel made space for her to sit next to her as she had done yesterday, and Oliver gestured for Cam to take up her allocated spot.

He settled himself before taking multiple photos, asking people to adjust their posture or lift their head. They whined and whistled at him for taking too many, but the atmosphere was excitable, and when Oliver had finished, they gathered around his camera trying to look at the photos he had taken, full of chatter about how stupid they'd all feel if they lost the championship and the article didn't make it into the magazine.

Cam hadn't dared tell them they might be on the cover. That would be one more surprise if Janie made good on her promise. She moved across to Oliver, pulling him to one side.

"Thanks, Oliver, you've been awesome. Let me know when I can buy you lunch."

"It's just nice to be able to do something to help. And I can't wait to see Liam's face when he sees the magazine."

"Yeah, that'll be something else you'll have to photograph for us," Cam said as Oliver began packing up his equipment.

Iris was talking to Hazel, her body language tense and her gestures betraying a degree of frustration. A couple of paralegals came into the kitchen from the main office, carrying platters of sandwiches, snacks, and cakes that they set out on the counter next to the coffee machine.

"Leftover from an execs meeting that just finished. Mr. Cottom said to leave them here for whoever wants them," the man said as he and his colleague disappeared as quickly as they had come.

A cheer went up and Cam headed across to the group, now hovering over the sandwiches and cakes. Iris popped some cake into her mouth, and Cam couldn't help but smile. She picked up a small triangular sandwich, not really hungry but wanting to join in. Her head was aching—too little sleep over the weekend—and she rubbed her temples.

"Hey, not still hung over surely?" Jess said.

"Erm, no, of course not, just a bit tired."

"You sure? You seemed pretty out of it on Friday. Switching to coffee is a dead giveaway that someone can't hold their drink." Jess sounded a little snarky, and Cam could feel the eyes of the group on her. She couldn't think of a response. Jess was playing mind games as usual. She caught sight of Iris leaning against the wall near the door, watching her curiously. She still said nothing.

"Diane and I went to a club after, but I was still up and out for my usual run on Saturday morning. Maybe Ryan needs to find himself someone with a bit more stamina." She paused. "He's a good laugh. We're gonna miss him when you guys go back to the States." Cam knew that every word was chosen to create trouble. Jess was calling Cam a lightweight and simultaneously suggesting Ryan deserved better. All in a few friendly sentences. She was good—pure poison—but good at it.

"Well, I'm never drinking and dancing again," Hazel said. "I think I was close to maiming Casey at various points."

Cam finally found some words. "Me neither. Friday night's a complete blur. I don't think I've been that drunk in quite a while. Talk about making a fool of myself. Next time I'll stick to soda water." Out of the corner of her eye, Cam caught Iris's sudden movement, as she turned her back on the group and left the room hurriedly. Cam went after her, not caring if it looked obvious. Iris was ahead of her in the long corridor that led to the main office.

"Iris?" she called out. "Iris, wait."

Iris turned slowly, looking in her direction but not really making proper eye contact.

Cam spoke quietly. "I wanted…I wanted to talk about Friday. I didn't get a chance Sunday. You didn't come to the pub. Could we go somewhere, maybe have lunch?" She sounded as unsure as she felt.

Iris studied her. Cam couldn't quite read the expression, but thought she looked guarded, not exactly hostile, but definitely ready to run.

"I'm pretty busy, Cam, sorry."

"Are you mad at me?" She stepped a little closer.

"Are you serious?" Iris didn't wait for her to answer. "I'm not mad at you, no. I'm fine with you touching me, almost kissing me, and then running off into the arms of your fiancé and ignoring me for the rest of the evening. It's not like I went home feeling completely ashamed of myself. And obviously I'm also totally fine with you blaming it all on the drink and letting me know that 'drunk you' did things you regret. I already got the message, Cam. You were drunk, you didn't mean it. I'm not sure we need to labor it over lunch."

"That's not what I meant."

"It's okay, Cam. It's my problem not yours. It's not that I didn't know you were engaged and a little bored. I should have seen it coming." She ran her hand through her hair, the exasperation clear.

"That's not fair." She couldn't bear Iris thinking that way about her, about them, but she couldn't find the words to tell Iris why she was wrong.

"Look, Cam, it's really okay. We had a little too much to drink and got a bit carried away. Luckily nothing happened so let's just forget about it, eh? Make sure it doesn't happen again." Iris sounded calm, but underneath Cam could hear the tension. She moved off toward her office, before turning back to Cam.

"Oh, and I didn't listen to the voice mail."

"I wasn't sure, but after this," she indicated the corridor and the two of them in a sweeping gesture with her hand, "I guessed you hadn't."

"You asked me not to, Cam."

"I know I did, maybe I shouldn't have." Cam sighed.

"You wanted me to listen to it?"

"I don't know what I want, Iris. I'm sorry. I'm a mess right now. And the one person I need to talk to about it, won't let me."

Iris stood silently in front of her.

"He warned me off, you know."

"What?"

"Ryan. He told me to stay away from you, told me I shouldn't try to take advantage of our friendship, of your good nature. He said that I was in danger of making a fool of myself."

"I don't understand." Cam drew in a breath.

"At the dance. At first, I thought maybe he'd seen us and had come over to confront me. But he hadn't. He just wanted to tell me that I shouldn't be pining for you."

"God, Iris, I am so sorry he did that. I had no idea." She moved closer to Iris and her heart hurt as Iris reacted by stepping away.

"Don't be. You're engaged to him. He's right to be possessive. It was just a little embarrassing…whatever. It doesn't matter."

Oliver came past them, nodding a greeting as he headed into the main building. The others would soon follow.

"We can't talk here," Cam said. "If we can't do lunch, let's go somewhere after training. Please."

Iris shook her head. "Sorry, Cam, I just don't think that's a good idea. I actually think we need a bit of distance. We nearly kissed, for God's sake. You're engaged, I'm…we're supposed to be friends." Iris shook her head, turned and left her alone in the corridor, and Cam had no choice but to let her go.

Ryan wouldn't expect Cam to be home so soon after training. She considered calling out to him as she heard him drop his keys onto the table in the hallway and his bag on the floor, but something stopped her. He'd been to Frankfurt and got back late last night. They'd barely seen each other since Sunday. He didn't come into the living room as Cam had expected but instead went straight up the stairs to the bathroom. Cam heard the shower running. She tried to remember how often, when she was home, he showered straight after work. Not often. Her mind was racing. He had been working late a lot recently; he obviously thought Cam was still out or he would have greeted her, but why did he need to shower before she got home?

Like a burglar in her own house, Cam quietly went up the stairs and looked across the landing to where the bathroom door was slightly ajar. A thought darted in and out of her consciousness. Ryan could be having an affair. He could be washing away the evidence. The notion froze Cam to the spot, and at that moment, Ryan emerged from the bathroom in just a towel, still glistening wet. He started slightly when he saw Cam in the doorway and gave her a broad, open smile.

"I wasn't expecting you to be home so early. Did you skip drinks?" He noticed Cam's expression. "You okay? You look like you've seen a ghost." He made a pose like a strongman. "Or is it the sight of my hot sporty physique?" He teased, nodding toward the bag at the foot of the stairs. She could see the handle of a squash racquet poking out of the top. "I played two games and got very sweaty in the process. Thought I'd jump in before you got home and I had to fight you for it." He kissed her on the cheek before padding down the stairs in his towel.

"Want some tea?"

Cam stood and watched him go. His back with its soft dark fuzz, his broad shoulders, and his strong, stocky legs. What did she feel? Not desire. Not even relief that he wasn't cheating on her. What came up instead was anger, at herself, at him, at Iris. She joined him in the kitchen as he set the kettle to boil.

"How was training?" Ryan's tone was light, the question routine. Cam usually answered with a few observations about her game, her fitness, how cruel Megan had been, but the scene earlier with Iris had left her feeling upset and frustrated for reasons she didn't quite want to face up to. Ryan set two mugs on the counter and began hunting through the fridge, looking for something to eat.

"I'm starving. You must be too." He pulled some pastrami and salad vegetables from inside and set to slicing some bread.

"Do you care?" Cam said it quietly but with enough meaning for Ryan to stop what he was doing and look at her directly.

"What do you mean, do I care?" He put down the knife. "What's that supposed to mean?"

"Do you care how training went? Do you care if I'm starving, or are they just questions you feel obliged to ask me? That's what I mean."

"Cam, what's up? Why are you being like this? Come on, I don't want to argue." He stepped toward her as if to take her into an embrace, but Cam stepped back. The movement seemed to rile Ryan more than her words.

"I'm tired and I'm not having another stupid argument with you. Maybe you didn't play well, maybe it's your time of the month. I don't care. I can't face it now. I'm hungry and I'm tired. C'mon, Cam."

The "C'mon, Cam" was, she knew, tacked on to make his words sound less harsh. They seemed to get to this place more often lately and more quickly. What usually happened was that one of them backed down, Ryan went off to check his emails or to turn on the TV, Cam went to cook something, and between them they found a way to keep it from escalating.

"What did you say to Iris?"

Ryan took his sandwich across the room and sat on the couch. He took a large bite of his sandwich and looked back at her as he chewed.

"So that's what's eating you. Has she been complaining to you about me? Well, you know what, I don't care. She had it coming. Am I supposed to just sit around and watch her ogle my fiancé? I don't think so. If she was a guy, I'd probably have punched her by now."

Cam couldn't believe he was being such a jerk. "What did you say to her?" She wanted to hear it from Ryan, to make him say it.

"Go ask her." He looked away, reaching across the coffee table for the remote control.

"I would if she was speaking to me, but since she's not, I can't. And she's not speaking to me because of you." It wasn't true but she didn't care.

Ryan kept eating his sandwich, sitting on the couch in a towel, showing her complete indifference. How had they come to this?

"Look, if she's that sensitive about it, it's probably because I hit a nerve. She'd have brushed it off otherwise." He shrugged.

"My friendship with Iris is the only thing I have here and you've gone out of your way to ruin it for me. I don't know why you'd do that to me. It's almost as if you're jealous." He turned to her. There was a flash of annoyance, before he controlled himself.

"I'm not, trust me. I'm just being protective. Maybe you'd prefer a fiancé who doesn't give a fig about other people lusting after you, but this one does. She might be your friend but she's also a lesbian. A lesbian with a reputation for screwing around. And you're not exactly streetwise…" He stopped himself from saying more. "You should just thank me for saying something, for making sure she's clear on the rules of engagement." He paused again. "And while we're talking about talking," he sneered slightly as he said the words, "let's talk about us for a change. Why we haven't set a date for our wedding, why we don't have sex anymore, why you seem to prefer spending time with everyone but me. I'm here, Cam, any time you really want to talk. Maybe now that Iris isn't speaking to you, you might find the time." He turned back to his sandwich.

Cam felt her chest tighten and the room close in. She put out a hand to catch the back of one of the dining chairs. This was impossible. Maybe he was right and they needed to talk about those things, but right now she couldn't see past Iris and her need to somehow make things right between them. She wasn't sure she had anything left for Ryan, not words and not even feelings.

She sat down with her laptop at the dining room table and busied herself putting the finishing touches to the article. Later, she would call her sister and try to figure out what the hell she should do.

CHAPTER TWENTY-ONE

Hey, beautiful, something looks good." Iris pinched a square of feta cheese from the chopping board that Casey was bent over, nodding approvingly at the taste of it. She glanced across at Hazel, who was arranging beers in a large ice-filled bucket.

"Why is the birthday girl wearing tropical beach shorts? Thirty is a bit early for a midlife crisis isn't it?"

"What can I say? She's in a barbecue mood. She only has to smell the charcoal and those shorts come out. Rain or shine."

Hazel walked over and handed Iris a beer. They clinked bottles. "You're completely overdressed, mate. The invitation clearly said barbecue, and that means beachwear."

Iris ran a hand over her shirt and jeans. "I've got my bikini on under here. When the time's right, y'know." She mimicked the motion of pulling down a giant zipper.

"Beth is going to love that. Though I kind of promised her a sensitive poet rather than a stripper, but I'm sure she'll adapt." Hazel sipped her beer.

"Oh no, I completely forgot about Beth." Iris groaned.

"Hey, you agreed I could invite her. You said it might be time to start dipping your toe back into the lady pool."

"I think we all know that I would never say such a thing."

"Okay, I might be paraphrasing, but you did say you didn't mind if I invited her." She put her hand on Iris's arm. "She's a writer. And really cool. You'll like her."

Iris pushed a hand through her hair. She'd completely forgotten she had agreed to meet Beth. She'd said yes just to make Hazel shut up.

And because she needed to stop thinking about Cam, to stop missing her.

"You sold me to Beth as a poet? Nice one, Haze. No pressure there. Maybe once she sees I am completely without any kind of banter, she'll just think it's a sign of my moody creative genius."

"You can manage without us for a bit can't you, love?" Hazel took Iris by the arm as she addressed Casey.

The lounge had already been readied for the party. The armchairs and couches pushed against the walls, the long dining table covered in rows of glasses, bottles of wine, and plates of nibbles. Hazel sat on the long leather couch and invited Iris to sit with her.

"Aren't we supposed to be doing helping stuff?"

"We will. I just wanted this beer before we got started on the chores." Hazel sounded a little shifty and Iris spotted it straight away.

"What's going on?"

"C'mon, Iris, you know we need to talk. You need to talk. About Cam. What the hell is going on with you two lately? The atmosphere at work sucks. Everyone's noticed."

Iris needed to talk to someone; she just wasn't sure it was Hazel. But she probably wasn't going to survive another evening with Cam and Ryan if she didn't speak to someone. She sighed and put down her beer in the space between her feet, leaning forward so that her elbows were resting on her knees and she didn't have to face Hazel.

"I don't know where to start and I know you're going to tell me I'm an idiot. You were right, okay? I denied it, but I wasn't being honest. I do have feelings for her. I know I should have kept my distance and cooled it down once I knew I had feelings for her, but I didn't. I tried, well, I kind of tried, but I couldn't stay away, and she wouldn't let me." She turned to Hazel.

"In the beginning, it was just attraction. I mean, you've seen her, she's beautiful."

Hazel nodded.

"But then I got to know her and we got close and, well, she's just great and my feelings got stronger, they changed and now I've—" She stopped herself from saying it, not able to face up to having fallen for Cam. "I've gotten too close and I've made a fool of myself and I'm hurting. I thought—" Her voice cracked. "I thought it was all me, that I was wanting things to be there that weren't, that I had to be careful with her in case I did something I shouldn't. And then, at the dance—"

She stopped. The memory of it even now, days later, causing her to flush, making the muscles in her stomach tighten.

"At the dance, we almost kissed. We were dancing, and she touched me, she almost kissed me."

Hazel swore under her breath.

"And it's ruined everything between us. It's not just that it's wrong and I shouldn't want it—it's that, despite that, I wanted it to mean something to her. But it didn't. She was drunk and she was bored and she was playing with me. I hate to say it, but maybe you were right about her."

Hazel put her arm around Iris's shoulders. "I guessed it must have been something like that, but I'm sorry, I didn't really want to be right, mate."

"Yeah, you did." Iris nudged Hazel, trying to lighten the mood. It was more than she could manage.

"And the worst of it is that he knows, Ryan knows. Not what happened, thank God, but he's guessed that I have feelings for her. I think Jess said something to him about me and Cam a while back, and he made sure to warn me off at the dance. He told me I was embarrassing myself by pining for her." She couldn't help a small sob escaping, she felt so miserable. "It was so humiliating, Haze. All I could do was deny it. What could I have said? She's the one who had her hands all over me on the dance floor. I couldn't do that to her. I didn't say anything. I told him he was wrong and then sat and watched him put his hands all over her for my benefit until I went home understanding just how much of an idiot I've been."

"Have you talked to her about it at all?"

"No, I've been avoiding her. She wants to, but what's the point. She left me a voice mail the night of the dance but then texted and asked me to delete it without listening."

"And you did?"

"I did."

"So you don't know what she said."

"I don't, but I do know that when Jess asked her about the evening, she made a point of telling everyone that she'd drunk too much and regretted making a fool of herself. I was standing right there so her message was pretty clear."

"If she just called to say she'd made a drunken mistake why would she tell you to delete it?" Casey spoke up from the doorway.

"That's what I thought at first, but then I figured that maybe she hadn't said it in a very nice way and she didn't want to be rude."

"Yeah, exactly." Hazel shot a warning look at Casey.

"And you really haven't talked about it since?" Casey asked.

"She tried to get me to go to lunch with her, said she wanted to explain. I just said I was busy. I've avoided the pub so I don't have to see her. I can't be around her right now. I don't want her to apologize and tell me we can only be friends, and she shouldn't have let things get out of hand. I know it's true, but I can't bear to hear her say it. And, anyway, I can't just go back to being her friend, not feeling like this." Her voice caught with the effort of keeping her feelings damped down.

"And, yeah, I know she's coming tonight with him, and I'm going to have to watch them be together. I mean, I don't even know whether she's told him. I don't really know how I'm going to cope."

"You'll cope by being polite but mostly ignoring them, having a few more beers and letting Beth—an actual available woman with zero baggage—charm you for an evening. And we'll be here. If she says anything, if he dares to say anything, I'll throw them both out. I don't care how good she is at football." Hazel was emphatic.

Casey shook her head at Hazel. She crossed to the couch and ruffled Iris's hair. "And if a forced blind date with Beth is a little much for you to take on right now," Casey said with a pointed look in Hazel's direction, "you can hide in the kitchen with me, honey. There'll be food, my delightful company, and lots of washing up to do...and I probably should have said this earlier, but Cam texted last night to say that Ryan isn't coming. I didn't think to mention it till now, sorry."

Iris felt something like relief. She didn't want to face Cam, but she especially didn't want to face Cam with Ryan in tow, with him thinking he had put Iris in her place, with him seeing Cam and Iris being so weird around each other. She didn't like him but he didn't deserve to be in the middle of this mess. Iris knew that better than anyone.

"Now, there's work to be done, you two, stop slacking." Casey looked at the floor and frowned. "And one of you needs to vacuum in here before the guests start arriving. It's a mess."

Iris put up a hand to volunteer. The place looked immaculate, but she would happily run a vacuum around and take the time to think about just how she was going to manage things with Cam. They worked together, they played together—if she got through tonight, she knew there'd just be another one and another one to get through, but what could she do?

When she goes back to America, it'll be a lot easier. Iris bent over as if winded at the thought. The idea of never seeing Cam again hurt more than the pain she felt at having let her feelings fuck up their friendship.

Casey came into the room with the vacuum as Iris righted herself. Casey put it down next to them, pulling Iris into a hug. Iris buried her head in Casey's shoulder.

"Hey, don't tell Hazel I said this, but I'm not sure that Cam's call was to tell you she made a mistake. I've seen the way she is around you, Iris, and I mean sober as well as drunk, and, well, I dunno, but I don't think she's without feelings for you, honey."

Iris groaned. It was all too much.

"I'm sorry—shouldn't have said it. I know it doesn't really help you any. I just hate to see you feeling so foolish. There might be more to it, more to her, than you think is all."

It was all Iris could do not to turn around and leave. She couldn't bear the idea of letting herself feel hope. She had no right.

"Do you really think so?"

Casey nodded and Iris tried to make herself believe it, but the twin memories of Cam sitting with Ryan after the dance and then talking about making a fool of herself to Jess just seemed too fresh.

She bent down to pick up the cord for the vacuum.

"Hazel's warning me off and you're urging me on. You guys are quite the double act. Ever thought of comedy?" She made herself smile.

"We did, but neither of us wanted to be the straight man." Casey took a bow and retreated back into the kitchen.

Iris plugged in the vacuum. None of it mattered. Cam was in a relationship, and Iris had plenty of her own reasons for not getting in the middle of that. She switched on the vacuum, happy to lose herself in a menial task for a while.

❖

Iris finished her third beer in double quick time. She went outside to claim a can of Diet Coke from the ice-filled barrel in which they were floating, knowing that she couldn't drink any more if she was going to drive home. And knowing that, regardless of whether she was driving or not, the one thing she couldn't afford tonight was to not be sober.

The chairs in the garden weren't quite as full as those in the lounge, but there were still plenty of hardy souls outside, cradling wine glasses and balancing plates of food on their knees, willing to brave the falling temperatures now that the sun had set.

Iris saw Hazel waving at her, her body language suggesting that she wanted to dance. Iris shook her head. She pointed inside the house and mouthed the word "Beth" in Hazel's direction, earning an enthusiastic thumbs-up as Hazel waved her back inside.

Iris was lying of course. Beth was currently in a corner of the living room, chatting to Amanda and had been for most of the past hour. The two of them looked like they were getting on famously. Iris had introduced herself to Beth when she arrived and they had chatted briefly, but she was in the wrong mood to get to know someone new. She had excused herself after a few minutes, hopefully without being too rude, and then hidden upstairs for a bit, expecting that Beth would have started to talk to someone else by the time she reappeared. And she had—Amanda. If it worked out for them, Amanda could thank her later.

Iris kept telling herself she was here to see her friends, to mingle and to forget about Cam, but neither her body nor her mind was listening, and she knew from the way she remained acutely aware of who was coming and going that really all she was doing was waiting for her.

When Cam finally arrived, she was on the other side of the living room, chatting to Oliver. Cam was alone, and Casey greeted her warmly, taking the wine and the square cake box Cam held out before shepherding her into the kitchen.

She looked stunning in a dark purple dress. Her hair was loose, her makeup light. Cam reappeared from the kitchen and scanned the room. When their gazes connected, Cam lifted a hand and gave her a hesitant wave. Iris nodded and raised her hand in a matching gesture. Her insides were in knots. She turned back to Oliver, realizing that he had been staring too. Of course he had, Cam looked incredible.

As Cam crossed to the drinks table and poured herself a wine, Iris tried to stop her eyes from following but found that it was impossible, as impossible as the first time she'd seen Cam in the changing room, all those months ago.

"It'll annoy the hell out of Liam if you guys win the league. I really hope you do."

She brought her attention back to the conversation. "Yeah, me too. Everyone has trained so hard, played so well. Megan deserves it more than most for everything she puts into the team."

"And Cam of course," Oliver said, "I mean, she's been the best player by miles this season. No offense meant."

"None taken. Cam's been great all season." Iris could see Jess headed over toward them. She couldn't face Jess, not tonight. She said a quick good-bye to Oliver and turned away, almost bumping into Amanda.

"Hey, how are you? I keep trying to catch up with you but you keep disappearing. Anyone would think you didn't like parties." Amanda's voice contained a hint of a tease.

"I've been around. You've been keeping yourself busy with Beth."

"I know. She's really nice. Said she didn't really know anyone so seemed happy for the company." Amanda blushed.

"Don't be so modest. I'm sure she's more than happy to spend time with you whether or not she knows anyone."

"She said she was here to meet someone actually—sort of a blind date—but they didn't seem very interested. Maybe their loss is my gain."

Iris couldn't hide the guilt she felt. Amanda knew her well and caught it immediately.

"You?" She laughed. "No way. Oh, that's just brilliant." She touched Iris on the arm. "Hey, should I be backing off?"

"God, no. I mean she seems lovely, it's just that…"

It's just that I think I've fallen in love with our star midfielder? It scored well for accuracy but low on sensible. *It's just that every time I let someone get close to me, people get hurt.* Also pretty accurate but scoring a little high on the self-pity scale. She shook her head, shook the thoughts away.

"It's just that I'm not looking for someone right now." She couldn't help how sad she sounded.

"I know what you mean. I know it looks like I'm stealing your blind date." She smiled. "But being single seems so wonderfully uncomplicated sometimes." Amanda sipped her wine.

Iris was very single and it didn't feel uncomplicated at all, but she couldn't say that to Amanda. She just nodded.

"There has to be so much more than sexual chemistry, surely?" Cam was chatting with Vicki about whether she was going to try for the reunion that Harry was pushing for, but she was also talking to herself about Iris, and about Ryan. "I mean, you have to get on, have things in common, make each other feel good."

"Yeah, totally. It's a mystery to me that she's so self-centered in life but so amazing in bed. Usually when someone is a dick and isn't interested in you, it shows up in the bedroom, but she's the opposite. It's really confusing." Vicki had just admitted that, although they had ended their relationship, she and Harry were still hooking up and having "incredible sex." Vicki's facial expression as she said it, already convincing Cam not to ask any supplementary questions.

Cam had found herself complaining about Ryan to Vicki. She'd said he was self-centered and not really interested in her or her life, that she wasn't even getting the sexual benefits that Vicki was. She felt guilty for being so harsh. He wasn't that bad. And she hadn't been honest enough to tell Vicki that she wasn't even sure she wanted him that way anymore. That was part of the problem. And now, knowing that she wanted Iris, had probably wanted Iris for longer than she had let herself admit, she knew she was in trouble. She tuned back in to Vicki who was still looking for advice about what to do.

She wondered what her answer would be if someone asked her if she and Ryan should stay together. Months ago, even weeks ago, she'd have answered in the positive without even thinking about it, but now she wasn't so sure. She blamed him for being so disinterested, but he had offered to come with her tonight, had seemed like he actually wanted to spend the evening with her for once, and she had lied and said that partners weren't invited. Their lack of connection, the drifting apart, she just couldn't pretend it was all his fault.

Iris had avoided her all week and they needed to talk. Cam knew it was all on her. The dance, the voice mail, the way she'd handled herself in the office afterward. She wanted…no, she needed…to try to fix things with Iris and the only way she knew to do that was to finally be honest about everything and hope they could find a way through it. She just didn't know yet what getting through it meant.

"I'm too fed up to party." Vicki got up. "I'm heading home."

Cam gave Vicki a hug before she trudged off, feeling guilty that she hadn't done a better job of listening to her. Her attention drifted, and she kept checking to see what Iris was doing and who she was talking to. It felt to Cam as if opposing magnets were working to keep them apart, keep them in opposite corners of every room, moving Iris away every time Cam got close enough to try to start a conversation. The pain of being so close to Iris and yet them seeming so far apart was stronger than she expected.

It was properly dark now, and there was nowhere near enough light from the patio to illuminate the whole length of the garden. It suited Iris. She had found a spot on a bench, sitting within a wrought iron gazebo, almost at the bottom of the garden. The urge to get away from everyone had been overwhelming. She had said her good-byes to Beth. They'd exchanged phone numbers, without any real expectation that either of them would call.

"Hey."

Iris looked up to see Cam, buttoned up in her coat, standing a few feet away. She felt both the pull of her and the impulse to run away. Cam smiled at her, and Iris hated the way her body reacted, undermining her intention to play it cool.

"You're pretty brave sitting out here. They don't even have patio heaters. Maybe I could go get you a blanket to fall asleep under."

As jokes went, it was pretty lame, and Iris couldn't believe that Cam thought they were ready to joke about things. She felt anger bubbling under the hurt.

"I was waiting for a chance to talk to you, but you missed drinks again on Wednesday, and tonight, well, it kinda feels like you've been avoiding me," Cam said softly.

"I haven't. I've just been hanging out with my friends. I do have other people to talk to you know." Iris wanted Cam to feel the sting of the comment.

"Sure you do." Cam's expression hardened. "And there's always Beth of course. You guys looked like you were swapping numbers. I'm confused about you dating again though. I thought you 'liked' being single, I thought that was 'your thing.' You told me it was, like, a dozen times."

Iris hated this, hated them arguing, but she couldn't stop herself. Cam had hurt her.

"Yeah, well, maybe I figured I should try and spend some time with women who are available and not just using me as a plaything because they're bored and drunk." As soon as she said the words, she felt bad. She put up her hands in a gesture of apology.

"Look, Cam, I'm sorry. There was no need for that." Iris pushed her hands through her hair. "And I don't want to argue with you. We don't need to. We don't even have anything we need to talk about really. Bottom line: you got drunk and a little carried away with a friend and you regret it. You should. You have a fiancé and he doesn't deserve you fucking him about like that. I know it happens but it shouldn't. And I know it didn't really mean anything and I should be able to just forget about it, but I can't." She finally took a breath. "Because if I'm honest, maybe I actually wanted it to mean a little more to you than it did and I feel crappy about that for lots of reasons. But that's my problem. I should have managed my feelings better." She wasn't exactly telling the truth, but she wasn't lying either. She was guarding herself from Cam while also trying to be honest enough to help Cam understand why she was upset.

"I hate your version of what happened, Iris. It's bullshit." Cam had her fists clenched at her sides. "I'm not some bored housewife, fooling around with a friend for a bit of excitement."

"Aren't you? I think that's exactly what you are. But it's my fault not yours." Iris kept her tone gentle. "Hazel warned me not to get too close for this very reason, and I didn't listen. We got close and I let myself become attracted to you. I let things get out of hand. I'm sure I'll survive the embarrassment. I just need a little time. But please don't expect me to talk to you about it."

"You're attracted to me." It was a statement from Cam, not a question.

"You really didn't know?"

"I mean, I thought maybe, when we danced, y'know, you looked at me, you touched me, it was like…" Cam started to speak and faltered. "But I thought it was because you were drunk not that you were… attracted to me. You've always been so inscrutable—"

"Well, okay, now you know and that's why I need some distance. I need to get over this silly crush and how stupid I feel. It may take some time." She muttered the last five words to herself.

"I'm attracted to you too." Cam said it quietly, her eyes lifting uncertainly to meet Iris's gaze. The words landed like arrows in Iris's chest, but before she could react or respond, Hazel called her name from just inside the house.

"Come and say good-bye to Megan." She was being summoned. Did Hazel know she was here with Cam? Maybe she was attempting a rescue effort. If so, her timing was perfect. And yet totally crappy.

Cam looked toward the door. "Iris, please, let's go somewhere and talk. I know this is hard but we…we can't just walk away from each other. Please."

Iris wanted to go with Cam, she wanted so badly to talk about this, even as she knew what a terrible idea it was. She took in a breath and let it out again.

"The car is parked at the bottom of the street, left when you come out of the house. If you go now, I'll follow on in a few minutes. Let me say good-bye to Megan, and to Hazel and Casey." Iris wasn't at all sure why she'd agreed.

"You don't want to be seen leaving with me."

"I'm sorry," Iris said, holding Cam's gaze, trying to look calmer than she felt.

"It's okay." Cam reached as if to touch Iris on the arm. Iris stepped backward leaving Cam's hand in midair. She looked hurt. "I was just going to say thank you."

"Just give me five minutes."

Cam nodded and walked off ahead of Iris back toward the house.

When Iris approached her car, a few minutes later, Cam was leaning against the passenger side door. The car was parked under a streetlight, and as she got closer, the sight of Cam waiting for her made her heart race. "Where shall we go?" Iris spoke first.

"I don't mind," Cam murmured her response.

"It's not too late for a pub." Iris didn't want to drink, but she couldn't think of anywhere else. "We could be back in Hampstead by ten and stop in at the Black Sheep?" Cam nodded, her eyes cast down.

They got in the car and Cam turned to her.

"I'm not toying with you, Iris. You couldn't be more wrong."

Iris swallowed, her throat full of words she wanted to say but couldn't. She put on her seat belt, fumbling slightly. Cam had sat with her in this car so many times, talking and laughing as they grew close. But tonight, if they couldn't find a way to get past their attraction, to get back to being friends, it would probably be the last time.

CHAPTER TWENTY-TWO

The Black Sheep was tucked away on the edge of the Heath and they settled themselves at a corner table. Iris went to the bar. Cam's mind was racing. She had asked Iris to let them talk about what had happened, about what they were feeling, but she didn't really know what to say. And she kept coming back to wanting to tell Iris about Mia. She couldn't help but think it would probably make things worse, but she also knew that, if she didn't, Iris would never take her feelings seriously. Maybe they couldn't do a thing about the way they felt, but Cam really needed Iris to know that she hadn't just been fooling with her.

Iris came back to the table with two tumblers of clear liquid. "Lime and sodas. Thought we should stay sober." She put them down and looked at Cam uncertainly.

Cam ached for her when she looked like that. She was beautiful of course, but she also seemed vulnerable and a little lost, and it was impossible for Cam not to feel responsible.

She angled her chair so that it was a little closer to the fire. "Maybe we can swap places when you start to smell my flesh burn." Cam picked up her glass. She was trying to make things less tense. "To cozy British pubs." She touched her glass to Iris's, feeling a little feverish.

Iris sat back in her chair and lifted her face to the beamed ceiling, her eyes closed. If they weren't indoors, in the half light of a pub, Cam would swear she was holding her face to the sun, hoping to catch some rays.

She waited for Iris to bring her attention back to the table, trying to find the courage and the right words to say what she needed to and convince her that they could have these feelings and still stay in each other's lives. Her anxiety heightened by the sense that, if she got this wrong, it would cost her Iris. Iris was about to walk away, and Cam had to let her know there was no need.

"I am so sorry about the dance. I was a little drunk…"

Iris shifted in her seat. "Don't—"

Cam put up a hand. "I'm not blaming that. I knew what I was doing. I wanted to do what I was doing. The drinking just stopped me understanding how wrong it was, but…" she hesitated. "I wanted to kiss you. And, if you'd listened to my voice mail you'd have heard me say that, and also heard me admit that somewhere along the way I caught feelings for you—"

"I don't think we should—"

"Iris, I know you don't want to talk about this, but I have to. I can't let you just walk away from our friendship without trying to fix things, without trying to make you understand. There are things I haven't told you, and I don't know why I'm making such a fuss about it, why I've taken so long to tell you. You've told me lots about you, and I want you to know this about me. It doesn't change things, not really, it's just that—" Cam stopped.

"There's no pressure from me, Cam. Whatever it is, you can tell me or not tell me. I'm not sure what difference it'll make anyway."

"It might. It might help you take me more seriously when I tell you that I'm not just some stupid straight girl crushing on her best friend."

"Cam—"

"Just let me tell you, Iris." She leaned forward. She thought she could trust Iris and had to hope that she wouldn't be judged. And even if she was, Cam still wanted Iris to know.

"At college, I wrote for the student newspaper. I was a journalism major. They advertised for writers, and I figured it'd be great experience. The paper wasn't exactly popular—it was a bit of a shitty gig to be honest—but I didn't care, it meant I could call myself a journalist and I felt proud of myself. We were pushing out a paper full of arty reviews and pointless stories of campus life, but now and then we'd stumble over a proper story about college funds being misspent or how professors were neglecting their students, and I loved it. The editor—Mia—was this super confident, super accomplished student who was a real player. I mean player as in women falling at her feet, not player as in soccer." Cam gave Iris a wry smile.

"Every other Wednesday, after we put each edition to bed in the early hours of the morning, she would head off into the night on her motorbike with her latest girlfriend on the back." Iris raised an eyebrow.

"I know, I know, a motorbike, leathers, all of it. Ridiculous but also, well, kind of sexy." Cam shrugged. "I used to try not think about the evening she was having and how badly it would contrast with mine. I always went home alone, and if I was feeling decadent, I might have a beer in front of the TV to unwind. I had friends, but I wasn't really dating. Sometimes guys would show an interest, but I couldn't really get excited enough about any of them to actually date.

"Meantime, I was feeling closer and closer to Mia and more and more bothered by those other women. I was surprised I was jealous but the feeling was unmistakable.

"And then at some point, I noticed that when we finished work on the paper, rather than zooming off into the night, Mia would wait for me. She started to offer me a ride home. We lived on the same campus so, once I'd admitted I didn't have plans, it was hard to say no. Not that I wanted to. I loved being on the back of that bike, the feeling of being able to put my arms around her." Cam watched Iris's eyes widen.

"We started hanging out, outside of doing the paper, and one night, after she took me home, she said that she was sorry if it made things a bit awkward, but she'd fallen for me, and while she could keep being my friend if that's what I wanted, she actually wanted more than that. I was so surprised, I just hadn't seen it coming." Cam blinked then and looked up to see Iris gazing at her.

"I wanted to tell her that I felt the same way, but I couldn't. I wasn't brave enough. I said I was confused—which wasn't really true—and needed time to think.

"The next time we saw each other, it was difficult. I couldn't see past the declaration she'd made, and I knew I wanted her but I was terrified at the same time. I mean, I'd never slept with a woman. We passed a few agonizing days and then arrived at Wednesday. After submitting the paper to the publishers, Mia suggested going for some food, but I knew I couldn't eat so I said I wasn't hungry and asked her to take me home. I know she must have felt like she'd blown it, but I just couldn't seem to find the right way to tell her she hadn't.

"When we got home, I didn't know what to do. I had all these feelings and I didn't want her to leave, but I couldn't seem to speak so I leaned across and kissed her. It was the only thing I could think of.

"We had sex that night. It was my first time with a woman and so kind of awkward but also kind of great." She sipped her soda, feeling embarrassed, guessing that Iris hadn't expected this.

"After a few weeks together, Mia wanted me to meet her friends and to meet my friends, but for some reason I found that very difficult to do." Cam stopped talking and started to pick at the edge of the table.

"Go on."

"It was all so new to me. I'd never thought of myself as a lesbian or bisexual, or whatever, and I struggled to imagine telling people I was. My mom was...is...conservative about most issues, but she's at her worst when it comes to gay things. I hated that I let her affect the way I thought about me and Mia, but I was younger then and it wasn't until much later that I understood just how much I must have internalized some of her crap."

Cam lifted her eyes to address Iris directly. "I know you came out at seventeen and you probably think all this makes me a ridiculous coward, but this is who I was back then."

Iris tried to say something, but Cam held up a hand, knowing she had to get to the end of this before she lost the courage.

"Anyway, Mia really wanted us to spend Thanksgiving together. She knew we couldn't be 'out' about our relationship but said she really wanted to meet my family anyway. We'd been dating a few months, it seemed reasonable, and I was convinced I could pass her off as a friend.

"It was a disaster." Cam couldn't keep the hurt from her voice. She swallowed and made herself carry on. "I think my mom figured Mia was a lesbian almost straight away—I mean, she fit my mom's stereotype after all—but it hadn't dawned on her that we were dating. Why would it? She'd only seen me with guys and I'd introduced Mia as a friend.

"But we were careless. We thought my mom had gone shopping, we were making out and my mom walked in and caught us. It was awful." Cam took in a breath.

"She blamed Mia for corrupting me. She blamed Chicago, she blamed the fact I was at a liberal arts college, she blamed everything and everyone but me. I tried to tell her it wasn't like that, that I was just as responsible, that it was something I had wanted, but it was like she couldn't bear to hear me say it, she just brushed it away. She was paying my college fees and she...she just stopped. She said I needed to come home and stop messing about with the kind of people I was hanging about with there and that it wouldn't matter if I didn't graduate because she hadn't gone to college and it hadn't hurt her. She said I'd thank her for it one day."

Cam had tears in her eyes at the memory of it, and Iris put a tentative hand on her arm. She let herself enjoy the touch for a long moment and then pulled away, rubbing away the tears.

"I know I should have stood up for myself, for Mia, and for my career, but I didn't. I didn't see that I had any choice but to do what she wanted—I couldn't afford to pay my own fees after all—but it left me feeling like I was the worst kind of coward. I was scared of her disapproval and scared to be the person I wanted to be."

Cam looked at Iris, waiting for her to speak. She could see her trying to process what Cam had just told her.

"Shall I get us another drink?" Iris stood.

"Don't rush off, Iris. You're gonna leave me thinking you can't bear to sit here with me now that I've shown you how pathetic I really am." Cam could practically hear the alarm bells going off in Iris's head. She looked like she was ready to bolt.

"Not pathetic, Cam. Not at all. Please don't say that. I...my head is so full of questions. I just don't know what to say."

"Ask me. That's the point of us being here. We need to talk about this stuff." Cam sounded surer than she felt.

Iris sat down. "How did you end up with Ryan after all that with Mia?"

Iris was biting the inside of her lip, her hands gripping her knees and Cam could only imagine the effort she was making to stay seated.

"I broke up with Mia, obviously. It was humiliating for us both and I couldn't expect her to put up with my family, with how little I had to offer her. And I felt like I had no choice but to leave college. I went home to Seattle, left journalism behind, and got a boring job in finance that wouldn't remind me of any of it. And I hated myself for giving in so easily. I hid for a long while, and then threw myself into dating. Into dating guys of course. I had dated guys before Mia. I mean, before Mia I didn't know I was anything other than one hundred percent heterosexual. And after Mia, well, I felt that I'd proved I wasn't ready to love women so I decided to go back to where it all seemed so comfortable, to where my mom wanted me to be.

"Ryan was a friend of a friend. We hung out as part of a group and we got along okay. Eventually, he asked me out and we started dating. I wasn't sure at first and then, well, I guess I grew to love him and we found a way to be happy together. At least for a while anyway."

Cam couldn't help but connect with some of the humiliation she'd felt at the time.

"I think it must have been an awful decision for you to let someone go that you loved. I'm sorry and I really appreciate you telling me." Iris sounded so formal, so cold, and Cam hated hearing it. She stood up, needing to compose herself. "I'll go and get the drinks." She rushed away from the table.

Iris couldn't stop thinking about the story Cam had told her. She now understood Cam's relationship with Ryan. He was Cam's safe harbor when she'd needed one. A port in a storm, and even more importantly, someone Cam's mother would never disapprove of. She sighed imagining just how painful it must have been for Cam to have a mom like that, and was even more grateful that her own father had loved her and her sexuality unconditionally.

Cam came back to the table with their soda waters and sat with a small shiver. The fire was dying and she slipped her coat back over her shoulders. They were silent together. Cam traced her fingers around the rim of her glass.

"So I guess that's a kind of long-winded way of telling you I'm not straight. I mean we both have to face that fact. I wasn't straight when I loved Mia, and the way I feel about you—wanting to see you all the time, wanting to kiss you—means I'm not exactly straight now."

Iris reeled at Cam's admission that she had feelings for her, that stone cold sober she still wanted to kiss her. She wanted to talk to Cam about it, to talk about her own feelings for Cam, but she made herself stop and tried to focus.

"Okay, let's agree that you're not straight." She shrugged and Cam smiled shyly at her. Iris took in a breath as she felt her heart skip. She had fallen in love with Cam. She wasn't prepared to admit it to anyone but herself, but that meant the stakes were too high for her to leave things hanging.

"It doesn't really change anything. In fact, it makes it worse. We can't—"

Cam interrupted. "It doesn't change everything, but it changes something. I'm just trying to tell you I'm not some stupid straight girl crushing on you in a way I don't understand. I know what these feelings are. I'm a grownup and I've spent a lot of grownup time with you that's convinced me that you're wonderful, and I know I did the wrong thing at the dance, but that was because I have all these feelings for you and I wanted to kiss you, but I only let myself do anything about it when I was drunk." Cam slowed her speech. "And I still want to kiss you—so damn much—and I know I'm not supposed to but I want us to at least be honest about what's going on. If we're not honest, I don't know how we can get past this, and I want to, because I miss you and I want to find a way to keep you in my life."

Cam slumped back in her chair, and Iris felt her resolve weakening. It would be so easy to say yes to her, to pretend they could find a way past this, but Iris didn't trust either of them now. Cam's admission that she had feelings for Iris put them in even more in danger of doing something they shouldn't. Now she just had to find the words to break both their hearts.

"Cam, you're engaged, to a man you've been with for more than four years and a man you've always said you're planning to marry. You sat by his side a week ago at the dance as his fiancé talking about your wedding venue. It doesn't matter if I have feelings for you, it doesn't matter if you loved Mia five years ago, or even if you want to kiss me right now." She couldn't help the twist in her insides as she acknowledged Cam's desire for her. "You're not in a position to be kissing anyone but Ryan, and you know that or you wouldn't have run back to him the way you did that night." Iris said the words in a rush, feeling the truth of them land deep and hard in her own chest. Cam had nothing to offer her and she had no right to expect her to.

Knowing about Mia made it clear to Iris that Cam could love a woman—and her body couldn't help but react to that—but it didn't change a thing. They couldn't feel like this about each other and expect their friendship to survive.

"It's late. We should probably go." Iris said the words as she stood. There was no point carrying on, no point telling Cam how she felt about her. It would only make things worse.

"Iris…don't…it's got to be possible for us to at least stay friends. I want us to be in each other's lives. I can fight these feelings if you can—" Cam stopped when Iris held up her hand.

"We should go. Ryan will be wondering where you are." Iris felt actual physical pain in her chest as she said the words. The look on Cam's face said she wasn't doing much better. This was hard for both of them.

Cam picked up her bag and Iris waited for her to pass by before following her out of the door.

Outside the pub, they leaned on Iris's car and looked up at the sky. It was jet-black and full of bright stars. London's pollution meant the stars were rarely that visible in the sky, but the Heath was one of the few places where it was possible, on a clear night like this, to get a really good view. Iris had already unlocked the doors to her car, but neither of them was making a move to climb inside and begin the process of going home. The drive would take barely a couple of minutes along the main road to Cam's house, and Iris wondered if, as she had, Cam had figured out that this was it. This would most likely be the last time they would be able to be together like this, just the two of them. Their friendship could not survive the feelings they now knew they had for each other and the fact of Cam's relationship with Ryan meant the feelings couldn't take them anywhere. Iris felt numb, but she knew that the pain would follow as surely as the sunrise.

They had stopped staring at the sky and were now just looking at each other, neither of them speaking. Iris knew that if she moved forward just a step, it would be all that was needed. The momentum, their desire for each other, would carry them together into a kiss, the kiss they had both wanted on the dance floor, the kiss Cam had admitted she still wanted. They could kiss against this car and then go their separate ways, neither of them having to talk about it ever again.

Iris wanted to sit with Cam in the car, wanted them to make out like carefree teenagers, wanted Cam to reach under her clothes and caress her like a lover would, to allow Iris to do the same. She wondered if these thoughts were visible to Cam in the dark of the car park, wondered what she would do if Iris spoke them out loud. She took in a breath, knowing she'd never let it happen.

Cam took her hand and she shivered as Cam gently stroked the back of it with her thumb. They were standing so close, Iris only needed to take a step. She knew Cam would respond, could only imagine how sweet the kiss would be, but she didn't move. One small step. To show Cam how much she actually meant to her, before it was too late.

Cam sighed, pushed herself off the car, and let go of Iris's hand. Iris felt a wrench inside at the idea that this was it, Cam was ending the evening.

"I don't want to go home, but I'm cold. Can we sit in the car?" Cam sounded calm, but Iris could hear something underneath the words.

They got in the car, the light stayed on for a while and then left them in darkness.

"You said I meant something to you, that you had feelings for me. That has to mean something. This can't be the end for us, Iris, it can't."

"Don't." Iris had her hands by her side, and she moved them to the steering wheel, feeling agitated, knowing she should just drive Cam home and put an end to this.

"Can you drive us somewhere? Can we please keep talking?" Cam's voice caught as she spoke. She was suffering just as much as Iris was at the idea of them saying good-bye.

Iris knew she needed to sound a warning. "We agreed that staying away from each other is—"

"We didn't agree, Iris. You did. You've decided we can't have this."

"Dammit, Cam, that's not fair. You have a fiancé. There are three people involved here, and if we don't put a stop to this, all three are going to get really hurt. I know what that's like. It's horrible. I stopped hurting people a long time ago, I won't…we can't—"

"I know." Cam cut across her, shaking her head, sounding weary. "I'm not asking you to do that. But I can't not have you in my life." She turned to Iris and looked at her in the dark of the car. "I just can't. You mean too much to me. Don't you know that?"

Cam reached for Iris and stroked her cheek. Iris couldn't help but lean in to the touch. Cam grazed Iris's bottom lip with her thumb. It was what she had done on the dance floor, and Iris felt herself shiver. Cam moved closer and her mouth followed where her thumb had been, grazing Iris's lips tentatively. Iris moaned. It was all the encouragement Cam needed to deepen the kiss, reaching one hand behind Iris's neck, reaching her fingers up into her hair. Cam had her other hand on Iris's jacket, pulling her into the embrace, and her whole body responded. She leaned into Cam, letting her mouth be taken, opening it to Cam, moaning as Cam darted her tongue inside.

"Oh God." Iris murmured the words, her insides turning molten, the sparks igniting her center, making her swollen and aroused. She reached for Cam without meaning to, wrapping her arms around her waist, pulling her closer, letting her tongue explore Cam's mouth, loving the taste of her, feeling Cam writhing in her arms, wanting even more than Cam was offering. They were both breathing heavily, the kisses taking what breath was left. Cam's mouth was so soft, her kisses so certain, Iris wasn't sure she could stop this, wasn't sure she wanted to. She was dangerously close to losing control, but then she pulled something from her depths and put a hand on Cam's chest to push her away.

"No, Cam, stop, we can't…"

Cam looked at Iris, as if just realizing where they were and what they had been doing. Her hands dropped to her side, and she looked straight at Iris, arousal and hurt visible in her eyes.

"I know, I know we can't. I'm sorry." The words came out as a low whisper as Cam turned her back to Iris and got out of the car, running away, up the main street toward her house, taking the route that Iris should have driven.

Iris stayed sat in the car, put her head on the steering wheel, and wept.

CHAPTER TWENTY-THREE

Iris stopped at the white bench that was her usual halfway point of her jog. She leaned against it as she made the necessary moves to stretch her calves and hamstrings. It wasn't that she particularly needed to stretch mid-run, but she definitely needed a breather and felt this was a more dignified way of doing it than to slump breathlessly into the seat while people were watching.

She had pushed herself much harder on this morning's run. She looked at her watch, knowing she had gotten here several minutes quicker than usual. No wonder she felt the burn in her chest and legs. It was painful, but she didn't mind. It took her mind off the other pain in the way she had hoped it might.

She had woken before five a.m., after tossing and turning for most of the night. She was struggling with seeing Cam, and struggling with not seeing Cam, and wasn't handling any of it well. Other than an awkward hello, they hadn't spoken for more than a week, and every time Iris saw Cam—in the kitchen, at the printer, in meetings—she was reminded of just how much she missed having her in her life. And every time she felt sorry for herself about it, she reminded herself that she had been the one to turn her back on Cam, not the other way around.

Iris wasn't willing to even consider the possibility of them finding a way through whatever this was, and now Cam looked haunted, a shadow of herself, and Iris felt responsible. Iris was hurting. She had never felt this miserable, not even after her breakup with Amanda, but she didn't want that for Cam. The sad fact was that she couldn't do anything to make Cam feel better that wasn't eventually going to hurt them, and Ryan, more. It was insane.

She'd sat next to Hazel in the lunch room yesterday and listened to Priti casually ask Cam about her plans to return to Seattle. She'd felt a panic in her chest that made her literally breathless. Cam had been noncommittal, suggesting they didn't have any firm plans, that they were still deciding, but Iris hadn't been able to sleep for thinking about never seeing Cam again, which was crazy since seeing Cam caused her nothing but pain. What the hell was wrong with her?

The feeling of confusion made Iris want to start running again, to physically try to drive the thoughts away, but she was too washed out to carry on.

They had problems at the Dubai office and Mr. Cottom wanted someone to go. He hadn't dared ask Iris again after last time, but as she sat on the bench feeling defeated by everything, she decided to offer to go. It would be four weeks starting at the end of the month and she couldn't help but feel it would be good for both of them not to have to see each other every day. And maybe she'd come back and find her feelings for Cam had changed. *Or maybe she'll already have gone home with Ryan.*

Iris leaned back and sighed, feeling the headache and the confusion she had woken up with settle back in. She rubbed away tears for the second time that day. Yeah, she was coping with it all pretty well actually.

"Hey." Vicki waved her hands in front of Cam's face. "Lost you again there for a bit. Want to tell me what's going on? You seem a bit out of it and, mate, let's be honest, you look terrible. I'm chuffed to have you buy me lunch at the cafe opposite my office, but the fact you came all the way over here to buy me lunch at the cafe opposite my office, says you may have something on your mind."

Cam poured sugar into her coffee, desperate for the energy she hoped it would give her. She hadn't been sleeping and it was taking its toll.

"I'm in trouble." Cam spoke the words quietly.

"Go on, mate, I'm listening." She tilted her head toward Cam.

"I don't know where to start." Cam sighed. "You know Iris pretty well I guess?"

Vicki had just put a forkful of salad into her mouth. "Does anyone really? I mean, apart from maybe Hazel and Casey. She's a pretty closed book. I like her a lot and we get on well, but I wouldn't say we're close."

"But you guys, I mean, I thought maybe because, you know…" Cam didn't want to say the actual words.

"We had sex? You can say it, mate. It's not like it meant anything."

"It didn't?"

"No, not really. We were drunk, she was lonely I guess. Though I didn't know that at the time. I thought it was just me being impossible to resist." Vicki sipped her juice. "And it was purely a one time thing. Kind of great, bit awkward afterward, but we talked and agreed to be grownups and not let it get in the way of us being friends."

"Wow." Cam wanted to be Vicki at that moment. Sure and confident—and past it all. She shook her head.

"What?"

"That, I mean just agreeing to put it behind you like that and be friends."

"It wasn't hard. It was something that happened out of nowhere. We just happened to be single, drunk, and horny in the same place at the same time. It's not like we had real feelings for each other."

Cam couldn't stop the breath escaping. Mostly the hurt felt like a silent hollow ache, but sometimes, like then, it was like a hot spear. She fought back the tears that threatened to fall. Vicki looked across at her with concern until Cam saw the jolt of comprehension hit.

"Ohhh." Vicki put down her fork. "Oh, I see. I mean, okay, so you two…?"

Cam put her head in her hands, leaning her elbows on the table, as if she was trying to keep herself upright. She sat like that for a moment until Vicki reached across and cupped her hand around one of the elbows.

"Cam? Looks like you got something you need to say. Don't worry, mate. I'm not gonna judge you."

"We didn't…I mean, we kissed, that's all." Cam shook her head, knowing the kiss wasn't all it was. "But I've tried to get past it and I can't because I think I'm in love with her and—"

"Holy crap."

"And I think she, well, I'm pretty sure she has some kind of feelings for me too. But she won't talk about it, I mean, she's closed it down, closed us down, says we can't even be friends now. She won't see me. And it really hurts." Her eyes watered and Cam swiped her hand across them, annoyed with herself.

"I did not see that coming."

"Neither did I. We'd been hanging out a lot obviously, getting on well. And then, well, I couldn't stop thinking about her, couldn't stop wanting to see her. I realized I was thinking about her in ways I don't usually think about my friends."

"Not even me?" Vicki winked.

Cam shook her head. "Not even you."

"Wow. I thought…I just assumed…I mean, I didn't even know you were bi."

"I don't know what I am and I'm not sure it even matters. I know we've been having problems, but I honestly thought Ryan was it for me, that I'd settled on him. I didn't expect to fall for Iris like this. I didn't want to, obviously. But I think I can manage the feelings…over time, I mean…I want to try. I really miss her and want her back in my life somehow."

"What did Ryan say about it? He can't be happy with the idea of you still seeing Iris, even just as friends. I know I wouldn't be. Not if you've already kissed and you're saying it meant something and you're finding it hard to fight the feelings."

Cam looked down at the table.

"I haven't told him." She sighed. "I know I should. It's just…well, we're not doing great, we haven't been for a long while if I'm honest, and I don't want to make things even worse. I'm trying to fix things. It might not seem like it, but I want my relationship to work, I want us both to be happier." She sat forward. "And the problems we're having aren't anything to do with Iris, with how I feel about her. They were there before I even knew her."

"But I can see why Ryan would think they do, why he'd want to know."

Cam said nothing. Vicki was right, of course.

"How can you 'fix things' with him if you're keeping secrets?" Cam felt the weight of Vicki's judgment. She deserved it. "And you can't really say that it has nothing to do with Iris either. If you were happy with Ryan, you'd either have been too busy hanging out in your happy relationship to spend all that time with her or you'd have gone back to America by now to get married and left her far behind." Vicki sat back in her chair.

"And if you've both caught feelings and you're already kissing, then her doing anything other than staying away is an inducement for you, at the very least, to cheat on your fiancé. Come on, Cam, you know Iris. She must have told you some of what she went through with Amanda."

"She told me all of it."

"Then you know she's not gonna get in the middle of you and Ryan. You're telling anyone that asks that you're going home soon to get married. What the hell is Iris supposed to do? Even if she loved you, there's nothing she can do about it but stay away." She reached across the table and put her hand on Cam's arm. "I love you, babe, but you're being a bit dense."

Cam hadn't thought of it that way. She assumed she'd fallen for Iris because she was wonderful and kind and sexy as hell, but—Vicki was right—she couldn't separate that out from the fact of her failing relationship with Ryan. She poked at her own food, her appetite still missing. And she'd been dumb enough to kiss Iris while she was still with Ryan. Even if she loved her, it was still cheating. No wonder Iris ran a mile in the opposite direction.

"I should tell him, beg his forgiveness."

"You should."

Cam felt out of her depth. Vicki had a better grip on this than she did and Vicki had known about it for two minutes while Cam had thought about nothing else for two weeks. She picked up her fork, not knowing what to say. She needed to talk to Ryan—of course she did—but she just wasn't sure she could cope without having Iris in her life and, right now, she couldn't see past that.

"She's impossible to really know. When we kissed she—"

"Careful, I'm eating here." Vicki interrupted, pointing at the remnants of her salad with her fork. Cam smiled sadly.

"I was just going to say that I could feel how much she wanted me, but she pushed me away. And now I don't even know if she misses me, if it's as hard for her as it is for me. And I don't know if she's waiting for me to do something, if she'll ever let us have a friendship or if she's really just moved on like that." She hesitated.

"Seems pretty important. Ask her."

"What?"

"Ask her." Vicki shrugged. "For the life of me, I'll never understand why people don't just ask people the things they wanna know. It saves a lot of heartache. Admittedly, rom-coms would be shorter and we wouldn't enjoy Jane Austen novels, but life would be a lot easier to navigate."

"But what would I say?" Cam couldn't just ask Iris, surely. For one thing, they'd already agreed to keep away from each other.

"Well, what do you really wanna know?" Vicki looked at Cam thoughtfully.

"If she loves me or if it's just an attraction." Cam surprised herself with how quickly she knew what it was she needed to know.

"How would knowing that help?"

"I really don't know." Cam put her head in her hands, feeling tears well up again.

"Cam?" Vicki leaned in and pulled her hands away. "I don't want to be brutal, but it doesn't really matter whether she loves you or not. You've got nothing to offer her right now. Surely your priority has to be figuring out what you're going to do about Ryan." Vicki sounded so emphatic that Cam sat up straighter in her chair.

"I know. I'm trying to find the courage to have the conversation we need to have." Cam felt like Vicki was interrogating her, but it wasn't unhelpful. It was making her face up to things, giving her more clarity.

"Which is?"

"He wants us to go home and get married, and I don't think I can do that."

"Because of Iris?"

"Because of Iris and also not because of Iris, because it's not what I want."

"But you love him?"

"I do. But sometimes I think…" she paused. "I think that the way I love him might not be enough. For either of us. Not enough to build a marriage on, to build a family on. He deserves more, we both do. I thought London would save us, and he thinks going back to Seattle is the answer. Maybe there isn't an answer. Maybe there never was. But I don't even know what the options are for us because I haven't been very good at letting him know what I'm really feeling."

"Sounds to me like you have some talking to do with people who aren't me." Vicki sat back in her chair.

"I do." Cam looked at Vicki across the table. "Thank you."

"No problem. I definitely owe you some angsty relationship chatter after the way I've gone on about Harry this past couple of weeks."

"Still the same?" Cam was relieved to get on to another topic.

"Yeah. We're not gonna make it." Vicki sounded a little sad.

"I'm sorry."

"Me too, kinda, but it just wasn't right. Though I very much miss the sex."

It was Cam's turn to point at her food. "Ew, eating."

"It was so good though. Posh girls are the absolute dirtiest." Vicki grinned.

"Too much information."

"She's not as good a kisser as Iris though." Vicki winked.

The memory of Iris pushing her away after the kiss they had shared in the car forced its way to the front of Cam's mind, and she felt something close to panic course through her body. She groaned.

"Sorry, mate, lame joke." Vicki held up her hands.

"Bit too soon maybe." Cam tried to smile, but the memory of Iris's mouth on hers had taken hold again and she couldn't. She shook the memory away and tried to concentrate on her lunch, knowing already that she wouldn't finish it.

❖

Cam entered the lunch room with her coffee cup in hand. Like every day that week, she was dreading, and yet desperately wanting, Iris to be in there. It wasn't that they didn't see each other at work, it was that they didn't speak. Not about anything that wasn't work and, even then, it felt like Iris was only saying the words that were absolutely necessary. And, worse, Iris always avoided her gaze. The fact that Iris—who had always made her feel so seen—didn't even look at her anymore hurt Cam as much as anything else.

Megan, Iris, and Jess sat at one of the tables, each of them holding one of the magazines that had arrived earlier that day.

"This is amazing." Megan waved a copy of the magazine at her, pointing excitedly at the cover. Cam made herself join them at the table.

"I know. I was really pleased with it. The photos Oliver took turned out really well." She had spent far too much time looking at them. Far too much. "I wasn't sure Janie would make good on her promise about the cover, but us winning the league didn't really give her a choice." She tried to smile.

"We've left a few copies on Liam's desk." Megan chuckled.

Cam moved across to the counter to pour herself some coffee. She had no energy for the banter.

"Has Graham seen it?" The voice was Iris's. Cam didn't answer, assuming the question wasn't meant for her, but when she turned, Iris was looking in her direction. Cam gripped the coffee pot a little tighter, feeling a tension in her chest.

"I think Sylvia slipped one into his briefcase." Her throat felt so dry.

Iris nodded and turned back to the table. Cam leaned against the counter, willing herself to pick up her cup and just walk out but Iris's presence made it difficult. She couldn't not want to be around her.

"When do you go to Dubai?" The question came from Jess.

"End of the month."

"How long this time?"

"A month. I'm gonna embrace the sobriety this time and think of it as a detox."

Cam was "moving on" with Ryan, trying to be a better fiancé, and seeing Iris every day made it so much harder, so the news that she wasn't going to be around for a few weeks should have been welcome. But as she picked up her coffee and headed back to her desk, she was feeling—if it was possible—even shittier than she had five minutes ago.

CHAPTER TWENTY-FOUR

Cam had another restless night. She had been up half the night and had slept in, only waking when Ryan made a noise looking for something in the chest of drawers. She was trying to eat some breakfast, and was still not dressed, despite it being nearly eleven.

It was Saturday, and she had nowhere to be, so it didn't really matter, but it wasn't like her to be so slow to get going at the weekend. Ryan had said nothing, seeming completely oblivious to her mood and the turmoil of these past few days.

At three a.m., Cam had given up trying to sleep and got up, hoping to reach Alison for a call but only getting her voice mail. She'd sat in the dark for a long time, thinking about the mess she was in. A mess that wasn't going to sort itself out without her doing something. Eventually, she'd given in and texted Iris. A simple message, but heartfelt. *I can't bear us not being in each other's lives. Can we at least try?*

Cam picked up her phone for the umpteenth time that morning, realizing, with an ache in her heart, that Iris was not going to reply. Why would she? She'd made it pretty clear that they needed to stay away from each other, and it seemed like she was getting on with her life without Cam in it, getting on with things like going to Dubai. Cam felt foolish. She read the text back to herself again, wishing she hadn't sent it. But it wasn't embarrassing, not really. It was the truth and the truth was something Cam needed to be speaking more often, not less.

Ryan had his head in the paper, but he was humming and seemed happier than he had in a while. Cam felt knots inside her stomach, knowing that she had to find a way to talk to him about what had happened, to tell him that she wasn't happy, and something needed to change. But the idea of saying it, of hurting him, made her back off and lose courage every single time.

He peeked at her from around the paper, smiling at her.

"Hey, babe, is that what you're wearing for the movie? I mean, I know it's a matinee, but I was kinda hoping you wouldn't be wearing your pj's." He was in a good mood. Cam offered him a weak smile, feeling tension in her belly.

She had been determined for them to do something nice together this weekend, wanting to prove that they could still enjoy each other. Iris was moving on, and Cam needed to try to do the same.

Ryan had been raving about the new Marvel movie, so she had bought tickets for them and booked a table at the Shard for dinner afterward. It was London's tallest building and had a Chinese restaurant on the thirty-second floor. Ryan loved Chinese food, and when she'd told him the plans last night, he had looked delighted. Cam had been surprised at just how happy he seemed and then understood, with a pang of guilt, that the last couple of weeks had probably been just as miserable for him.

He'd also been paying her a lot more attention lately. She tried to think when it had started. Maybe after the dinner dance? She wasn't really sure. It was nice but she couldn't convince herself that it would change anything now, it felt just too little too late. She shook the negative thoughts away. She had made a silent promise to them both that she would do what she could to make them work better. They had a lot of history and she cared about him deeply, and if Iris had taught her anything, it was that talking and trying was better than watching the train crash. She would enjoy the movie and the meal they'd planned and remind herself of just why it was they had managed to be together so happily for so long.

"I've got hours to get ready yet, I'm guessing you're gonna play squash first." Cam knew that nothing would keep him from his Saturday squash game.

"Yeah, I owe Rory a hammering. He beat me the last two times we played and hasn't shut up about it." He spoke the words into his newspaper.

Cam felt lost, like being here with Ryan was suddenly strange to her. It didn't matter how often she pushed it away, the kiss she had shared with Iris was on repeat in her mind, and she didn't know how to stop it. She touched a finger to her lips and closed her eyes. In her mind, Iris's eyes warned her away and pulled her in at the same time, her desire unmistakable. The memory of Iris's tongue in her mouth having the power to make her aroused every time she thought about it.

But Iris had pushed her away. Cam let the memory of that, and the fact of Iris's continued indifference to her at work, sober her. Iris had made it clear that they couldn't even have a friendship, let alone anything else.

She sighed out loud, not meaning to. But she needn't have worried. Ryan didn't even notice. She tried to force herself to say something to him, to ask if they could talk, to ask if he was as unhappy as she was. *Anything to get the damn conversation started.*

"I can't believe I have to go on that golfing trip to Scotland next weekend. I can't even play the game, and can you imagine having to spend a weekend following a little ball around with those jerks in the exec team and then watching them getting drunk on overpriced whisky? Not fun." Ryan sounded weary at the idea of it.

"I've given the rental agency your number. They said they'll keep you posted about any viewings that weekend. Hope that's okay. You don't need to stay in, they've got keys. They just asked that we keep it reasonably tidy." He pulled a face. "I asked them to define 'reasonable' but they didn't think I was funny."

Cam stopped what she was doing, feeling a sudden chill in her body.

"Sorry?" She had heard every word but couldn't manage a better response.

"Viewings." Ryan looked at her, peering around his paper. "You know, for people who might want to rent the house after we're gone." He spoke to her as if she was being a little dim.

"I know what a viewing is. But why now? Isn't it a bit early? We haven't even given notice yet." Cam caught the lowering of his eyes, saw his body grow tense.

"I told them we wouldn't be renewing the lease once the year was up. It's only a few weeks away. They want to get some new tenants lined up, so they don't have a gap, y'know? Makes sense really." He shrugged.

Cam stood up, not knowing what else to do. "We didn't agree to that. I don't want...what the hell, Ryan. We haven't even discussed it." Cam didn't want to go and he had to know that.

Ryan lowered the paper, folding it in half carefully before putting it on the table. Something about the deliberateness of the action made Cam feel even angrier. She could guess what was coming next. He would talk to her with an exaggerated patience, like she was a small child who needed things explained to her.

"We have talked about this."

Cam stayed still, stayed silent, watching him, knowing he would act all restrained and reasonable and make her feel like she was being overly emotional.

"You know we need to go. I'm not happy, work is unbearable. And the stress is making us unhappy here. We both know that. I spoke to your mom."

"You spoke to my mother?" Cam was ready to burst. She couldn't believe what he was trying to do.

"Yeah, she said of course we can stay with her until we find our own place. You know what she's like. She's just happy we're going back."

"I know what she's like, she's my mother, or did you two forget about that?" Cam spat out the words.

Ryan crossed to where Cam was standing and tried to take her hand. She snatched it away and stalked to the other side of the room. She looked at him, wondering who the hell this person was, still not believing that Ryan would do this without talking to her first.

"It's not working out here, Cam. You know that really. We've been wrong...unhappy even, especially lately. London doesn't suit us. We'll be better once we're home."

"Maybe London doesn't suit you, but it suits me. Did you even stop to think about that, to think about me? Of course not, you didn't even ask me, for chrissakes." Cam was close to shouting now.

"We talked about it plenty of times." His posture was defensive and his voice louder, matching hers. "Work is crazy, I'm never home. And we need to get married. You were the one who said you wanted to do that in the States. It doesn't make any sense to extend the lease, to stay here any longer. And anyway, I told Bob I was coming back. They've kept the job open for me." Ryan was serious about this. He had made plans.

"And what if I want to stay?" Cam tried to sound calmer than she felt. Faced with the reality of it, she knew she couldn't go. "Did you ever think that I might want to stay?"

"Cam, you hate your job, you hate your boss, and you hate being away from Alison, your friends. You're as unhappy here as I am."

"That was before. Weeks ago, months ago." She shook her head.

That was before she'd started at Cottoms, before she'd joined the team, before she'd met Iris. Cam couldn't say it, couldn't even allow herself to think it. The panic surged, making it hard for her to talk, to breathe. Going home would mean leaving Iris. For good. She wouldn't...she couldn't do that.

Ryan regarded her closely, something in his eyes she couldn't read.

"Before what?" He paused. "Before what, Cam?"

Cam felt his gaze; it made her uncomfortable. She picked up her plate, her cup, the knife from the table and carried them to the kitchen, needing some time. She put them carefully in the sink and turned to face him.

"Before the football team, before the friends I made there, before I had a social life—"

"Before Iris."

Cam felt trapped. She wouldn't lie, but she wasn't ready to tell him the truth. Not like this. Not now. *Why not, why not now?* She was afraid. Of course she was. Scared to hurt him, to want things for herself, scared that Iris didn't even care whether she stayed or went.

"I've got a life here Ryan. For the first time in nearly a year. People to do things with, people I care about. I'm starting to love London, and you don't even care. You're telling me it's time we went home and got married because you want to, because my fucking mother thinks it's time. Dammit, Ryan, I'm not ready to get married, and I'm not ready to leave. I have to have a say in this."

Ryan came closer and stopped a foot away from her. Cam couldn't meet his eyes. "I'm not a fool, Cam. I know you think I am. That I'm too busy to pay attention, but I'm not." He sounded tired, beaten. "I can see what's going on."

Cam made herself look at him. She could feel panic rising in her chest. He took her hand, and this time she let him.

"It's time we went home. I think that London…that your friends… they're changing you. Sometimes I think that I'll lose you if we don't get away. I don't want that. Let's go home, get back to the way we were. Please." He made it all sound so reasonable, and it made Cam want to respond reassuringly. She didn't like to see him hurt, needing. But she couldn't. Whichever way she considered this, he was trying to make a really important decision without talking to her, choosing to talk to her mother behind her back, trying to force her into doing something she wasn't ready for. Maybe old Cam would have gone along with that, but she wasn't that person any more. She pushed his hand away.

"This, Ryan, this treating me like a child, this putting yourself first like always, coming to London because YOU wanted to, leaving because YOU want to. Thinking you know what I need without ever bothering to ask me. This is what's going to make you lose me. I don't want this anymore, I can't…"

"What the hell is that supposed to mean? You don't want this anymore or you don't want me anymore? Come on, Cam, out with it. I know you can barely stand to touch me these days."

"I can't…I don't…" She had tears in her eyes, but she needed to say it. "I can't leave London, Ryan. I can't. And I don't…want to get married. I just don't think I feel the same way anymore." Finding the courage to say everything she needed to was close to impossible, but she had said something. It was a start.

"I don't want—"

"But what do you want, Cam?" He paced as he spoke. "I mean I literally have no idea. You don't talk to me. I'm not sure you ever really have. I know everything about what you don't want, what you don't like, but you've never fucking told me what you want from your life. How am I supposed to have a chance at making you happy when I don't even know what that looks like?" He was upset but trying not to show it.

"London makes me happy." Cam felt a dam burst. "And Iris makes me happy." She couldn't not say it, couldn't not feel it, even as she knew there was no coming back from having said it out loud. "I don't think I knew what I wanted, what I needed, until she came along. And I'm so sorry, I didn't mean to feel that way about her. I tried not to."

Ryan moved toward her and put his hands on her arms, holding them next to her side. He stood inches away from her.

"You don't mean it. You don't need her, Cam. You...you're not like that, not really. I think I'd know. She's got you confused. You're not happy and she's been paying you all that attention. And I haven't. And I'm sorry. We need to leave. We'll get home and we can get back to normal. I'll work less and we'll get married and be happy, like we were before."

"No." Cam found her voice. "Not like before. Don't you see? I wasn't happy then either, not really. I haven't been happy, felt right, for a long time." She knew this would hurt him, but she had to be honest. "Iris...she's made me feel things I haven't felt before, helped me understand I'm only living half a life, that I've denied myself things that make me happy. I don't have a career, I'm twenty-eight and I'm still scared to be disapproved of, and I settled for a relationship which isn't enough for either of us, not really. You deserve m—" He cut her off.

"Of course she's helped you understand all that. She is trying to get you on your back, Cam. Are you that fucking stupid? She's filled your head with all this stupid stuff so she can swoop in and save you." His eyes betrayed how furious he was. "Newsflash, Cam, she'll fuck you if you let her, of course she will, I mean who wouldn't." He was squeezing Cam's arms hard now, his breathing heavy. "But that'll be that. She has nothing to offer you. Have you not been paying attention to anything people have said about her? You're a much bigger fool than I thought."

He dropped his hands, knowing he had gone too far.

"Cam, I'm sorry. It's just...don't do this...don't make a fool of—" He couldn't finish the sentence; his body trembled with the effort it had taken him to calm down.

"She's not that person. You don't know her." It was all Cam could say.

"If you don't come back home with me, that's it, Cam. No way back. I'm not gonna wait around for you to get this stupid crush out of your system and then come crawling back to me when you figure out she's not what you wanted." He held her gaze.

"I know." She looked back at him until he turned his eyes away from her and stalked out of the kitchen and up into their bedroom.

Cam had no idea whether Ryan was right. Iris wanted her, she knew that much, but that didn't mean she loved her. She sat on the edge of the armchair, her body shaking, and the self-control she'd managed in Ryan's presence evaporating. She didn't want to cry, but she couldn't stop the tears from spilling out. She clenched her fists in her lap, willing herself to gain some composure, trying to think straight, and flinching as she heard the front door slam shut.

Of course Ryan had gone out. If he really cared about her, about them, he would have stayed and insisted they talked it all out. And he should have raged at her for finally admitting she had feelings for Iris. But he didn't take any of it seriously and she knew that, instead, he'd go and hammer a squash ball for an hour and come home hoping that she'd seen sense. It was a fair assumption for him to make. She normally went along with him, her moments of resistance fleeting. He thought she would leave her "crush" behind and follow him to Seattle and marry him. He was used to her doing what was expected of her. But that was before.

Before Iris.

She lay down on the couch, curled up on her side, and let the tears fall. Her head was pounding, her heart hurting. There was no way through this without hearts being broken. What could she do? What did she want? She could imagine leaving Cottoms, leaving Graham, and she'd be happy to leave this house. She'd never really liked it, never liked the feel of it, not really ever trying to make it feel like home, but leaving Ryan after more than four years together was a big step. Could she do it? And could she do it without the promise of a life with Iris?

Cam sat up and swiped her eyes with her sleeve. It was no good. She couldn't avoid her feelings, couldn't just lie there and wait for Ryan to come home. She knew one thing for sure. She wasn't ready to leave Iris. She loved her. Cam didn't know if Iris felt the same, if Iris would want her to stay, if Iris would be devastated at the idea of Cam leaving, but she had to find out.

Iris had said she had feelings for Cam. That was something, not nothing, and Iris had kissed her, kissed her like she wanted something more. But this was Iris. She had kissed a lot of women she didn't really love. Cam had to see her, tell her that she was leaving Ryan and hope Iris loved her enough to take a chance on being with her.

If Iris sent her away this time, she would be heartbroken but she would stay in London without Ryan and try to honor Iris by being something more of the person she felt she should be.

But first she'd fight for Iris.

Cam headed upstairs, hoping a hot shower would help her think, help her find the words she needed to convince Iris they should be together.

CHAPTER TWENTY-FIVE

The windows of Cam's car had started to mist up. A voice inside her head told her it was a sign she'd been sitting there too long already. This voice was more reasonable than the one that had spent the best part of the last hour telling her she was crazy and destructive and should just do as Iris wanted and leave her alone.

Cam was outside Iris's flat, had been outside since eleven thirty, too scared to go and ring the bell, but too scared to leave. She didn't even know if Iris was home. Her car was parked outside, but that didn't mean a thing. She could have been out for a run, out having brunch with a friend, anything.

Cam had the car radio on low. The DJ gave a time check. It was twelve fifteen, and all the clarity she'd felt when she left her house had evaporated on the short drive over to Iris's flat.

Cam had come intending to tell Iris about Ryan leaving, to tell her she loved her and ask her if she would be with Cam if she stayed. And then she had sat there, and sat there some more, and felt stupid for imagining that Iris would be interested in loving her.

Yes, Iris had kissed her, but she'd also made it clear that she didn't want drama, and Cam could think of nothing more dramatic than a woman leaving an unhappy relationship turning up on her doorstep asking Iris for a commitment that she herself was terrified of making.

The DJ played a song that reminded Cam of Ryan. He had sung it to her once, badly but sweetly, at a karaoke bar soon after they got together. Mentally, she added the words "when we were in love," knowing that she wasn't any more. She wasn't even sure now that she ever had been, knowing he'd never made her feel the way Iris did, that simple fact causing a tightening in her chest.

Iris thought Cam was bored and looking for excitement and an easy way out. She was right and she was wrong. Iris excited her, but there was nothing easy about choosing Iris. Iris didn't represent an escape hatch to Cam, she represented the upending of everything Cam had ever thought her life would be about for the past four years, and Cam had to be sure it was what they both wanted because she knew the fallout was going to be terrible.

Iris's front door opened and she stepped outside. She was barefoot and dressed casually in sweatpants and a T-shirt. She put a small bag of trash into the trash can next to her front door and looked up at the sky where rain-filled black clouds had formed. The sight of Iris brought Cam back to her senses. Maybe it was a cliché to say that she couldn't live without Iris, but she certainly didn't want to have to try. Looking at her now made Cam's heart beat faster, and she knew without a shred of doubt that she loved every beautiful inch of her, inside and out, and it would be enough to get them through, but only if Iris loved her back.

"Iris." Cam got out of her car and called Iris's name while running across the street. She reached the small paved area that passed for a front garden in front of Iris's apartment and stopped as Iris turned sharply. Iris looked surprised and then concerned. The visit was unexpected, Cam knew that, and she guessed that maybe she didn't look her best. She hadn't bothered to stop and put on makeup, hadn't even dried her hair properly. But she had wanted, needed, to see Iris. And here she was, looking at Cam warily.

"Cam, what are you doing here? Is everything okay?"

"Can I come inside? I really need to talk to you."

Iris hesitated.

"Please," Cam pleaded.

Iris pushed open the door and indicated for Cam to go inside.

The hallway was a small square containing a door to the left marked 6A and another immediately ahead of them marked 6B. Iris closed the door to the street and passed within inches of Cam on her way to reach across and push open the door to 6B. Cam fought the urge to reach out to her, to pull her into the kiss that she so desperately wanted. What stopped her was not just the uncertainty of how Iris would respond but understanding that above all else they needed to talk. She needed to know how Iris felt about her, and make Iris understand that she meant enough to Cam for her to end her relationship so they could be together. Vicki had said Cam had nothing to offer Iris. It wasn't true, she was ready to offer her everything.

The door opened inward onto a flight of stairs. Iris took them two at a time. Cam followed slowly. Her legs feeling like lead.

"I'll put the kettle on," Iris said over her shoulder. "Make some tea." The tension in her voice was obvious to Cam.

Cam settled herself onto a stool next to the small breakfast bar that separated the kitchen from the living room, watching Iris busy herself with cups and a teapot. She looked around the room, willing herself to calm down. At one end were two large armchairs next to a solid oak coffee table, sheaves of paper scattered across its surface. A laptop was balanced on the arm of the chair nearest the window. On either side of the chimney breast stood two tall oak bookcases, both overflowing with books. The room was decorated a soft yellow color. The armchairs were dark gray with yellow cushions, and colorful framed prints brightened the walls. A small TV sat in the corner looking unloved, a throw draped over one end. Cam had not been inside before, but the apartment had an ambience that made her feel safe and made her feel at home.

"Iris?"

Iris stopped what she was doing and turned to face Cam. Her dark eyes gazed at Cam with concern. Cam felt the power of the gaze ripple through her body.

"Oh God," Cam exclaimed, not really meaning to say the words out loud, knowing she sounded a little crazy.

Iris took a few steps forward, putting down the teapot on the breakfast bar between them and reaching across to take Cam's hand.

"Is everything okay?"

Cam gazed downward, looking at Iris's hand holding her hand, not able to meet her eyes. She took a breath. "No...no, it's not okay. None of it."

Iris grazed her thumb across the back of her hand. Cam felt the heaviness in the air between them, knowing Iris was waiting for her to say something.

"Ryan has—" Cam's voice cracked. "Ryan has given notice on the house, so we can go home, back to Seattle. He's arranged to get his old job back, arranged for us to stay with my mom for a while, until we find somewhere else." She shook her head, saying it out loud made her feel nauseous.

Iris pulled her hand away as if suffering an electric shock. "You're leaving."

"We argued. I told him I wanted to stay, that I wasn't ready to go." Cam dared to look at Iris. Her expression was closed now, the concern was gone.

"I told him I didn't want to leave, that I had reasons to stay, people I really care about. That I had you...but...I need to know if..." She wanted to say more, to declare herself more fully, to ask Iris to finally talk to her about how she felt. But Iris's face was like a mask, her blank expression was making Cam lose courage.

"But you came here to tell me you're going. Whatever you say you feel about me, you're prepared to leave me behind because Ryan wants you home. And your mom, let's not forget your mom. Has she texted you the date of the dress fitting yet? All that to look forward to. It's going to be so much fun." Iris's voice was stronger now but bitter, sarcastic. Cam felt panic rising in her throat.

"He didn't tell me what he was doing, didn't ask me, he just assumed I'd go. I told him I can't go, Iris. I don't love him enough. And, we...this...I mean I've only just let myself admit how much you mean to me." She had come to Iris. It had been the first thing she'd wanted to do. She had to make her understand. "Iris, I can't leave you. I think you know that. I love you. I told him that. And that I want to be with you, if you want that, I mean. Help me. Please. I just don't know what to do." Cam swallowed the sob that she felt in her throat.

Somehow it was the wrong thing to say. Iris stood stiff and straight in front of her, wrapping her arms tightly around her body.

"Help you do what, Cam? Help you by begging you to stay and telling you that to lose you is something I don't think I'll ever recover from?" Cam heard her voice break.

"Or maybe you want me to be the friend who rises above it all and helps you draw up a list of pros and cons about staying, with me on one side and Ryan on the other?" She took in a breath. "Well, I won't, and you can't bloody well expect me to. Decide what you want, Cam. Choose. Make a decision for yourself for once in your life and follow it through rather than doing what everyone else wants for you." Iris turned her head away, but not before Cam caught the glistening of the tears in her eyes.

"I'm not someone you can try out for size while you're deciding what you actually want, Cam. I just won't be...I can't..." She stopped speaking and leant back against the sink. "Just go, Cam." The words were barely a whisper.

The stool scraped the tiled floor as Cam stood up. She walked out of the kitchen and headed down the stairs to the front door and out into the street. She let both doors slam shut behind her.

❖

Fuck, fuck, fuck.

The understanding that she had probably lost Cam forever punched Iris in the gut. *Hadn't sending her away just made it certain that Cam would go home with Ryan?* Iris couldn't believe she hadn't been braver, hadn't asked Cam to choose her and to stay. And she knew why. She didn't feel worthy, didn't believe she would recover from the rejection if she showed Cam that she needed her and Cam still chose Ryan.

And I had the nerve to call Cam weak?

Iris grabbed her keys from the counter, slipped on her shoes, and ran as fast as she could down the stairs. She couldn't just let Cam leave like that. Finally, something had broken through and told Iris to fight for her.

A car screeched away in the street outside. Iris cursed, knowing she was too late. The pain made her stop still in the hallway. Her heart was hurting so much. After a few moments, she walked outside, needing the fresh air, not caring that it was raining.

Iris heard a sob. She turned toward the sound. Cam was standing with her back to the wall of the house, oblivious to the rain, crying quietly. Cam turned her head toward Iris and fixed her with a gaze that seemed angry. Iris hadn't expected that. Cam pushed her body away from the wall and faced her—not once moving her eyes from Iris's. Iris was holding her breath, waiting, expecting some form of argument or outburst. She wanted to comfort Cam, but she didn't know how.

"You have no idea, do you?"

Through the noise of the rain, Iris could only just make out the words. She looked at Cam. She was scared, scared this was it, scared she had gone too far, expected too much. All Iris could do to answer the question was to hold Cam's gaze and shake her head. The answer was plain to Iris—no, she had no idea, didn't know what this was, what they were going to do. She loved Cam, and she wanted her. She knew that being her friend had stopped being enough weeks ago, and, now that she was about to lose Cam altogether, she felt like that man who knows a hurricane is coming but who battens down his house and stands in the face of it, refusing to leave, refusing to back down, expecting nothing but to get flattened.

Cam's eyes left Iris's for the first time. She looked at her hands as she held them out in front of her. They were shaking. She seemed not to care that Iris was watching. She stepped toward Iris and pushed her back into the house. They stumbled slightly as they crossed the threshold into the hallway. Cam kept pushing, and Iris kept retreating, until Iris's back was flat against the door that led to her apartment. Cam's eyes were shining now, a deep watery green, and her hands were still on Iris's shoulders.

"People are always telling me to decide what I want, while telling me that I can't have what I want. I'm sick of it."

Without waiting for permission, Cam stepped closer to Iris and kissed her, her soft lips demanding and her warm mouth in contrast to the rainy coldness of her cheeks. Cam pulled Iris's face to hers, and Iris responded, threading her hand in Cam's hair, opening her mouth to meet Cam's searching kisses, pulling Cam closer. Iris's knees buckled as Cam's tongue flicked across her lower lip before entering her mouth.

"Oh, Cam." Iris moaned with the desire she felt—feeling completely lost, knowing she couldn't stop this, not this time. As suddenly as she began, Cam pulled away. She was no longer crying. She touched Iris's face tenderly, wiping the wetness from her cheeks, her fingers grazing Iris's lips.

"I'd already decided when I came to you…and you need to believe in me." Cam pulled Iris into a hug, and they stood there for a moment, holding each other tightly. Iris grabbed on to the words, wanting them to be enough, glorying in the feel of Cam in her arms, and when she felt her relax, Iris broke the contact to take Cam gently by the hand and lead her upstairs.

The apartment door closed behind them and they stood in the middle of the living room just looking at each other. Iris removed Cam's wet jacket, laying it carefully over a chair. She grabbed a towel from the bathroom and came quickly back to Cam's side to gently towel her hair. Cam leaned in to her touch and slid her hands around Iris's waist, moving closer, and nestling herself against Iris. Iris dropped the towel and gave in to the embrace. Cam felt soft and warm, and Iris put her lips to Cam's damp hair and pressed a tender kiss to the top of her head.

Cam tilted her head to look up at Iris. The unmistakable need written across Cam's face, the desire in her eyes, made Iris's throat dry. She stroked strands of hair away from Cam's forehead and marveled at the feeling, her fingers felt made for touching Cam's skin. Cam shivered at her touch and her eyes grew wider. Iris leaned down and pressed her lips to Cam's, the kiss was gentle but searching. Iris had wanted to be able to kiss Cam for weeks and now she could, she was going to take her time.

She deepened the kiss and, when Cam parted her lips, Iris darted her tongue inside. Cam sighed and opened her mouth a little wider, taking in Iris's tongue. The warm wetness of their kiss was so delicious that Iris couldn't help but moan Cam's name into her mouth. Cam pressed herself against Iris, her hands on Iris's backside, pulling Iris to her. When Cam took her lower lip between her teeth and bit softly, Iris arched in pleasure. The movement seemed to encourage Cam as she bit a little harder, before pulling away. Her lips were full and red now, her eyes hooded.

"I can't not want you." Iris spoke almost to herself. She couldn't stop this. Everything had been about what they couldn't feel, what they shouldn't do, but now Cam was in her arms, telling her they could finally have this and she was powerless.

"I don't want you not to want me. We can't keep fighting what we feel." Cam stroked Iris's cheek.

Iris nodded and kissed Cam again. She had one hand on the back of her neck, the fingers threaded in Cam's hair, and the other hand inside Cam's sweatshirt so she could touch the bare skin of her lower back. Iris could feel the throbbing between her legs and knew already that just kissing Cam, being kissed by Cam, had made her wet. She moved her hands, and slowly, very slowly, unzipped Cam's sweatshirt, watching as Cam shrugged it to the floor. Her breath caught at the sight of Cam in just her bra. It was sheer and practically transparent, and Iris longed to have her hands and her mouth on the dark buds she could see through the fabric. She began to lift her T-shirt, wanting Cam's hands on her own breasts.

Cam shot out a hand to stop her. "Let me." Her voice was husky, deeper than usual.

Iris dropped her hands and held her breath as Cam lifted her T-shirt. She heard Cam's soft gasp as she saw Iris wasn't wearing a bra. Cam threw the T-shirt to the floor and moved her hands unhesitatingly over Iris's breasts. As Cam grazed her palms across her nipples, Iris stiffened and felt her breathing becoming a little ragged. She was mesmerized by Cam's hands, moving across her back, into her hair, caressing her breasts, never keeping still. Cam's lips moving from her mouth, to her neck and now tracing soft kisses across her collarbone. Iris felt like she was made of liquid, not sure how she was still standing.

"I take it you have a bed in here somewhere." Cam's voice sounded low, sultry and sure.

Iris took Cam by the hand and led her to her bedroom door, in the far corner of the living room. She pushed it open and Cam followed her inside. A king-size bed with a wrought iron frame sat in the center of the room. Cam moved over to the bed, kicked off her shoes, and sat down.

"Get over here." She held out both hands toward Iris.

Iris felt the command register. She had let herself imagine being with Cam like this, but she hadn't dared to imagine Cam would be so bold. It was intoxicating. She dropped onto the bed next to Cam and leaned in to capture Cam's mouth again in a kiss, teasing, insistent, and urgent. Cam reached for her breasts, caressing the soft flesh and pinching the nipples, driving Iris crazy.

"Beautiful." Cam sighed the word into the space between them before Iris silenced her with another kiss. Iris moved her hands over Cam's breasts, hating the fact that the sheer lace of Cam's bra was stopping her from tasting them.

"Take it off." Cam spoke, as if reading her mind, the urgency of the request unmistakable. Iris reached behind Cam and unhooked her bra a little clumsily before tossing it to the side of the bed, her fingers shaking slightly. It wasn't just that Iris was out of practice, Cam had her senses on overload.

Iris traced her fingers across the warm curves of Cam's breasts and enjoyed feeling the shudders that accompanied every graze of the nipples, watching them get harder. She pushed Cam backward onto the bed and closed her mouth over one and then the other. She explored them with her tongue, teasing a spot just under each nipple that had Cam writhing underneath her.

Iris moved her mouth down Cam's torso, tracing her tongue across her ribs, along her abs, into the hollow beneath her stomach, giving gentle fluttering kisses as she moved. Iris looked up at Cam, seeing nothing in her eyes but want, seeing a pleading that was all the answer she needed.

Iris unzipped Cam's jeans and pulled them off along with her panties, marveling at the sight of Cam naked now beneath her. Her insides contracted and she felt the heat of the arousal in her core. She shifted position so she could push Cam's legs farther apart and trailed kisses from her navel to the inside of her thighs, permitting herself only the lightest of kisses brushed against Cam's center before pulling away and teasing her again by moving back to kiss the soft skin inside her thighs. Iris felt Cam's hand in her hair, urging her not to wait any longer. Iris hadn't dared think about it, but right then she knew that she wanted to taste Cam more than she had ever wanted anything else in the world.

Iris dipped her tongue into Cam's wetness and felt Cam arch her body. She stroked her tongue up and down the length of her folds, stopping to make circles around Cam's clitoris, flicking her tongue across the swollen tip. Cam's breathing was rapid now, her body grinding into the bed to the rhythm of Iris's tongue, one hand grasping the bed sheets tightly and the fingers of the other wrapped in Iris's hair.

Cam's moans became louder, more urgent. She was close to the edge. Iris had her hand cupping Cam's breast and she moved her thumb back and forth across the nipple. Cam moaned more loudly, lifting her hips from the bed, pushing herself into Iris. Iris closed her mouth over Cam's center, sucking gently, before pushing her tongue deep inside. She felt Cam cresting beneath her and cry out. The sound of her name in Cam's mouth was intoxicating, and Iris didn't stop sweeping her tongue to and fro across the hard knot of Cam's clitoris as she ground into the bed underneath her.

"Oh God, Iris. Please, oh fuck, I'm coming." Cam swallowed the last word and tightened the fingers in Iris's hair into a fist as the wave hit. She let out a cry of pleasure, and Iris felt Cam shudder violently, as the orgasm seemed to ripple through her body, leaving her panting as she tried to come back down.

Iris pulled her mouth away to look up at Cam as she climaxed. Her head was back, her body arched and her eyes closed. She had never looked more beautiful. Iris rested her cheek on Cam's thigh, unwilling to move, feeling a closeness and a wonder she had not experienced before.

"Iris." Cam said her name, her voice sounding throaty with desire. "Get back up here."

Iris lifted her head to see Cam smiling sexily at her, her eyes still hazy. She moved herself up the bed, not able to resist trailing kisses along Cam's body as she moved to lie next to her. Cam was lying on her back with her head turned and Iris was lying on her side so they were facing each other, Cam traced her fingers up and down Iris's arm, causing Iris to shiver.

"Wow." Cam lifted her hand and kissed her palm. "That was... just...amazing." She leaned over and gently pressed her lips to Iris's, and Iris gloried in the tenderness of the kiss.

"You kind of made it easy for me. You're so..." She hesitated. There were so many words she could choose, but she was too full of feelings.

"Hold on, are you calling me easy?"

Iris laughed, the first she had managed in days. She leaned in to return the kiss, a soft, searching kiss. Cam sighed and then closed her eyes. Iris touched her fingers to Cam's lips, not quite able to believe they were finally hers to kiss, before tracing a path down her neck, down her breastbone, and all the way to her navel. She felt Cam tremble; it was a wonderful feeling. She stopped and tapped her fingers on Cam's stomach.

"Well, you are kind of naked and on your back while I'm still half dressed. It might suggest easy to some people."

Cam stroked Iris's arm. "If I'm easy, then it's your fault." She ran her fingers across Iris's stomach and let them rest just underneath the edge of Iris's sweatpants. Iris couldn't help but move beneath her hand, her body was straining to meet Cam's touch, and humming with arousal as Cam leaned in and kissed her, harder this time. Her hand moving to cup Iris's breast, to pinch the nipple between her finger and thumb. Iris moaned softly and closed her eyes.

"You are breathtaking," Cam said into the kiss, "and you're mine." She pulled herself up onto her knees, pushing Iris gently onto her back and leaning down, using both her hands to slide Iris's sweatpants down her legs. Iris kicked herself free of them. Cam had been careful not to remove Iris's panties, knowing that she wanted to take her time. Her center throbbed at the sight of Iris stretched out beneath her, her long legs, her toned torso, the white cotton panties leaving nothing to the imagination, the thin damp fabric allowing Cam to see through to the dark stripe of hair. Cam played with the edge of them, dipping in and out, tracing lines across Iris's center. She brushed her thumb across Iris's swollen ridge. Cam knew Iris was watching her, waiting, her breath hitched, her eyes full of desire.

Without stopping the movement of her fingers across the fabric of Iris's panties, Cam claimed Iris's breasts. She tasted first one then the other, running her tongue over the taut buds. Being the one to make Iris writhe beneath her was exhilarating. She moved her mouth back onto Iris's, not able to resist the taste of her lips and the feel of her tongue. She kissed Iris hard, possessively.

Cam used the heel of her hand now to exert more pressure, rubbing it harder against Iris's core, applying the friction Cam knew she wanted. Iris grabbed her wrist, yearning written across her face. Cam glowed red hot between her own legs, an unceasing throbbing linked to being able to finally have Iris like this.

Iris guided Cam's hand inside her panties. "I can't...Cam, don't make me wait any longer. Please." Her voice was a low growl.

Cam filled Iris, pushing her fingers deep inside, feeling Iris open to accept her and then tense around her fingers as her orgasm began to build. Cam moved in and out, deep and slow at first and then more rapidly as Iris's breathing changed and she lifted her hips to meet her thrusts. The feeling of being inside Iris, feeling how wet she was, how wanting, was incredible, and Cam felt her own core hungering for more. She moved so that she was straddling one of Iris's legs and without ceasing the in and out strokes that were now causing Iris to gasp and grab at Cam blindly, Cam moved her slick and swollen center against Iris's thigh, the pressure almost sending her back to the point of orgasm. She clenched and waited, wanting to come with Iris, wanting them to come together. She curled her fingers slightly as she pushed deeper inside and Iris bucked beneath her as she found the sweet spot.

As Iris grabbed her wrist to hold her inside and pushed herself up from the bed to meet Cam's hand, her thigh pressed harder between Cam's legs and brought her closer. She was barely able to stop herself from coming. Iris's muscles tensed around her fingers. She arched her back and cried out in pleasure as the juddering climax washed over her. Cam let go and her own orgasm hit at the same time. She writhed against Iris's thigh, the liquid pleasure spreading around her body until she could no longer sit up and she fell next to Iris on the bed, the two of them panting and slick with perspiration.

Cam had her fingers in Iris's hair, softly twisting the strands. They were lying down, looking at each other, face-to-face.

"I spend so much time looking at you." Cam traced a finger across Iris's lips, making her shiver. "And still I had no idea you could be this beautiful."

Iris wanted Cam to gaze at her this way forever. She ignored the voice that told her how crazy this all was. They had been in bed for about two hours and not said a word about what they were doing and what might happen next.

"You've seen me naked plenty of times. We've showered together, remember." Iris raised an eyebrow.

"Yeah, but with, like, ten other people blocking my view and us mostly covered in mud and bruises. Now I can look at you without pretending not to."

"You used to look at me secretly?" Iris chewed her lip, trying not to enjoy the idea of it too much.

"I'm afraid I did." Cam looked at Iris a little sheepishly. "More than was decent actually."

Iris's eyes widened. "So, it's official, Cameron Hansen is a pervert. And you have such a sweet, innocent face too." She shook her head playfully. "It's always the quiet ones."

Cam stroked Iris's cheek softly, tilting Iris's face downward and placing a chaste kiss on her lips. Iris's stomach fluttered. She couldn't seem to get enough of Cam's kisses. "Don't tell me you never did the same." Cam's eyes held hers and Iris felt the contraction in her stomach, the pulsing between her legs. She was powerless to stop her body from reacting when Cam looked at her like that.

"I noticed how hot you were the very first time I saw you, before I even knew your name. Hazel caught me staring and never let me forget it." Iris nibbled on Cam's bottom lip, grazing her tongue along the inside as Cam stiffened in pleasure. "I always looked the other way in the showers though."

Cam laughed. "I bet that's not true."

"It is," Iris insisted. "I'm very well brought up, English manners and all that." She paused. "Now though..." Iris let her gaze travel slowly up and down Cam's naked body. "Well, let's just say that I'm definitely enjoying being able to look now."

Cam shifted closer so that there was no longer any distance between them, pushing herself against Iris and crushing her lips in a passionate kiss. Iris held Cam to her, enjoying feeling the length of Cam's body against hers. She pressed one hand to the small of her back, and the other in her hair, as if to prevent her from pulling away. They kissed and stopped and kissed again before Cam took Iris's hand in hers, lacing and unlacing their fingers. This felt so right to Iris, so special. Cam bit her lip. The gesture still a giveaway that she had a question she was trying not to ask.

"When did you..." Cam faltered. "When did you know you had feelings for me...like this I mean, not as a friend?"

Iris knew they had to talk. They had a lot to say about their feelings and where they were headed, but despite the sex, despite Cam coming to her and saying she was choosing her, she was still nervous about exposing herself too much until she knew for sure that Cam was here for good. Cam and Ryan had a lot of history and Cam hadn't always been brave. The thought was overwhelming. Iris pushed it away.

"I'm not sure I should answer that. What's that thing they always do in American cop shows to avoid incriminating themselves in court?"

"Taking the Fifth," Cam said.

"Yeah, well I'm taking the Fifth."

"Why?"

"Because, if I answer, it'll make me look like I've been pining for you for longer than is decent and I don't want to seem like a sad case."

Cam said nothing, but her eyes were focused on Iris and she stroked her fingers up and down Iris's arm, before lightly scratching

Iris's stomach, tracing a path from her navel to her breastbone and back again. It was exquisite…and completely irresistible. Iris had already come to understand that she had no defenses when it came to Cam's touch.

"But if you were being tortured and had to answer…" Cam let the sentence tail off as she dipped her fingers between Iris's legs for an instant before resuming her stroking on the path between Iris's chest and navel. She arched an eyebrow in Iris's direction. It was a very special form of torture, and Iris felt her skin grow hot under Cam's touch.

"Don't judge me, okay. I meant to tell you sooner that I had feelings for you, but I just couldn't."

"Go on."

"It was when we had the curry. We had such a great day together and you were so lovely about the thing with Amanda, after I'd been dreading telling you, worrying you'd think I was pathetic. We held hands in the cab on the way home, and I remember hating myself for feeling so good about it, feeling like I shouldn't. And I knew, when you got out at your house, that I had no right to feel as madly jealous as I did that you were going inside to Ryan." Iris hadn't meant to be so honest. She felt exposed in just the way she hadn't wanted to be.

"What about you?" Iris pushed her anxiety away.

"When we had dinner at my place and I woke up to find you sleeping on me. It felt too good, and my feelings weren't exactly just friendly." Cam sounded a little unsure. "I called my sister that night intending to talk to her about you, about how I was feeling but I didn't have the courage to say what I needed to." Cam paused. "I guess neither of us has been very honest—"

"We were being sensible—" Iris interrupted but then stopped herself from finishing the sentence, knowing they were naked in bed together, not feeling very sensible.

"Until now." Cam finished the sentence for her.

"Until now."

Cam lifted Iris's hand and placed a kiss in the middle of her palm, holding her gaze. Iris lay silently for a while, just staring back at Cam.

"I bet you get tired of people telling you how beautiful your eyes are." Iris trailed her fingers across Cam's collarbone, marveling at the softness of her skin, at the fact she was allowed to touch it at all. Her eyes held Cam's. "But they really are beautiful."

Cam shook her head slightly. "I don't know who you think has been telling me that. I'm not exactly...I mean...well, I'm not as experienced as you, Iris."

Iris raised an eyebrow.

"Experienced is a very polite word for it. Thank you." Iris leaned in to kiss Cam, pressing her lips softly against Cam's, then scattering kisses across her mouth, from one corner to the other, and back again. She laid her head on Cam's chest, enjoying the feel of Cam's fingers playing with her hair and loving the sound of Cam's heartbeat against her cheek.

"But this is the only experience I want."

Cam tilted Iris's head upward till she could see her face. "That's smooth, damn smooth actually. How am I supposed to resist that?"

Iris smiled back at her. "You're not. Though I'm not trying to be smooth, I'm being truthful." Iris bit her lip, feeling a little embarrassed.

"I had no idea you were such a softie." Cam stroked Iris's cheek with her thumb.

"Neither did I."

Iris couldn't ever remember feeling this way. Not even with Amanda. She felt content, but behind the contentment was fear. She loved Cam, she was letting herself be vulnerable, and that meant Cam could hurt her. Cam frowned at her as if able to see from her expression what she was thinking about.

"Hey?" Cam pulled her tightly into an embrace, holding her head against her chest and pressing her lips to the top of Iris's head. "It's okay."

"Are you hungry?" Iris wanted to change the subject. Cam had come to her, she had to accept that Cam meant to love her, meant for them to be together. She didn't want her insecurity to ruin things.

Cam nodded. Iris lifted her head and leaned up to kiss Cam. The kiss was possessive rather than gentle. She was signaling her intent in some way. As they broke the kiss, Iris leaned her forehead against Cam's and closed her eyes. She might not be good at saying the words that were needed but she wanted Cam to know that she loved her, that she really wanted this. She moved off the bed and rummaged in the tall chest of drawers next to it. She pulled out and slipped on a tank top, before passing Cam a red T-shirt with the logo of the bookstore printed across the front. Iris went out into the living room. The door closing behind her.

Cam blew out a breath and stared up at the ceiling. This was where she wanted to be; she had no doubts at all anymore. How had it taken her so long to realize? She smiled for a moment and then felt the weight of what would come next settle on her shoulders. She had to convince Iris that this could work and then go home and badly hurt the man she had once agreed to marry.

"I'm coming up empty." Iris shouted from the room next door. "I can do beans on toast or it's gonna have to be a takeaway."

Cam slipped on Iris's T-shirt and padded into the living room. Iris was peering into the open fridge in just her tank top. Her delectable ass on full view and her long legs causing Cam's heart to beat faster.

"If I say that I'm easy either way are you going to give me some trouble about being loose again?" Cam crossed to Iris and ran her hands up the back of her legs, stopping at Iris's backside. She placed wet kisses on the back of Iris's neck, biting down slightly into the flesh. She reached around and brushed her hands purposefully across Iris's breasts. Cam sighed as Iris pushed back against her, moaning slightly.

"I thought we were hungry." Iris's words came out ragged.

"Oh, I'm hungry all right." Cam turned Iris to face her, crushing her lips with a kiss, not wanting to be gentle, her need too urgent. Iris's tongue sending bolts of arousal between her legs every time Iris slipped it inside her mouth.

Iris moaned with desire and Cam leaned behind them to slam the fridge door shut, pushing Iris up against it, wanting to press herself against the length of her. Iris reached for her, reached inside the T-shirt. Cam stopped her, pushing Iris's hands behind her back and holding them there, pinning Iris against the fridge.

Cam relaxed her grip so she could slide her hands up and down Iris's torso, lifting her top so that she could taste first one and then the other nipple. She gently grazed her teeth across the erect buds and felt Iris writhe next to her. Cam enjoyed the fact that she already knew exactly what Iris liked her to do to her nipples. She trailed her fingers down Iris's body, to her hips, her backside, down the outside of her thigh and then, slowly, feeling Iris tense beneath her touch, up the inside of her thigh, arriving where she knew Iris wanted them to be. Cam's fingertips slid into the wet folds between Iris's legs, softly moving across her clitoris. Iris's body responded with tremors and Cam felt herself heat up as her own body reacted to Iris's pleasure, knowing that touching her made Cam feel like nothing else she'd experienced. She kept her touches light and feathery until Iris pushed against her, straining for more contact with her fingers.

"Inside." The plea made Cam impossibly aroused. Cam made sure she could see Iris's face, her eyes closed now, her head tipped back against the fridge, and she entered Iris, finding the rhythm that Iris wanted, sliding her fingers in and out. Cam snaked a hand behind Iris's neck and pulled her into a kiss. Iris gripped Cam's T-shirt tightly, bunching the material and using it to pull Cam closer. And still Cam moved her fingers in and out. Iris lifted herself slightly, pushing up on her toes, her thighs tensing. The moans, the words, told her Iris was close.

"Don't stop, don't stop, don't stop." Iris spoke through gritted teeth.

Cam had spent hours getting to know this body, greedily laying claim to every inch, but this—right now—was everything she had wanted to do for months. Cam felt Iris stiffen and she pushed herself against Iris. She had her tongue inside Iris's mouth, and she felt Iris shudder against her as she came. Iris's orgasm came in waves, her breathing rapid and she clasped her hand around Cam's, not letting her withdraw, keeping her inside. Her eyes were clamped shut.

Finally, Iris opened her eyes and looked at Cam. Her eyes were shining, bold, holding not even a shadow of embarrassment. "That was incredible."

"You are incredible." Cam placed a soft kiss on Iris's lips as she gently withdrew her hand. "And indescribably hot." She looked Iris up and down, leaning back as she did so. Iris pulled her back into the embrace. She kissed Cam, soft and slow at first, and then harder and wanting. Cam felt her body respond and she lost herself in the kiss until she made herself put her hands on Iris's chest, pushing herself away, breaking the contact. Iris looked confused and hurt, her hooded eyes showing the lust she still felt. Cam leaned in and whispered in Iris's ear. "If we don't eat something, I'm gonna die."

Iris pulled a pan from the cupboard and set some bread in the toaster. The simple pleasure of making a snack for Cam almost as enjoyable as the sex that had gone before. She felt a wave of arousal looking across the breakfast bar to see Cam watching her with a sweet shy smile. The bar between them a practical necessity to stop them from reaching for each other, to give Iris the chance to make the food they both needed to eat. She put the beans in the pan and set it on the stove.

"And what are you smiling at, my angel?" Iris tilted her head in Cam's direction. Cam met her gaze.

"I'm looking at you fixing me some food and wondering why this feels so natural when we've never done it before. And jeez, I love it that you just called me angel."

"Sorry, it just slipped out. That wasn't me trying to be smooth." She stirred the beans one last time as the toast popped up.

"I guess not," Cam said. "Anyway, smooth would've been having some champagne on ice and smoked salmon in the fridge. Not beans on toast."

Iris buttered the toast before pouring beans onto each slice. She handed one of the plates to Cam.

"This is the 'you-totally-caught-me-unawares' version of smooth. If I'd known you were coming, I might have managed a bit of cheese as well." She waggled her eyebrows at Cam. "I'm a council estate kid who can't cook, you might as well know what you're getting into."

As soon as the words came out, Iris regretted them. It was a figure of speech. She hadn't meant to assume that Cam was getting into anything, that this meant anything close to what she wanted it to mean. But the idea that it might not took her breath away for an instant. She made herself sit down across the bar from Cam and fork some beans into her mouth, feeling uneasy. Cam reached across the bar and entwined her fingers with Iris's.

"Iris." Cam waited for Iris to look up at her, to meet her eyes. "Next time—and I intend for there to be lots of next times—I'll bring the cheese."

Iris slowly pulled herself out of sleep. Cam was propped on an elbow next to her, watching her closely.

"Hey." The single syllable from Cam was probably the sexiest she had ever heard.

"What time is it?" Iris yawned out the question.

"Nearly six." Cam reached her fingers down to stroke Iris's hand, leaning in to place a kiss on her lips. Her expression looking serious in the soft lamp light. Iris felt that something had come between them.

"You okay?"

"Yeah. Of course. Just thinking about how cute you look when you're asleep, and…" she hesitated, "just hating Amanda a little bit for daring to leave you feeling so bruised."

Iris hadn't expected that. She had been trying not to think about that whole situation, trying not to recognize the parallels. There was so much for her to worry about without that. She frowned and rubbed her face, wanting to feel more awake.

"What are you thinking?" Cam used her thumb to smooth out the frown.

That I love you with all my heart and I need to know that you really mean this. Iris left the words unspoken, her heart beginning to hurt with all the things they weren't saying to each other. They had to find a way to have the conversation somehow.

"What do you think happened to Gina?" Iris said the words softly. She was flat on her back, her hands folded on her stomach, gazing at the ceiling.

"What do you mean?"

"In the story I told you, it was all about me and Amanda, Gina doesn't have anything but a supporting role. Don't you understand? Amanda used her to break things with me, because we were having problems, and she wanted a way out." Iris wanted Cam to understand.

"But after Amanda and I broke up, Gina was just cast aside. It might have taken Amanda a couple of weeks to do it but she didn't really want Gina, she wanted some way to get away from me. Gina was just—" Iris's voice broke. "She was just collateral damage."

Cam sat up in the bed.

"Iris, this isn't like that, you know it isn't." Cam's voice betrayed how upset she was.

"Isn't it? Aren't you just using this…me…to get away from Ryan? You're not happy and you weren't happy long before I came along. Doing this, with me, it gives you a way out." She looked away from Cam, not able to meet her eyes. She needed the reassurance but didn't want to ask for it.

"That's not true. I wasn't totally happy, no. But I wasn't looking for a way out. Not until I got to know you. I tried to resist you, Iris, but I couldn't, I can't." She reached for Iris's hand. "I don't know how to convince you that I want this, that I'm serious, that I love you. I don't have the words."

"I don't want words, Cam." Iris whispered her response and they looked at each other, not speaking.

After a few moments, Iris pulled Cam toward her. She still feared that Cam wouldn't be brave enough for this, that somehow love wouldn't be enough—but the woman she had fallen in love with was sitting in her bed, naked apart from a T-shirt and offering to try. It was something.

Iris kissed Cam hard, crushing her lips with her own, not caring if it was too hard. She pushed Cam onto her back, heard the groan of pleasure as she pushed her tongue into Cam's mouth, saw the want in Cam's eyes. Iris pulled off her own top as Cam removed her T-shirt, revealing her breasts, the nipples hard and perfect. Iris pushed her thigh between Cam's legs, finding her still so wonderfully wet.

Cam gasped as Iris slid down and bit her nipple gently and then not so gently. She moved upward, kissing Cam between her breasts before raking her neck with kisses. Iris felt as if she and Cam were melted together. Cam moved to wrestle Iris onto her back. She grabbed Iris's hands and pushed them above her head, pinning her down so she was unable to move. Cam leaned her mouth close to Iris's ear.

"The difference is that Amanda didn't have a reason to stay with Gina afterward. I do, Iris, because I love you."

Before Iris could reply, Cam's mouth came down hard on hers. She moved it down Iris's body, pausing to kiss her collarbone tenderly and then, as Iris wrapped her hands in her hair, Cam bit down, sucking the flesh, tasting her skin, and biting a little harder when Iris moaned loudly with pleasure. Cam stopped to look at her face.

"I know you don't want my words but I'm gonna show you how much I want this. Not just here, in bed, but tomorrow and the next day and the next day. In the daylight, with everyone watching, with my actions not my words."

Cam gave her a smile that was ridiculously shy given the position they were in. Iris couldn't help but react to Cam's words. She grabbed Cam's shoulders, reversing their positions again, wanting to be on top, wanting to claim Cam all over again. She moved her hands across Cam's breasts, in her hair, on her behind, pulling them closer, never feeling they were close enough. She ran her tongue over Cam's taut stomach, salty with sweat from the lovemaking, and down between Cam's thighs, desperate to taste her once more. Iris pushed Cam's thighs apart far enough to allow her to be able to run her tongue along the swollen flesh, using her hands to hold Cam's backside slightly off the bed. She moved her tongue in circles, delighting in the noises Cam was making, enjoying that she was the cause of them.

Iris stopped to nip at the soft, smooth flesh on Cam's inner thigh and Cam moaned before guiding her head back to where it was before. "Please, Iris, please." Iris took all of her, greedily. Cam's head was thrown back and her fists balled. "I love you, Iris," she growled the words as she arched her back, giving in to her orgasm.

Iris eased herself out of bed and crossed into the living room, flipping on the lamp next to her favorite armchair and switching on her laptop. Cam had fallen asleep, but she was wide-awake. If she wasn't going to sleep, then she should at least use the time to write. Writing always helped her sort through her feelings.

Through the open door to the bedroom, she could see Cam sleeping on her side, her face pointed toward the door, the covers draped across her hips but leaving her upper body and legs uncovered. Iris drank in the sight of her before turning back to the keyboard and waiting for the words to come. Her whole being had been shaken from head to toe today, and she felt full—full of feelings, full of fear and, yes, full of love. She opened a new document and began to tap out a slow steady rhythm—the words coming easily for once.

A phone rang in the bedroom. It wasn't hers, she could tell from the tone. Cam moved slowly, seeming to force herself awake. Iris crossed to the doorway, picking up the jeans that Cam had been wearing and passing them to her. The phone had stopped ringing by the time she had fished it out of the pocket, her movements slowed by sleepiness. Cam's forehead creased as she moved her thumb across the screen, checking something.

"Who was that?" Iris knew the answer but asked the question anyway.

"Ryan."

Iris waited.

"He was worried…he sent a text, but I didn't answer, so he called." Cam scratched a spot on her arm.

"Does he know where you are?" Iris held her breath, needing the answer to be yes, knowing it would signal the right kind of intention on Cam's part.

"I don't know. He left the house before me so—" Cam sat up. "He might think I'm here. Or at Vicki's. He knows we're close, that I might go there."

"Why doesn't he know you're here…with me?" Iris swallowed down a rising feeling of panic. "I mean, you left him to be with me. You said you told him that. Why wouldn't he think this is exactly where you'd be?"

"He might. I don't know…I mean, he probably does. It's not important."

Iris couldn't stop herself from pacing in front of Cam. Her senses were on alert and she felt sick in her stomach. "Of course it's important."

Cam got off the bed and reached for her. "Iris, don't—"

Iris moved out of reach.

"I just don't know why he'd think you were at Vicki's. If you told him…if you broke up with him and told him you weren't going to Seattle and you were staying here because you loved me, because you couldn't leave me." Iris used the words that Cam had used hours ago. "Why the hell wouldn't he think you were right here?"

"I'm sure he does. I just—"

"Cam, please tell me that he knows it's over. That you ended it with him before coming here."

"He…yes…but…" She couldn't meet Iris's eyes. "He walked out. We didn't get to say everything we needed to."

"Dammit, Cam." Iris felt the breath leave her body.

"But I told him I loved you, that I didn't want…that I couldn't… leave you. I told him I was staying to be with you, but he left in the middle of the argument." Cam had her hands pressed together in front of her body and Iris could see distress written clearly across her face. She didn't want to hurt her, but she had to know.

"He's calling and texting to see where you are, Cam. That doesn't sound like someone who thinks you're over."

"We are." Cam moved closer. "We are, Iris. I promise you that. I only want you, this. I love you so much."

Iris could hear the tears behind the words, but she couldn't afford to care. She hadn't wanted this, had gone out of her way to avoid this exact fucking situation.

"But does he know that? I told you I would never..." Iris made herself calm down, made herself concentrate on her breathing, on the words she needed to say. Her heart was beating loudly in her chest and she felt her throat constricting as she spoke. "I didn't want it this way. I never wanted you to do this to him. In fact, I did everything to make sure this didn't happen. Fuck, Cam, I would've waited for you to end it, for you to be free. It would've been better, surely you knew that."

"I didn't know that. I thought I was losing you. I wanted—"

"You wanted what, Cam? To hedge your bets, to take me for a test drive before you traded in the old car?"

"Iris—" Cam cut across her. "I know you don't mean that. Do not do this."

"Do what, Cam? Want the person I'm with to not still have an actual fiancé, to want you to be able to commit to me before we spent the day fucking each other senseless, cheating on your fucking fiancé."

Iris couldn't believe she'd been so stupid. She should have asked more questions, been more careful. Cam had come to her and it was everything she had wanted for months, but it wasn't everything, it wasn't anything actually. Cam said she loved her, but she hadn't loved her enough to break off her engagement first. She felt nauseous and utterly heartsick.

"I think you should go."

"Iris, don't. Please don't. I'm sorry if I've not done this right, but I want to be here with you. This isn't me hurting you. I won't do that."

Iris turned her back on Cam and crossed into the living room. She would not cry, not in Cam's presence.

"Iris, try to trust me. I just need a little time—" The voice came from behind her. She turned. Looking Cam in the face was like looking directly into the sun—it hurt and she couldn't do it.

"I would've given you time, all the time you needed, but you didn't ask for it. You came here and acted like you'd decided and you haven't, not really."

"I have. It's just…it's four years, it's complicated. You know that. I just need to talk to him some more, make sure he understands."

Everything Cam said made things worse. "So go and talk to him. But I don't want you to come back here. You got what you came for and I think, deep down, we both knew how this would play out. You won't leave him. He's your port in a storm. I knew you wouldn't be brave enough, wouldn't love me enough." She paused and took in a deep breath, willing the tears not to fall. "Just go, Cam. Before it gets so late that he won't believe whatever lie you're going to have to tell him about where you were today."

Cam reacted to Iris's words as if they were a slap. Iris felt a sliver of regret and then pushed it away.

"I'll go, Iris." Cam's voice was shaky. Iris could tell she was trying not to cry. "But I mean this and I'm sorry you won't let me show you just how much I love you." She walked away from Iris into the bedroom. Iris wanted to say something, to believe her, to stop her from going even as she sent her away but she did nothing. She couldn't watch Cam dress and leave, knowing it would hurt too damn much, so she moved into the bathroom and shut the door.

CHAPTER TWENTY-SIX

Iris." Her dad waited a moment and called her name again, knocking lightly on the door. "I've made some dinner. Come and eat with me."

Iris had been for an early run and then spent the day upstairs, in her old room. She knew she needed to talk but wasn't sure she'd be able to do so without sobbing and she was far too old to still be wetting her dad's shirts with her tears. She headed downstairs and into the kitchen to see her dad plating two omelets.

Iris sat in the chair opposite him. He passed her the brown sauce.

"Try and eat, sweet pea. Look, I fried chips for you." He smiled. She sat up a little straighter in her chair, picked a chip from her plate, and bit the end off.

"Any better today?"

Iris shook her head. She'd turned up asking if she could stay for a couple of days, handing him her phone on the doorstep, knowing she didn't trust herself not to weaken and call Cam. She wanted to apologize and beg Cam's forgiveness, and she wanted to shout at her for making Iris feel so hurt and foolish. It was for the best that she couldn't do either.

Iris cut off a corner of the omelet with her fork, lifting it to her mouth uncertainly. She chewed and swallowed. "I've fucked up, like I always seem to."

"Want to tell me about it?" Her dad's voice was low and kind.

"What's the point?"

"Need a dad cliché? Better out than in. A problem shared is a problem halved. Talking is a cure. Enough yet?" He shuffled his chair a little closer to her, and put a hand on her arm, stroking it gently. "I'm worried about you, but I'm not going to pry."

Iris swallowed and looked up at him, fighting not to shed more tears.

"Cam...I...we...we got together. And"—she ran a hand through her hair—"it was amazing and I've fallen in love with her. I mean I already had, but..."

"And that's bad?" He wrinkled his face in confusion.

"Yes. She's still with her fiancé. She came to me and made it sound like she'd left him to be with me, but she hadn't, not really. We cheated on him and I hate myself for it. She said she loved me but...I don't think she knows what she wants, or who she is. And I think that, even though she loves me, it isn't enough." Iris shook her head, the memories too painful. "I threw her out, I wasn't kind. And I hate myself for that too."

"Oh."

"It's breaking my heart to have come so close to having her and losing her." She rubbed the tears away with the napkin her dad gave her.

He held out his arms and Iris moved into the space, letting her dad hug her while she cried for her own stupidity and for the loss of Cam. It wasn't enough to erase the pain, but it was a start.

"Are you sure?" Her dad held up her phone, a frown on his face. "It's been buzzing like crazy. And I'm guessing they're not all work related." Iris smiled at him. She wasn't sure, but it felt like the first she had managed in two days. She'd got up this morning feeling a little brighter and determined to just get on with her life.

"I'm sure, Dad. I have to get back to work and I'd rather know what's waiting for me." Iris was only half telling the truth. She also badly wanted to know if Cam had called or texted. The thought of Cam leaving London still had the power to hurt, to make her draw breath, but she'd spent most of the last two days in her room, playing around with her poems, listening to music and she'd had plenty of time to think.

What had happened wasn't on her. She had trusted Cam, believed her to be free. She had opened up her heart to her, not just her bed, and if Cam had come to her before she had a right to, without really meaning to leave Ryan, that wasn't her fault. The pain was the same, but somehow not feeling completely responsible for the mess helped Iris to think she could survive this better.

"I'm taking this upstairs so you don't hear me swear." Iris tried for a joke as she took the phone from her dad. "I know you already think I have a potty mouth."

"Something else you got from me." Her dad laughed. "And I put your laundry on your bed. There was some stuff in your pockets that I left on the dresser, don't forget to pick it up before you go."

"Thanks, Dad." Iris gave him a quick hug before disappearing upstairs. She sat on her bed, almost too nervous to look at her phone. When she finally steeled herself, Iris could see multiple texts and missed calls from work, and from Hazel and Casey, but nothing from Cam. She opened the most recent text from Hazel. It just said, *Cam has given in her notice. Thought you should know.*

Iris put the phone down and put her head in her hands. Her feelings—shame, sorrow and loss—were an absolute whirl in her chest. Maybe Cam just hadn't loved her enough. Or maybe Iris's behavior had made it impossible for her to do anything but go to Seattle with Ryan. Iris felt the rejection like a knife. She had let herself fall in love with Cam, but she couldn't give Cam the courage she needed to choose her. She barely had enough of her own.

Iris picked through the items her dad had fished out of her jeans. She put the coins and USB stick back in her pocket and unfolded the small piece of paper, knowing exactly what it was. She'd carried it around for weeks, ever since Cam had given it to her. The well-worn creases created black lines on the paper, but it didn't matter. Iris knew the date, knew the venue, knew she had promised Cam faithfully that she would perform at the event all those weeks ago. But that was before, what felt like a lifetime ago.

Iris stuffed the remaining bits and pieces into her backpack, slipped her phone into her pocket, and headed down the stairs. She was going home, she was going to try to keep her head straight for the day, and maybe tomorrow she would go and perform one of her poems. But if she did, she'd do it for herself, because it was bloody well time that she started living in the world rather than hiding from it. If loving Cam had taught her anything, it was that.

CHAPTER TWENTY-SEVEN

Y ou don't have to move out straight away. We've got a few weeks till the lease is up." Ryan stood leaning against the kitchen counter, looking defeated and sounding weary. "We can be civilized with each other after all this time, surely. Unless it's that bad that you really can't bear to be around me that is." He added the last sentence a little bitterly, trying for a smile but not quite managing.

Cam felt such fondness for him. She wanted to give him a hug but knew that the contact would not be helpful for either of them. She hated that she was the reason he was hurting right now. He was waiting for her to reply, to reassure, but she said nothing. What could she say?

"You'll have to leave your keys after you've finished moving. The agency will want both sets back at the end of the tenancy." He choked slightly on the words, and Cam moved toward him, despite herself.

"Don't." He said the word quietly, holding up a hand.

Cam sat back down on the couch. The purple blanket was folded neatly next to her. She ran her hand across the fabric. It was impossible for her not to associate the blanket with Iris, with her realization weeks before that she had the wrong kind of feelings for her. Feelings that turned out to be the very right kind of feelings. Even if Iris wasn't willing to let Cam prove it.

Cam yawned. Neither of them had slept the night before. They had spent hours raging, crying and despairing, calming down enough to eat a stilted breakfast together, both of them understanding by then that it would probably be their last, and then arguing again for what felt like hours. Finally, thinking there was nothing more to say, Cam had gone up to their bedroom to throw a few things into a bag. Ryan had come upstairs to watch her, not really believing she was going to leave, and starting the same conversation they'd had several times already.

"You can't love her. You've only known her for a few months. And you're not even a lesbian—I think I'd know. This is just some stupid crush." Ryan kept returning to Iris. It was like he could accept Cam leaving him, but he couldn't accept Cam with Iris.

"I'm not leaving you for Iris." Cam said it again, feeling the pain of Iris's words, of her rejection, all over again.

"How can you say that? That's exactly what you're doing." Ryan rubbed his forehead.

"We aren't happy together. We haven't been for a while. We've just stopped working. You know that really. I know it's hard after so long together, but we both deserve to be happier, to be with people who love us the way we deserve to be loved."

"And you think that's Iris for you? Bullshit." He shook his head.

"I want it to be." Cam was quietly emphatic and Ryan got up and walked out, slamming the bedroom door behind him.

Iris clearly didn't feel the same way, and every time she thought about what had happened between them, she felt the same searing hurt. But, on one level, it didn't matter. She couldn't stay with Ryan now that she'd experienced how Iris made her feel. Living with Ryan was like living in black and white, whereas with Iris everything felt Technicolor.

When she had returned from Iris's on Saturday evening, he was waiting for her, and as soon as she got through the door, he asked her outright if she had spent the day with Iris. She couldn't lie to him; she didn't want to. She had nodded, her eyes cast down, still full of the tears she had shed when Iris had told her to go. Ryan had raged, and for a time she had felt fearful. He had run through every insult he could throw at Iris—called her manipulative, a slut, a relationship wrecker, accused her of seducing women for the buzz of it—and when Cam told him that she was the one who had gone to Iris, that Iris had always been the one to try to stay away, that Iris had thrown her out telling Cam that they couldn't be together because of Ryan, he looked at Cam with a mix of disbelief and fury in his eyes and his fists clenched at his sides.

"Why would you do that to me? To us?"

"I love her. I can't be without her."

She had repeated a version of that truth so many times as they argued and talked that eventually he had been forced to accept that she meant it. That she loved Iris in a way she had never loved him, never loved anyone, and she had meant for them to be together.

"I can't really believe you're gonna do this. I know we kind of drifted, but I didn't think..." They were sitting side by side on the couch. It was close to four a.m. "I thought we'd go home, get married, and have kids. That it'd get better. I thought we just needed something to focus on. I didn't know you felt like this."

Cam turned to him. He looked tired, drawn. Whatever she said would hurt him, but she had to be honest. She hadn't ever trusted him with her truth.

"I've been so scared of what people thought of me—you, my mom, our friends—that I let myself be talked into doing things I didn't really want and give up the things that make me happy. And I settled for a relationship that isn't really enough for either of us. I want to be with someone I can't be without—and who can't be without me—who wants me to be me, the best me I can be. I didn't expect to feel this way about her and I can't go back to what things were like before. I can't."

"And when she's finished with you, you'll be left feeling like a fool on your own in a country that isn't even home, writing obituaries for the Hampstead free paper because you always wanted to be a fucking journalist and are somehow still blaming me for keeping you from your dream."

He was angry now. Cam had pushed him too far. But she couldn't stop; they needed to do this.

"I'm not blaming you. I'm blaming myself." She took in a deep breath. "And I don't have Iris, Ryan. She doesn't want me. Okay?" Cam could feel the pressure in her chest. It felt like a heavy weight pressing down on her breastbone. She slowed her breathing, wanting to get the words out. "She threw me out...after we...I mean, she actually told me I was the one fucking with her. So you're right about us not making it. She doesn't want any part of this drama."

She could see Ryan trying to process what she'd told him.

"But I'm not leaving you for her, Ryan. I'm leaving you for me. Iris has shown me that I can have the kind of life I want here, that I deserve to have things I want. I have my friends, the soccer team, I can start to write again." Cam paused. "And she's helped me to love London, even to love myself a little more." Her eyes filled with tears again.

"I'm going back home, I'm not waiting to see if you change your mind," Ryan said eventually. "I deserve to have what I want as much as you do."

"I know."

They both sat silently.

"I hope you'll be happier." Cam meant it, but it was far too soon for Ryan to accept her sympathy. He shot her a look of disbelief.

"Oh yeah, it's gonna be a blast. I mean, London was such a great move for me and I get to go home having failed at all of it. I'm sure I'll be skipping through the fucking airport when I get home." Ryan was bitter. Cam knew he had a right to be. "And, Cam, when it doesn't turn out the way you want, don't come running back to me." Ryan had said the same thing several times. He walked out of the living room without waiting for a reply.

"I won't," Cam said to herself.

She hadn't been stupid enough to think that four years of a relationship could be unraveled without hurt and recriminations, but this was hard. Harder still because, without Iris, she was hollow and hurting.

Cam had wanted to call her so many times but kept coming back to the appalled expression on her face when she had understood that Cam had not yet properly ended things with Ryan. Iris had said that she didn't want Cam, that she was sick of Cam's cowardice and Cam couldn't stop the small sob that escaped as she remembered it all over again. She had told Iris that she would prove her wrong, that she meant to love her out in the open, forever. But she could only do that if Iris was willing to let her, if Iris loved her back with the same righteousness. And Cam had no reason to believe that Iris loved her enough to give her another chance.

CHAPTER TWENTY-EIGHT

Iris sat in one of the chairs reserved for performers to the right of the makeshift stage. Next to her another performer, an older woman with a mop of curly hair tied up in a bandana, was reciting the words of her poem under her breath as if incanting a meditation. Iris had always had a dread of performing, but forgetting the words was not something that made her anxious. Tripping, being unable to actually form words with her mouth, walking off stage to complete silence—those were the things that she worried about.

The woman swore softly and fished several pieces of paper from her handbag, riffling through them manically. Ordinarily, Iris would have wished her luck, offered some words of encouragement, but tonight she wanted to focus on her own performance, on the poem that she had written for Cam, surprising herself that that was the poem she'd chosen to perform. It was the one she was surest of, but it was also the most exposing. It was almost as if she was throwing herself in the deep end. The obvious question being whether she was going to sink or swim.

Iris remembered the conversation where she had promised Cam she would perform at tonight's event like it was yesterday. Cam's shining eyes, her belief in Iris, her encouragement and confidence all making it seem as if it would be easy. Cam had made her pinkie swear, and Iris was nothing if not a keeper of pinkie promises. Of course, Cam had also said she would be cheerleading from the front row. At the time, Iris had thought the idea wonderful. She imagined herself—not like this, not as she was now, full of heartache and pointless courage—but being with Cam, performing for her, the two of them against the world.

But Iris had made sure that wouldn't happen. Cam had come to her and Iris had sent her away. And now she was leaving Cottoms and going home with Ryan. Iris inhaled, feeling the distress at just how spectacularly she had blown it, course through her body, and the woman next to her stopped what she was doing and looked across at her with concern.

"Sorry, just thought of something I forgot to do." Iris's voice sounded strange to her own ears and she worried about her ability to do this.

The poem she was going to perform described her love for Cam. She'd written it that night as she'd watched Cam sleep in her bed. It was an attempt to describe the bravery they would both need to show to turn the evening they'd shared into a week, a month, and then into a life together. She rubbed her eyes and hoped that, having repeated it often in practicing for tonight, it no longer had the power to move her to tears.

A young woman with a clipboard appeared and spoke to the performers as a group. There were six of them, all women, all first timers. The woman was lively and excited.

"More than ten minutes and we hook you off. Don't stand too close to the microphone or you'll burst eardrums, and no bad language please. The old people don't like it." She raised her eyebrows. "And enjoy yourselves, if you can. We've got a good crowd in." She disappeared off as quickly as she had appeared only to reappear on the stage to welcome the audience and introduce the first performer.

Iris sat back to listen to the young woman speak of the recent death of her father and how the loss had left her feeling. Her performance was angry and moving. Iris let the words wash over her, giving in to feeling her own loss. The loss of her never-quite-was relationship with Cam.

The warm applause of the audience brought Iris back from her reverie. The young woman looked uncomfortable with the acclaim and exited the stage quickly as if not expecting it. As the next performer, the nervous woman with the sheaves of crumpled paper, climbed onto the stage, Iris looked around at the venue once more. All the seats were taken, and those without seats were standing across the wall at the back of the bookstore.

Scanning the audience, Iris felt everything slow down, as a woman who had been bent down and fiddling with something in her bag, stood and turned around to face the stage and Iris found herself staring at Cam's beautiful face. Hope and warmth surged through Iris and left her just as quickly as they had arrived when Cam looked away without reacting, without even seeming to see Iris, and threaded her way around the edge of the room to the drinks table.

Of course she didn't come to see me, Iris thought coldly. She didn't even know I'd be here. But the small voice inside her head told her that maybe, just maybe, Cam had come to keep her side of the promise and there was some way back for them.

❖

Cam's legs felt heavy as she climbed the stairs to the second floor of the bookstore. She'd been running on the Heath that morning and got a little lost, taking a route that added a couple of miles that her calves were already complaining about. She'd gotten to the top of Parliament Hill eventually and sat there enjoying the view, and thinking of Iris. Of course. There weren't many hours when she wasn't thinking of her.

She'd taken a photo and almost sent it to Iris, finding it impossible not to reach out, wanting to tell her that Ryan's flight was booked, that they were over, wanting it to make the difference. It was a way of asking Iris to let them try again. She hadn't sent it. It didn't matter how much she wanted it, or how right they felt together, Cam had to accept that Iris just didn't feel the same way.

Cam reached the second floor and headed for the table against the back wall. Empty wine glasses sat on one side and wine bottles on the other. Behind the table, a bearded man in a black turtleneck sweater was handing out drinks. Tonight's event was a fundraiser and the tickets were more expensive than usual, but included a free glass of wine. She pointed to the bottles of wine to the man's right hand side.

"White, please."

She took the glass and turned. The room was pretty full, but her calves really wanted her to sit down. Cam felt her breath catch in her throat as she spotted Iris sitting next to the stage. Her head was bowed and her hands pressed together as if she were meditating, but when she lifted her head, it seemed as if she looked straight at Cam. The sight of Iris made her tremble. It was a mixture of want and fear. She turned toward the back of the room without acknowledging her, her heart beating loudly in her chest. She wasn't sure Iris would come. She desperately wanted it to mean something that she had, something about the promise she'd made to Cam, but a hard little voice in her head told her it was just as likely that this was part of Iris moving on with her life. Her life without Cam.

Moving across the back of the room, she spotted a single seat near the window in the far corner. It had a view of the stage but not the side where the performers were seated. She could no longer see Iris, and it both settled and unsettled her.

Cam had come tonight on a whim. She'd spent the day moving into Vicki's houseshare and come out intending to buy some stuff she needed for her room. But as she sat at the lights on Archway Road, knowing left would take her to IKEA, she found herself pushing down on the indicator and turning right. To Hampstead. Her mind, her heart, not really letting her forget that tonight was the slam. She hadn't stopped to change. Hell, she hadn't even stopped to consider if maybe putting herself in the way of Iris again was a good idea. She just had to come.

Cam wasn't sure she'd be able to settle down enough to concentrate on the rest of the poetry, but she made herself try. The performer on stage now had a strange speaking style that matched the staccato rhythm of her blank verse. Cam appreciated the woman's intensity even if the poetry wasn't to her taste. She looked down at her wine and saw that it was almost finished. She'd clearly needed the liquid courage. She didn't know if Iris wanted her here. She didn't know if Iris would care that she was finally free to love her. The words Iris said as she threw Cam out of her apartment settled like a stone in Cam's chest.

Iris scanned the room looking for Cam but couldn't see her anywhere. She wanted to flee, sure she could not read her poem with Cam in the room, but she was frozen to the spot and doubted that her legs would be able to carry her away even if she was able to get them working. As she completed the thought, the crowd burst into applause as the nervous woman finished her turn. The emcee stepped onto the stage to introduce the next performer. Iris made herself calm down, made herself breathe and fix her attention on what the woman was saying, but she couldn't tune in. She looked for Cam again, and she spotted her at the end of the back row. Iris swallowed as Cam caught her gaze. She still couldn't believe that Cam had come.

"Now, please welcome to the stage Iris Miller. As with everyone on stage, it's her first time here with us tonight so a nice warm welcome would be great." The emcee stopped off the stage to the left, waving Iris forward.

Iris stood unsteadily and took the few short steps to the stage as if on autopilot. She climbed onto it and turned to face the audience. The round of applause that had accompanied her passage to the stage had long died down, and Iris felt the expectation, the waiting.

She had waited a long time to do this, and Cam had been the one to give her the encouragement and the courage to perform her poetry. Iris had dared to imagine that Cam would have been there at her first performance, but not like this, not after everything that had happened. Iris hadn't expected Cam tonight and now wasn't sure she could read her intended poem in the circumstances. She would be exposed, it would be clear that she was heartbroken and that she loved Cam more than she had ever loved anyone.

Iris looked at her shoes, felt the audience's energy shift from anticipation to uncomfortable tension. She lifted her head slowly and looked toward Cam. They gazed at each other for an instant before Cam moved her hand to place it flat against her heart and nodded. Iris felt the power of the gesture from across the room. Her throat full, she cleared her throat and looked out across the audience. She began to speak the lines of the poem she had prepared. The poem she had written about Cam, about her love for Cam, about the hope she had, about the courage they needed. She had never imagined reading it in these circumstances, but she really wanted Cam to hear her say the words. Her voice grew steadier and stronger, and the rhythm of the poem established itself, and she felt glad that Cam was there, glad that she finally had the chance to say to Cam what she felt, even if it was too late. She spoke the final stanza:

The smallest steps are hardest to make
Much easier the big mistakes
If you let me I will leap,
Your love and your life mine to keep

Tears were gently rolling down Iris's cheeks as she finished, but she didn't care. Her voice had stayed strong, the words and the feelings had been expressed, and she'd done it. Iris stood frozen to the spot as the audience clapped enthusiastically. There were even one or two whistles. She stumbled from the stage, embarrassed, and headed to the right hand side of the room, as the emcee introduced the next poet. Someone patted Iris on the back as she passed by, but it barely registered. She couldn't make herself look at Cam, to see her reaction; it all felt too overwhelming. She headed out of the nearby fire door and stood outside breathing deeply, forcing the air into her lungs. It was a cold evening, a welcome relief, and Iris tried to calm herself to focus, to think.

The door banged to her left and Iris felt time slow down as Cam walked in her direction. The look on her face was unreadable, but her eyes held Iris's, only leaving her face briefly to navigate around the chairs set out on the fire escape landing where Iris was now standing. It had been days since Iris and Cam had seen each other. Days, not weeks, and not months, but still Cam's beauty was a surprise. And still Cam had the power to make Iris forget everything there was in the world but her.

"Iris?" A single word, spoken so quietly. Iris could see that Cam had been crying. Her cheeks were still wet with tears, and her eyes looked a little swollen. Cam stopped in front of Iris, a yard away and looked down at her feet before slowly bringing her eyes up to look at Iris.

"That was…" Cam paused. "That was incredible. I loved…they loved it." She gestured toward the door leading back inside the store. "I'm so…" Cam stopped. "I'm not sure I have a right to say it, but I'm so proud of you." The words brought tears back to Cam's eyes, and as she stifled a small sob, Iris stepped forward, wanting to comfort her, wanting to pull her into a hug. She stopped herself from doing it.

"I didn't think you'd come."

"I couldn't not come. We…I promised. I keep my promises." Cam seemed uncertain. The dark shadows under her eyes making clear to Iris that the last few days had been hard for Cam too.

"Look, Cam. I'm sorry. I was horrible. I just…" Iris was having trouble finding the right words. "I know that I did the right thing but I could…I should…have been nicer. I felt foolish because after everything we said, after everything we did, I really thought you'd chosen me, and then when I realized that maybe you hadn't I was heartbroken. It wasn't just the cheating, it was that I loved you. I wanted you, I wanted us, but you just didn't seem as sure. It hurt." Iris couldn't believe she was being so honest. Reading the poem for Cam seemed to have unlocked something.

Cam reached for Iris's hand and entwined their fingers. Iris let her, feeling happy to be touched by Cam again.

"You should've believed in yourself, believed in how much I loved you." Iris felt Cam's use of the past tense like a punch to the stomach, not sure what it meant and dreading the worst. Cam took Iris's other hand, they were face-to-face now, holding each other's hands.

"I told Ryan everything. Everything that I hadn't already made clear. About just how much I loved you, about not loving him anymore, about not being sure that you and I would make it but really needing to try. I left. And moved into Vicki's place. He's going home in a couple of weeks, his flight's booked, the house is packed." Cam shook her head. "I'm so sorry that I didn't handle it better, that I didn't wait until I was properly free. I was just...overwhelmed and not thinking straight. I had all these feelings for you and I didn't know what to do with them. I know I've messed it up but, after everything we said, after everything we did," Cam repeated Iris's words back to her with a soft, shy smile. "How could you possibly think I didn't love you with all my heart, that I wouldn't choose you? I'm not the coward I once was."

Cam bit her lip to keep from crying. For Iris it was too much, she stepped forward, just one small step, and took Cam into her arms, tilting her face upward and leaning in to touch her lips gently to Cam's. She pulled away, though the touch had been gentle, Iris felt the power of the contact ripple through her body. Cam blinked, her eyes showing surprise at the kiss, showing desire.

"I want you to know that, if I wasn't already head over heels in love with you, I don't think I'd have stood a chance after that poem." She grinned and pulled Iris toward her, wrapping her arms around Iris's waist. Iris let herself be held by Cam. "Will you please give us another chance? I want this, Iris, I want you and I'm prepared to prove it to you in any way you need me to." Iris felt the intensity of Cam's gaze.

"I mean every word of that poem. I always meant it. I just didn't find the right way to say it to you. Maybe if I had...well, maybe you'd have found your way to me sooner." Iris held Cam tightly. "But I love you, I really do." She murmured the words into Cam's hair as they hugged. Iris lifted her head from Cam's shoulder and tilted her face downward, searching Cam's eyes for permission that wasn't needed as Cam's mouth found hers and took her hungrily. Iris rocked under the force of the feelings.

Cam's hands reached under Iris's jacket and caressed her back. "I've been so stupid and I don't want to spend another day without you, I've missed you so much." She kept kissing Iris softly, their bodies pressed against one another. "And I've missed this."

Iris moved her hands to Cam's hair, holding her head now, making sure the kiss could not be broken. Cam's thigh settled between her legs and pressed into her causing a heat to rise in her body. Iris kissed back, she pushed against Cam, her hands roaming over Cam's body, digging them into her back and moving them across her shirt to caress her breasts. Cam moaned and arched her body, gripping Iris tighter. She hadn't dared to imagine this, thinking she had lost Cam for good, but now she didn't care who could see them. Iris shifted position so as to grip Cam's leg more tightly between her own. She pushed her tongue into Cam's parted mouth and bit down on Cam's lower lip. Cam's hands were on her back, pulling her even closer.

The fire door banged shut behind them. With some effort, they both pulled away, gasping for breath, gazing at each other. Iris could see the desire in Cam's eyes, her lips were full and her face flushed. She felt sure her own arousal would be just as clear to see.

"I don't know if you have plans, but…" She grinned at Cam, taking her by the hand and leading them both down the stairs to the back of the bookstore. "But I only live a few minutes' walk from here and…" Iris was teasing, walking slowly. "I mean, you'd be welcome to come back for tea." She felt Cam pull her hand, encouraging her to walk quicker as they made their way along the alley beside the bookstore. "And maybe we could drink the tea and talk a little about the poems we've heard today."

"Dammit, Iris." Cam pushed Iris inside a shop doorway, one that had thankfully already closed for the day. She held Iris by the lapels and leaned up to kiss her long and hard. "If you don't get a move on and stop teasing me, I will have you in this doorway."

"This is Hampstead. You'll get us arrested."

"Then hurry us home, sweetheart. We have a lot of making up to do."

"Two minutes and we'll be naked on the floor, I promise." She raised an eyebrow at Cam.

"Now that sounds like a better plan for a Wednesday evening than watching Vicki watch TV." Cam kissed her hard before pulling her out of the doorway and hurrying them up the street.

EPILOGUE

Baby?" Iris nudged Cam gently, stroking the hand that was sticking out from under the blanket. Cam shifted and Iris waited for her to pull herself out of sleep. She felt Cam snuggle in closer but could tell from her breathing that she was awake. She leaned down to plant a kiss in her hair.

"We have to move the seats upright. We're thirty minutes from landing." Cam looked up at Iris and the sight of those green eyes, inches away from her own, made her heart swell. Would she ever get used to being looked at like that by Cam? She doubted it.

"Okay, okay." Cam shook herself awake, moving the blanket that Iris had draped over them onto the empty seat next to her.

"Remind me why we're flying to Vancouver when you live"—Iris pointed at the small screen above their heads, showing the flight path and location of their plane—"all the way down there in Seattle?"

Cam took Iris's hand, bringing it to her lips to kiss it softly. "Because I wanted some time with you on my own before I inflict my family and friends on you. You'll be quite the celebrity when we get to Seattle." She bit her bottom lip and Iris leaned down to kiss it. "I might have gushed about you these past few months, given you quite the buildup."

Iris groaned playfully. "That's fine. I've been not living up to people's expectations for decades. They'll adjust."

"They'll love you as much as I do." Cam's eyes turned serious.

"As much as my dad loves you?" Iris raised an eyebrow. Cam and her dad had fallen for each other the first time they met and Iris loved how well they got on.

"At least that much." Cam smiled.

"And, er, they know I'm a woman, right? I mean, you did come out to everyone—eventually?" Iris couldn't believe that after everything they'd been through to get to this point, she could tease Cam about this kind of stuff.

"Loud and proud, jackass." Cam punched Iris's thigh playfully. It was a joke between them now, but Cam had worried about it at the beginning. She'd told her sister right away, and Alison had been fine, excited even. Most of Cam's friends were surprised, but happy for her, with one or two deciding they couldn't handle it and throwing their loyalty in with Ryan. But of course, her mother had been the one that Cam couldn't face talking to. Ryan had made sure he got his version of things in first so her mother knew the outline of what had happened, but she didn't reach out to Cam, waiting for Cam to get in touch. It was a master class in passive-aggression that Iris would find it hard to ever forgive.

Eventually, Cam decided on an email, and they worked on it together until Cam was happy it said what she needed to not just about Iris and about Ryan but about the way her mother had made her feel about Mia all those years before. Cam had left the door open for her mother to contact her if she could be accepting about Iris, but sadly for Cam, so far she had chosen not to. Coming to Seattle and not seeing her mother would be hard, but it was Cam's choice, and Iris respected the lines she drew for herself. It showed a strength of character that she wasn't sure she possessed herself.

"I still can't believe your boss gave you two weeks off a month after starting there." Iris felt for Cam's hand, wanting to hold it.

"I know. I had to explain the trip was already booked and I couldn't cancel it, and anyway, I think she kind of likes me so…" Cam left the sentence hanging.

Cam had left Cottoms within days of starting her relationship with Iris. It had just been too weird for her being at Cottoms with Iris, Hazel, and Jess in the same building. Her parting gift to them all had been a copy of Graham's incriminating email about the funding of the football teams. Their reaction to the contents teaching Cam a few more of the English curse words she hadn't already picked up from Iris.

After a few weeks in which Vicki claimed Cam was turning out to be the worst kind of unemployed lodger, Cam had joined a publishing company as a general assistant to the editor in chief. It wasn't glamorous, but it brought her closer to what she really wanted to be doing. And, as Cam had told Iris with a big grin the day she got the job, it was words not numbers.

"She's sixty, right? And a grandma. I don't have to worry about you two? You're not gonna go all Sarah Paulson on me." Iris feigned a worried look and Cam laughed.

"It's about as likely as me and Graham getting together."

"I dunno, Cam, seemed like there was a lot of sexual tension in that room sometimes. Or was that you and Sylvia?" She raised an eyebrow playfully.

Cam pretended to be considering the idea of Sylvia, and Iris gave her a playful pinch at the bottom of her back, leaving her hand behind in the gap between Cam's shirt and the top of her jeans, caressing her skin softly, never tiring of the fact that she could touch Cam in that way.

They fell into silence for a few minutes before Cam rubbed her hand across Iris's shoulders in a gesture that was half caress and half massage.

"What are you thinking about?" Cam looked across at Iris.

"A poem, actually. One I wrote about you that time you got injured."

"You were writing poems about me even then?"

"I know, I had it bad." She shrugged. "It was just something about how fragile we are and how easily hurt. I don't know what I did with it. I don't think I finished it and I'd like to. Seeing someone in physical pain, watching someone get kicked or hit by a car or whatever, you know what to do, how to offer comfort, how to help someone heal, but when people hurt emotionally it's much harder to know what they need because you can't see the bruises or the cuts. It's hopeless."

"Maybe you can finish it and perform it at the slam that Alison is taking us to." Cam was excited that Iris was performing regularly.

"Maybe."

"Are you okay?"

"I'm more than okay. I'm as happy as I've ever been." Iris brushed her lips tenderly across Cam's and Cam responded, deepening their kiss, no longer self-conscious about public displays of affection. "And this trip is a great way to celebrate being thirty."

"Well, I was going to book us to run a marathon together you know, but..." Cam smiled teasingly at Iris.

"You did not just say that."

"I'm afraid I did. Can I still blame my tactlessness on being American?" She grinned and Iris leaned down to capture Cam's smiling mouth with her own, enjoying the soft full lips.

"You can. Right now you can do anything you want."

"I love you."

"I love you too." Iris had to accept that her thirties were turning out to be pretty damn good after all.

THE END

About the Author

MA Binfield is a hopeless romantic living in the UK with her long-term partner. She loves books, food, traveling, food, theater and food. She is a frustrated linguist who is overly tall and has always wanted to be left-handed. She's a passionate public servant and, randomly, a qualified football referee. Home is always where the heart is.

Books Available from Bold Strokes Books

Date Night by Raven Sky. Quinn and Riley are celebrating their one-year anniversary. Such an important milestone is bound to result in some extraordinary sexual adventures, but precisely how extraordinary is up to you, dear reader. (978-1-63555-655-1)

Face Off by PJ Trebelhorn. Hockey player Savannah Wells rarely spends more than a night with any one woman, but when photographer Madison Scott buys the house next door, she's forced to rethink what she expects out of life. (978-1-63555-480-9)

Hot Ice by Aurora Rey, Elle Spencer, Erin Zak. Can falling in love melt the hearts of the iciest ice queens? Join Aurora Rey, Elle Spencer, and Erin Zak to find out! (978-1-63555-513-4)

Line of Duty by VK Powell. Dr. Dylan Carlyle's professional and personal life is turned upside down when a tragic event at Fairview Station pits her against ambitious, handsome police officer Finley Masters. (978-1-63555-486-1)

London Undone by Nan Higgins. London Craft reinvents her life after reading a childhood letter to her future self and in doing so finds the love she truly wants. (978-1-63555-562-2)

Lunar Eclipse by Gun Brooke. Moon De Cruz lives alone on an uninhabited planet after being shipwrecked in space. Her life changes forever when Captain Beaux Lestarion's arrival threatens the planet and Moon's freedom. (978-1-63555-460-1)

One Small Step by Michelle Binfield. Iris and Cam discover the meaning of taking chances and following your heart, even if it means getting hurt. (978-1-63555-596-7)

Shadows of a Dream by Nicole Disney. Rainn has the talent to take her rock band all the way, but falling in love is a powerful distraction, and her new girlfriend's meth addiction might just take them both down. (978-1-63555-598-1)

Someone to Love by Jenny Frame. When Davina Trent is given an unexpected family, can she let nanny Wendy Darling teach her to open her heart to the children and to Wendy? (978-1-63555-468-7)

Tinsel by Kris Bryant. Did a sweet kitten show up to help Jessica Raymond and Taylor Mitchell find each other? Or is the holiday spirit to blame for their special connection? (978-1-63555-641-4)

Uncharted by Robyn Nyx. As Rayne Marcellus and Chase Stinsen track the legendary Golden Trinity, they must learn to put their differences aside and depend on one another to survive. (978-1-63555-325-3)

Where We Are by Annie McDonald. Can two women discover a way to walk on the same path together and discover the gift of staying in one spot, in time, in space, and in love? (978-1-63555-581-3)

A Moment in Time by Lisa Moreau. A longstanding family feud separates two women who unexpectedly fall in love at an antique clock shop in a small Louisiana town. (978-1-63555-419-9)

Aspen in Moonlight by Kelly Wacker. When art historian Melissa Warren meets Sula Johansen, director of a local bear conservancy, she discovers that love can come in unexpected and unusual forms. (978-1-63555-470-0)

Back to September by Melissa Brayden. Small bookshop owner Hannah Shepard and famous romance novelist Parker Bristow maneuver the landscape of their two very different worlds to find out if love can win out in the end. (978-1-63555-576-9)

Changing Course by Brey Willows. When the woman of your dreams falls from the sky, you'd better be ready to catch her. (978-1-63555-335-2)

Cost of Honor by Radclyffe. First Daughter Blair Powell and Homeland Security Director Cameron Roberts face adversity when their enemies stop at nothing to prevent President Andrew Powell's reelection. (978-1-63555-582-0)

Fearless by Tina Michele. Determined to overcome her debilitating fear through exposure therapy, Laura Carter all but fails before she's even begun until dolphin trainer Jillian Marshall dedicates herself to helping Laura defeat the nightmares of her past. (978-1-63555-495-3)

Not Dead Enough by J.M. Redmann. A woman who may or may not be dead drags Micky Knight into a messy con game. (978-1-63555-543-1)

Not Since You by Fiona Riley. When Charlotte boards her honeymoon cruise single and comes face-to-face with Lexi, the high school love she left behind, she questions every decision she has ever made. (978-1-63555-474-8)

Not Your Average Love Spell by Barbara Ann Wright. Four women struggle with who to love and who to hate while fighting to rid a kingdom of an evil invading force. (978-1-63555-327-7)

Tennessee Whiskey by Donna K. Ford. Dane Foster wants to put her life on pause and ask for a redo, a chance for something that matters. Emma Reynolds is that chance. (978-1-63555-556-1)

30 Dates in 30 Days by Elle Spencer. A busy lawyer tries to find love the fast way—thirty dates in thirty days. (978-1-63555-498-4)

Finding Sky by Cass Sellars. Skylar Addison's search for a career intersects with her new boss's search for butterflies, but Skylar can't forgive Jess's intrusion into her life. (978-1-63555-521-9)

Hammers, Strings, and Beautiful Things by Morgan Lee Miller. While on tour with the biggest pop star in the world, rising musician Blair Bennett falls in love for the first time while coping with loss and depression. (978-1-63555-538-7)

Heart of a Killer by Yolanda Wallace. Contract killer Santana Masters's only interest is her next assignment—until a chance meeting with a beautiful stranger tempts her to change her ways. (978-1-63555-547-9)

Leading the Witness by Carsen Taite. When defense attorney Catherine Landauer reluctantly becomes the key witness in prosecutor Starr Rio's latest criminal trial, their hearts, careers, and lives may be at risk. (978-1-63555-512-7)

No Experience Required by Kimberly Cooper Griffin. Izzy Treadway has resigned herself to a life without romance because of her bipolar illness but wonders what she's gotten herself into when she agrees to write a book about love. (978-1-63555-561-5)

One Walk in Winter by Georgia Beers. Olivia Santini and Hayley Boyd Markham might be rivals at work, but they discover that lonely hearts often find company in the most unexpected of places. (978-1-63555-541-7)

The Inn at Netherfield Green by Aurora Rey. Advertising executive Lauren Montgomery and gin distiller Camden Crawley don't agree on anything except saving the Rose & Crown, the old English pub that's brought them together. (978-1-63555-445-8)

Top of Her Game by M. Ullrich. When it comes to life on the field and matters of the heart, losing isn't an option for pro athletes Kenzie Shaw and Sutton Flores. (978-1-63555-500-4)

Vanished by Eden Darry. A storm is coming, and Ellery and Loveday must find the chosen one or humanity won't survive it. (978-1-63555-437-3)

All She Wants by Larkin Rose. Marci Jones and Tessa Dalton get more than they bargained for when their plans for a one-night stand turn into an opportunity for love. (978-1-63555-476-2)

Beautiful Accidents by Erin Zak. Stevie Adams and Bernadette Thompson discover that sometimes the best things in life happen purely by accident. (978-1-63555-497-7)

Before Now by Joy Argento. Can Delany and Jade overcome the betrayal that spans the centuries to reignite a love that can't be broken? (978-1-63555-525-7)

Breathe by Cari Hunter. Paramedic Jemima Pardon's chronic bad luck seems to be improving when she meets police officer Rosie Jones. But they face a battle to survive before they can find love. (978-1-63555-523-3)

Double-Crossed by Ali Vali. Hired thief and killer Reed Gable finds something in her scope that will change her life forever when she gets a contract to end casino accountant Brinley Myers's life. (978-1-63555-302-4)

False Horizons by CJ Birch. Jordan and Ash struggle with different views on the alien agenda and must find their way back to each other before they're swallowed up by a centuries-old war. (978-1-63555-519-6)

Legacy by Charlotte Greene. When five women hike to a remote cabin deep inside a national park, unsettling events suggest that they should have stayed home. (978-1-63555-490-8)

Royal Street Reveillon by Greg Herren. Someone is killing the stars of a reality show, and it's up to Scotty Bradley and the boys to find out who. (978-1-63555-545-5)

Somewhere Along the Way by Kathleen Knowles. When Maxine Cooper moves to San Francisco during the summer of 1981, she learns that wherever you run, you cannot escape yourself. (978-1-63555-383-3)

Blood of the Pack by Jenny Frame. When Alpha of the Scottish pack Kenrick Wulver visits the Wolfgangs, she falls for Zaria Lupa, a wolf on the run. (978-1-63555-431-1)

Cause of Death by Sheri Lewis Wohl. Medical student Vi Akiak and K9 Search and Rescue officer Kate Renard must work together to find a killer before they end up the next targets. In the race for survival, they discover that love may be the biggest risk of all. (978-1-63555-441-0)

Chasing Sunset by Missouri Vaun. Hijinks and mishaps ensue as Iris and Finn set off on a road trip adventure, chasing the sunset, and falling in love along the way. (978-1-63555-454-0)

Double Down by MB Austin. When an unlikely friendship with Spanish pop star Erlea turns deeper, Celeste, in-house physician for the hotel hosting Erlea's show, has a choice to make—run or double down on love. (978-1-63555-423-6)

Party of Three by Sandy Lowe. Three friends are in for a wild night at billionaire heiress Eleanor McGregor's twenty-fifth birthday party. Love, lust, and doing the right thing, even when it hurts, turn the evening into one that will change their lives forever. (978-1-63555-246-1)

Sit. Stay. Love. by Karis Walsh. City girl Alana Brendt and country vet Tegan Evans both know they don't belong together. Only problem is, they're falling in love. (978-1-63555-439-7)

Where the Lies Hide by Renee Roman. As P.I. Camdyn Stark gets closer to solving the case, will her dark secrets and the lies she's buried jeopardize her future with the quietly beautiful Sarah Peters? (978-1-63555-371-0)